DOUBLE BLIND

The Seneca County Courthouse Series: Book Two

A.X. FOSTER

Copyright © 2024 by A.X. Foster.

All rights reserved. This book or any portion thereof may not be reproduced or used in any manner whatsoever without the express written permission of the publisher except for the use of brief quotations in a book review.

Published by Paper Raven Books LLC

Printed in the United States of America

First Printing, 2024

Paperback ISBN: 979-8-9876997-2-0

Library of Congress Control Number: TXu 2-451-303

This is a work of fiction. All names, characters, places, and incidents are the product of the author's imagination or are used fictitiously. Any resemblance to actual events, locales or persons, living or dead, is purely coincidental.

DEDICATION

"It is better to have ten guilty men escape Justice, than to have one innocent man suffer."

Sir William Blackstone
Commentaries on the Laws of England
1783

CHAPTER 1

July 5, 2002
2:22 a.m.

The first shot was not fatal. It skipped down the center of J'Mal's scalp from front to back, parting his hair like a comb. Blood cascaded in equal quantities down both sides of his face, curving around each of his ears in semicircles.

The second shot killed him.

The copper-jacketed hollow-point bullet hit J'Mal's cheekbone, sending a hailstorm of metal slivers and bone fragments through his brain, exiting from the back of his skull. His large body crashed downward onto a glass coffee table beneath him, smashing it into pieces. By the time he hit the table, his brain had ceased functioning, and his heart, no longer receiving signals, stopped beating.

"What the fuck?!" screamed Makayla as she frantically brushed her long, stringy blonde hair from her face. She turned away, cowering and pressing her body into the corner of the room, praying she wouldn't get shot next. Protectively covering her eyes with her hands, she heard footsteps as the thin, young man with dreadlocks dashed out of the apartment and ran down the stairs to the street.

As Makayla's ears were still ringing from the sound of the two pistol shots in the small one-room apartment, she wiped her hands reflexively on her faded jeans. The smell of smoky gunpowder hovered in the air as she moved forward to look at J'Mal's body lying on top of the demolished coffee table. He was on his side, and his eyes were open. A splinter of sharp broken glass was embedded in his right eye. Underneath J'Mal's body, she saw part of a silver gun camouflaged in the glinting glass shards.

Oh my God! Oh my God! I gotta get out of here!

Then she noticed a small plastic sandwich bag with a twisted, knotted top near his left hand. Inside the plastic baggie was a collection of white irregularly shaped rocks, jumbled together like a bag of dice. She leaned forward and grabbed it. She stuffed it into her front pocket, turned, and sprinted to the door, which was still swinging open, back and forth, in the summer storm. Even with the door open, she did not notice it was raining. She hurried down the stairs and stumbled out onto Rotterdam Street, looking both ways to see if anyone was rushing toward her. No one was. She glanced down the street to look for cars, and, seeing none, she dashed across the wet pavement to the other side. Her Converse sneakers splashed rhythmically in the puddles as she ran.

Jesus, no one heard that? You've got to be kidding. That was so loud. OK, get your shit together. I've got to call Harp!

Makayla stopped and used the window of the QuikStop convenience store as an impromptu mirror. She saw her own reflection staring back at her: a tall, thin woman with a nest of disheveled, wet hair and green eyes bulging with fear. She ineffectively smoothed the jumble on top of her head, pulled her damp T-shirt from the waistband of her jeans, and arranged it to hang down to hide her bulging pocket. The logo on her shirt said WORLD SERIES CHAMPION ARIZONA DIAMONDBACKS. She patted her thighs.

Money, ID, keys and the baggie with all that crack. This is a disaster! That dude shot J'Mal! I'm in so much trouble!

She went inside the QuikStop. Luckily, it was open 24/7. She shivered like a wet dog, crossed her arms across her chest, and approached the counter. The store was empty. No one was inside except the sales clerk, a familiar elderly Latina woman.

"Ana, can I use your cell phone, please? It's an emergency."

Ana smirked and, with exaggerated effort, pulled a pair of headphones from her ears. She stood up from her stool, put her portable CD player on the grimy counter and pulled a Motorola Razr flip phone from her back pocket, saying, "Girl, you gotta get your own damn cell phone one of these days. Everyone's got one now. I ain't Verizon, y'know."

Taking the flip phone from Ana, Makayla thanked her, "I'll just be a minute. It's super important. I really appreciate it!"

Makayla stepped toward the rear of the convenience store, looked back to see if Ana was paying attention, and then pulled the door open on the floor-to-ceiling cooler compartment. She felt the frosty, refrigerated mist waft across her face as she inventoried the assortment of colorful, unhealthy, cold drinks assembled in rows before her. She looked back toward the front counter. Ana had put on her headphones and was peering down at a cracked plastic *R. Kelly* CD cover in her hand, examining it carefully, as if looking for clues. Ana began bobbing her head.

Makayla reached as far back into the cooler as she could and took out a bright pink Watermelon Splash Gatorade from the last row of bottles positioned in the top rack. She reached into her pants pocket, took out the baggie, and stuffed it into the back of the cooler in the space where the last bottle had been. She would get that tomorrow.

Satisfied no one could hear or see her, Makayla pushed the buttons on the cell phone.

"Harp! It's me."

"What phone is *this*? Our unit has Caller ID now. I can tell everyone who calls. What's going on? Did he make the buy? We're two blocks away."

"No! He shot J'Mal and ran! He shot him and stole the baggie!"

"Jesus Christ! Are you kidding? Me and Sergeant Ricky will be there in three minutes. Where exactly are you?"

"I'm in the QuikStop on Rotterdam across the street from J'Mal's apartment. I'm in the back of the store. Hurry!"

"Look, Makayla, if you're going to do these undercover informant jobs for us, you gotta pay attention and set these buys up better than this! I thought you knew this guy who wanted to score some drugs."

"I'm sorry. I'm *sorry*! No, that guy didn't show up. This was just some random guy on the street who came up and asked me where he could get some rocks. So I took *him* up to J'Mal's because you and Sergeant Ricky wanted to catch someone. I was just trying to help. And then all *this* happened."

Makayla started to cry.

Harp ignored that and said, "Did you get a good look at the guy who shot him?"

"Yes, I mean—I think so. I'm not sure."

"Well, you better be sure! If you wanna get paid, you've got to do better than that, Makayla. Right now, you're an accomplice to a homicide, and who knows how the State's Attorney's Office will think about this."

Makayla sat down on the floor of the QuikStop.

"We're pulling up now. Give the phone back to whoever you borrowed it from and come outside. We will think of something."

CHAPTER 2

May 18, 2022
7:34 a.m.

Mac MacIntyre pulled his badge from his back pocket and used it to tap on the opaque glass door of the State's Attorney's Office, as he had done hundreds of times before. Like all the prosecutors in his office, Mac loved having that badge. A useful perk, it folded into a cell-phone-sized rectangle of black leather. Mac used it as an improvised wallet, sliding his credit cards and driver's license into one of the side slots; if pulled over by a cop for speeding—one of Mac's foibles—he would deliberately hold the wallet open to give the patrol officer ample opportunity to see the bronze disk imprinted with the words: SENECA COUNTY STATE'S ATTORNEY'S OFFICE. Without saying a word, he always got off with just a warning.

A buzzer sounded, and Mac pulled the door open and stepped into the office. Lupe, a young Latina woman, was sitting behind the reception desk, twirling a pen in her hair. She said, "Look who it is first thing in the morning, Mr. Memory Man! You're here awfully early. Like they say, early bird catches the worm."

"*Buenos dias*, Lupe. You know what a cliché is, right?"

"I forget. I can't remember trivia things like you, Mac! Do you have an office day today? Or court upstairs?"

"No, I'm taking it easy today," Mac replied. "Yesterday, we got a nice verdict in that crazy trial with the rich, preppie kid, so I'm off for a couple of days, and, trust me, I could use a break! But you know how it goes around here. The *mierda* could hit the fan at any moment."

"Oh, congrats, Mac. Yeah, I saw you on CNN. Looking good! So, since the jury came back with a guilty verdict, does that boy go to jail or somewhere else, like a hospital?"

"We don't have sentencing until August, so I'm pretty sure they'll try to get his hands—or stumps, I guess—fixed up by then. But, hey, it's not *my* problem."

"Kind of sad. College boy blew his own hands off. For what?"

"Right. Well, that's what happens when you try to make a bomb from some stupid website on the Internet. You know how much I hate clichés, Lupe, but if you play with fire, you get burned. So, he has no one to blame but himself."

Slapping her hands together rhythmically, she said, "Let me give you some applause, because I guess *he* won't be clapping any time soon! Well, have a nice day off, Mac. You deserve it. And then it's on to the next case, I guess."

"Right. *Gracias.* Hey Lupe, page me if Mr. Fischbein gets

off the elevator. He'll want to do a press conference before the noon TV shows and get credit for my work, as always. He will need me to draft up a media release about Clapping Boy. I just hope he doesn't order me to stand beside him on that stupid podium like a mannequin. It's so ridiculous when prosecutors do that lineup thing. Anyway, catch you later."

As Mac strolled down the hallway, he dodged other prosecutors like a downhill skier swooping around the gates of a snowy slalom racecourse. ASAs, victim/witness coordinators, and administrative aides were hustling to handle the daily business of a big suburban prosecutor's office. With trials, pleas, sentencings, violations of probation, bond reviews, and a wide variety of assorted legal proceedings, there was never a sense of calm or completion in the air. Crimes kept rolling in endlessly, like waves on the beach, and the Seneca County State's Attorney's Office handled a myriad of malfeasance: from misdemeanors like DUIs, fistfights, and shoplifting thefts, to major felony jury trials for the most serious criminal offenses. Mac MacIntyre was a Senior ASA who handled the SAO's homicides and other attention-getting, high-profile crimes.

From far down the hallway, as he approached his corner office, he saw a sky-blue case file lying on the floor in the space where a doormat would be. As Mac got closer, he saw it had a yellow sticky note attached to it with a message written in petite black ink characters. He recognized the florid, expressive handwriting. He reached down and tore the sticky note off.

> *MAC, THIS IS AN OLD CASE JUST REVERSED BY THE COURT OF APPEALS. THEY GRANTED A RE-TRIAL. PLEASE PREPARE IT AGAIN. MEET ME AND ARI AT 8:30 SHARP. VERY IMPORTANT. JO*

Mac walked into his office, closed the door behind him, and plopped the case file on his desk.

Meet with Ari and Jo? Damn. There goes my day off.

He took off his suit jacket and hung it on a hanger on the inside of the door. Sitting down at his desk, he leaned back and sighed.

His desk phone rang. The Caller ID said BLOCKED.

Someone's calling me from inside the courthouse. I bet Lupe saw The Fish come into the office.

Mac lifted the receiver and said, "This is Mac MacIntyre." He paused. He could tell someone was listening, and he could hear faint labored breathing. Puzzled, he said, "Hello? Is anyone there? Lupe? Is that you?"

He hung up.

Never a break. Well, my office number is published on the SAO website, so any nut or angry defendant can call me with some stupid heavy-breathing crank call. At least this new case file is thin. Can't be too bad.

His desk phone rang again. The Caller ID said BLOCKED.

Mac squinted and picked up the phone.

"Hello, this is..."

"Hey, Mr. Fischbein just left the floor and went down to the cafeteria," Lupe blurted. "He walked right past me and didn't even say good morning. *Idiota*! He's been the State's Attorney for like two years, and I bet he still doesn't even know my name."

"Ari Fischbein. The Fish. This guy has a gigantic ego for such a small man, Lupe. That big ego is his Achilles' heel. No doubt."

"His what? Did you say his heel?"

"His Achilles' heel. It's a reference to Greek mythology."

"How do you know all that super-random stuff?"

"I'm sorry. Things just stick in my mind. I can't help it."

"Well, nobody asked you about his damn heel, Macaroni. How come whenever I say something basic to you, you always come back sounding like a human encyclopedia or Google? Can't you just have a normal conversation without bringing up things no one's ever heard of?"

"Well, according to the myth, Achilles was dipped into magical waters by his mother, Thetis, when he was a baby. The water protected him like a coating, but—here's the thing, Lupe—she held him by his heel, so it was his only vulnerable part. And, yes, you guessed it, he ended up getting hit with an arrow right in the heel, and, well, the rest is history. Literally."

"Oh, I get it," said Lupe. "You mean like my Achilles tendon down by my shoe. So, that's why they call it that, huh?"

"Lupe, if The Fish heads down to my office, call me, OK? At the risk of sounding totally crazy, it's exactly 88 steps from his office to mine. The front desk is halfway. 44 steps. So, if you see him walk by, you'll still have time to warn me."

"Next time I see that creep, I'm going to shoot him with an arrow, and I'm aiming for the back of his foot. Got that?" Mac smiled and hung up the phone. He took a deep breath and exhaled slowly.

Mac reached down to the lowest desk drawer and slid it open. Inside, face-down, was a small, framed postcard. He lifted it out and gazed at it. The photo depicted a tiny red house with a slope-backed stone bridge in the foreground. To the side of the house, a canal with rippling green water appeared. Printed on the bottom of the postcard were the words:

HET OOIEVAAR HUIS, AMSTERDAM, HOLLAND

He looked at the tiny red house and squinted. Above the door, a stone sculpture of a stork standing in a nest appeared, frozen in time perpetually. Mac closed his eyes. Fortified, he opened them and returned the framed postcard to the drawer. He looked down at the blue case file lying on his desk. As his pupils focused, he noticed the typed lettering on the file's tab: ***St. v. Edward Stephens*** **– Murder 1st.**

Mac pulled his cell phone from his suit pants pocket and dialed Detective Andre Okoye, the top investigator for the SAO.

"Hey, Mac. What's up?"

"Hey. I just got assigned a new murder case. I need you to swing by police storage or wherever the hell they keep old case files. It's a murder case from 2002, but it was reversed on appeal, so now we have to do the whole damn thing over again. All I have is a thin case file with a snotty note from Jo Newgrange."

"No problem. I know a guy from the Police Academy

who now works as the custodian of records in archives. Did you say Jo Newgrange was already on your ass? I swear, that woman is kinda hot, but she's so annoying. Stay away from her, Mac. If you lie down with dogs, you get fleas!"

"Stop!"

"So, you know what a female dog is called, right? Hey, I know she's the Deputy State's Attorney and runs our whole office while The Fish does nothing but look in the mirror, but there's something a little too slick about that woman, even if she has a sexy body, y'understand what I'm saying?"

"I know exactly what you mean. I've got a meeting with them at 8:30. Hey, I just learned a new Spanish word from Lupe: *idiota*."

"OK, I'll zip down to police archives right now and let you know what I find ASAP. Later, bro."

Mac flipped open the thin case file. It had only 20-odd pages inside. Each page had been perforated by a two-hole punch, and then impaled by metal prongs bent forward to secure all the papers, like an owl's claws grasping a doomed field mouse.

The only document in the file was a copy of the Maryland Court of Appeals opinion reversing the original guilty verdict and sending it back to the Seneca County Circuit Court for a retrial. The file had no Statement of Charges, no interview notes, no witness statements, no autopsy report and no ballistics analysis. Nothing.

How the hell am I supposed to prepare a murder trial with just this?

He read the brief opinion.

He learned that in 2002, a drug dealer was shot and killed in a tiny apartment on Rotterdam Street. A teenager named Eddie Stephens was convicted of first-degree murder and sentenced to life in prison based on a positive identification from a female eyewitness who was actually inside the apartment and saw the shooting. Eddie was picked out of a photo lineup almost immediately. The police served a search warrant at Eddie's parents' house, and a handgun consistent with the bullet fragments was seized from inside a sneaker hidden in a shoebox under Eddie's bed.

I like my chances. I'll win this case easily.

Eddie insisted all along that he was the wrong man and elected to have a jury trial.

He lost.

Mac's desk phone rang, piercing his thoughts. The Caller ID said BLOCKED.

He answered. "Hello, it's Mac."

"Hey, it's Lupe. Mr. Fischbein is back, and he seems really pissed off. He just got off the elevator with Jo Newgrange." She lowered her voice to a whisper and continued, "He was all huffy and stomped right past the front desk again."

Mac glanced at his wristwatch.

Lupe continued, "I heard a glimpse of what he was saying as they walked by. He mentioned your name. He said, 'Get Mac into my office right away before that judge calls me *again*.' And he said 'again' real hard-like."

"Yeah, Jo left me a note. I've got to meet with them in eight minutes."

"Good luck."

"But wait, Lupe. Are you sure you heard him say the word 'judge?'"

"Yes. Definitely. I get a weird feeling, Mac. Like, maybe they're going to try to blame you for something."

"Me? I had nothing to do with this fiasco. They can't blame anything on me."

"Well, it's just my woman's intuition. You may have a photographic memory, but I've got a woman's intuition. And I don't trust that Ms. Newgrange at all. She smiles a lot, but it's always very fake, like she's got too many sharp teeth in her mouth."

Female dog, Andre said.

"And Mac, she always stares at my clothes like I'm a homeless woman or something. Stuck up. Women pick up on stuff like that."

"OK. Well, I have to deal with them right now. And Lupe, by the way, Zaria from the Public Defender's Office is going to stop by at around noon. She's got a Presentence Report in that case I did with the deaf girl who was attacked. Remember that one?"

"No," Lupe replied. "But I sure as hell know who that Zaria is! Wasn't I just talking about a woman's intuition? I know what's going on. Please, Mac, I'm not blind."

"Shit, I have to go literally right now."

CHAPTER 3

May 18, 2022
8:34 a.m.

Marcel St. Croix parked his classic 1978 Datsun 270Z in the visitor's parking lot of the Broad Run Regional Correctional Center and turned off the ignition, letting the purring engine slowly wind down to a halt. He picked up the thick case file on the passenger seat and the package of travel-size sanitary wipes, and then put his cell phone in the Datsun's console, knowing it was not allowed inside the maximum-security prison. He slipped off his large copper bracelet too; no metal would get through the Mag without tripping the alarm.

As he walked to the entrance of the facility, he brushed his long, perfectly straight, black-and-grey hair out of his face. The cool spring wind sparred with him, attempting to disorganize his fastidious attempts to orchestrate every detail of his outward appearance. Marcel knew from his many years inside courtrooms that an impressive deportment was as important, if not more so, than any of the brilliant legal strategies or clever business decisions swirling around in his mind, swirling like his hair in the wind.

His long career as the preeminent criminal defense attorney in Seneca County had given him many opportunities to display his prodigious talents—he had the natural gifts of a charismatic stage actor, and he commanded the attention of any audience he faced with wit, confidence, and style. His orations before juries were legendary, and, knowing that his Native American heritage sparked curiosity, he capitalized on his ethnicity to draw attention to it without appearing to be an obvious self-promoter. He therefore—quite intentionally—let his hair hang down to his collarbone, and he wore a single turquoise stud earring in his left earlobe. Although he was part Mi'kmaq—an indigenous tribe in the north of Quebec—the earring was purchased in Taos, New Mexico from a Navajo jeweler sitting cross-legged on a blanket in the radiant sunshine selling handmade items in the Plaza. Marcel correctly calculated that no one here in Seneca County, Maryland, would ever know the difference. It was all about image. He was the only attorney who wore an earring to court. He was, after all, Marcel St. Croix.

He opened the grimy outer door to the prison and then, before entering the lobby, took out his pack of sanitary wipes. He vigorously wiped his hands with a cluster of moist wipes and then dropped them into a large trash can by the front door. As he walked up to the front desk, he pulled out his Seneca County Bar Association ID card and his driver's license.

"Good morning, sir," he said to the young corrections officer sitting like a bank teller behind a glass partition. He was a large, very muscular man with pink skin and a blond military-style haircut.

This young man is clearly more familiar with barbells than with books.

The officer did not look up and turned away, apparently suddenly preoccupied with the contents of a clipboard. The name tag over his beige uniform shirt pocket said, "Taylor, M."

"Good morning," Marcel repeated in a louder tone. "I'm here on a scheduled professional appointment with my client. Here is my Bar card and my driver's license."

Officer Taylor completely ignored him.

Marcel cleared his throat and said, "I arranged a visit yesterday with Warden Simpson. It was approved and sent back to my law firm—would you like to see the confirmation, sir?"

Upon hearing the word "Warden," the officer looked up and slid the clipboard to the side of his desk.

"OK, let me see that ID."

As the officer carefully examined Marcel's identification, he robotically said in a flat tone, "No cell phones are allowed inside the facility. No eating, drinking, or smoking inside. Any disruptive behavior will be subject to ejection. All visits are monitored and recorded. Got that?"

"This is a professional visit, Officer Taylor. Perhaps I have not been clear, but let me repeat myself: I am an attorney. There will not be any recording of any kind as this is, as I've already said twice, a confidential meeting with attorney/client privilege."

Marcel took out the official permission slip that had been sent to his office as an email attachment and held it up for the officer to see.

Scrutinizing the driver's license, Officer Taylor said, "OK, OK, you don't have to get snappy about it, Mr.—how do you say this name? Crocks? Saint Crocks?"

"Croix. The *X* is silent. It rhymes with '*boy*.'" He emphasized the word 'boy' for an extra beat, as if to underscore the age difference between the two men.

"OK, Counselor. Put all of your stuff here in this basket and step through the Mag."

Marcel walked through the metal detector, then reached around the side of the rectangular-shaped frame and picked up his wallet and keys from the basket.

"Who is the inmate you're here to see?"

"Edward Stephens."

"Oh, Eddie!" the officer exclaimed. "Yeah, I know him good. He's been here since I started back in 2018. He's been here a long time, long before I even got out of the Academy. He didn't tell me he got a lawyer like you. What's going on?"

Sensing the tension in the air had dissipated significantly, Marcel decided to capitalize on the opportunity.

"Well, Officer Taylor, I can't get into the details because that is privileged information, but I can tell you this much—since this part is public information—Eddie's case was reversed on appeal, and he's been granted a new trial."

"No shit. That's awesome. Good for Eddie! He's always been, like, one of the coolest dudes in here. Never causes any problems. He's a genius at checkers. Nobody in here—inmates or COs—can beat him. He says he can think six moves ahead, and I believe him."

"Checkers is a lot more complex than it seems. Just like a jury trial: you have to think six moves in advance. Of course, in checkers, if you can get a piece all the way across to the other side, well, then it's crowned a king. That's my favorite part of the game."

"Well, head on back to Interview Room One and wait there. I'll radio up, and he should be transported down in just a few minutes."

Eddie Stephens stepped into Interview Room One. The heavy metal door clanked shut behind him.

"Mr. St. Croix! So glad to meet you."

Marcel stood up and bent forward to shake hands. He leaned over a raised wooden barrier that bisected the table, a long horizontal plank about six inches high, ostensibly erected, like a miniature wall, to prevent the transference of contraband. A different corrections officer was standing outside the door; the back of his head was visible through a small square window in the door. The window was dirty and thick. A small dead insect—perhaps a wayward bed bug—was stuck to the glass.

"Eddie, my pleasure. Ms. Katz and your mother told me you've done some very impressive things while in here. Got your college degree. That's excellent. Ms. Katz asked me to convey to you that she is fully committed to your cause and will sponsor you all the way."

They both sat.

"So, I got a new trial?" Eddie asked.

"Yes. The Court of Appeals agreed with our brief and found that there was obvious ineffective assistance of counsel in violation of your Sixth Amendment rights at your original trial way back in 2003."

"So, do you really think we have a chance to win a retrial?"

Marcel slid out a multipage legal document from his case file and started to hand it to Eddie.

"Here's a Xerox of the Court of Appeals's decision."

"Oh, I read that already," Eddie replied. "Ms. Katz mailed me a copy. Must've read it 10,000 times. I also showed it to a guy in here who's real smart with law and cases. He's doing life without parole. Helps inmates read these court opinions, and he writes their *pro se* appeals. Trust me, he's won a bunch. If he was on the outside, he'd be one of the top criminal defense attorneys in Maryland. Maybe not like you, Mr. St. Croix, but pretty close."

"Well, the appellate court said your public defender was ineffective, so they're giving us a second chance," said Marcel.

"He was a complete idiot, man. His name was Dick Finsey. And he *was* a total dick. He didn't question those cops at all, and he didn't say shit about that dumb crackhead girl who identified *me* as the shooter. I swear, I've never seen that girl in my life. First time I ever saw her, she's walking into the courtroom ready to string me up. And the jury believed her. I was in shock. *I* could have asked better questions than that PD. He sold me out bad."

"You had poor legal representation. And the Court of Appeals agreed with us, so at least we are making progress. I filed a *Writ of Corum Nobis* bringing up the right arguments, if I do say so myself, but that's all water under the bridge, Eddie. We can't go back and re-litigate all of that now. We can only move forward."

"Has the Circuit Court set my case in for any hearings or given us a new trial date yet?"

"Yes. But there's a new judge assigned. Old Judge Barnette died after your first trial, so it's been reassigned to a new judge. Someone better. A woman judge. Judge Roberta Ryan. She was a prosecutor before taking the bench, so I think she'll be good for us."

"A prosecutor? Shit. That's not good."

"No, Eddie. Some of them are actually fair. She will not like the witnesses if they are shady. I think she's a good draw for us."

"Well, I hope she's good because that Barnette judge was horrible. So fat he could hardly get up those little stairs to the bench, and then, when he got up there, he didn't do shit to stop anyone's lies. Useless. Like a big ol' frog sitting on a fence until it falls off. That guy was a joke."

"And don't forget: he gave you life."

"Don't *forget*? Believe me, I haven't forgotten. That's like my mom. She keeps saying, 'be patient,' and I say, be *patient*? I've been locked up for 20 years for a crime I didn't do, and she's telling *me* to be damn patient! I've been patient for more than half my life. I want to get out of here!"

Marcel shuffled the legal opinion back into his file. He leaned back in his chair and remained silent, sensing the need to let the storm of Eddie's emotions quell. When a few moments had passed, Marcel said, "Well, I'm very glad your mother contacted Ms. Katz for assistance. She's been very helpful."

"Damn right. There's no way my family could afford to hire you without her help. Ms. Katz has always been in my corner, going all the way back to high school. I think she knew this case was bullshit from the beginning. Just another Black kid lynched, except in a courtroom instead of hanging from a tree branch in Mississippi. You should hear the stories she tells. Selma, Dr. King, John Lewis—Ms. Katz's seen it all! She's a warrior."

"I've always held Ophelia Jackson Katz in the highest regard," Marcel replied.

"Amen to that."

"So, Eddie, I read the transcript of your original trial. It was 16 volumes, all packed up in boxes. I also filed a Motion for Discovery with the new prosecutor. He's obligated to give me everything they have against you. That's a rule. All of their evidence. We're entitled to it all."

Eddie reached up to his face with both hands and wiped them down from his forehead to his jawline, as if he was removing a mask. He glanced back at the door behind him, then back to Marcel. Quietly, he said, "I got proof it wasn't me. We can blow their case right out of the water. Do you wanna know about it?"

"Yes. Tell me."

"OK. First, let me just say this, Mr. St. Croix: Merry Christmas!"

CHAPTER 4

May 18, 2022
8:30 a.m.

Ari Fischbein held the top position in the SAO, and he rarely let anyone forget it. Not yet 40, he was one of the youngest State's Attorneys in Seneca County history. He looked older. His lumpy, soft body was slowly transforming into a pear shape, and his once perfectly fitting, custom-tailored suits now looked tight. He stood about five-foot-seven, much shorter than Mac, who towered over him.

Mac, Jo, and Ari were sitting around a polished wooden conference table at the far end of Ari's large corner office. Eight people could sit around the table, three on each side, one at the head and one at the foot. Ari territorially sat at the head of the table, a position he demanded for himself and no one else, like a cat who had marked his litter box. Jo and Mac sat on either side of him, creating a triangular formation of three levels of prosecutors: State's Attorney, Deputy State's Attorney, and Senior Assistant State's Attorney.

Ari brushed his thinning blond hair across the top of his head, adjusted his wire-rimmed glasses, and said to Mac, "Well, *I'm* the State's Attorney, and it's going to be *me* who has to get elected, not you!"

Mac calculated that the next election would—in effect—be *a fait accompli*, since Ari was running unopposed. Without any opposition, Ari had a 100 percent probability of being reelected for another four-year term. As that nauseating prospect dashed through Mac's mind, he jolted himself back into reality and said, "Jo dropped off this Stephens case for me today. I read the Court of Appeals's decision, but the file is otherwise completely empty. I'm happy to work it up for trial again, but is there anything I need to know—I mean, from a political perspective—or is this merely a retrial of some random drug deal gone bad?"

Ari's office looked like the archetypical prosecutor's office, with floor-to-ceiling bookcases filled with books which no one had read since all legal research was now done online. There were mementos of Ari's career scattered about the room, framed newspaper articles, and photographs of Ari standing next to dignitaries and politicians. A white plastic lacrosse stick was propped up in the corner of the office, a relic of Ari's benchwarming days at boarding school much earlier in his life. Visitors to his office rarely acknowledged the lacrosse stick, although Ari hoped they would, so he could regale them with imaginary tales of his youthful athletic prowess.

Oblivious, Ari didn't realize that absolutely no one saw him as dexterous or athletic.

Jo Newgrange was an intense, stylish, petite woman wearing a forest green Max Mara tailored suit. While demure in physical stature, she projected a commanding aura, like a small but beautiful silver switchblade. She had the look of a crisp TV news anchor with coiffed, dyed red hair augmented by luxurious hair extensions. While she was unquestionably an excellent courtroom litigator, there was something ineffably dangerous about her. With her faint Southern accent, she said, "This is the case with Judge Bennington. Mac, we need to tread softly and make this whole thing quietly go away. We can't let the press find out about it, if possible."

Ari chimed in, "I'm going to need the support of the judges for my reelection. I've already hired two of their clerks as rookie ASAs. The timing on this is terrible, understand? I can't afford any screw-ups, Mac."

"Well, as always," Mac replied, "I will try my best, Ari. But I'll need more information than what is in this file. I understand from reading the Court of Appeals's opinion that Judge Bennington handled this case when he was the original prosecutor. Everything I've read so far looks like a simple, basic, garden-variety homicide. So, I'm not sure why there's a need for all of this secrecy. Am I missing something?"

Mac had a blank legal pad in front of him next to the thin blue case file. He hadn't written anything on the pad yet.

Jo said, "So, listen—Ari and I run a tight ship here. We don't want any type of controversy, especially with the next election in mind. The last thing we need are questions from the press about this old murder case. Got it?"

"Sure, Jo," said Mac. "But why would anyone in the media be interested in this? We probably handle half a dozen of these drug rip shootings every year, and nobody cares. Most of the time, the media doesn't even cover a case like this, and the dead guy rarely has any family members pestering us for justice. So, what's the big deal?"

Jo didn't answer and looked deferentially at Ari.

Ari was looking directly at Jo and remained silent.

Mac's question lingered in the air like a candy wrapper floating in the wind, swaying back and forth, unguided, eventually succumbing to gravity as if gently being pulled down to earth.

After an uncomfortably long pause, Mac looked at Jo and then back at Ari, and then back at Jo again.

Finally, Jo began whispering, although no one else could possibly hear through the closed office door. She said, "OK, so we spoke to Judge Bennington. He knows the case was reversed. He's in a terribly awkward position. He doesn't want to testify as a witness in a murder trial in the same courthouse where he's a judge. Obviously."

She looked around Ari's office as if searching to see if anyone else was there, even though the room was empty except for the three of them. Continuing, she said, "When Judge Bennington prosecuted this case 20 years ago, he was one of the top ASAs in this office. He was winning all his trials back then. And not long after the conviction in this Stephens case, he was appointed to be a Circuit Court judge, skipping right past District Court and going directly to Circuit Court. The judge who handled this case back then was Judge Barnette. You remember him, right? He gave Stephens a life sentence. Everyone says Barnette was a racist, but that's beside the point."

Mac picked up his pen to write something on his legal pad, but Jo raised her hand up in a "stop" gesture, and Mac put his pen down.

"Then," she continued, "Judge Barnette died of a heart attack sitting on the toilet. That was like a year after the sentencing. Stephens goes off to Broad Run and has been rotting away there ever since. No one ever thought about this case again. But, Mac, if this is a retrial risen from the dead, Bennington's involvement in what happened will get scrutinized by the press, and that's—well, that's going to be messy. We need to protect him from that. That's very important to us—as an office. We can't allow one of the judges here to be raked over the coals."

"Raked over the coals. I understand," Mac replied.

"Bennington says there were 'irregularities' with how the original prosecution unfolded," Jo continued. "He wouldn't tell us any more than that, but he used the word 'irregularities,' which is an extremely peculiar word for a former prosecutor to use. He also specifically mentioned the name Sam Harper."

Mac asked, "You mean Assistant Police Chief Sam Harper?"

Jo replied, "Yes, him. Harper was working on the Vice Squad or Vice Team, or whatever it was called, in 2002. That whole unit was disbanded shortly after this case, and no one knows why. This was down around Rotterdam Street, which was a pit. After this case was done, Harper kept getting promoted. Corporal Harper, Sergeant Harper, Lieutenant Harper, etc. And now with Chief Levy about to retire, Harper is next in line to become the Chief of Police, they say. So, he's got a lot riding on this Stephens retrial too. That old Vice unit working the Rotterdam area was pretty rough back in those days, I hear. So, who knows what kind of 'irregularities' the cops did to catch bad guys back then?"

"We don't want to open up a can of worms!" Ari chimed in. The cliché clanked around in Mac's brain.

"Well, I understand," Mac said. "Ancient cases like this can be problematic. Witnesses may have died, evidence might be lost, and people's memories have definitely faded, that is, if they can even remember anything at all. I really don't want to get up in front of a jury and have nothing to say. So, let me dig into this a bit and see what I can discover. Obviously, if we can work out a plea—maybe we can just offer Stephens time served and call it a day? That would be the path of least resistance."

"Yes," said Ari. "Plead it out. For Christ's sake, the guy's already been locked up for 20 years for shooting a drug dealer. No one gives a fuck about a dead drug dealer."

Jo jumped in, "We also need to keep Assistant Chief Harper out of this mess, too. Last thing we need is the whole Fraternal Order of Police complaining about how our office doesn't support the police department. The rank-and-file cops love Harper, so we don't need to open up a Pandora's Box with this old crap."

Mac said, "Pandora was sent by Zeus to Prometheus with

a box as a gift. Zeus told her not to open it. But she lifted the lid, and all of mankind's evils poured out by accident."

Jo replied, "Mac, we don't have time for all of that nonsense now, OK?"

Having received his marching orders, Mac picked up his felt-tipped pen and slotted it into the breast pocket of his suit jacket. He pushed himself away from the edge of the conference table. He paused just a moment in case either Ari or Jo had anything left to say. They didn't.

"OK. I'll see if I can find out if we even have any witnesses left. Judge Bennington and Assistant Chief Harper are obviously still around Seneca County, but the Court's opinion mentioned another undercover cop, too. A cop who was Harper's partner back then by the name of York. I never met him, but he shouldn't be too hard to find and interview. But the key to the case is this: a woman named Makayla. She's the eyewitness who allegedly saw the shooting. Well, if we can't find her, that will pretty much wrap things up. Without her, we can drop the case, and no one is the wiser. If we *do* find this Makayla, then I'll just go through the motions and offer Stephens a plea to second-degree murder with credit for time served. We can also agree to his immediate release. He'd be completely stupid not to take that plea."

"Right. Take a plea. We can't just drop it. That will look like we have something to hide," said Jo. "No. Stephens has to plead guilty to *something*—anything, really, even a manslaughter, and then we all move on. Judge Bennington moves on. Assistant Chief Harper moves on. We *all* just move on. But, Mac, this is important: we can't just *nolle* it. That will arouse all kinds of suspicion."

"Yup," Mac confirmed. "A can of worms. Pandora's Box."

"And whatever happens," Jo emphasized, "we don't want any bad press. We have to be especially careful with Don Morris at the *Seneca Journal*. He already wrote an editorial criticizing Ari. Watch out for him. We do not want him writing some article about this case. Understand?"

CHAPTER 5

May 19, 2022
7:30 a.m.

Maryland Edition

MAN SERVING LIFE SENTENCE TO GET NEW TRIAL. CLAIMS WRONGFULLY CONVICTED BY POLICE MISCONDUCT.

By Don Morris — Seneca Journal

Eddie Stephens has served nearly twenty years of a life sentence at Broad Run Regional Correctional Facility outside Baltimore. The Maryland Court of Appeals has reversed his first-degree murder conviction based on "ineffective assistance of counsel" and has granted him a new trial. Stephens was represented in 2003 by the late Dick Finsey, who resigned from his position in 2004. The appellate court's opinion cited numerous deficiencies by Finsey in his capacity as defense counsel, highlighting failures at trial to investigate possible misconduct by the Seneca County Police Department almost two decades ago.

Stephens is currently represented by the well-known criminal defense attorney Marcel St. Croix, who successfully argued to the Court of Appeals for a new trial. "What happened here was a complete miscarriage of justice," St. Croix stated. "This is a classic example of faulty eyewitness identification. Here, a totally innocent man was misidentified. His former attorney didn't ask a single question about that."

Seneca County State's Attorney Ari Fischbein (D) responded, "We have full faith in the Seneca County Police Department and, of course, the integrity of our experienced staff of prosecutors. We fully expect this Defendant to be convicted again, and we will oppose any attempt to have him released on bail. He is a murderer now, and he will always be a murderer."

A copy of a 2002 Application for Statement of Charges in the original case was obtained by the Seneca Journal. The charging document[1] states that on July 5, 2002, a shooting occurred in the Rotterdam Street area of Seneca County resulting in the death of a local man, J'Mal Quantavious Jefferson. A homicide investigation at the time revealed that a female eyewitness to the event positively identified the Defendant as the shooter.

Stephens was arrested a few days later by Vice Unit Team officers Samuel Harper and Richard York. A subsequent search of Mr. Stephens's parents' home resulted in the seizure of a handgun linked to the crime. Samuel Harper is currently an Assistant

---

1: See Appendix One.

Chief with the Seneca County Police Department, and his name has been widely circulated as a top candidate for the position of Chief of Police pending the imminent retirement of the current Chief Douglas Levy. Officer York retired in 2005 and now lives in Colorado Springs, Colorado. Attempts to reach Harper and York were unsuccessful. The original Assistant State's Attorney who handled the 2003 trial, Daniel Bennington, is now a Seneca County Circuit Court judge, having been appointed to the bench in 2006. It is unclear if Judge Bennington's involvement in the case will require a change of venue.

Veteran Senior Assistant State's Attorney William MacIntyre has been assigned to the retrial.

A Scheduling Hearing has been set in the matter for tomorrow morning with a trial date set for September.

CHAPTER 6

May 19, 2022
3:18 p.m.

Robbi Ryan had always wanted to be a judge. From the time she was a young girl, she was fascinated with the concept of justice. But what exactly did justice mean?

She was a bright and cheerful child who excelled in school, always garnering the teacher's favor and achieving easy success with classroom projects, tests, and discussions. Yes, she loved to talk. She graduated from Seneca County's top magnet high school, where, as a senior, she was voted Student Council President. She also triumphed on the soccer field and was named as an Honorable Mention to the All Seneca County team. It would not be the last time Robbi was called "Honorable."

She was book smart, yes, but her real talent was managing people and understanding human motivations. Her father worked long hours and was rarely home. As a girl, Robbi wasn't sure what he did all day. He was an insurance agent, but she didn't know exactly what that was. She sensed, however, that it was something to do with helping people who had suffered various tragedies or damage to their property.

Once, when Robbi was in seventh grade, she went along with her father to view a mansion that had been struck by lightning. She never forgot the smoky scent in the air and the way the vinyl siding had been melted, twisting up from the roof in curlicues of plastic, splayed in all directions like spaghetti. Mostly, she remembered how kind and quietly authoritative her father was. He was seeking justice in his own way, trying to make something that was broken whole again.

"But, Papa, why did lightning decide to hit this very house and not another?" she mused at the random serendipity and chance ferocity of nature.

"Because, Robbi, life isn't fair. Some people call it 'an act of God,' but not everyone believes in God. I call it 'fate.' You could also just say it was bad luck, I guess."

"Fate?"

"Sometimes bad things happen to good people for no reason, and you just can't make sense of it," her father explained.

She never forgot those words. Yes, life wasn't fair at all.

Her mother had died of severe complications during childbirth. Her father had worshipped her mother, so she was named Roberta in her memory, but little Robbi carried an impossibly unattainable burden her entire childhood: she wanted to be loved by her father as much as he had loved her mother. It was futile to compete with a ghost.

But every time Robbi looked down, she knew her father was correct about fate.

She was born with three fingers on her left hand. Her thumb and index finger were normal, but the remaining three fingers had been fused together into a fleshy wedge. In the late 1950s and early 1960s, the use of a drug called thalidomide was prescribed to help pregnant women with morning sickness. Tragically, it caused horrific birth defects to countless unsuspecting, innocent infants. A generation of babies came into the world missing whole limbs, or toes, or fingers, until the connection to the use of thalidomide was established. For Robbi, it was too late. Lightning had struck. Life *was* unfair.

Her condition was technically called Phocomelia Syndrome, but that fancy name did not protect her from the bullying and taunts she endured from cruel kids. In the sixth grade, one obnoxious boy called her "Lobster Girl." The second time he said that to Robbi, they were in the school cafeteria. Without hesitation, she took a tray and broke it over his head. She was suspended for a week, but no one called her names after that.

That incident modified her behavior in a paradoxical way: while she was proud of herself for fighting back, she also subconsciously started hiding her left hand as much as possible. She refused to be defined by—what was it called? Fate? So, she kept her hand balled up into a fist, or deep in her pocket, or under the table, or hidden from view as much as possible. She also wore gloves. Robbi was determined to be judged on her talent and character, and not on her deformed left hand.

Midway through high school, Robbi decided she would first become a lawyer, and then a judge. If life was truly unfair, then she would try to right as many wrongs as she possibly could. She enrolled in the University of Maryland, where, after tearing her ACL on the very first day of soccer practice, she rehabbed in the library, voraciously studying her pre-law textbooks, and reading all she could find on criminal law and procedure. She scoured the library shelves to find books about infamous criminal cases, and became an expert on a nefarious parade of historical world criminals: Jack the Ripper, Charles Manson, and Ted Bundy. She devoured biographies on wrongful convictions, like the Scottsboro Boys, the Rosenbergs, and the Lindbergh kidnapping. She was fascinated by conspiracy theories, like the JFK assassination and dozens of other crimes, criminals, and courtroom trials. It became more than a hobby; it became her passion and her private obsession.

She was accepted into the University of Maryland School of Law in Baltimore, where she thrived academically. Her first year, she studied Constitutional law and contracts and property, but it was criminal law that captured her full attention. Robbi's entire first-year class—they were called "1Ls"—had a mandatory requirement to participate in the schoolwide moot court tournament.

There were 250 1Ls. Robbi killed all of them. The tournament was a single-elimination format where each victory brought her a step closer to the top of the winning pyramid. Confident, logical and extremely articulate, she won not only first place, but was also awarded the prestigious Best Oralist prize. Upon graduation, she was offered jobs at several top law firms throughout Maryland, but she wanted more than anything to come home and help her local community. She was thrilled to accept an appointment as an Assistant State's Attorney at the Seneca County State's Attorney's Office. Her rise there was unprecedented. After only five years, she applied to be a District Court judge, and easily got the recommendation from the Judicial Nomination Commission.

She hid her left hand less and less after that.

"Kristen," Judge Ryan said. "We have a Scheduling Conference in that case the Court of Appeals reversed and remanded back, don't we? It's set for tomorrow morning at 10:00. Correct?"

CHAPTER 7

May 19, 2022
3:19 p.m.

"Yes, Judge, we do," said Kristen Voice, Judge Robbi Ryan's law clerk. Kristen was a tall, lithe young woman who had been a ballet dancer before attending law school. Dressed in an eggshell-colored Anne Klein sleeveless sheath dress suit, she wore a gold chain with an Australian ironstone opal pendant hanging down into her subtle cleavage. Kristen combed her long fingers through her spiky, short, jet-black hair and turned to face Robbi.

"Y'know, Kristen, I never asked you about your last name. Voice. That's very unique. I don't think I've ever met anyone with that surname before. Do you know your genealogy? Is that an Eastern European name?"

"Yes, Judge. That's right. My father always said our heritage was Hungarian or Romanian, I can't remember which. But the original name was Weiss. It's Jewish. We were the Weiss family once. But at Ellis Island, when my great-grandfather first got off the boat, some immigration guy asked him what his name was, and he said 'Weiss.' But, because of his thick accent, it sounded like 'Voice,' and we've been the Voice family ever since."

The two women were standing in Robbi's chambers, a large rectangular room on the ninth floor of the courthouse. The walls were adorned with framed diplomas and landmark achievements of Robbi's career, including a shiny State's Attorney's bronze badge mounted onto a mahogany plaque. Kristen had a small office adjoining Robbi's spacious chambers, but Robbi encouraged her to sit on the couch in the main open area of her chambers so they could keep each other company, and simultaneously bear witness to all the meetings, Zoom calls, in-person arbitrations, and conferences with squabbling attorneys.

"I saw the Lines of Appearance in that Stephens case. We could be in for a slugfest," Robbi said.

"We have two Lines," said Kristen, flipping through the judge's file. "One for—oh, my God—Marcel St. Croix. I love that guy! He is hysterical. I saw him do this cross-examination of a police officer once. The cop said he couldn't hear anything because he was sitting in his cruiser with the windows up. It was amazing. The cop kept saying over and over that he 'rolled up the window.' He kept repeating that he 'rolled it up.' Then Mr. St. Croix asked him to demonstrate *how* he rolled it up, and the cop does this ridiculous stirring motion with his hand, making fast little circles in the air. And then Mr. St. Croix shows him a photo of the inside of the car door, showing it had levers and not one of those old-fashioned window crank things. He proved it was an automatic window which didn't roll up at all! One tiny fib ruined this lying cop's whole testimony."

Robbi smiled and said, "Marcel is a good listener. Sometimes when a witness lies, it's like he's been given a little gift. Rolled up the window. Totally unnecessary detail. But a good cross-examiner will take that embellishment and accept it like an unexpected donation. Then, Marcel will slowly unwrap it, like a gift, right in front of the jury."

"Yes," Kristen continued. "He said in his closing argument—I'll never forget it—that a lie was like a pin. And the truth was like a big balloon. And a little pin, with just one prick, will pop the whole balloon and burst a witness's credibility. And he clapped his hands together really loudly right when he said the word 'burst.' It was so good! He's a great lawyer."

"A not-guilty verdict?"

"Yes, not guilty. I think the jury went out for about thirty minutes. That's all. That lying cop was pissed."

"And did you see? The ASA is Mac MacIntyre. He's no slouch, either. Have you seen him before a jury yet?"

"Oh, yes! Not a full trial, but I saw him do this presentation for all the new law clerks last month. It was about prosecuting big cases and what to expect in the courtroom with handling exhibits and stuff. Oh my God, Judge. He is really *hot!*"

"Kristen! I guess you weren't paying attention to the presentation?"

"I'm sorry, Judge. I didn't mean it to sound that way. But,

seriously, that guy is intense. The way he moves around the courtroom. It's like he's a fencer or something. So smooth."

"Yes," said Judge Ryan. "He certainly knows his way around a courtroom."

"But the thing is, he's so *smart*! And I don't just mean book smart. There is something about him—I can't even describe it. His eyes remind me of a wise old owl. Well, no. More like a hawk. There is something about that look he gets. Like he will swoop down and sink his claws into you. Like you're his prey."

"Don't get carried away."

"Judge, do you know what the word sapiosexual means?"

"No. I'd have to look that one up! Pansexual, polysexual. I get all of those mixed up."

"Never mind," said Kristen. "But do you know what I mean about those green eyes? They're so penetrating. I introduced myself to him after his presentation, and when I looked into his eyes, I just stopped *thinking*. It's like his eyes drilled right into my brain and, like, everything froze. I swear, I think he could hypnotize women with those things!"

"Oh, Kristen."

"And, Judge, he's so tall and slender."

"Tall, yes. But slender? I'd say skinny, if you ask me. If not downright bony. He's all elbows and knees."

Kristen said, "I noticed he wasn't wearing a wedding ring. Do you know if he's dating anyone? You don't think he's too old for me, do you?"

"Ms. Voice! He's *way* too old for you! I'm not exactly sure how old he is, but let me think—he joined the SAO when I was still working there. So, we must've overlapped by about a year. I know him mostly from doing cases up here in Circuit Court. I agree with you: he's very smart, but more importantly, he seems like a good guy, too."

"So, you think he's about 40? That's not too old," said Kristen.

"Well, let's see. He's been an ASA for, I'd guess, 20 years. So, that would make him about 45. That's *way* too old for you!"

"OK, OK. But it's going to be fun to look at him during this Stephens trial. I'll have a front-row view of all the action. Can't wait!"

"Well, you only have to wait until tomorrow's Scheduling Hearing."

CHAPTER 8

May 20, 2022
10:02 a.m.

"All rise!" said Kristen, as Judge Robbi Ryan walked into the courtroom and ascended three small steps to her chair on an elevated platform. From that position, Judge Ryan's perspective allowed her an unobstructed view of the entire space. In authority, and in location, she was now literally above everyone else in the room.

Mac was already standing before the judge entered; he was well versed in the expected choreography of courtroom decorum. He had his day planner spread out on the well-worn counsel table in front of him, but no notes or outlines. Marcel also stood, but he unfolded his body slowly, like a penknife with an old rusty blade. Marcel had his trademark wooden briefcase placed flat on the table. He had used that briefcase for at least two decades; it looked like an artist's slender box of oil paints, and it held only a sliver of the necessary legal documents, but it looked impressive, and Marcel St. Croix always wanted to look impressive. There were two sheriff's deputies in the courtroom, as was usual protocol, since this was a criminal case and the deputies were charged with the responsibility of maintaining security inside the courtroom.

Judge Ryan sat down and flipped open her laptop, activated it and added, "Ms. Voice, hang on a sec..." as the computer noisily whirred into action. Mac and Marcel stood patiently.

"OK, it's up and running now," the judge said. "Deputies, you can get the Defendant. We are ready." One deputy left the circular courtroom through a side door, and Mac could hear a clanging sound as a metal door, just out of view, was unlocked.

Within seconds, the deputy returned with Eddie Stephens, who was dressed in an olive-green jail jumpsuit. Since this was merely a scheduling matter, and no jurors would be present, the rule that all defendants must be dressed in civilian clothing—and not prison garb—did not apply. Eddie's arms were still handcuffed behind his back. When he got to his seat at the defense table next to Marcel, he paused and turned his back toward the deputy to allow the unclasping of his cuffs. Eddie had done this pirouette thousands of times. He briefly rubbed his wrists and glanced around the courtroom, which was empty except for his mother, Tamika, sitting in the last row. Eddie looked at Tamika, smiled, and silently mouthed to her, "I love you." Tamika was a large woman wearing a burgundy-and-gold Washington Redskins hoodie and white sneakers. She sniffled loudly and used a large cluster of crumpled, wet Kleenex tissues, like a white carnation, to dab at her runny nose.

Mac followed Eddie's glance and saw Tamika sitting in the back row.

Judge Ryan said, "OK, everyone is here. Please call the case, Madam Clerk."

Kristen announced, "State of Maryland versus Edward DeLawrence Stephens, case number 2407777300-02-C."

Mac turned to face Judge Ryan, who was still preoccupied with her computer screen, and said, "Mac MacIntyre for the State, Your Honor. Good morning."

"Good morning, sir," the judge replied, peering toward Mac. She shifted her gaze to the defense table where Marcel remained standing and Eddie was now sitting down next to him, listening intently.

"May it please the Court, Marcel St. Croix for Mr. Stephens, who is present in the courtroom and sitting next to me to my right."

"Good morning to you as well, gentlemen," Judge Ryan repeated, addressing both Marcel and Eddie. "So, we are here on a Status Conference," she said. "First of all, we've cleared some dates with the Assignment Office for a five-day trial. Mr. MacIntyre and Mr. St. Croix, we have blocked out the week of September 19th. Is that time frame acceptable to both of you?"

Mac flipped through his day planner and responded, "Yes, judge. I have a plea calendared for that Monday, but I think that's going to be rescheduled, so, yes, we can reserve that week. I would estimate that we are looking at a five-day jury trial, that is, unless we can resolve this matter before then."

"Mr. St. Croix?" Judge Ryan asked.

"Your Honor, that week comports with my calendar as well, but frankly, I don't anticipate a five-day retrial. I'm very hopeful the State will use its discretion in this case."

Mac knew instantly that the phrase "use its discretion" was courtroom code for "hopefully, the State will drop this case." He did not respond, knowing that Marcel was baiting him.

Judge Ryan said, "Well, let's just set the dates and reserve that time frame with AO in case there is no meeting of the minds. Of course, let my law clerk, Ms. Voice, know if you gentlemen reach a resolution before July 25th."

"Certainly, Your Honor," said Marcel, who was intentionally deferential but bordering on obsequy. "I trust the Court's judgment."

Mac said, "That week is fine with me, Judge."

Jesus, Marcel, do you have to lay it on so thick? You've been inside this courthouse since it was built, and you were probably an attorney before Robbi was even born.

"Ms. Voice," the judge said, "Please call down to AO and tell them those dates are acceptable. Thank you." Kristen picked up a landline phone on her small desk and covered her mouth as she whispered into the telephone receiver. She was looking at Mac as she murmured into the telephone receiver.

"So, gentlemen, let's set a date for Motions. Something a bit earlier, perhaps in June? Are we anticipating any Motions, Mr. St. Croix?"

"I'm sorry, Your Honor, may I have the Court's indulgence?"

This was a proper, overly formal way for Marcel to

request a very brief pause so that he could discuss something confidential with his client. With some effort, Marcel leaned down close to Eddie's ear and softly said something. From years of experience, Marcel knew that the circular design of the courtroom produced awkward acoustics; the round, curved walls tossed fragments of private conversations all the way around the room like a boomerang, allowing experienced attorneys moments of uninvited eavesdropping.

Marcel put his hand in the small of his back and grimaced slightly. He sat down next to Eddie.

"Thank you, Judge," Marcel said. "Yes, should this case proceed further, we will have a Motion to Suppress an Identification, specifically a photo array which was conducted in this case. We will object to that extrajudicial identification pretrial at Motions."

Judge Ryan, acknowledging Marcel's statement, said, "Very well. Mr. MacIntyre, you are on notice. Mr. St. Croix, I expect that if you have any other Motions, or any Motions in Limine, that you will notify the State and the Court promptly."

"Yes, of course. Certainly," Marcel confirmed.

"Well," said Judge Ryan, "Let's set a date for Motions, too. I'll block out the morning of Friday, June 17th. So, gentlemen, are there any other issues which need to be resolved at this time?"

Marcel turned toward Mac and then back at Judge Ryan, and said, "There is the matter of discovery, Your Honor. As the Court knows, this is a retrial from a case that was previously litigated back in 2003. We do have trial transcripts available to us, and the original trial exhibits have been recalled from the Circuit Court archives, so we are satisfied with the production of those items. However, at this time, we would make an oral Motion and Demand for Discovery. Of course, we will supplement our oral request with a written Motion forthcoming. But, Your Honor, as the Court well knows, we are *entitled* under law to have *all* discovery that the State is possession of."

"Mr. MacIntyre," said Judge Ryan. "Any response? Does the State aver that you have already provided full discovery in accordance with Maryland rules?"

All I have is a practically empty case file. I don't even have the evidence myself.

"Your Honor, I am awaiting the delivery of the original evidence box from police archives. Once I receive it, I am happy to share the entire contents of the box, except, naturally, any privileged items such as work product or confidential internal notes. I should be able to have all of the discovery copied, scanned, and e-filed with Mr. St. Croix's office by the end of the week. It'll come as a big file with PDF attachments, but if there are any issues downloading any of the materials, I would be happy to facilitate the transfer should it become necessary, Judge."

Marcel began to stand up quickly, but his sore back betrayed him.

Mac smiled slightly, recognizing what Marcel was doing.

Oh my God, can you please spare the theatrics? There's no jury here.

As he was rising, Marcel loudly announced, "Judge, just to be clear, we are requesting the entire contents of the evidence box, not just the items the State *feels* is appropriate to share. In a case that's two decades old, the defense is in a difficult position, and we need to be fully prepared. As Your Honor knows from reading the Court of Appeals's decision, there was gross ineffectiveness and incompetence by my client's former attorney. We certainly do not wish for a repeat of that unfortunate injustice. Therefore, we are requesting *all* of the evidence in this case and not, shall we say, just the evidence the State deems relevant. We request all of it."

"Mr. St. Croix," Judge Ryan said. "As you know, Mr. MacIntyre is an experienced prosecutor. We've both known him for many years. I am sure he understands his obligations with respect to both the SAO open-file discovery policies and, also, with respect to any potential *Brady* material. If this becomes a problem, Mr. St. Croix, I trust you know how to file the appropriate Motion to Compel Discovery. I am also available for an *in camera* review of any contested material. However, I am positive that this will not be an issue."

She turned her head toward Mac and said, "Correct, Mr. MacIntyre?"

"Yes, Judge Ryan. Absolutely," Mac answered.

"Gentlemen, anything else?"

"No, thank you," Marcel said.

"Nothing from the State," Mac confirmed.

"Thank you both. We will see you in June," the judge said. She stood up and walked down the steps toward the doorway to her chambers.

Kristen announced, "All rise! Court is in recess," as she followed the judge out of the courtroom. Before she stepped through the door to chambers, she glanced back one last time to see if Mac was watching her. He was.

Eddie stood up, turned, and shook Marcel's hand. He then waved to his mother in the back of the courtroom.

Tamika blew kisses toward Eddie.

The deputy shackled Eddie's hands behind his back and escorted him out of the courtroom.

Marcel said to Tamika across the empty courtroom, "Mrs. Stephens, I'll meet you outside in a minute." He then made a shooing motion with his hand, indicating she should wait for him in the hallway. Tamika picked up her large black leather shoulder bag and slowly walked down the center aisle and out through the double doors.

Marcel turned to Mac. They were the only two people left in the courtroom.

"Mac, I tell you, some shady things happened back when this case went to trial the first time around. Stay in touch with me on this one, OK? Please examine that old discovery carefully, will you?"

"Of course. On any plea offer, I will need to talk with Mr. Fischbein and Deputy State's Attorney Jo Newgrange. You know how it is. These things are not my sole decision, y'know."

"I trust you, Mac. You've always been very upfront with me. So, let me repeat—I trust you." They shook hands, and Marcel picked up his thin, stylish wooden briefcase and walked down the center aisle toward the hallway.

Mac took an extra moment to gather his day planner and his thoughts.

Where is Andre with that evidence box?

CHAPTER 9

May 20, 2002
11:51 a.m.

"Oh, Kristen!" Judge Ryan said, raising her voice so it could be heard across her chambers.

"Yes, Judge?"

"Can you please bring this Motion down to Mr. MacIntyre's office in the SAO? It's one of those boilerplate things—State's Motion in Response to the Defendant's Motion to Suppress. They file them automatically in every criminal case, so it's nothing special. But Mac's admin forgot to have him sign it, and rather than ordering him to file the whole thing over again, it'll be easier if you take this original copy down to his office. Just get his signature and bring it back."

"Sure. No problem. I've got nothing planned. Just another quiet, boring lunch break."

Mac sat at his desk and finished his toasted bagel. As he crumpled up the paper plate and tossed it across the room into the wastepaper basket, his desk phone rang.

"Mac, hey, it's Lupe. Your girlfriend Zaria from the PD's office is here. She says she has a report to drop off for you. I sent her down the hallway to your office. OK?"

"She's not my girlfriend, Lupe."

"Whatever. Like I always say, *cuidame mis secretos*. All of your secrets are safe with me, Macaroni."

"I trust you."

"Well, enjoy reading her report," Lupe said.

"It will be my pleasure."

"Oh, Mac, I forgot to tell you, one of the new law clerks came down to the front desk asking for you like half an hour ago. I figured you were busy with that new case, so I told her to come back after lunch."

"Which law clerk was that?"

"I forgot to ask her name. Sorry. It's crazy up here right now. Everyone's coming and going. There's like a crowd waiting for the elevators. It was that new law clerk. The tall, pretty one. She has big eyes and short black hair."

"Does she look like the young woman in *The Girl with the Pearl Earring*, the painting by Vermeer?"

"Mac," said Lupe. "What the hell are you talking about? You always do that. Refer to some trivia from history long ago and I have no idea what you mean."

"Oh, sorry. There is this famous painting. It's by a Dutch

artist named Johannes Vermeer. He lived from 1632 to 1675. One of his most famous paintings has a girl who looks exactly like Kristen, Judge Robbi Ryan's new law clerk."

"Hey, Mac, I don't have time to talk about stuff like this from 400 years ago, Mr. Trivial Pursuit. OK? If you want to go on *Who Wants to Be a Millionaire* and split the money with me, I'm good with that. Otherwise, I'm on my lunch break now. I'm heading down to the cafeteria. Need anything?"

"No thanks, Lupe. I already grabbed a bagel and coffee from the snack bar. I'm good. See you later."

Zaria stepped into Mac's office and shut the door behind her. She was wearing a dark blue turtleneck blouse, a short black miniskirt, and flat shoes that looked like slippers. The hemline of her skirt accentuated the length of her thin legs, and, while she stood nearly six feet tall, her arms and legs seemed even longer. She leaned back against the inside of the door but did not reach down to the doorknob to lock it. Her dark hair glistened in the harsh overhead office lights, contrasting sharply with the paleness of her skin. Her grey eyes narrowed, like a cat, as she peered directly at Mac.

She said, "*Dipendenza*."

Mac whispered, "You never told me how to say that in Slovenian, Z. But I remember you said that's the Italian word for *addiction*."

Zaria tossed the manila envelope she was carrying onto the couch and put her forefinger up to her lips. Mac glanced at the closed but unlocked office door, and then turned to look directly at Zaria.

Their eyes locked, and she stood still, staring back at him.

He reached out with his right hand and very gently touched her elbow. He could feel a nearly undetectable tremor through the soft texture of her cotton turtleneck.

"Are you sure?" Mac whispered.

She leaned forward, just slightly, and nodded while staring into his eyes.

With a soft touch, he delicately guided her toward him.

Mac said, "We have to be quiet." The staccato tapping of footsteps scurrying outside in the hallway penetrated his closed plywood door.

All of the logical and rational thoughts that constantly swirled in Mac's mind evaporated, giving him the transitory relief he craved, and something else—something at once intoxicating and also stimulating—washed over his mind.

She pressed her open lips inquisitively against Mac's mouth, as if seeking permission for his surrender. Feeling no resistance, she hungrily kissed him and wrapped both of her arms around his head. She grasped his red hair tightly with both hands and possessively pulled him against her chest. Conquered, he thrust his tongue into her mouth and swirled it around, two tongues sparring in moist circles.

With his right hand, he reached up behind his head and encircled her left wrist like a handcuff. She pressed her entire body against him, her small breasts flattening against his chest. He guided her hand to his lap.

She brushed against his hardness with the back of her hand and gasped loudly.

Someone ran down the hallway.

Mac said, "Don't make a sound."

She pressed her palm down into his lap, sensing warmth through the cloth of his suit pants. She grasped him hard and felt his body heat pulsating in her fist.

He moaned, but Zaria quickly raised her other hand and covered his mouth.

"Shhhh!" She smiled, saying, "People can hear."

Mac leaned back and placed his arms behind him, making his torso into a tripod shape for balance.

She quickly unbuckled his belt and adroitly unzipped his pants. As she reached down to free him from the tightness of his clothes, Mac looked up at the ceiling and then closed his eyes. She held on to him tightly with her hand at the base of his groin and felt him throbbing against her encircled fingers. She said, "Just relax," and then she knelt down on the carpeted floor before him.

His breathing became quicker and more urgent.

Zaria rocked her head slowly, then quickly, then, as she could feel him rising, she sprinted furiously until he could hold back no longer. He collapsed backward onto his elbows. When he stopped quivering, she rose from the floor, but still held on to him, feeling him soften in her hand with exhausted satisfaction.

She stood, leaned against Mac's chest, and wrapped her arms around him.

He shifted and sat on the edge of the desk again while she stood between his legs.

His hands became very active.

He gently reached up under her skirt and circumvented her sheer damp panties.

Zaria buried her face into his shoulder, leaving a black smear of mascara smudged on his white dress shirt. She closed her eyes and pressed her mouth against his firm convex deltoid to buffer or attempt to silence any uncontrolled gasps she couldn't possibly suppress.

His fingers quickly found her most sensitive spot. Gently, then very gently, he swirled his index finger clockwise round and round. He teased her until her passion rose inexorably to a surrender, like an untethered helium balloon drifting haphazardly higher and higher into the wind.

As she was carried away to her zenith, she bit down hard into Mac's shoulder, sinking her front teeth completely through the fabric of his shirt and into his flesh like she was biting into an apple.

He did not react to the pain.

As her heartbeat gradually slowed, he lifted both of his arms and held her tightly. She stood, wobbly, leaning against him, her legs trembling.

After a moment to bask in the intensity of the electric currents coursing through both of their bodies, Zaria opened her eyes and saw two spots of bright red blood staining the white cloth covering Mac's shoulder.

"Oh my God! I'm sorry!"

"Don't worry," said Mac. "It's nothing."

"Jesus, I tore a hole in your shirt!"

"It's fine. I'll just wear my jacket, and no one will ever know."

Zaria straightened up her skirt and ran her fingers through her hair. She looked at Mac again.

"That was incredible."

Mac smiled, tilted his head, and said, "There's more where that came from. You know I'm addicted, Z." He reached into his bottom desk drawer, retrieved a box of Kleenex, and quickly fashioned an improvised bandage.

Zaria frowned and softly exclaimed, "I've hurt you. I'm so sorry."

"I love it. I hope it's a scar. Something to remember this moment forever."

"A scar?" she asked.

"He jests at scars that never felt a wound."

She couldn't form any intelligible words, so she softly moaned a primal sound in response.

Mac clarified, "That's from *Romeo and Juliet*."

She purred, "I've got to get back to the PD's office."

"The balcony scene. Act Two, scene two."

Leaning forward, she kissed Mac's lips farewell and looked deeply into his light green eyes one last time before she left his office. Turning, she said, "*Hvala vam*. You remember how to say 'thank you' in my language?"

As Kristen walked past Zaria in the hallway, she noted Zaria's miniskirt and disheveled shirt. Kristen turned to watch Zaria walk unsteadily away from her, wrinkled her brow in thought, and then approached Mac's office. She knocked on the door.

Mac stood, dropped his coffee cup into the wastepaper basket, and opened the door.

Kristen smiled and looked up into Mac's eyes. She immediately forgot what she was going to say, gulped, and said, "Hi, Mr. MacIntyre."

"Oh please, call me Mac," he replied, standing back and gesturing with his left arm in a sweeping motion inward. "Come in. You need me to sign a Motion?"

She took two steps into his office.

He closed the door behind her.

Kristen said, "Oh, it smells like perfume or something in here."

"No, that's just my lunch," Mac replied, gesturing at the trash can.

"Um, well, oh, right," Kristen stammered. "Judge Ryan asked me to bring you this." She handed him the document. "You filed this in the—the—I can't remember the name of the case right now. God, that's embarrassing!" She reached up and used her fingers to fork her hair backwards.

Mac asked, "The case we just did the Status Conference for today? The Stephens case?"

"Yes. Sorry. I'm not thinking straight."

He sat on the edge of the desk facing her and picked up a pen.

"Um, it's not signed," Kristen said. "Judge Ryan asked me to…" Her voice faded away as Mac preemptively took the paper from her and placed it flat on his desk.

"I always sign the original Motion in blue ink. That way, I can tell the difference between the original and a Xerox copy."

"Oh. I get it. That's smart," she said.

Mac flipped the pages of the document over and signed the last page. Done, he picked it up and handed it back. He smiled and said, "Thank you. You are very nice to bring this Motion down. It saves me tons of work. I really appreciate it."

She didn't move.

After a moment, Mac said, "Well, I'll see you up in court soon. I've got to get back to work now. Thanks."

Kristen looked up at a framed drawing directly over Mac's desk. It was a child's sketch in crayon colors depicting a stick-figure of a man with red hair. The handwritten caption said:

"TO THE STAIT'S ATTOURNY MAC. YOU ARE VERY NICE AND THANK YOU FOR HEPLING MY GRAMMA. LOVE MADISON"

"What's this?" she asked. "Do you have kids?"

"Oh, no. No," Mac said. "This is a thank-you note a victim gave me years ago."

"You got it framed, Mac?"

"Yes."

Kristen turned back, made eye contact, and said, "You said it was OK to call you Mac, right?"

"Of course! Take care."
Kristen smiled, turned, and left the office.

CHAPTER 10

May 20, 2022
3:32 p.m.

"Andre, did you see yesterday's paper? The Stephens case was all over the front page. Talking about possible police corruption and change of venue. Someone talked to the reporter. Probably his attorney trying to pollute the jury pool. Tactical move."

"Defense attorney is slick."

"So, I met with The Fish and Jo Newgrange. For some reason, they desperately want to keep this case quiet, and they are going to be freaked out by all this press." Mac paused and said, "The cat's out of the bag."

"You're hysterical, Mr. Cliché! Cat's out of the bag."

"Wait, I can hardly hear you. Where are you? Somewhere with shitty reception, obviously. You're not playing basketball instead of working again, are you?"

"No. I'm digging through this archive place, and I found

your box of evidence. Took me two days to find this shit. So you can say 'thank you' right now."

"Thank you. What did you find?"

"I've never been down to this dungeon before. My buddy showed me where to look. It's a dusty basement at the old Sixth District station. Row after row of old boxes. Looks like an Amazon warehouse. Took a while, but I found it. Mac, something's weird about this box, though."

"What?"

"It's all taped up with like layers and layers of duct tape. Never seen this shit before. Is there a gun or a bomb in this box?"

"I highly doubt that. Can you cut it open and look while I'm on the phone and we have a connection?"

There was a pause in the conversation. Mac could hear cutting noises and shuffling of papers.

"Got it open," Andre said. "Just a normal-looking evidence box. I see about 20 legal pads with notes—the handwriting is print, no script—and a bunch of manila envelopes. There's a stack of forensic reports and a few photographs, too. I see a floor plan of the apartment where the shooting took place. Cops must have gotten that from the rental office at the complex where the dead guy lived. But why the hell was this box secured so tight and taped round and round? Whatever. I'll bring this up to your office. Be there in fifteen minutes."

"Oh, I almost forgot: Marcel St. Croix is the lawyer representing Eddie Stephens. Did you see that in the newspaper article?"

"Oh shit, not him. Not that French guy. He's such a hot dog in court."

"He's Canadian, French Canadian, from Quebec. Somewhere way up there by the North Pole."

"Whatever. French, French Canadian. Same thing. Maybe the dude is Santa Claus? Maybe he's an Eskimo?"

"He's a really good attorney, Andre. Yeah, I know, he likes being in the spotlight, but a jury trial is kind of like being on a stage. We are all actors in a way."

"*You* are, for sure. You against Frenchie? That's going to be prime time."

Mac lifted the evidence box from the floor, placed it on his desk, and then tugged at a strip of the fraying, grey duct tape wrapped around the box. Andre was sitting on the couch scrolling through his phone.

Mac said, "Damn, you're right. Someone really wanted this box shut tight."

Andre stood and stepped over to the desk, discarding his black leather motorcycle jacket, dumping it unceremoniously on the floor, where it lay in a clump, like a dog on a rug before a fireplace.

Mac gingerly lifted the cover off the box. Silently, both men gazed down into the square opening. There was obvious water damage to the entire right side of the box, as if it had once been soaked in a minor flood, or had actually been rained upon, and had then dried slowly after years of seclusion. The brown cardboard was wrinkled and discolored with blotches of grey, and the papers directly under the damaged lid were stained. Someone long ago had written STEPHENS on the box's top in large block letters. Now, the ink was faded to a ghostly green tint, and the two right-most letters had disappeared entirely, so that the writing said STEPHE only.

Mac started gently examining the box's contents, carefully shuffling through the manila envelopes and notepads like a croupier handling cards in a casino.

Andre said, "Hey, what the hell is *that?*" He pointed at a manila envelope that was also incongruously sealed with several pieces of the same grey duct tape. The two once-sturdy, thick elastic bands around it had cracked over time and split, lying sideways like a twin pair of dead worms.

Mac stared at the envelope but did not pick it up.

"Do you have your Leatherman?" Mac asked.

Andre stepped over to his motorcycle jacket, reached down to the floor, poked around in the side pocket, and retrieved the utensil. He handed it to Mac.

Flicking his fingernail to release a small, sharp blade, Mac carefully sliced the top of the envelope, reached in with his index finger and thumb, and pulled out a single sheet of paper. It was a page from one of the familiar yellow legal pads that were used by every attorney in the SAO. In addition to the stains, which gave the page the appearance of a blurry watercolor sketch, the page had been folded and refolded several times: first in half, then in quadrants, then eighths, then sixteenths. When fully folded, it would be small enough to have once sought refuge in a wallet many years ago.

Mac shook the paper flat and then laid it on the top of the box.

It was a handwritten note. Some letters were nearly invisible with decay and some totally absent, vanished with the passing of time.

Mac and Andre studied the mysterious page carefully but could not make any sense of it.

"Look there!" Andre exclaimed, pointing to words written on the paper.

CHAPTER 11

May 20, 2022
5:15 p.m.

B U N A S E R A
H R B &
$750 – GJT.
$750 – T.

For   vices ende d."

B: Mark work prod . 911*

CONFIDENTIA

CHAPTER 12

May 23, 2022
9:00 a.m.

"Good day, this is Marcel St. Croix speaking."

"Mr. St. Croix—um, Marcel, this is Mac MacIntyre calling from the State's Attorney's Office. Is this a good time to talk?"

"Well, well, *c'est magnifique*! If it isn't the most brilliant prosecutor in the State of Maryland calling. To what do I owe the pleasure?"

Mac leaned back in his swivel chair and picked up a felt-tip pen. He reached across the desk and grabbed a legal pad. He wrote in the corner of the first page:

T/C Marcel St. C. 5/23 9:00

Mac smiled and said, "OK, OK, Marcel, enough with the soft sell. I know how you operate. Seriously, do you have a few minutes?"

"*Mais oui! Certainement*. Sure. I'm in my car heading to

Baltimore, so if I need to put the phone down, I'll let you know. Last thing I need is a ticket from another one of these corrupt cops swarming all over Seneca County."

"I'm sure you could smooth-talk your way out of a traffic ticket, *Monsieur*."

"*C'est vrai!* So, Mac, I hope you've decided to drop this Stephens retrial. Excellent decision."

A small, wry grin involuntarily formed in the corner of Mac's mouth. Gamesmanship, banter, panache, and psychological warfare were the tools of the criminal defense attorney's trade.

"Maybe I didn't read the same newspaper as you did?" Mac replied. "I missed the part about entering a *nolle pros*. But I did see that *someone's* been talking to the press. Pretrial publicity and all that good stuff. Are you really looking for a change of venue, *mon ami*? Because, Marcel, if we take this show on the road and try this case in, say, Allegheny County, or somewhere on the Eastern Shore, your client might not do so well."

"Slow down, Mac. No one said anything about a change of venue. I haven't done any demographic studies recently, but can I ask you: are there *any* Black people in Allegheny County? And I'm not so sure a long-haired hippie Indian like me would impress the jurors out there on the West Virginia border. So, we will be very happy to stay home in liberal, left-leaning, highly educated Seneca County for this one."

"Me too. It's easier to take the elevator from my office to the courtroom than drive out toward West Virginia. Works for me."

"Oh, and easier for Judge Bennington to walk across the hallway to testify, *n'est-çe pas?*"

The phone call was disconnected.

Marcel must be going through the Baltimore Harbor Tunnel. No reception there.

Mac dialed Marcel's number again but heard, "You've reached the law office of Marcel St. Croix and associates. I'm sorry, but I cannot take your call. Please leave a detailed message when you hear the tone, and I will return your call as soon as I can. Thank you and have a nice day."

Mac hung up. Immediately, his phone rang.

"Hey Marcel, did you get cut off?"

There was no answer. Mac glanced down at the Caller ID. It said BLOCKED.

Oh Jesus. Not this shit again.

He could barely hear what sounded like someone panting, but the sound was muffled, as if a hand was placed over the telephone receiver.

Mac said, "Hey, who is this? Listen, whoever you are, I have some work to do so can you please stop with these hang-up prank calls? Do I have to ask my detective to trace these? I really don't want to file an Information for telephone harassment, OK?"

Mac listened. Whoever was calling was still listening. Mac hung up. After a short pause, Mac redialed Marcel again. The call went through.

"Sorry, Marcel. I lost you for a sec. Bad reception. You must be away from a cell tower. What were you saying?"

"You damn well heard me. I was saying before you hung

up the phone on me—are you absolutely sure you want Judge Bennington pulled into this hornet's nest? My client is telling me some very interesting stuff. I don't think I've ever heard of a case where a sitting Circuit Court judge testified as a witness in a murder trial—let me think. No, sir. And I've been around these Seneca County courtrooms for fifty years."

"There's a first time for everything, I guess," Mac replied. "I think he would make a very impressive witness, don't you?"

Mac jotted down on a legal pad: **BENNINGTON MY WIT OR MARCEL'S AS A DEF WIT?**

Marcel shot back, "Well now, I guess that all depends on what he has to say? Were you planning to call him as a State's witness? Or leave him for me to testify on behalf of the defense?"

"I guess that all depends on what he has to say," said Mac, trying to mimic Marcel's exact tone of voice.

"Then there's that redneck liar, Assistant Chief Harper," Marcel said, continuing to pry and poke. "Not to mention that alcoholic dirt bag Sergeant York. This retrial is going to be quite a freak show. A real three-ring circus. Maybe you've got the Bearded Lady and the Siamese Twins on your witness list, too? Hey, any way you slice it, it's great publicity for my law firm. You know how shy I am when it comes to press conferences and TV appearances, right?"

"Shy? You? The Magician Marcel St. Croix? I know how much you love to pull a rabbit out of a hat inside the courtroom. But these witnesses? I'm not worried about them. They are all professionals with many years of experience testifying."

"True. But this time *I* will be doing the cross-examinations, not some *ineffective* public defender." Marcel let the word 'ineffective' hang in the air.

Mac said, "OK, can we both stop with all the posturing? Listen, Marcel. I am inclined to offer your client a plea and agree to his immediate release. He's been at Broad Run long enough. But I just can't drop this case. I've got strict marching orders from Ari Fischbein. He is insistent that your client plead guilty to a lesser charge. He and the Deputy State's Attorney—Jo Newgrange—have you had any cases with her, Marcel?"

"That woman with the fake red hair? Yes, I have met her and, keep this between us, I was less than overwhelmed with her sincerity."

"Underwhelmed?"

"What's that? I can't hear you very well."

"Never mind. But, Marcel, *mon ami*, Stephens will have to plead guilty to something. Anything. How does a manslaughter with time served sound? It's a great offer."

"No, sir. That will never fly. Mr. Stephens is innocent. Your girl Makayla picked the wrong guy out of a bad photo lineup, and your cops didn't exactly play fair, to put it mildly. Mac, Stephens is adamant. And his mother, too. He's not pleading guilty to anything. He actually *wants* a trial so he can prove his innocence. So, it's either you *nolle* the case outright and we'll call it a day, or we go to trial and everything—including the ugly stuff—will see the light of day. Those are your two choices."

"That's impossible, Marcel. I can't just drop a murder trial where the guy already got convicted beyond a reasonable doubt by a jury! You know I'll never get approval for that."

"You are the prosecutor, Mac. Impossible, you say? You're the one with all the power. You can *easily* make it happen. Just file a Motion to Dismiss and you'll get no opposition from me. Hang on, I'm going through the tunnel."

Mac could only hear a buzzing sound on his phone as Marcel was zipping underground and the reception was interrupted. It gave Mac a chance to pause his thoughts, recalculate, and analyze his choices. He wrote on his pad:

WILL NOT TAKE A PLEA AT ALL. SAYS IT'S A TRIAL OR A NOLLE?

Marcel's voice reemerged from the phone receiver.

"Sorry. The E-Z Pass lane is blocked. Baltimore is a dump. I don't know why I even come here anymore. So, as I was saying, Eddie Stephens has been locked up at Broad Run for 20 years based on lies and incompetence and possibly worse. Do you really want *your* name attached to this pile of stinking garbage?"

Mac didn't respond but wrote on his pad:

NEED TO TALK TO BENNINGTON.

Marcel continued his pitch, "*Nolle* this case and you'll be a hero. Let this innocent man go free. Explain it like that to Ari Fischbein. Listen, I know a narcissist when I see one. Tell him if the case is dropped, he can spin this to make it look like he's a champion of justice. If he takes that route, could be lots of good press? I'll get that Dan Morris of the *Journal* to write a great article. And we all know that publicity is his drug of choice."

"The Fish. Ink runs in his veins."

"What did you say?"

"Never mind."

"I *know* you, Mac. We've had many cases together over the years. You are a good man, and I know you have a conscience. Let this guy go free. Do the right thing."

"Let me see what I can do, but don't get your hopes up, OK?"

"Trust me," Marcel said. "I'm psyched for a trial with dirty police officers and an unethical Circuit Court judge. Definitely would be interesting. Hey, and another thing: let me know when you talk to this airhead Makayla Schweitzer. If *she's* your star witness, I like my chances."

Mac wrote:

ANDRE: DID YOU FIND MAKAYLA????

CHAPTER 13

May 23, 2022
9:00 a.m.

Makayla O'Reilly popped open a can of Fancy Feast Minced Chicken in Gravy cat food, picked up a tablespoon, and scraped out the lumpy wet contents into a small oval-shaped bowl. She reached down and placed it on the floor by the bottom of the dishwasher and said, "Coconut! Time to eat." An ancient white cat, with a belly whisking across the floor, slowly walked over and sniffed the bowl. Satisfied, Makayla turned and slid open a trash container under the sink and tossed the empty can into the garbage. She held the spoon up to her nostrils and wrinkled her nose.

She looked around the spacious kitchen of her large suburban home, readying herself for the day.

Mail those bills, call the lawn care service, and check on Colin's dry cleaning at the Korean place next to the mall. Anything else?

Life was pretty simple now, at least compared to how it used to be.

Let me think: Colin won't be home from work until around 6:30, so I'll still have time to get in my steps on the Peloton. Then I'll grill some salmon for dinner.

Her cell phone rang. She pulled it out of the back pocket of her purple Lululemon Align yoga pants and glanced at the Caller ID. It said UNKNOWN.

Oh, Lordy, not another scammer or solicitor! Or maybe it's another survey asking if I still vote for the Republican candidates.

"Hello, this is Makayla O'Reilly. Can I help you?"

"Good morning. My name is Andre Okoye, and I'm a detective with the Seneca County State's Attorney's Office. Is this Makayla Schweitzer O'Reilly?"

She dropped the spoon on the floor.

"I found her, Mac," said Andre.

"Jesus. Good work, man. Where the hell was she?"

"She lives in Ashton, Virginia. Very nice neighborhood. Must be million-dollar homes out there. Real rich, cul-de-sac kind of place. And her name is changed. She's been married for 16 years, according to the Civil Clerk's Office in Loudon County. Her husband is a guy named Colin O'Reilly. He's owns a Toyota dealership, possibly two. He definitely makes decent money."

"You're on fire today, Andre."

"I've got her Facebook page open here on my computer

right now. Instagram, TikTok, they are all over social media. Look like the perfect, happy, blond, privileged couple."

"Barbie and Ken, huh?"

"No. His name is Colin, and she's Makayla, Mac."

"I know. I was being sarcastic. I meant they probably look like perfect little white privileged dolls."

"10-4. Copy that."

"Barbie and Ken dolls. They were introduced to the American toy market in 1956 by Mattel."

"I know what a Barbie doll is, Mac. But we didn't play with that shit on West 127th Street. Too busy with pigeons and rats."

"Sorry. But, I have to say, I'm surprised. I would have thought Makayla would be dead by now, or incarcerated, or wasting away in some homeless shelter."

"I'm seeing something here online about a rehab center, too. It's called Noah's Ark in Elkins, West Virginia. Christian bullshit, born again and all that propaganda. I went to their website, but I can't get into any of their confidential records. Let me work on that and try to get around their firewall. But, anyway, it looks like Barbie and Ken have given several large donations. I'm guessing she got cleaned up a long time ago, and now they feel indebted or whatever."

Mac said, "I would have never guessed she'd make a transformation like that."

"Well, some people actually *do* turn their lives around. Hey, if she's going to testify for us, it's a hell of a lot better that she's no longer some scuzzy street addict trading blowjobs for rocks of crack, right? So, this is a good development."

"Andre, did you tell her why we want to interview her?"

"Not really. Not in detail, but I explained you were the prosecutor, and you needed to talk with her right away. She didn't seemed surprised, which was weird."

"But did she agree to come in and talk to us, or are we going to have to do an Interstate Material Witness subpoena for her? Technically, it's Virginia so we have to jump through all of these hoops to get her back here in Maryland. You know what a pain in the ass that process is."

Andre replied, "She said she would come to your office tomorrow. I did mention the word *subpoena*. I know that Interstate bullshit is a drag, but there's no way she will figure that out, so I think she'll come in voluntarily for an interview."

"Let's say 11:00 tomorrow. You go pick her up and drive her here so she can't bail in the middle of the meeting. She'll need you for a ride back to Virginia."

"I'll go get her. Good idea. Reserve the SAO conference room for 11:00."

"Did you actually tell her that the Stephens case was reversed for a new trial?"

"I didn't have to. Seemed like she already knew. Not sure how. Just as we were about to hang up, she said, 'I've been trying to forget about that shooting. I had nightmares for years.' She either saw something about it on the news, or maybe Frenchie's already gotten to her. But she said she would come in tomorrow, so we just gotta roll with that."

"Excellent work finding her, Andre. Nightmares, huh?"

"That's what she said. Oh, man. You're not doing that insomnia thing again, Mac, are you? You OK?"

"Um, I'm fine. Thanks."

"No, I can tell. Are the dreams coming back? You know I deal with that PTSD shit too, man. It's nothing to be ashamed of, y'know?"

"I'm not ashamed."

"Are you thinking about your wife? Does Celine come back to you in your dreams?"

"Sometimes. When I feel stressed."

CHAPTER 14

May 18, 2004
11:02 a.m.

Celine swooped her rental bicycle down Noorderstraat, whizzing over the well-worn herringbone pattern of the rust-colored bricks. The sound of her wheels buzzing matched the bumblebees down by the water's edge. She was as confident as an Amsterdam native born to the skill, not an American tourist on her honeymoon.

"Hey, babe! Be careful!" Mac shouted from behind as he trailed her, trying to keep up with her pace, but Celine was a free spirit and not easily tamed. Her long, light brown hair plumed out behind her in the cool, springtime breeze. Mac churned the wheels on his creaky bike to catch up, mounting the ancient humpbacked bridge over the glorious Prinsengracht canal. Celine pumped her athletic legs, quickly advancing further ahead of him.

He stopped at the apex of the bridge to catch his breath,

resigned to watch Celine glide downward and proceed further up the canal side roadway. The scent of blooming flowers was in the air, mixed with the salty aroma of the brackish water sluicing through the canal. An elderly man wearing a cap was in a rowboat beneath the bridge, his oars rhythmically splashing in the green water. Celine was wearing light blue denim cutoff shorts and a white tank top. Her multicolored Reebok running shoes were a blur of bright shades, swirling like a kaleidoscope, as she pedaled away.

A small, red townhouse with prominent bell gables stood at the corner of the street at the base of the bridge. Only three stories high, it was a typical slender structure, with an exterior that had remained unchanged for centuries. Like most classic townhouses along the canal, it was positioned in a long row of buildings that tilted like dusty books leaning against each other for support on a library shelf.

Legend had it that these dwellings were actually built from ship blueprints, and then, instead of floating horizontally on the water, were turned vertically, and slotted upright in rows. Ancient architects in Holland—borrowing designs from their shipwright brethren—had simply recycled maritime charts to build these tall, narrow homes.

On the façade over the doorway of the red townhouse were the numbers "1675." A shelf-like platform protruded over the door, which provided shelter from the ubiquitous rainstorms in this wet, coastal land. Above the platform stood a large figurine, a carved stone statue, of a stork. A circular nest, also carved in stone, lay at the bird's webbed feet.

The building was known as the Ooievaar Huis, or the

Stork House. Dating to the Golden Age in Dutch history hundreds of years earlier, this small structure was the legendary home of countless generations of midwives. Inside, hearty women—the wives of fishermen, merchants and sailors—had come to deliver their babies, to bring new life into the world. Even then, when almost none of the citizenry could read or write, pregnant women knew where to go. The statue of the stork drew them here, just as similar sculptures above the doorways of other buildings notified the illiterate populace what services or products were for sale: a sculpture of a cow over the butcher's store, a bouquet of stone tulips at the flower market, a pair of sculpted scissors over the tailor's shop.

However, the Stork House was not just a place of birth; it was also a place of death.

Expectant mothers in 17th century Amsterdam did not always face an easy process. Science, medicine and hygiene were evolving practices, competing with superstition and myth. Pregnancy, successful or not, was in the hands of Fate, with the vagaries of chance and luck mixed with the skill of the midwife. Inside the Stork House, a twisted umbilical cord, an uncontrolled hemorrhage, or a minor infection doomed inestimable souls. Despite the risks, giving birth here was a much safer choice than having a baby on a bed of vermin-infested straw somewhere in the maze-like back alleys of the bustling seaport town. Even then, in medieval times, Amsterdam was already centuries old, having developed from a tiny fishing village in Roman times to a mercantile trading post growing rapidly on either side of the Amstel River's dam.

As Celine whipped down the bridge, she did not see that

there was a stick, camouflaged by some leaves lying across the bricks in the roadway. When her front bicycle tire hit the stick, she swerved and, trying to overcorrect her momentum, crashed into a large elm tree directly in front of the Stork House. From 50 feet away, still on the top of the bridge, Mac heard her head crack into the side of the tree with a sickening thud. Celine fell to the street and landed flat on her back, her bike spinning out from underneath her, both tires twirling around like roulette wheels of mortality.

Mac raced down the bridge. "Celine! Are you alright?!" he yelled hopefully, knowing that she was in desperate danger.

But when he got to her as she lay prone on the bricks, he knew she was gone.

Someone—a local woman pushing a stroller—came running from the courtyard of the Amstelveld church across the canal. She exclaimed something to Mac in Dutch. He wailed, "Help me! We need to get her to a hospital!"

Hearing Mac speak English, and noticing the markers on the bikes indicating they were tourist rentals, the Dutchwoman said, "I speak English. I'll call for an ambulance on my mobile phone!" Mac cradled Celine's head in his lap and watched her forehead swell and expand like a balloon slowly being inflated. Her eyes were open and staring upward, reflecting the same hue of blue as the spring sky above, but her pupils were dilated pinpoints of black. A straight-line incision gaped in her hairline at the top of her forehead, and crimson-red blood flowed backwards, discoloring her hair. Mac sheltered her head in his arms, but, as he held her, he could feel her body draining limp and lifeless in his grasp.

She died before the ambulance arrived.

The tragedy was frozen in Mac's mind. Like a video looping over and over, the images of that day haunted him in a ghostlike repetition that usually appeared in the still of the early morning calm, stealing his peacefulness at sunrise. Mac remembered every detail. Nothing could erase the images. He took comfort, paradoxically, in his conviction that he and Celine were interlocked eternally in grief, but the pain of accepting the loss of their unrealized life together forever changed his view of the universe. He did not believe in God, or any deities, and he did not believe in Fate as something preordained, but as something you could affect by performing good deeds and helping other people. As a prosecutor, the pain helped him understand the victims he represented. He despised the cliché that "everything happens for a reason." He wondered, "Where is the 'reason' in Celine's accident?"

The agony was compounded when, later on, her body was examined at the Academsch Ziekenhuis, the nearest hospital in Amsterdam, and it was discovered that Celine was nine weeks pregnant.

Mac lost a wife *and* a child in front of The Stork House.

CHAPTER 15

May 24, 2022
11:02 a.m.

"Good morning, Ms. O'Reilly. It's nice to meet you," said Mac, as he rose from his chair at the head of the table in the SAO conference room.

Andre shut the door after Makayla stepped into the room. She turned, walked confidently toward Mac, and offered her hand. "It's very nice to meet you, Mr. MacIntyre. I've read some articles about you online. You've had quite a busy career!"

Andre followed behind her and sat down inconspicuously in the corner behind her field of view. He reached into the side pocket of his motorcycle jacket and slid his Dictaphone out. Surreptitiously, he activated the "on" button on the device and placed it on the empty chair next to him. He dialed the volume up to "10." It would record for 120 minutes.

The conference room was large, and voices seemed to echo off the far walls. There was a row of large windows facing the Courthouse Square five flights below. The trees were bursting with fresh green leaves, and people were scurrying between the four buildings in the Square. The Circuit Court, which housed the SAO, was the dominant, largest building. It was built in 1972 in a monolithic, concrete upright rectangular shape. When it rained, water discolored the beige concrete exterior, giving the building the appearance of a gigantic chocolate cake with black frosting dripping down from the top. In the adjacent corner of the Square, the sparkling new District Court rose. There, misdemeanor crimes were handled. The District Court was a modern jumble of faux white marble and reflective glass. Unfortunately, the architect never anticipated how all those windows would trap and retain the sun's heat like a greenhouse, making the hallways unbearably hot, even in winter. In summer, the District Court hallways were like a sauna.

There was a small park in the center of the Square with a memorial for the victims of the 9/11 terrorist attacks. Thirteen residents of Seneca County, all of them unlucky passengers on those fateful flights, perished. The memorial had been cleverly designed with a large sundial that was situated so precisely that each year, on September 11th at exactly 8:46 a.m., the time the first plane disintegrated against the North Tower of the World Trade Center, the rising sun would light up a plaque with the names of the victims. Sadly, the new District Court had been constructed in 2014 in a manner that unintentionally blocked the sun from hitting the sundial, rendering the memorial's concept entirely defunct.

The third courthouse in the Square was the Grey Courthouse, built from sandstone during the New Deal in the 1930s. It housed the current location of the Juvenile Court and various administrative offices. The fourth building anchoring the Square was the tiny but majestic Old Colonial Courthouse. With its red bricks and pointed white steeple sticking up like two hands in prayer, it was once the most significant and prominent building in Seneca County during the Revolutionary War. Although not confirmed, legend persisted that George Washington himself had once been inside, and, since that time, the structure grew in significance, symbolizing the founding of Seneca County, Maryland. Of course, eons before that, before Europeans had arrived with government, land ownership, firearms, diseases, and endless flows of new immigrants, the indigenous Seneca tribe had once walked these footpaths and stalked these hunting grounds. Where the Interstate now carved the county in half with eight lanes of traffic in both directions, the Seneca had once marched for thousands of years along the same route.

"Have a seat," Mac politely said to Makayla, while he glanced over at Andre. Mac saw the Dictaphone lying innocuously on the chair beside Andre. It looked like a cell phone, but Mac knew that it was now taking the place of a stenographer to capture every word of the interview.

"Thank you," Makayla said. "Please, if you don't mind, can you turn that recording device off? I'd prefer if you didn't take notes of our meeting."

Mac shot a quick glance at Andre, who picked the Dictaphone up and clicked it off. Andre added, "Don't need it anyhow. Mr. MacIntyre's got a photographic memory, they say. He'll remember every word. He never takes notes. Doesn't have to."

Makayla smiled and looked at Mac.

"That must be useful. No grocery lists for you, eh?" she said as her shoulders seemed to relax. She was wearing a crisply tailored, dark blue Ralph Lauren pantsuit with six large, metallic, gold-colored buttons that formed two vertical lines down each half of her jacket. Her hair was stylishly bound in a long blonde ponytail running neatly down her athletic back from the nape of her neck. Mac noticed that her fingernails were recently manicured and adorned with cherry-red nail polish. He glanced at her wedding ring; the emerald-shaped diamond was approximately two carats, large, but not ostentatious.

"I assume you want to talk about that old case from 2002, Mr. MacIntyre. Correct?" she said.

"Yes, that's right. But please call me Mac. May I call you Makayla?"

"Certainly."

"As you know, the conviction has been overturned by the Court of Appeals, and the case is now back in a trial posture.

So, I wanted meet with you. I'm happy to answer any questions you may have about the process and, also, to prepare you for the possibility of testifying again."

"You're kidding. Testify again? How is that possible after all these years?"

"Yes, you're right. This is a bit unusual, but sometimes these cases can go on and on. Even for years. But the bottom line is that it was reversed, and we just have to face the reality that it's starting all over from scratch."

Makayla tilted her head slightly and tugged at her ponytail. With a barely perceptible sigh, she said, "How old is Mr. Stephens now? Must be 30-something?"

"Thirty-seven. He's been locked up at Broad Run for 20 years. It's a maximum-security facility outside Baltimore."

"Wow. A man now. All I can remember is a skinny teenager with, I think, long dreadlocks, if I've got that right. He probably looks completely different now."

Andre interjected, "Well, we *all* look a lot different now. That's a long time."

Deep in thought, Makayla stared down at her reflection on the polished conference room table.

Mac paused to let her have a moment to unscramble her thoughts. Sometimes silence prompted a response more effectively than an endless, rapid-fire barrage of questions. After a few seconds, she said, "A long time. You got that right. I try not to remember those days, actually. I've blocked out as much as I can. I had to."

Mac, sensing her thoughts drifting away like an unmoored boat floating further and further from a dock, tried to refocus her. He said, "Makayla, I understand this is difficult, and I wish we could put this case back in a dusty old box and stick it up on a shelf somewhere. But the reality is we can't. This case is back, and all of us need to buckle down and face it. Can we count on you to do that?"

"Yes. I can do that. I remember that night perfectly."

Andre jumped in. "But you just said you *not* to remember those days. You know what PTSD is, Makayla? You just said you *think* he had long dreadlocks. How can you be sure that...?"

She interrupted him sharply and said, "I just told you, Detective Okoye, I remember that night perfectly. It's frozen in my mind like a photograph. I remember *everything*. Every detail. I'll never forget that kid's face. He shot that guy right in the head. Twice. I was standing right there, closer than you are to me right now. I saw it all. I told everything to Harp."

CHAPTER 16

May 24, 2022
12:16 p.m.

Mac walked into Sushi Queen and looked around the crowded lunchtime restaurant for Assistant Chief Harper.

A hostess came up and said, "Lunch buffet for... one?"

"Thank you, but I'm looking for someone—oh, there he is." Mac waved toward the back where Harper was commanding a full booth. Mac walked to the rear to meet him and said, "How'd you get this big table? This place is always jammed at lunch. This all-you-can-eat buffet is great."

"I never ate here before, but these Orientals love cops. All you gotta do is walk in wearing a police uniform, and they treat you like you're the Emperor of China or something. We'll probably get free egg rolls."

Assistant Chief Harper was 52 and had been with the Seneca County Police Department for 30 years. He was a stocky man, and, while he didn't look obese, he had a solid, husky build. He was prematurely grey, and his hair was closely cropped, standing up on the top of his head like the bristles of a giant overturned white toothbrush. He had a wide smile of unusually large white teeth, giving him the appearance of a man with a mouthful of dice. His piercing blue eyes were always darting around, constantly searching for danger even when there was none.

"Have a seat," Harper said, gesturing toward the opposite side of the square booth.

A very petite Asian woman, with black hair scooped up in a bun on top of her head, approached and said, "Drinks?"

Harper said, "Just ice water for me. Thanks."

Mac, taking his turn to respond, said, "I'd love some hot tea, please. Thank you."

The server asked, "Buffet for both of you?"

Harper gave her a thumbs-up gesture, and Mac confirmed, "Yes. Thanks."

As the server turned away, Harp asked, "So, what's the deal? You just take as much as you want? You wanna talk now or should we load up first, then talk?"

"Go ahead, Chief. I'll go up after you're done," Mac said as he pointed toward the buffet spread in the rear section of the restaurant, an elaborate assortment of sushi, a huge cauldron of miso soup, and a variety of salad items. It was an enormous display which ran across the entire width of the restaurant. There were four men in white jackets with matching paper hats behind a counter who constantly restocked the buffet with prepared plates of fresh sushi. As the chefs plopped down new platters for consumption, customers milled around the food like pigs before a trough.

"Hey, I'm not the chief, yet! The announcement doesn't officially come out until July, so let's not jinx it."

"Right. But my money is on you. That's what everyone at the SAO says."

"Just call me Harp, OK?"

"Sure. I'll wait here and keep the table. Go get your food. Batter's up," Mac replied, adding, "I see your tattoo. Nice touch."

Mac gestured toward Harp's forearm, where a prominent triangular-shaped tattoo of a harp emblazoned his thick, tanned muscle.

"Yeah. I got this on the boardwalk at Ocean City. Like it?"

"Yes. That's one big harp, Harp. That looks like the classic Celtic harp, or I should say the Gaelic harp, y'know, the national symbol of Ireland. I like it."

"What do you mean, a 'gay' harp?"

"No," Mac replied. "Gaelic. You call anything Irish or from Ireland Gaelic."

"Oh, I didn't know all of that. Just saw it on a Guinness beer can and asked if they could do it bigger for me. Well, since I'm Irish, I guess that was a good move, right? You're Irish too, Mac, with a name like MacIntyre."

"No. Actually, my heritage is Scottish. Not Irish," said Mac.

"Pretty much the same thing, right?"

"Well," said Mac. "Ireland and Scotland are two different places. They don't even share a border. They're not contiguous. Just like you wouldn't say someone from Colorado was Mexican. My ancestors, the MacIntyre clan, came from Scotland, and yours came from Ireland. Close, but not the same thing, Harp."

"Yeah, now I know why the cops say you're the guy who always corrects everyone."

Harp left the table, and Mac pulled out his phone to check his texts and messages. Before he could clear all of them, Mac looked up and saw Harp returning from the buffet, heading back toward the booth. Harp balanced a large china plate—it looked more like a serving platter—with a gigantic pyramid of stacked sushi piled several layers high. He placed the bounteous haul down on the table and slid into the seat on one side of the booth.

"I got tons of these fish cutlets on rice, and these wrapped-up things. What are these called?"

"That's called a California roll. Avocado, cucumber and fake crab stuff."

"Looks good. And I hate California, so ain't that something?!"

Mac went to the buffet and chose a modest portion from the wide assortment of sashimi, sushi, and soup. He returned and sat down in the booth. Mac noticed that the other customers' eyes followed Harp in his tan police uniform as he moved about the space. Dozens of eyes peered at his utility belt, watching his Taser, flashlight, and jangling handcuffs bob as he walked by. His ominous Glock 9 millimeter handgun was holstered on his right side.

"OK, so Mac, let me tell you," Harp began, speaking

with a full mouth and occasionally spraying grains of white rice as he spoke. "This Stephens kid is a total shithead. He got what was coming to him. If you ask me, he should've got life without parole and not just life."

Mac replied, "He's done 20 years at Broad Run."

Harp reached up with his right forefinger and lifted his lip, exposing his front teeth. "See these? These are four implants. I had to get 'em after this punk Eddie Stephens poured a can of paint from a second-story window on my windshield. This was about a year before he shot the guy down on Rotterdam. I'll never forget. Kid was a total troublemaker. Thought it was funny to throw paint. Well, caused me to smash into a parking meter. Busted out my teeth on the steering wheel. We couldn't prove he was the one who tossed it from the window, but I saw it was him."

Mac said, "That's an assault. Probably second-degree assault, but possibly a first-degree, since you got a serious injury. Was Stephens prosecuted?"

"No. Some dumbass ASA said they couldn't prove beyond a reasonable doubt who actually threw the paint. So they didn't charge anyone and all I got out of it was four fucking implants."

"Damn. Sorry to hear that."

Harp continued, "And the Court of Appeals—what the hell?—they gave him a new trial? Unbelievable. Hey, did you find that girl, Makayla, yet? Can't do the case without her. God knows where that crackhead is now. Dead in the gutter somewhere most likely."

"Yes. Actually, we found her. She's changed a lot. I met with her this morning."

"What's that broth stuff with those white things floating in it?" Harp inquired.

"Miso soup," Mac clarified. "With tofu and seaweed."

"That looks disgusting."

"It's an acquired taste," Mac said, slurping a spoonful of the warm, comforting liquid.

"Wait! You said you *talked* to that junkie girl? Oh, great! Stephens will definitely plead guilty now. I can't believe you found her. That airhead was fucking every crack dealer on Rotterdam Street just to support her habit. If you got her on board, then this case is locked up good." Stuffing his mouth, Harp continued talking, "Now you've got a direct eye witness who IDs him actually doing the shooting. Then, she picked him out of a photo array like the next day, I think. Plus, we found the gun used in the 0100 at his parent's house. Under his bed. I mean, what more do you need? He'll plead guilty and take time served. No doubt."

Mac finished his soup, placed the white porcelain spoon in the bowl, and pushed the pair to the edge of the table.

"This kid Eddie was nothing but trouble back in the day," Harp continued. "Always hanging around, a total nuisance. Once, he popped our tires with a nail. Man, I tell you, that punk's got a real smartass mouth on him, too. Used to yell '5-0' when we rolled up in our undercover car. No respect for law enforcement. Then that shit with the paint can. Finally, we caught him robbing that drug dealer. And old Judge Barnette sure stuck him good. Serves that little Eddie right."

Mac squeezed a rectangular slab of sashimi between two wooden chopsticks and dipped it into a small bowl with a mixture of soy sauce and green wasabi. He decided to just let Harp keep talking. He did that with witnesses who were lying: let them ramble and just listen carefully.

"So, Mac, well, I'm glad we could meet right away because we've gotta wrap this case up. We don't want no retrial. I'm sure you can work something out. Offer him a time-served plea and make this shit go away, OK?"

Mac swallowed the piece of sashimi and put the chopsticks down on his napkin. He didn't respond.

Harp continued, "I'm telling you, this Eddie guy doesn't want a new trial. He's not going to risk getting re-sentenced and going back to Broad Run all over again. He'll jump at a plea, and we can wrap this up. I don't give a shit if he gets out *today*."

"I understand," said Mac. "I'm not too psyched about doing this trial over again either, to be frank."

"Plus, I've got all kinds of stuff to do at the Police Academy to get ready for a huge organizational reshuffle, and if I *do* get the chief's position, it's going to be a major transition. I have to make all new appointments for commander at each district station, and we're switching the department over to e-filing, and that crap is confusing as fuck."

"Oh, I agree with you on that," Mac concurred. "That e-filing system is terrible, and all of the prosecutors in my office now have to do all of our own pleadings, Motions, and discovery by email. The system is horrible. Everyone agrees on that."

Discovery! I have to provide everything to the defense in discovery. Marcel is expecting that stuff, and Judge Ryan just ordered it to be sent. Damn.

Harp rambled on, "There's also a big retreat scheduled for September in Orlando for new police chiefs, and I don't want to miss that either. Last conference there, I stayed at that airport hotel, and God, Mac, you wouldn't believe how awesome it was!"

Mac asked, "The airport hotel in Orlando? Not exactly the French Riviera."

"Yeah, apparently that hotel is a hub for Delta, and all the stewardesses stay there. So, all you gotta do is look out your window, and there's a million of 'em in thongs strutting around the pool. I ain't missing that seminar, man."

"I mean," Mac said, "let's get our priorities in order: a murder case versus flight attendants in bikinis."

Harp emphasized, "So make this retrial go away. Can't you, Mac?"

"I'll try. But I'm dealing with this defense attorney, Marcel St. Croix. Do you know him?"

"Oh, my God. Everyone in the Department hates that queer. He's gotta be LGBQT for sure."

"LGBTQ," said Mac.

"What?"

"Never mind, Chief."

"You're talking about that French asshole with the long hair? The guy who wears an *earring* in court? Are you kidding me? How in the world can Eddie Stephens ever afford a hotshot lawyer like that!?"

"He's got a lady from D.C. sponsoring him."
"Who the hell is that?"
"Her name is Ophelia Jackson Katz."

CHAPTER 17

May 24, 2022
1:04 p.m.

Ophelia slowly stepped into Marcel's office and said, "It's a pleasure to finally meet you, sir."

Marcel stood and offered his hand. "No, it's definitely *my* pleasure, Ms. Katz. I've heard so much about you, and your reputation certainly precedes you. Please call me Marcel."

"Well, don't bother about all of that reputation stuff." She turned toward the doorway and gestured to Tamika who was following closely behind.

"This is Eddie's mother, Tamika Stephens."

Marcel turned and shook Tamika's hand.

"Yes, I know. Good to see you again, Mrs. Stephens. As you know, we are trying to do everything we can to help Eddie."

"Thank you very much, Mr. St. Croix," Tamika responded. She was wearing an oversized purple Adidas hoodie and carrying her large bulky shoulder bag, which held five notebooks. With some physical effort, she swung the heavy bag from her shoulder and put it down on the floor next to one of the two red leather chairs in front of Marcel's desk.

With his arms outstretched, Marcel said, "Please, ladies, have a seat."

Ophelia was a very thin woman with a caramel-colored complexion. She appeared to be about 85 years old. Her completely white hair was braided and then looped around her head in a crisscross pattern resembling an "X." She was dressed in a pair of elegant black cotton slacks and a tailored navy blue blazer. She labored to use a large, black ebony walking cane to steady herself.

Ophelia said, "Well, Marcel, what happens next?"

"Well, we had the Circuit Court Scheduling Conference, so..."

Tamika interrupted, "Why did they schedule a new trial? They should just drop this case and let us be. This ain't fair. Eddie has to do a second trial? What for?"

Marcel explained, "Well, I still have hope that the State will dismiss the charges, but until they do, we have to prepare for a new trial. There will also be additional dates for hearings and Motions, so..."

"Oh, I see. Motions? What do you mean?"

Ophelia jumped into the fray. "Tamika! Can you just sit still and be quiet for once? Let Marcel explain and then you can ask questions. Got it?"

"I'm sorry. I'm just so mad about all of this," Tamika replied. "My baby's been locked up half his life, and he didn't do anything wrong. Those police are devils. Framed him all those years ago. He was just 17."

Marcel began again, "So, I've already talked to the prosecutor, and he's a very reasonable guy. Someone we can work with, I believe."

Ophelia quickly replied, "Marcel, do you know how many times I've heard that exact thing? That 'oh, he's someone I can work with' line? Justice Marshall heard that malarkey back in '54 when he did *Brown v. Board of Education*. And I heard the same thing with my own ears from a prosecutor in 1967 when we challenged the Court in *Loving v. Virginia*. Lord knows Dr. King heard that nonsense from white prosecutors his whole life. So, forgive me if I'm skeptical, but I *deserve* to be skeptical. What makes you think this new prosecutor is any different from all the rest of these so-called law enforcement officers?"

"Ms. Katz, I understand your concerns, and, trust me, I am deeply skeptical of prosecutors and police, too. Always have been. Native Americans haven't fared so well over the course of history as you know, and I am part..."

Tamika burst into the conversation. "It's different! We are talking about Black people in America. Been different for, like, 400 years. And it ain't getting much better. Tell the George Floyd family about it."

"I assure you both, I am 100 percent on your side. You will never have to worry about that. I've been defending clients for a very long time. It's the State we need to scrutinize."

Tamika said, "The State?"

"Yes. The State of Maryland as personified by its agents. Here, I am talking about the police officers who arrested Eddie and any misconduct they may have engaged in, as well as the prosecution, if, in fact, *they* did anything questionable as well."

Tamika echoed, "Oh, the State. I get it."

"So, right now," Marcel continued. "We are in the process of getting what is called discovery. All that means—the word *discovery*—is that the new prosecutor is obliged to share with us all of the information he has relating to Eddie's case. Both favorable and unfavorable. He is not allowed—by law—to keep anything secret from us. Even if it hurts his case. We filed a formal Motion for Discovery, and we are entitled to whatever they have. And, then, the real digging starts."

Ophelia reached down for her cane. It was an elaborate thick stick, about the size of a baseball bat, with African themes chiseled into the black wood. Marcel glanced at it and detected giraffes, elephants, impalas—an assortment of sub-Saharan creatures—with a carved lion's head with a flowing mane at the very top. Ophelia's long, delicate bony fingers surrounded the lion's head and gripped it as she labored to stand.

"Thank you again, sir. We need to be leaving. But I am a quick judge of character. I have seen a lot in my days, and in the remaining blessed time on Earth that I have, I want justice for Tamika's son, Eddie. Trust me, I know justice can be elusive, but Marcel, all we ask is that you *try*. Truly try. Will you pledge to do that?"

"Yes, Ms. Katz. I will do everything I can. I promise."

Tamika rose and said, "You want these binders? They've got all the letters Eddie wrote from jail since 2003. He's studied the law and all of that procedure stuff and the Constitution too. They have it all in the library at Broad Run. And there's a really smart inmate friend of his who's helped him read up on all of it." Tamika gestured at the bag on the floor and said, "His whole story. It's all here."

"Yes," Marcel replied. "I'd love to read Eddie's letters. Absolutely."

Tamika unzipped the bag and placed five thick binders on Marcel's desk. Each woman shook hands with Marcel, turned toward the door, and started to leave the office.

"Oh, and Ms. Katz," Marcel softly said, "I'm very sorry about Mr. Katz. I never had the opportunity to meet him, but I know he must have been a great man. A real philanthropist. The Miles Davis School for the Performing Arts has helped generations of young people. You and your husband have so much to be proud of. Your school is known nationally. I should say internationally. Thank *you* as well for all the many contributions you've given not only to the Davis School but also to the wider community. Please accept my condolences on Mr. Katz's passing."

"Oh, thank you, that's very kind. Well, he was an old man! We should all be lucky enough to reach 100 years!"

"Amen," said Marcel.

Ophelia stopped and closed her eyes for a moment. She tilted her head as if she was trying to listen to something in the distance and said, "You know, Eddie was one heck of a musician himself. Unbelievable natural talent. He was destined for great things. We had a private audition scheduled at Julliard in New York. Such a shame all of this happened."

Marcel said, "Thank you for sharing. I didn't know that."

Tamika volunteered, "Well, you read those binders I just

gave you, Mr. St. Croix. You'll learn who Eddie really is. Not some killer, like the police said. No. He's still got half a life left. We really need him to come home. I haven't changed his room all these years. It's exactly the same as the day he was arrested. Even his trumpet. It's still in the case right on his bed. I haven't moved it in 20 years."

"Yes, Tamika, I totally agree. They really botched Eddie's case. And that will be our sole focus moving forward now that the case is back. Both of you are welcome to come to the Motions Hearing if you'd like to. Before then, I plan to discuss things with the new prosecutor. There is always a chance we can quickly resolve this case."

"What did you say his name was again?" asked Ms. Katz.

"MacIntyre. Mac MacIntyre."

CHAPTER 18

May 24, 2022
1:35 p.m.

"Mom,   July 7, 2012

I hope you are doing good and that your diabetes is not bothering you too much. Remember what the Dr. said you should cut down on carbs and sugar. I know you aren't much for diet Coke but that switch from regular Coke alone would be good. Carbs are big in spaghetti and bread too so be careful. I love you so much and want you to stay healthy. And try to walk more or even run haha!

So, OK, I've been locked up for exactly ten years! Yes, I keep track of every day. I try to stay by myself because there are a lot of dangerous guys in here.

When I first got here, it was very rough because I was the youngest inmate in my Pod. I figured out how to keep my head down and just try to stay out of trouble. Going back to school was a good idea. I was so proud when I passed my GED and started taking college courses by correspondence.

I just signed up for AVP, the Alternative to Violence Project, and Anger Management. A guest teacher also comes once a month now from the Seneca County community college. The lady Miss Elbereth runs this program for jail inmates called "Books Behind Bars." I've read a whole lot and she turned me on to a lot of Black writers. I especially like this Playwrite named August Wilson, if you don't know him, read some of his plays. They are excellent and really capture Black life for real.

I prefer stay by myself and read since it helps fill the time, and you wouldn't believe how these guys fight over who gets to use the phone.

It took me more than two years of applying, but I finally become a Library Assistant. I like going around the facility delivering book requests to the inmates. There is one man in here who has been locked up for more than 30 years, I'd say he is about 50 now. He is very smart and knows legal issues real good. His name is Muhammad Kalif Siraj. His born name is

Bobby Ray Seals, but he converted to the religion of Islam many years ago.

    I've been discussing my case with Mr. Siraj, and he says there were a WHOLE LOT of mistakes in my trial, which obviously I knew that. But he says there are ways to go back to court and challenge the conviction. Or at least try to get the main charge of first degree murder knocked down to something less, like manslaughter. If I could do that, my release date becomes automatic because manslaughter only is 10 years and I've done that much already. But since I got sentenced to Life, the rule is that I've got to serve a minimum of 30 years before I could even be considered for parole. Mom, I can't stay here another 20 years! I think we need to try to get help with a good private lawyer, not a Public Defender. That PD I had really sold me out. Mr. Siraj says to find a "benefactor." It's someone who can help us since there's no way we can afford the money for a real good lawyer. So, can you contact Ms. Ophelia again about maybe helping or doing something on account of The Davis School? She will know how to raise funds or help somehow. You are my mom and I love you to death, but Ms. O is like a second mother to me and she knows how all of this law and court stuff works. What we want is to file for a "Post Conviction" hearing. If the higher court agrees my PD was "ineffective," you get a new trial.

Well, keep writing those letters to me! I love to hear from you. I collect all of them. And come visit when you can but I know it's two long bus rides. I love you so much, Mom! I think you are the only one who believes in me. So try to get through to Ms. O. Hopefully, the school can do a fundraiser to hire a good lawyer, not a liar and drunk like that guy I had before.

I love you, your son, Eddie

PS Mr. Siraj knows a ton about jazz! He says it should be called "Black Music" and not jazz, and he said his father was a drummer when young and actually met Miles Davis and John Coltrane and Dizzy Gillespie back in the day in a part of New York called Greenwich Village.

PPS Mom, someday I'll be playing my horn again, I promise!"

Marcel put down the binder and called Mac. It went to voicemail.

"You've reached the office of Mac MacIntyre. I'm sorry I'm not available at this time. Please leave a detailed message, and I'll return your call as soon as I can. Thank you very much."

Marcel sighed and said, "Mac, this is Marcel. I'm calling

about the Eddie Stephens case. I was wondering if you've had a chance to send me discovery yet."

He looked at his wristwatch, and then continued, "It's only been a short while since we were before Judge Ryan, and I know you are quite the busy man, but if you get a chance, please try to get those materials over to me. Thank you. And Mac, take care."

CHAPTER 19

May 24, 2002
2:54 p.m.

"Mac, what the hell are we going to do with that weird note with all the missing letters?"

Andre took three steps across Mac's office toward the windows and looked out across the Courthouse Square. Mac slid the single sheet of paper with the handwritten note back inside the water damaged manila envelope. He placed it on top of the evidence box and said, "Well, the question is—is this note discovery or work product? That is exactly what we have to decide first. It says at the bottom of the note 'Mark work prod.' So, it says right on it that it's work product."

"Work product? But how does that rule operate when it's not *your* work product but the notes of the prosecutor before you who handled the case the first time around?" Andre responded.

"OK, well, when any prosecutor creates something him or

herself, like trial notes or personal observations or something like an outline used to prepare a case—those kinds of things are not mandatory to give to the defense. The defense is entitled to certain stuff, but not so-called work product, because that is a product of a prosecutor's personal work, and that makes it private."

"So that concept transfers to us from the first trial? That weird note that looks like freakin' scribble-scrabble is ours? And it's private and St. Croix can't see it?"

"It's not as simple as that, Andre. And Judge Ryan was clear. She said give Marcel *everything*. That means everything here in this box. Including the note."

"But we don't even know what the hell that note means! It's just a jumble of words. It's not even complete. Half that shit is missing! Shouldn't we at least figure out what it says before we give it to the defense attorney to twist around and use against us?"

Mac reached down into the evidence box and slid the note out again. He held it up to the window, trying to let the daylight illuminate it, hoping the bright light would resurrect the original letters from the dried paper like a phoenix.

Mac said with an irritated tone, "I have no idea what this first sentence even means. "BU NA SERA. We can't even tell how many letters are missing."

"I'm clueless on that part. I can't think of any words that match those random letters. What is this? *Wheel of Fortune?*"

Mac said, "But look down here. That part is definitely about money." He pointed at the two next lines. "See? It clearly says '$750' once and then '$750' twice."

"I agree."

Mac continued, "That's a total of $1,500 bucks. In 2002 money, that's a lot."

Andre asked, "What do you think 'GJT' means?"

"Not sure, but I always think of Grand Jury when I see the letters 'G' and 'J' next to each other. We use that abbreviation, 'GJ,' all the time, especially when we file for new indictments. That's *got* to refer to the Grand Jury."

"But, Mac, we don't pay witnesses to testify before the Grand Jury. We just subpoena them."

Mac and Andre simultaneously stopped looking at the note and looked at each other instead. Andre's eyes widened.

"You'd only *pay* someone if you needed them to *lie*," said Andre. "This shit is getting very sketchy, man."

Mac looked back at the note and said, "It says for 'vices ended.'"

"Vice squad works prostitution and gambling and shit like that. I'm 100 percent sure of that. When I was on SAT back in the day we worked with Vice all the time."

Mac stared at the paper, stumped, as if stuck in a stalemate.

"Andre, this is what we need to do: first, I'm going to get this whole box scanned by our IT guys in our Discovery Unit. They can email all of this right away. I'm going to send every single page to Marcel."

"But what about that funky note with the missing letters?"

"I'm keeping that for now. Just this one single page. Until we figure out what it means. In order to decipher it, we need to talk to Assistant Chief Harper, or even Judge Bennington, and ask them if they recognize this thing. And who wrote it? Notice it's unsigned?"

Mac's desk phone rang. The Caller ID said BLOCKED.

"Andre, oh, I forgot to tell you. I've been getting these crank calls ever since this Stephens case got assigned to me. Got your Dictaphone? Record this shit. I may need you to do some follow-up and trace this idiot."

Andre moved like a cat, picked up his motorcycle jacket from its customary spot on the floor by the small couch, grabbed the device from the inside pocket, and in a flash had it propped up next to Mac's landline desk telephone.

"Listen to this," Mac said. He picked up the receiver and said, "Hello, this is Mac MacIntyre. Can I help you?"

No one answered.

Andre looked at Mac and motioned with a stirring gesture in front of his mouth to indicate that Mac should keep talking.

Mac said, "Hello? Is anyone there? Hello?"

There was a wheezing sound, in an irregular pattern, like deep breathing, softly emitting from the telephone. Then it clicked off and disconnected.

Andre said, "What the fuck is that shit!? How long you been getting those freaky calls?"

Mac replied, "Like I said, they started earlier this week. Must be the third one. It sounds like someone breathing. Or buzzing. Did you hear that, Andre?"

"It said BLOCKED. That's an internal call. I'm sure about that. Gotta be either someone with a landline inside the courthouse, or maybe it's coming from those free phones down on the first floor. Y'know how they have those old phone booths converted down in the atrium to hospitality calls now? Lawyers use them all the time. Is someone mad at you?"

"I mean, Andre, everyone's mad at me! Just kidding, but it could be a defendant in a prior, unrelated case, or maybe an attorney who's pissed off at me with an axe to grind. When you've beaten as many lawyers in court as I have, it definitely stirs up some bad feelings. It could even be someone from right here in the SAO—you know how jealous these other ASAs can be, right? Jesus, for all I know, it could be Jo Newgrange or even The Fish himself. That guy's missing a few screws."

"That breathing was weird. Well, maybe you have a stalker, Mac. I've seen that many times before. Someone gets fixated on the prosecutor. Remember that homeless guy who kept crank calling Jo Newgrange a million times? The bailiffs always found that psycho sleeping in the courthouse stairwells, remember? So, don't blow this off, Mac. Take that shit seriously. I'm not joking."

"I know, I know. Trust me, I do take it seriously."

Andre said, "Are there any witnesses in this new case who might be trying to sabotage this shit?"

"Yes, all of them! And speaking of weird witnesses, we need to find that second cop from the night of the murder on Rotterdam Street."

"Right," Andre confirmed. "The sergeant from Vice. The guy who retired and moved to Colorado. Maybe *he's* hassling you? What's his name again?"

"Sergeant Richard York."

CHAPTER 20

May 25, 2022
10:01 a.m.

"This is Ricky York. Can I help you?"

"Good morning. This is Senior Assistant State's Attorney Mac MacIntyre. I'm calling from Seneca County, Maryland."

There was no response.

After a long pause, Mac added, "I hope I'm not catching you at a bad time. There's a two-hour time difference, I think. Is this too early in the morning for you?"

"No, I'm awake. Just enjoying the beautiful weather we have here today."

"Is this Richard York, formerly Sergeant York, of the Seneca County Police Department?"

"Yes, it is. But you can call me Ricky. What, may I ask, are you calling about?"

York was standing outside on the deck of the small

boarding house on Knob Hill where he rented a room. From the rickety wooden deck, he could see the Mining Exchange building downtown and, by turning his gaze toward Pike's Peak, he could spot the radio towers flashing atop Cheyenne Mountain. Across the valley, opposite from downtown Colorado Springs, stood the forest of burnt tree skeletons, torched in the devastating Waldo Canyon fire, sticking up like whiskers in a three-day beard. The morning sun was just reaching the apex of the mountain and would momentarily cast brilliant sunshine across the entire region, a peaceful swath of endless Western pine trees and rock formations, unchanged since pioneers rolling across the Great Plains first laid eyes on this majestic scenery.

York sat down in a cracked plastic lawn chair. A creaky, rusty tray table was arranged at his side. He held his cell phone in his left hand. With his free hand, he adjusted his aviator-style sunglasses, and then reached over to the tray table. He put his small wooden pipe down into a clunky glass ashtray and peered down into the bowl of the pipe, trying to judge how much unsmoked marijuana clung to the circular edges. He tapped the pipe gently with his brown fingernail to free the remaining greenish leafy flakes. Looking up at the uppermost crest of the mountaintop, he inhaled the crisp air, enjoying a lungful of clean oxygen. He reached back behind his head and tugged at the rubber band assigned to hold his long, thin grey hair into a ponytail. The sun was now just creeping into view. The sky was a brilliant, cloudless oceanic blue.

"That was a long time ago. Ah, Seneca County. What did you say your name was again?" York inquired.

DOUBLE BLIND

"Mac MacIntyre. I'm the prosecutor assigned to a case we need to talk to you about. I should tell you first—I am here in my office, and I've got you on speaker. My partner, Detective Andre Okoye, is here with me. Is that OK with you?"

York sucked on the pipe as the embers inside the bowl turned from orange to grey ashes. He exhaled. The sweet, intoxicating effects of the potent marijuana swirled across his brain, soothing and relaxing him, but dulling his concentration. York said, "Well, I guess that all depends on why you're calling me. I won't have to assert the Fifth, will I?"

Mac, sitting at his desk in the State's Attorney's Office, motioned silently to Andre to have him check that his Dictaphone was operating correctly. Andre picked it up, tilted it to check the battery's strength, and pointed to the read-out that said "97%."

"No, no. Nothing like that, Sergeant York. We're actually just calling you about a really old case that you once worked on before you retired from the SCPD."

"Yeah, definitely an old case 'cause I've been out here in the Springs for—wait—I think it's been at least 15 years—no, wait—gotta be more like 18 years now. My memory's not as good as it used to be."

Mac glanced at Andre and then pointed down to the Dictaphone. Andre lifted his thumb up, signaling "yes."

"So, we're calling about this old homicide case," Mac explained. "The Defendant is a guy named Eddie Stephens. It was a shooting of a drug dealer down on Rotterdam Street. He was a kid. He's been locked up for almost 20 years now. You recall that case?"

There was no reply.

After a lengthy pause, Mac said, "Officer York? Are you still there?"

"Oh, yeah. I remember that one. But I wasn't the investigating officer on that case. Do they still call them I/Os? I wasn't the I/O."

"Yes, Officer Harper was the primary investigating officer. At least it's Harper who signed off on the Statement of Charges. We're assuming he wrote the SOC. Is that correct?"

"Man, what did you say? You should see how the sun is reflecting off the rocks up there. It's gorgeous."

"So, listen to me, Ricky," Mac said with more volume. "I've already interviewed Harper. But weren't you his supervisor at the time? Your name appears several times in the SOC as Sergeant Richard York. That's *you*, right?"

"Well," said York, "I *used* to be him. That was definitely another lifetime ago. But, yeah, I remember that 0100. Harp. We called him that: Harp. He was all gung-ho working Vice, if I recall correctly. We were doing a clean-up job of Rotterdam Street back then. There was a lot of prostitution and street CDS hustling back in the day."

Andre mouthed the word "vice" to Mac and pointed to the dusty, cardboard evidence box.

Mac said, "Yes, that's correct. But we're not calling about a massage parlor or street hooker or anything like that. This was a drug dealer who got shot and killed. Remember that case? You actually testified in court about it. It was a jury trial before Judge Barnette. Does that ring a bell?"

"Oh, yeah. That drug dealer who got shot in the face and

fell on a glass table. I can still see that scene in my mind all these years later. There was broken glass sticking in his eye. Hard to forget that. Wish I could, actually."

Mac said, "That's right. That's the case. Eddie Stephens. Convicted of first-degree murder and sent to Broad Run. He's still there."

"Why are you calling me about that? And how the hell did you find me out here? I'm a long way from Maryland."

York reached into his front jeans pocket and took out a small, one-inch by one-inch plastic baggie. He opened the packet, picked out a bud of marijuana the size of a watermelon seed, pinched it between his right thumb and index finger, and placed it in the center of his pipe.

"The case was reversed. We have to prepare it for trial all over again," Mac said.

York reached back into his pocket and pulled out a plastic Bic cigarette lighter with a logo that said ROCKY MT HIGH DISPENSARY. He flicked on it to release a full flame and then toked deeply on the pipe, letting a lungful of soothing cannabis smoke fill his chest. He exhaled and watched the swirling pattern in the air the grey smoke made in the sunlight. Looking up at the crest of the mountain again, he said, "A retrial? But I'm in Colorado."

"We will pay for you to fly back to Maryland. We have a nice hotel you can stay at—no charge, of course. On us. Plus, per diem for each day you're here. But that's only if the case actually goes to a retrial. We are hoping to resolve it first."

York leaned back in his lawn chair and closed his eyes. He listened to the sound of an ATV buzzing off in the distance.

"Sergeant York? Are you still there? Sergeant York?"

York opened his eyes. "Yeah, I'm still here."

Mac added, "I'm sure you know how the Interstate Subpoena for Material Witness process works, right?"

York closed his eyes again, but didn't respond.

Mac bluffed, "So, we've already been in touch with the El Paso County District Attorney's Office."

"Just send the subpoena directly to me. No need for all of that legal mumbo jumbo. I'll come back."

"Voluntarily?"

"Yes," said York. "I want to testify. That shit's been on my mind for a long time. It's been bothering me for years, that one. I'd like to get that monkey off my back once and for all."

"Bothering you? What do you mean?"

York said, "Hey, did you find that girl? That hooker who was in the apartment when the guy got blasted. *She's* the one you really need to talk to. More than me. Her name was Makayla."

"Yes. She's important," Mac confirmed.

York interjected, "And that Assistant State's Attorney who did the case. You need to talk to him too. His name was Benningham or Billington, something like that."

CHAPTER 21

May 25, 2022
4:44 p.m.

To: jbennington.scct.com
From: mmacintyre.scsao.com
Date: 5/25/22
Re: St. v. Stephens, Retrial.

Judge Bennington, as you know, the above-referenced case has been scheduled for a trial in the Circuit Court before the Honorable Roberta Ryan. I would very much like the opportunity to review your anticipated testimony in person especially considering that it has been nearly twenty years since you prosecuted this case as a member of the SAO before you were appointed to the bench. May I schedule a time to meet with you soon? Thank you, Mac MacIntyre, ASA.

"I just sent him an email," Mac said as he pressed his cell phone against his ear.

"Well, maybe you should just keep all of your discussions in emails to protect yourself?" Andre said. "I mean, maybe you shouldn't actually meet with him in person. I can come to the meeting with you if you want—if the judge allows it. But if you keep it all in writing, he can't weasel out of something later on, right?"

"I can't ask him to keep it to emails! He'd pick up on that right away. I've got to meet with him face-to-face, but I would like you to come with me if he doesn't object. Trust me, I will remember every word the man says, but I need you to be my witness in case he starts changing his answers later on."

"OK. 10-4."

"Where are you right now? Playing basketball at the Police Academy again? How soon can you get down here to the Judicial Center?"

"Actually, I'm about five minutes from Rotterdam Street, Mac. I'm all the way across the county from you. I wanted to see the crime scene after reading that old SOC Harper wrote. Something didn't seem right. Like, why didn't Makayla just lock the door and stay inside? I mean, she says she saw the shooter run outside. So, why did she leave and go *into* danger instead of just staying there and shutting the door? Also, there was a landline phone in J'Mal's apartment. She could have used that to call 911. A bunch of things don't add up. The timing doesn't make sense."

Mac asked, "What do you mean the timing?"

"The SOC says she called 911. From where? There's no

pay phone anywhere. They all got vandalized on the street. Guys tearing them apart looking for coins. And this is before the days of cell phones in everyone's pocket. Cell phones were just getting popular in 2002. Remember? We used to have pagers. Now everyone's got a cell phone, even criminals. But the SOC says she called 911. From where?"

"And, Andre, the records from 911 show *no call* from Makayla. But Harper and York get to the dead guy's apartment within minutes. There's no record of a call placed *to* 911 from what I can see."

"Exactly my point. So how did Harper and York know to go to the scene? I'm thinking Makayla called one of *them* directly herself. Remember, I was on SAT once. Something is not right. Why would she have had either Harper or York's number?"

The desk phone on Mac's desk buzzed.

"Hang on. Someone's calling me." Mac looked down at the Caller ID panel on the desk phone and saw it said "BLOCKED." He spoke into his cell phone to Andre and said, "I've got to run. Call me later."

Mac picked up the landline phone's receiver.

"Good afternoon, this is Senior Assistant State's Attorney, Mac MacIntyre. Can I help you?"

"Mr. MacIntyre, good day. This is Judge Bennington calling. I just received your email."

"Yes, sir. Thank you for contacting me so promptly. I appreciate your quick response."

"Sure. Well, we finished up in court for today, and I'm just up here in chambers getting some paperwork done and reading Motions for a civil trial we begin tomorrow. I have a window of opportunity right now to meet with you and talk about the Stephens matter."

Mac subconsciously looked all around his office like a drowning man looking for a rope, searching for someone or something to rescue him. He was alone. Andre was far away.

Is this really happening? I've got fucking Judge Bennington on the line.

"Thank you, Judge. Let's set up a meeting, and then we can discuss what you remember about the case. As you know, it was reversed and is coming back."

That was a stupid thing to say! Obviously. He said he read my email.

"Come up to my chambers right now. We're on the seventh floor—well, I'm sure you know that already. But come up now. Tomorrow, I'll be starting this complex med mal litigation case that will take up the next two weeks at least. I'm free right now."

I need a witness to any discussions I have with this guy. I'll ask that his law clerk meet with us as a witness. That will work for now. I don't want to wait two weeks.

"OK, Your Honor. I'll be right up. See you in 10 minutes, Judge."

CHAPTER 22

May 25, 2022
5:00 p.m.

Judge Daniel Bennington enjoyed a life of great privilege. He had it all. He was born into a successful, wealthy family of attorneys. His father had once worked as the Assistant Secretary of Commerce in the White House administration of President George H. W. Bush. Bennington was educated at a prestigious local Seneca County prep school and then attended Yale University for undergraduate studies. He matriculated at the University of Virginia School of Law and graduated quietly, without much distinction.

His father helped get him a position right out of law school as a rookie Seneca County Assistant State's Attorney, skipping the usual track of first doing a judicial clerkship. Daniel was a modestly talented, but not gifted, courtroom litigator, satisfied to stay in the background of the SAO, churning out efficient, inoffensive prosecutions. He quietly marched up the ranks within the State's Attorney's Office's Economic Crimes Division, focusing on white-collar crime cases which rarely drew any attention from the media. When he was appointed as a judge on the lower-level District Court after only a few years as a prosecutor, some eyebrows were raised in the legal community. However, everyone knew and quietly accepted the reality that rich, privileged, connected people became judges—no one ever said it was a meritocracy. Subsequently, Judge Bennington was elevated to the Circuit Court when, shortly after the Stephens case concluded, old Judge Barnette dropped dead, creating a seat on the higher court. Bennington then steadily served on the Circuit Court bench without controversy, maintaining a low profile in a personal quest to achieve competency, but not brilliance.

He was a handsome man with a generic, All-American look. At 52 years old, he was still athletically built and seemed taller than his six-foot-one height. He had prematurely grey, nearly white hair that was extremely thick, giving him the appearance of a man wearing a white helmet. His hair was puffed up into a luxurious coiffure, always perfectly symmetrical, round and severely parted on the left side. His bangs lay diagonally across his forehead in the manner of one of his heroes, Robert F. Kennedy.

In the main atrium of the Seneca County Judicial Center, there was a display of all the Circuit Court judges going back all the way to the invention of the camera around the time of the Civil War. Row upon row of framed squares formed symmetrical lines of long-deceased judiciary. The first six rows depicted uniformly austere, unsmiling white men—some with magnificent full beards circa 1880, others with bow ties, and some with gradually modern details like eyeglasses and ever-changing hairstyles. It took six rows of portraits, and 150 years, before any faces other than white men appeared; the first break in the chain was a white woman judge around 1960. She was elderly and had snowy hair pulled back into a bun over a frowning face, the very first female Circuit Court judge. Then, in the second to lowest row, somewhere in the 1970s, a Black man appeared with a moderately puffed Afro hairstyle, the first African American judge. The bottom row was equally divided among men and women, with the first appearances of Latino and Asian members of the bench. There, on that last row, Bennington's portrait appeared, looking to the side of the camera's lens, unfocused, in the vein of an outdated high school yearbook photo, as if he was told not to look directly into the camera. His puffy, white hair was even more resplendent than it currently was, global in its convexity, and, yet, he looked as if he would have been right at home on the top row, sitting next to the judges who looked like Robert E. Lee. Yes, Bennington was a privileged man.

Bennington played golf religiously and had won the Seneca County Bar Association's annual golf tournament four times. The plaques were prominently displayed in a neat line on his chamber's wall. It was clear he valued his golf championships more than any of his modest legal accomplishments. Bennington symbolized the kind of comfortable, suburban man to whom much had been given, but from whom not much was required in return.

Mac exited the elevator on the seventh floor, but instead

of heading to one of the four courtrooms situated in each corner of the floor, he walked down a short corridor to the side, away from the courtrooms, toward Judge Bennington's chambers. Before Mac got to the door, he glanced up at a large security camera hanging from the ceiling. On the wall underneath the camera was a bright red, poster-sized placard bearing the warning: AUTHORIZED PERSONNEL ONLY.

Mac respectfully tapped on the chambers door, waiting for Judge Bennington's law clerk to open it. There was a running joke in the SAO that you had to have won at least one beauty pageant to become Judge Bennington's new law clerk. So when Mac knocked, he fully expected Judge Bennington's newest acquisition, Melody, to be on the other side.

"Hey, Mac. Come in," said Judge Bennington as he opened the door.

"Oh, yes sir," Mac replied, glancing over the judge's shoulder, expecting to see the sumptuously blonde Melody, who had reportedly won third place in the Miss Maryland pageant before going to law school. She was not by the doorway.

"This way..." Judge Bennington directed, sweeping his arm toward the main area of his chambers.

Mac stepped into the room and looked toward the little auxiliary office where Melody worked. The lights in her office were off, and the room was dark.

"I was hoping to see your new law clerk, Your Honor," Mac said, with a deliberate smirk intentionally designed to bond with the judge.

"Oh, I let her go home early today. She's been working overtime a lot lately. You didn't pass her in the hallway?"

"No, sir," said Mac. "I would *definitely* have remembered that."

"Yes, well, some law clerks are easier on the eyes than others," the judge said with a grin. "Now, have a seat and tell me—what do you need to know about that old Stephens case?"

There's no one here but myself and Judge Bennington. No witnesses at all.

Mac sat down in one of the big leather chairs in front of the judge's desk. Bennington crossed around to the back of the desk and sat down in his swivel chair. Turning toward Mac, he said, "Have you interviewed Assistant Chief Harper yet? He's the witness who knows this case best."

"Yes, Judge, I had lunch with him the other day. But I'd like to hear what you yourself remember about the case. Did you think it was a strong evidentiary case when you prosecuted it back in 2002?"

Judge Bennington leaned to the side of his desk and picked up a golf club that was balanced against a bookshelf. He grasped the putter with both hands and twirled it. Deep in thought, he looked down the shaft of the putter. After a moment of compulsively spinning the golf club, he stopped and turned to face Mac. He said, "When you're prosecuting a case with a witness like Harper, y'know, someone so headstrong and talkative, well, sometimes you just let *them* put the case together. You know what it's like, Mac, when you're a busy ASA swamped with major cases, right? Occasionally, you have to let your cops do the heavy lifting and help you, right?"

"Absolutely, Judge. I know exactly what you mean."

This fucker is already trying to blame Harper.

Bennington continued, "And then when the trial starts, the simplest thing to do is just to call your investigator up to the witness stand and let him explain everything. So, what I remember most about this Stephens case was letting Harper—and to a lesser extent, York—take the lead. Basically, I just called them to testify and asked them to tell the jury in their own words what happened. I basically kept saying, 'What happened next?' and "Then what happened?' over and over until they were finished testifying."

Mac did not reply.

Bennington continued, "But all I can recall is them both giving open-ended narratives. And that PD never objected. Never said a word. That's what I remember most."

"Judge, do you recall this woman Makayla? She picked Stephens from a photo array. What do you remember about her eyewitness identification?"

CHAPTER 23

June 17, 2022
10:00 a.m.

EYEWITNESS IDENTIFICATION
SENECA COUNTY POLICE DEPARTMENT DIRECTIVE #1818

1. Overview

Eyewitness identification is one of many tools used by the SCPD in the investigation of crime. It is critical that all eyewitness identifications be strictly conducted in a professional manner and supported by written documentation. The purpose of this directive is to establish guidelines consistent with the Annotated Code of Maryland, Public Safety Article, Section 3-506.

2. Photographic Arrays

A photographic [photo] array is a display of a photo of the suspect arranged in random sequence and mixed with five [5] other similar photos of other individuals whose physical characteristics closely resemble the suspect's appearance at the time of the commission of a criminal offense. The photo array must contain a total of six [6] photos:

the photo of the suspect mixed with five [5] other photos obtained from the arrest files of prior individuals in unrelated offenses. The photos of the five [5] other unrelated individuals must have similar features, such as facial hair, hair color, and hairstyles. The unrelated photos must be of the same race, gender, and approximate age as the suspect.

3. Process

This directive requires that two [2] officers participate in the presentation of the photo array. The first officer is the "investigating officer" who is familiar with the facts of the case. The second officer is the "presenting officer" who is <u>unfamiliar</u> with the case and, thus, unbiased as to the identities shown in the six [6] photos. To ensure fairness, the photo array process must be conducted in the following manner:

a) The "investigating officer" shall compile a collection of six [6] photographs which includes the suspect's photo mixed with five [5] neutral photos. The "investigating officer" shall then shuffle the photos and place them in a sealed envelope in random order.

b) The "presenting officer," who is unfamiliar with the investigation, participates only to the extent that he/she presents the full photo array to the eyewitness. This approach ensures neutrality because the "presenting officer" does not know which of the six [6] photos is that of the suspect, and therefore cannot influence the eyewitness's selection. This technique is called the "double blind" technique and is approved by the SCPD.

c) Eyewitnesses must be told the suspect "may <u>or may not be</u> among the persons presented in the photo array. The "presenting officer" is required to contemporaneously document the eyewitness's verbatim words upon viewing the full array, and must further document the level of confidence that the person identified is the perpetrator. The eyewitness must then sign the photo selected along with the date of the identification.

Judge Robbie Ryan announced, "Gentlemen, we are here on the Defendant's Motion to Suppress a Photographic Array. Are both sides prepared to proceed at this time?"

Marcel answered, "Yes, Your Honor, the defense is prepared."

"Good morning, Judge. Mac MacIntyre for the State of Maryland. We have Assistant Chief Harper outside in the hallway ready to testify."

"Call your witness, Mr. MacIntyre."

CHAPTER 24

June 17, 2022
10:07 a.m.

"Do you solemnly swear or affirm that the testimony you shall give is the truth, the whole truth, and nothing but the truth?" the courtroom clerk asked.

"Yes, I do," replied Assistant Chief Harper.

"Please be seated," said Judge Ryan.

Harper was dressed in a freshly pressed, khaki Seneca County Police Department uniform. His white hair was assiduously trimmed in his trademark bristly flattop. As he sat in the witness stand, his bright sky-blue eyes scanned the entire courtroom in the manner of a submarine's periscope sticking out of the ocean and peering for danger in all directions.

"Please state your name for the record, and spell it so the record is clear," Mac said, standing at the prosecution table. Across the room, at the defense table, Marcel sat still with his arms folded. Eddie sat next to him, wearing his olive-green jail jumpsuit. In the last row of the courtroom, Tamika sat alone, puffing heavily in a rhythmic wheeze. Ophelia wasn't with her.

"Sure. I'm Assistant Chief Samuel Harper. That's spelled H-A-R-P-E-R. Good morning, Mr. MacIntyre."

"And, sir, how are you currently employed?"

"I am a member of the Seneca County Police Department. My current rank is that of Assistant Chief. I have been with SCPD for, um—let me think. Well, I guess it's been over 27 years now."

Mac said, "Let me draw your attention to the date of July 5, 2002 and the subsequent days that followed. I know it's been a while, but do you recall the events of that day?"

"Yes, I sure do."

Mac continued laying a foundation. "Have you had the opportunity to review your records and reports from a case dating back to that date, specifically the State versus Edward D. Stephens?"

"Yes. I read a copy of the entire case file dating back to that time. You provided it for me, Mr. MacIntyre."

"First, Assistant Chief, do you see the Defendant present in the courtroom at this time?"

Marcel labored to rise from his table, but surrendered to the pain in his back and, halfway upright, he waved his hand toward the judge and said, "Stipulate as to the identity of the Defendant, Your Honor." He sat down with a thump.

Judge Ryan confirmed, "The defense stipulates that the Defendant has been identified as Mr. Stephens, who, I will note for the record, is sitting in the courtroom next to his counsel, Mr. St. Croix."

From the last row of the gallery, Tamika raised her hand and waved a tissue like a flagman at a railroad crossing. She leaned forward against a row of seats in front of her and urgently said, "He ain't do nothing, so how you going to identify him?!"

Mac, Marcel, Eddie, and Judge Ryan all simultaneously swiveled their heads to look back at Tamika. Marcel held his hand up in a "stop" gesture at exactly the same time Judge Ryan exclaimed, "Ma'am! Please, we are conducting court right now, and there will be no talking or outbursts. Do you understand me? If you cannot maintain your composure, I will have no alternative but to ask the sheriff's deputy to escort you out into the hallway. Are we clear?"

A burly young man in a deputy's uniform quickly stood from his chair behind Eddie. He stepped briskly toward the aisle leading from the well of the courtroom to the public gallery portion of the courtroom. The deputy had a completely shaved head with only a small patch of oval-shaped brown hair positioned on the top of his head. He had his hand on a bright yellow Taser device strapped to his thigh. A nametag over his chest pocket read FEENY, P.

"Deputy, that won't be necessary," said Judge Ryan.

Feeny stopped in his tracks, but his eyes were bulging. He was staring at Tamika. She held her hand up and gently waved it in quiet resignation. She leaned back in her seat and reached into her purse, extracting a small square plastic container of Tic-Tacs. She poured herself a handful of white, pill-shaped mints and put all of them in her mouth.

Satisfied the commotion was sufficiently quelled, Judge Ryan said, "Mr. MacIntyre, you may continue."

"Thank you, Your Honor." Mac turned toward the witness stand and said, "So, Assistant Chief Harper, let me ask you about a photo array which you conducted while investigating a homicide that occurred on Rotterdam Street in Seneca County, Maryland during the first week of July in 2002. Do you remember participating in that photo array?"

"Yes, I do."

"Who was the eyewitness to whom you presented the photo array?"

"Her name then was Makayla Schweitzer. She got married, I understand. Of course, I haven't seen her in something like 20 years."

"Thank you."

Before Mac could ask his next question, Judge Ryan jumped in and asked the witness, "Just to make the record clear, sir, what was your rank and duty assignment on the date of July 7, 2002?"

Usually, Mac detested when a judge took over the questioning process. He always wanted to maintain control. It was disorienting, like driving a car and having the front-seat passenger suddenly grab the steering wheel. Right now, he didn't mind, as there was no jury to wonder why the judge would suddenly start interjecting questions. Today, it was just Motions. In effect, Mac had only *one* juror to convince today, and that was Judge Ryan herself.

Harper answered, "I was working plainclothes on the Vice Unit on that date, Your Honor. I had been a cop for only a few years then. I mean, a lot's changed in the last two decades, obviously."

Judge Ryan continued to establish the facts. "I will take judicial notice that the witness conducted a photo array with an alleged eyewitness, who was then known as Makayla Schweitzer, but who is currently known as Makayla O'Reilly. Have I gotten all of that correct, Mr. MacIntyre?"

"Yes, Judge."

Judge Ryan looked at the defense table and said, "Mr. St. Croix? You agree?"

"Yes, ma'am. So stipulated, for the purpose of this Hearing. We do not dispute the chain of events leading up to the presentation of the photo array."

"Understood," said Judge Ryan. "Mr. MacIntyre, you may proceed."

Mac turned toward the witness stand and asked, "Was anyone else assisting you as you conducted the photo array?"

"Yes. My partner, Sergeant Rick York."

"Thank you," Mac replied. "Can you please describe for the Court the process of compiling the various photos used in the array?"

"Yeah, sure. First, we told Makayla she had to come in and identify the guy who shot the dead guy—I'm sorry, I forget his name right now."

Mac offered, "The victim was a young man named J'Mal Jefferson."

"Oh, that's right, him. Jefferson. I remember now. Well, anyway, me and Sergeant York had been working Vice all up and down Rotterdam Street for about a year prior, and when Makayla said the guy was named 'Eddie,' and that he was a light-skinned Code 3 male—Code 3 means an African American subject—and that he had long dreadlocks, we immediately knew it was the Defendant."

Mac said, "Let's get back to the photo array. How did you compile the six photos used in the array?"

"Well, me and Rick—that is Sergeant York—we dug through the file cabinets of Polaroid arrest photos down at the 4D Station. We had thousands of mug shots all separated into different categories. It's all done different now. Now, we use a computer program to assemble them. But this was long before the days of the Internet and cell phone cameras, y'know. So, back then, we had tons of Polaroids from other arrests. They were all divided by sex, race, age and physical characteristics like hairstyles and things like that."

Mac tried to steer him in the right direction. "So, you did your best to compile a group of five photographs gathered from prior mug shots that were all similar to the way the Defendant looked at that time? And all of them had faces very comparable to Mr. Stephens?"

Marcel didn't have the energy to properly stand, but said firmly while seated, "Objection, Your Honor. Leading question."

"Sustained. Please don't lead the witness," Judge Ryan quickly replied.

"My apologies, Judge. So, Assistant Chief, please describe how you selected the other five photos. How did you pick the ones to add in with the one of the Defendant?"

"We selected five other mug shots. All of them were young

Black males approximately the same age as Mr. Stephens, which was around 18 years old, if I'm not mistaken."

Harper reached across the witness stand and grasped the handle of a shiny aluminum water pitcher. He flipped over a white Styrofoam cup and poured water into the cup.

"Please continue, sir," Mac urged.

"So, we got these other five photos of young guys with light-skinned complexions. And we specifically picked ones with those dreadlocks, too."

"How did you have a photo of Mr. Stephens?"

"Oh, Eddie has a long record. There were several mug shots of him on file," said Harper, who then turned directly to face Judge Ryan. He added, "He had prior convictions for all kinds of stuff. Vandalism, graffiti, slashing tires on police cars. All kinds of stuff, Judge."

Mac continued, "Did you give the eyewitness any instructions?"

"Well, first we explained she was going to look at these six photographs, and one of them was the guy who we thought did the shooting. But we told her to be careful and not guess. Told her, 'If you see the shooter, point him out.' That's all. We didn't try to influence her choice in any way, shape, or form."

Mac said, "How did you actually do the presentation?"

"OK, so me and Rick—sorry, I mean Sergeant York—we was in the conference room at the 4D station, and we put the six photos out on the table. Spread 'em out in a line like you're supposed to do. It was just me, her, and Sergeant York. No one else. As soon as we put all six photos down, she immediately pointed at the one of Eddie Stephens and said, 'That's him! I'm 100 percent sure. I'll never forget that face as long as I live.'"

"And did she subsequently sign the photo of Mr. Stephens?"

"Yes, she did."

"Your Honor, may I approach the witness?"

Judge Ryan said, "Yes, you may."

Mac reached into his box of evidence and pulled out a thick envelope of the type used for ordinary mail, now yellowed around the edges. He walked up to the witness stand and placed it on the witness stand in front of Assistant Chief Harper.

"Sir, I draw your attention to State's Exhibit One for the purpose of this Hearing. What is it?"

"This is an envelope with the six photos we showed Makayla on that day back in 2002."

"Are any of the photos signed by Ms. Schweitzer?"

Harper shuffled through the six Polaroids, examining each one as he inspected them. On the fourth photo, he stopped and held it up for the whole courtroom to see.

"This one. Number Four. Makayla Schweitzer written here in her own handwriting at the bottom in ballpoint pen ink. This is the one she signed."

"And who is that a photo of?" Mac confirmed.

"Eddie Stephens. Him," said Harper, as he pointed accusatorily at the Defendant.

CHAPTER 25

June 17, 2022
11:06 a.m.

"Mr. St. Croix," Judge Ryan said. "The State has rested on the issue of the photo array's admissibility. On behalf of the defense, do you have any questions of the witness?"

"Oh, yes. Oh, yes, I do, Your Honor," Marcel replied as he rose. He picked up a single sheet of paper from the defense table and winked at Eddie, who looked up into his eyes. Eddie turned to face his mother, Tamika, and nodded.

"May I approach the witness, Judge Ryan?"

"Yes, you may."

Marcel deliberately walked up to the witness stand and said, "Assistant Chief Harper, I am showing you what is marked Defendant's Exhibit Number One. Do you know what this document is?"

Harper took the sheet of paper and inspected it. The

overhead fluorescent light reflected against the blueness of his eyes. He reviewed the page and then handed it back to Marcel. "Yes, Mr. St. Croix. I recognize that document. It's new, or I should say fairly new. It's a copy of Seneca County Police Department Directive 1818. We didn't have that back when we did this case in 2002."

"Thank you, sir," said Marcel. "So, Defendant's Exhibit Number One is the Department's current protocol, or I should say directive, on exactly how photo arrays are to be properly conducted by the police here in Seneca County, is that correct?'

"Yes," said Harper. "But, as I just said, we didn't have that back then."

"I understand. You've mentioned that twice already, and I didn't ask you anything about that. Sir, can we agree that you will answer the questions I pose and that you'll not add gratuitous extra comments? Will you answer my questions without embellishments?"

Mac interposed, "Objection. This is argumentative."

"Overruled," said Judge Ryan. Turning to Harper, she added, "Assistant Chief, please answer Mr. St. Croix's questions, and if Mr. MacIntyre needs to clarify anything, he will have an opportunity on redirect examination to do so."

"Yes, ma'am."

Marcel continued, "Can we also agree that Directive 1818 is the controlling document *currently*?"

"I'm not sure what you mean by controlling."

"Very well, let me restate the question in a simple way, so that perhaps you may understand. This document that I am now holding in my hand is a set of strict instructions, designed to give guidance to investigators on exactly how to properly conduct a photo array presently. *Currently*. Correct?"

Harper looked at Mac at the prosecution table. Mac reached down and lifted his case file, and pulled out his copy of Directive 1818. He laid it flat on the table as he reviewed it. He took his pen from his jacket's breast pocket and circled several different words on the page.

Marcel pounced. "You don't need to look at the State's Attorney to answer my question, do you?"

Harper said, "No, I don't need to look at him. But yes, sir. That's the *current* directive. You got me there. Yes."

Marcel continued. "Assistant Chief, let me draw your attention to this section of the directive, paragraph four. This section is entitled 'Process,' is it not?"

Harper conceded, "Yes."

Marcel said, "And paragraph four requires that every photo array be conducted with two officers, one who is the lead investigator, and a second who is *not familiar* with the case. The second officer is called the presenting officer. Am I right?"

Harper reached for his Styrofoam cup, but did not lift it. He hesitated, and then grabbed it and moved it across the witness stand, where he placed it next to the shiny aluminum water pitcher.

Marcel waited quietly while Harper fiddled with the cup.

Judge Ryan turned her head toward the witness stand.

Marcel cupped his hand around his ear as if he couldn't hear and said, "What is your answer?"

"Can you please repeat the question?"

Marcel asked, "You did *not* have a second officer assisting you with the presentation of the photo array. Isn't that true, Assistant Chief?"

"I've testified already that I had Sergeant York assisting me."

"But, sir, Sergeant York was your *partner* on the investigation! He wasn't neutral or 'blind,' as the directive requires. Surely, you don't disagree with me on that point?"

"Like I said, she picked him out and was 100 percent positive. What more do you need?"

Marcel pounced. "Sir, the rules of court do not allow me to answer *your* questions. This is how it works: I ask questions, and *you* answer them."

Mac shifted his weight but did not rise to object.

Marcel walked back to the defense table. Eddie was leaning forward, his chin in both of his hands and the points of his elbows sharply positioned on the table.

Marcel spun backwards toward the witness stand and asked, "Paragraph four also requires that—and I quote—'eyewitnesses must be told that the suspect may *or may not be* among the persons presented in the photo array.' Do you recall *that* section of Directive 1818?"

Harper responded, "Well, I'm not sure what your point is, but…"

Before he could complete his sentence, Marcel jumped in, "Sir, it's not important if *you* understand what my point is as long as Judge Ryan does."

Mac swung his feet underneath him to get his footing to rise, but before he could lift himself off his chair, Judge Ryan interjected, "Mr. St. Croix, please! That *is* argumentative, and I will sustain the State's objection. I may remind you that there is no jury here, so it would be helpful to the Court if you saved your theatrics until then."

"Yes, Your Honor," said Marcel with an apologetic tone. "I fully appreciate the Court's indulgence. Please excuse me. May I continue with cross-examination, ma'am?"

Judge Ryan waved her hand at the witness stand and said, "Proceed."

"So, I will ask you again: did you tell Makayla Schweitzer, when you and Sergeant York showed her the photo array on July 7, 2002, that Eddie Stephens may *or may not be* included in the six photos? Yes or no?"

Harper was trapped. No one, not Mac, not Judge Ryan, not Sergeant York, not even Makayla, could rescue him now.

"No. I didn't."

CHAPTER 26

June 17, 2022
1:31 p.m.

"We're totally fucked, Andre. Judge Ryan suppressed the whole photo array. She said we can't even mention it to the jury."

Mac leaned back in his office swivel chair and put both of his hands over his face. His shoulders drooped, and he let out an audible sigh.

"Hey man, you going to eat that extra California roll or not?" said Andre, pointing at the clear plastic box he had brought Mac from Sushi Queen for lunch. "I love this shit," he continued. "I would never have tried raw fish if it weren't for you, Mac. What's this one called again?"

"Salmon is *sake*. And yellowtail is *hamachi*. Tuna is *tekka*. That's all the Japanese you need to know, bro."

Andre tossed his empty plastic box and chopsticks in

the trash can to the side of Mac's desk and lifted a can of Diet Mountain Dew, draining the last few drops down his throat. Done, he crumpled the can in his fist and shot it like a basketball into the trash can where it landed with a crash.

"You should have seen how Marcel St. Croix destroyed Harper on cross," Mac said. "Just sliced his ass up. If that's any indication of what's in store for us at trial, we are really in trouble."

"Yeah, man. I get a bad vibe about Harper. He's holding something back. I can tell. I was on SAT for years. I know how it goes down there on Rotterdam. Lots of 'street justice.' Let's just leave it at that."

"Yeah, street justice. I've heard about that."

"One time, Mac, back in the day, I saw these three SAT guys take this obnoxious drunk dude behind the Target on Rotterdam, and, instead of arresting him, they smashed him in the head with their flashlights and left him there unconscious in the parking lot. Said it was easier than going to court. Man, makes me sick when I think about it."

Mac added, "This guy Harper? How did he ever get promoted? And he's going to be the new Chief of Police. Jesus help us."

"10-4 on that shit, for real."

"He did the photo array all wrong. Totally messed it up. Didn't follow the directive at all and then tried to act like it didn't matter."

Andre responded, "I bet Judge Ryan straightened him out. She don't play around."

"It was humiliating. And *I* had to take the spear right

in the chest. Ryan was lecturing *me* about *ex post facto* laws and retroactivity, and when she ruled, every word out of her mouth felt like death by a thousand cuts."

"*Ex post facto*. Whatever the fuck that means."

Mac passed his plastic lunch box over to Andre and said, "You can have this. I can't eat. Actually, I feel like I'm about to vomit. And not because of the sushi, but because of Harper, and because of this damn case." Mac crumpled up his small white napkin and used it to grab his used chopsticks, and then dropped the bundle into the trash can.

"So, how does that work in a trial if the photo array is blocked? Can't we just use Makayla in the retrial to point out Stephens in court, like, in real time in front of the jury?"

"Yes," said Mac. "We can. The photo array is technically called an 'extrajudicial identification.' That means that the witness pointed out the Defendant right after the crime, when her memory would have been fresh in her mind. That's why they do these photo arrays. It's like they try to lock in a solid ID right after the crime happened. Because witnesses' memories are so faulty."

"And Harper did it all ass backward."

Mac explained, "So, Ryan's ruling means we can't mention the photo array, but we can still go ahead with the case. A single eyewitness—if believed beyond a reasonable doubt—is all that the jury instructions require. But trust me, this case was weak to begin with, and now it's even weaker. The photo array would've at least supported Makayla when she identifies Stephens in court, and now that corroboration is lost."

"Yeah," Andre agreed. "You know that old saying about a

table? If you take out one leg, it gets wobbly. But if you take out *two* legs, it falls over. Feels like this case is about to tip over."

"Right. I'm going to meet with The Fish and Jo Newgrange tomorrow morning to tell them this trial is disintegrating. I'm going to recommend we just make whatever deal we can get with Marcel and zip this case up tight for good. I mean, *no one* wants to do this trial. Harper said to ditch it. Makayla doesn't want to be here. And Judge Bennington definitely doesn't want to rehash this old nightmare. He's going to have to take the witness stand! He's a judge here in the same courthouse. That's never happened in Seneca County before, I'm sure."

"And *we* don't want to do this jury trial either," Andre echoed.

"Exactly. So, why the hell are we doing it?"

They sat in silence for a moment. Andre asked, "Do you think Stephens killed that guy down on Rotterdam Street? Do you think we even have the right man?"

"I don't know. 20 years ago, a jury said he did it, so I've got to respect that decision, but, I tell you, I'm not even close to confident about this case. Not even close."

"Well, Makayla *saw* it happen right in front of her with her own eyes. Nothing else really matters, right? The rest of it—the screw-ups by Harper and York—they don't mean shit if Makayla saw what she saw."

"That's true," said Mac. "But I don't think that's going to be enough to convict Eddie a second time."

"But if you drop the case, the whole world will think you're dropping it because the cops and that dope Bennington were corrupt. If we let Eddie walk, the press will crucify that judge, and then you get into all that political shit. That will be the hook in the papers: a Circuit Court judge cheated. That judge will be toast. And The Fish will point his stubby little finger at you. Trust me on that. Shit slides downhill, and he's above you, Mac."

"I know," said Mac. "It slides downhill. Laws of gravity."

"Maybe you just have to put the trial up and let the jury decide? Then at least you're off the hook if they acquit him."

Mac looked up at the framed child's drawing over his desk. His eyes settled on the words, STAIT'S ATTOURNEY. After a pause, he added, "And if Makayla's telling the truth?"

"But why would Makayla lie? She seems so damn sure. What's she got to gain by pointing out the wrong guy?"

Mac turned to look at Andre, and said, "We need to figure that out. But I can think of a couple of reasons, actually. But we can't keep going down all these rabbit holes."

"What exactly does that mean? I've heard people say that—rabbit holes. Usually it's a lawyer who says that."

"It's an expression, Andre. It means going off in the wrong direction or getting lost or off track. It comes from a book called *Alice's Adventures in Wonderland*. It was written in 1865 in England. The author was a guy named Lewis Carroll. Alice fell down a rabbit hole, and, well, then she went on a very strange trip."

"I'll take your word for that. Hey, Mac, have you ever convicted a guy, and then you found out later he was innocent?"

Mac stood up and walked to the window. From up on the fifth floor, he looked out over the Courthouse Square. He watched the people crossing the diagonal pathways bisecting the small park area between the four main buildings that anchored each of the corners. From this perspective, the rectangular layout resembled a leafy Ivy League campus. A variety of people were shuffling between the different courthouses. He had worked in all of them: delinquents in the Juvenile Court, misdemeanors in the District Court, ceremonial functions in the Old Colonial Courthouse, and here, where he stood at his office window, jury trials in the Circuit Court. Lawyers, witnesses, police officers and courthouse employees were scurrying along the pathways after enjoying a lunch hour in the warm mid-June weather. A young man and woman at the far end of the Square had spread a plaid blanket out on the grass and were taking picnic items out of a boxy lacquered straw basket.

"I had a jury trial once about ten years ago. You helped me with it, Andre. Remember the Jamaican taxi driver? I almost put that guy in jail for a sexual assault he didn't commit. I mean, the jury was well on their way to convicting him."

"Oh my God. Yes, the taxi driver. I remember that trial. And the girl from England, right?"

"No. She was from Edinburgh, Scotland," said Mac.

"Same thing."

Mac looked out the window over the Courthouse Square and didn't respond.

Andre said, "That was a long time ago, man. What was that taxi driver's name again?"

CHAPTER 27

June 17, 2022
1:59 p.m.

"Simms. His name was Tybalt Simms. It's been nine years since I did that trial, but I remember it like it was yesterday."

The Simms trial was in its third day. Mac picked a jury on the first day, and he was pleased it had 11 women seated. The public defender was way in over her head. She didn't even raise a *Batson* objection when it was obvious to everyone in the courtroom that Mac was striking as many men as possible from the jury pool. Even the worst PD knew that the Supreme Court, in *Batson v. Kentucky*, had ruled that an attorney couldn't strike jurors based on their race. Then, in the years after the *Batson* ruling, the concept of ensuring fairness in jury selection had been extended to include gender and age. Every halfway decent attorney watched for patterns when opposing counsel struck jurors, and, if a lawyer kicked off a series of potential jurors of the same type of demographic, it could be objectionable. But if the PD wasn't going to object, Mac kept trying to seat as many female jurors as possible. He'd take 12 if he could.

Women were usually better for the prosecution in any kind of sexual assault case. There were virtually no women alive who had not experienced some type of sexual harassment, from simple catcalls on the street to unwelcomed touches or worse. In the Simms case, female jurors would subconsciously identify with a young woman who was assaulted by a random taxi driver. Without even thinking, they'd put themselves in the victim's place.

After the jury was selected, Mac gave a compelling opening statement.

He described Paige Evans, a 19-year-old *au pair* from Scotland. She was working in Seneca County while taking a gap year before heading to St. Andrews University. She had met a nice guy named Geoff, who worked as a lifeguard at the country club. One Friday in August, when her host family was away at Rehoboth Beach, he asked Paige to come along with a bunch of his college friends for a fun, warm night of barhopping in Georgetown. He knew a place that didn't check IDs very closely. After a night of Jell-O shots, tequila-heavy margaritas, and green bottles of cold Heineken, Geoff noticed that Paige was intoxicated—she could barely stand—so, in gentlemanly fashion, he called for a taxi to take her back to the house in the Maryland suburbs where she was spending the summer.

As Geoff walked with Paige out of the bar into the summer night, he watched as the taxi came down the street toward them. He squinted his eyes against the glare of the oncoming headlights. As the cab pulled up, Geoff gave Paige a quick hug, said goodbye, and gave her a $20 bill for the fare home. As the taxi drove off, he went back inside the bar, hoping to hook up with one of the pretty college girls crowded inside, grouped in enthusiastic, gyrating clusters on the dance floor.

In the taxi, Paige held up her cell phone showing her home address through the partition separating the back seat area from the driver, and then she sprawled across the seat and fell asleep. When Paige awoke, she realized she was still inside the taxi, but it was parked in the rear, not the front of the house where she was staying.

As Paige regained her senses, she saw the house was dark. Startled, she realized that the taxi driver was in the back seat with her, not up front behind the driver's wheel. She felt a searing pain and looked down, confused as to why her light summery sundress was pulled up around her waist and her panties pulled down to the middle of her thighs. Her mind momentarily cleared, and she realized he was penetrating her with two fingers. She screamed. The cab driver jumped up and said, "Sorry! You said I could. Why are you yelling so loud?"

Paige shrieked, "Get off me!" She immediately passed out again, but, somehow, when she regained consciousness, she found herself lying in the grass in the backyard. As she saw the red taillights of the cab quickly sprinting away, she pulled her panties up and reached for her small purse, which, luckily, had gotten tangled with the spaghetti straps of her sundress and was still wrapped around her shoulder. Fumbling in the darkness, she opened her purse and found her keychain and cell phone. Amazingly, she now felt completely clearheaded. She ran around to the front door, clumsily negotiated the lock with her house key, and scrambled inside. She slammed the door behind her and slid the deadbolt lock into place. Now safe, she grabbed her cell phone and called 911.

"911. What is your emergency?" she heard a voice calmly state.

"I've been raped!" she exclaimed. "Come right away! It was a cab driver. He's still in the neighborhood!"

"What is the address you are calling from, ma'am?"

Paige gave her location and added, "He's a Black guy driving a taxi. He can't be far."

"Units are on the way, ma'am. Stay inside and turn on your house lights and make sure your door is locked. A police cruiser is close by. Hang tight."

Within seconds, two patrol cars raced into the driveway. The first cruiser's door popped open, and a female officer jumped out with her service weapon drawn. Watching from the peephole in the door, Paige flicked the lights on and off in the front hallway to alert the officer, who came running toward her. Paige opened the door, and the police officer cautiously entered the house with her service weapon in her hand. The officer looked quickly around and asked, "Is he still in here?"

"No! He just drove off like three minutes ago!"

The officer holstered her handgun and leaned over to

speak into a radio transmitter clipped to her shoulder. She announced, "All units in the Thomas 4 sector, look out for a taxi with a Code 3 driver."

Over her crackling radio, another officer immediately chimed in, "We have him stopped. Code 3 driver. Subject is in custody. Just six blocks from your location. We're bringing him by for a show up. Stand ready."

Paige was told they caught the guy who tried to rape her and that she should step outside into the driveway to identify him. When she was escorted to the front lawn, there were six patrol cars jumbled in the front yard, all with bright headlights on and blue lights swirling, illuminating the entire space like a giant pinball machine. Paige could see a Black man sitting in the back seat of the second officer's cruiser, his arms behind his back. The windows to the cruiser were rolled down, and two other cops were shining huge, powerful flashlights in his face. Paige was accompanied by the female officer toward the cruiser and stopped ten feet away.

"That's him," Paige said. "I'm sure."

The cab driver was arrested, charged, and indicted for a slew of sexual offenses. Mac took the case. Very strong direct evidence. Proof beyond a reasonable doubt.

And now they were in day two of the taxi driver's jury trial.

The public defender, a quiet young woman named Kusha Rora, came up to Mac in the middle of the trial and said, "Mr. MacIntyre, you have the wrong guy. My client didn't do this. He says it was a different cab driver. He swears to God."

Mac said sarcastically, "Oh, he swears to God? I guess *that* means he's innocent, huh? Funny how God only gets involved in these cases after my opening statement."

Kusha replied, "The girl picked the wrong cab driver. My client speaks with a very thick native Caribbean accent. Your cops said the girl told them the taxi driver who assaulted her was an African American guy. My client is not, I guess technically, African American? He's from Jamaica. You can hear it in his voice immediately."

"Maybe the victim doesn't know the difference? She's from Scotland."

"Can you please ask her about that? I'm serious, Mr. MacIntyre. And ask her about his teeth, too. My client, Mr. Simms, has never had any type of dental care in his life, and he's missing almost all of his front teeth. She'd definitely remember that."

Now, that's hard to fake. Accents can come and go, and a good actor can change his voice. But missing all of his teeth? That's something she'd remember. Maybe he wears a bridge or some dentures?

"OK, I'll ask her about that when we are done for the day. She's scheduled to testify tomorrow."

After court concluded, Mac went down to his office on the fifth floor and called Andre.

"Where are you, man? Something's really weird in this taxi driver case. Can you swing by?"

"Yeah, man. Be there in 15."

When Andre arrived, he was carrying two containers of hot coffee from Starbucks. He said, "I figured you'd be stressed, so here you go: a venti skim mocha latte with five Splendas."

"Thanks, All Star," Mac said. "So, listen, Andre. The public defender came up to me during the lunch break. She's this young woman they just promoted to Circuit Court. I don't know if she's ever done a jury trial before. But, anyway, she says we have the wrong guy, blah, blah, blah."

Andre went to the couch, sat down, and then reclined flat on his back as if the couch was a bed. He said, "Oh my God. I mean, she must know you've done over 100 jury trials by now. I bet she's intimidated as fuck by you, Mac. Which PD is this? Do I know her?"

"Kusha Rora. Have you seen her in court before?"

"Oh, yeah. That tiny little girl with the shaky hands? She speaks so quietly, I'm surprised the jury can even hear her. I've seen her in District Court. I thought she was an intern. They promoted *her* to Circuit Court? Lord have mercy."

"She's not a bad lawyer, actually," Mac said. "She's very smart and works hard. She's just not much for public speaking. To be good in front of a jury takes a bunch of different skills, Andre. You have to be bright, and you have to have a strong work ethic. You also have to be a fighter and competitive, but most of all, you have to enjoy the show. Some people do, some people don't. The PD's office seems to just promote whoever's next in line by seniority, no matter if they're good or not. It's like a factory in that office, and all the PDs are just cogs in a wheel that keeps spinning."

"Sounds like the damn police department. I mean, if you really suck as a police officer, they give you an award for meritorious service and then promote you. That's how you know a cop is completely incompetent: they keep getting promoted."

Mac smiled. "Same here in the SAO. I guess everywhere."

"That Kusha? Once I was in court on a bond review or something, and I saw her pick up a sheet of paper. And, as she's talking to the judge, the paper was rippling back and forth like she was in a hurricane."

"Yeah, she may be an inexperienced courtroom attorney, but the facts are the facts. No lawyer can change them. I've seen great lawyers lose cases and completely horrible ones win them. The lawyer can only do so much. It's like poker: an idiot with four aces is better than a genius with none. But something feels off with this trial. This Scottish woman seems—I'm not sure. I told the jury in my opening statement this was her first time visiting America. When I interviewed her before trial, she never said anything about a thick Jamaican accent. She also never mentioned the guy had no front teeth. That's weird. You'd remember both of those things, even if you were with him just a minute or two, wouldn't you?"

"Maybe he was wearing like fake teeth? And maybe he softened up his accent? I know some guys from the Islands who can do that real good. I play basketball with this guy from Tortola, and he can switch back and forth easily."

"Let's call Paige and ask her right now."

CHAPTER 28

June 17, 2022
2:33 p.m.

"Hey, Paige, this is Mac. I need to ask you about a few things, OK?"

"Sure. No problem. What's going on?"

"Did you notice whether or not the taxi driver spoke with an accent? A foreign accent?"

Mac looked at Andre and motioned for him to take notes, so he could be a witness if something went haywire. Andre reached across the desk and grabbed a new legal pad. Mac handed him his pen.

Paige said, "An accent? I don't know what you mean. He spoke normally."

"Did you have any conversations with him? Did you talk to him when you first got into the cab down in Georgetown?"

"I don't remember. I was so tired. I showed him my address off my phone. I may have spoken to the guy—I just can't recall. I didn't have any money left, so Geoff gave me a $20 bill. I must've fallen asleep, because the next thing I remember is being back in Seneca County in the back of the house where I'm living. Which was super weird. I was wondering, why are we in the backyard instead of in the driveway up front?"

Mac said. "Did you tell the police he yelled something when you woke up and he was in the back seat with you?"

"He said 'Stop yelling!' or 'Be quiet!'—something like that."

"So, you could hear him speak, right? And he would've been right next to you in the back of the taxi?"

"Yes," Paige affirmed. "I guess so."

"And did he speak with any type of accent?"

"No. Just a normal African American dialect."

Mac confirmed, "But Paige, let me ask you this: do you know the difference between a typical African American accent and a Caribbean accent? Have you ever heard a Jamaican accent before, for example?"

"Yes, of course," Paige replied. "We have tons of immigrants in the U.K. Jamaica used to be a colony of England. You know that, right? I have many friends from all over the world, and I've been hearing Jamaican accents my whole life. It's very diverse where I come from in Scotland, actually."

Mac looked at Andre. Andre opened his mouth and tapped on his front teeth.

Mac asked, "Paige, while we're talking about the taxi driver, did you ever notice anything unusual about his teeth?"

"His teeth?"

"Yes. Anything memorable about them?"

There was a long pause. Andre put his pen down and shook his head. Mac pointed to the legal pad in front of Andre on the desk and made a scribbling motion with his hand. Andre picked up the pen, and instead of writing any words, he drew a huge question mark across the top half of the page.

"Paige?"

"Well, to be honest, nothing comes to mind. Is there something about his teeth I need to know?"

"Just something we're working on. Don't worry. It's nothing you've done wrong. We are just trying to put all the pieces to this puzzle together."

Andre started drawing a series of question marks across the legal pad. Dozens of question marks. Flocks of them.

"Let me ask you this, Paige," Mac continued. "After the incident with the cab driver, when was the next time you saw Geoff?"

"I never saw him again. He ghosted me big time."

"No contact at all?"

"No. He deleted my Instagram and blocked me on Facebook too. He never even said he was sorry for what happened. I went to the pool about two weeks later, and he completely ignored me. Is he going to be here for the trial? Am I going to have to see him? That's super awkward."

"Yes, he's been subpoenaed. We have him set to testify tomorrow morning. But if you don't want to see him, we can shuttle you up to the courtroom. Detective Okoye can escort you. Don't worry. Hey, can you do me a favor, please? Can you keep your cell phone with you today in case we need to touch base again?"

"No problem."

"OK. Thanks. Talk to you later."

Mac gave the cell phone back to Andre, who tapped on the screen and said, "She's going to be a horrible witness, dude. She can't remember squat. How is a jury supposed to convict this taxi driver guy beyond a reasonable doubt based on that flimsy shit?"

"Call that Geoff guy. Let's see what he remembers."

"Geoff, this is Mac MacIntyre calling from the State's Attorney's Office. How are you?"

"Hey, Mr. MacIntyre. Is everything OK?"

"I'd like to ask you about your interaction with the cab driver. When he arrived at the club in Georgetown, did you have any conversations with him? Did you speak directly with him?"

"Um, let me think. I mean, I asked him to take Paige back to her house. He never got out of the cab, so I was just, like, on the curb. I remember her holding up her phone and showing it to him. And then he gave, like, a thumbs-up sign and drove off."

Mac followed up. "Did you talk to him?"

"I remember I asked him what the fare would be back to Seneca County, and he said it was 14 bucks. So I gave Paige money to cover that plus a tip. That's all I can remember."

"Did you ever hear the taxi driver speak?"

"Well, briefly. He said thanks for the tip. But that's about it. Nothing out of the ordinary."

"Based on his speaking voice, was there anything unusual about that?"

"Not that jumps out. Just a normal guy."

"Did he have a Jamaican accent?"

There was a pause as Geoff digested the question. Andre looked up at Mac and cupped his hand behind his ear, as if to signal, "Listen."

Geoff said, "No. Definitely not. I'm sure of that."

Mac added, "Anything about his teeth that stood out?"

"His teeth? I don't understand."

"Did he have any noticeable missing teeth? Could you see his mouth when he talked to you?"

Geoff said, "No, there was nothing special about his teeth. He had a full set of teeth. I would've remembered something like that. Did Paige say he had missing teeth?"

Mac didn't answer that question. Instead, he asked, "Can I ask you point blank: how drunk were you at that exact point in time?"

"Well, Mr. MacIntyre, I wasn't totally messed up. I'd say I was buzzed. I'd had about five or six beers. That's it. Paige was the one who was messed up real bad. She said it was a bad mix with her medications. I think she even vomited in the ladies' room in the club. That's why I called the cab. She had had enough and was ready to go home."

Mac motioned again to Andre and made the scribbling gesture more urgently. Andre wrote the word "medications" on the legal pad, held it aloft for Mac to see, and then added another string of two dozen question marks.

"Did she tell you exactly what type of medications she had taken?"

"She's got a bunch of mental health issues. That much I know for sure. She was talking about bipolar disorder or something like that. Or schizophrenia. I can't remember exactly. But she takes a ton of stuff. Mood stabilizers. And they don't mix well with alcohol."

"How much alcohol did you see Paige consume?"

"Oh, she was shit-faced. Sorry for the language. But she had shots. A *lot*. Like 10 or more, I think. Guys were buying her shots, and she was guzzling them down."

"Last thing," Mac asked. "Let me ask you about the taxi cab itself. Do you recall which company or type of cab it was?"

"Seneca Yellow Cabs, I think."

"Can you describe the cab? Any physical features that stick out in your memory? Dents? Or anything about the cab itself which helps to identify it?"

"It had a big sign going down the roof, y'know what I mean? Like an advertising billboard-shaped thing. It went down the center from front to back. Like a shark fin. I definitely remember that sign. Like an ad lit up brightly. Must've had light bulbs inside it. It was an ad for cigarettes, and I was thinking I had just emptied my pack of Newports out, and I needed to buy a new pack. So that cigarette ad sticks out real clear in my memory. I'm super positive about that detail."

Andre wrote a note and held up the pad so Mac could read it. It said "Defendant's cab has no sign on the roof."

Mac said, "Thanks, Geoff. Talk to you later."

"OK. Goodbye."

Mac looked at Andre and shook his head. "This is a disaster."

Andre tossed the legal pad back on the desk and replied, "She was drunk as a skunk. And she takes all kinds of fucked-up medications for split-personality disorder or whatever the hell is wrong with her. And, on top of all of that, she didn't even notice the thick accent *or* the missing teeth?"

Mac added, "And she's got the wrong cab. Simms drives a taxi with no advertising sign on the roof. I've already shown the jury *photos* of Simms's cab."

"What are you going to do? You're halfway through this trial!"

"Well, I'm not going to put an innocent Jamaican dude with no teeth in Broad Run based on *this girl's* flawed testimony. She has the wrong guy."

Andre responded, "Well then, the question is—why are we prosecuting Tybalt Simms? And how did *he* get tagged with this crime?"

"His PD said he was the wrong guy all along. He just happened to be another Black guy driving a cab in the same rich, white neighborhood at the same time."

"Wrong place at the wrong time."

"Andre, please. I hate that cliché."

"It's true, Mac."

"Andre, when I was in law school, we learned about this guy named Blackstone. He lived from 1723 to 1780 in England. He was a famous lawyer and judge. Anyway, he wrote scholarly articles—books, actually—about the law. He once said that it was better to let 10 guilty guys go free than to convict one innocent man."

"Seriously? You read that shit years ago when you were back in law school? How the hell do you remember details like that?"

"Once I read something, it sticks in my mind. I can't explain it."

"Hey, so this guy Blackstone said a prosecutor should never convict an innocent man?"

"Right."

"Did they even have taxi drivers in England back then?"

Mac thought about his options overnight, and early the next morning, he called Kusha, the public defender, and told her he would be dropping the case. Ethically, if Mac himself thought there was a reasonable doubt as to the Defendant's guilt, he was obligated to end the prosecution, even if a jury had been sworn and the case was steaming down the tracks toward a conviction.

Mac never forgot Tybalt Simms.

CHAPTER 29

June 20, 2022
11:31 a.m.

Mac marched into Ari Fischbein's office. Ari was standing next to his desk with his back turned, looking at his cell phone. He did not turn around when Mac entered. Jo Newgrange was sitting at the conference table at the far end of the office focused on an iPad arrayed before her on the table.

Ari looked up momentarily and said, "So, you wanted to meet with us about this Stephens retrial? Can you make it quick? I have a lunch fundraiser for the Young Democrats Club, and I have to leave soon."

"I'll get right to the point, Ari," Mac answered, as he stepped up to the conference table. "Stephens will not plead guilty."

Jo was still looking intently at her device's screen. From where Mac stood, he could see there was some type of legal document on her screen, but, from his position, it appeared upside down, and he could not make out the content. He memorized the image on her screen and attempted to flip it right-side up in his mind.

Mac sat down and said, "And the evidence in this trial is looking extremely weak. I've been interviewing witnesses, and I'm hitting major roadblocks in every direction. As you know, this case is 20 years old, so most of these people have dispersed all over the country. One of the lead cops we need for the trial now lives in Colorado, for example."

Jo said, crisply, "So what? Get him here. Use the Interstate Witness Agreement and just subpoena him. That's not hard to do."

Mac ignored that comment because it was, as he knew from his actual experience, a very cumbersome and difficult process.

Mac did not take the bait. He said, "The main problem is this eyewitness, Makayla O'Reilly. She is the whole case, basically."

Ari turned, put his phone in his pants pocket, and reached down for his suit jacket that was folded on the arm of his chair. After he slipped his jacket on, he stepped toward the mirror mounted on the inside of his office door. Over his shoulder, he said, "We can't drop this case, Mac. If they won't plead guilty, just do the damn trial and stop complaining. Let the jury decide if this guy's guilty or innocent." He reached the threshold of his office, turned back, and said over his shoulder, "You know, it's not *your* job to decide the verdict. It's your job to present the damn case and let the chips fall where they may."

"Well, Ari, it's a little more complicated than that," Mac

responded. "This eyewitness Makayla is worthless. She doesn't seem to remember what happened at all. And this is even more important: Judge Robbi Ryan suppressed Makayla's extrajudicial identification at Motions, so we can't even tell the jury she had previously identified him. We lost that."

Jo said, "Well, if she can still ID him in the courtroom in front of the jury, that's all you need, at least according to the Maryland Common Jury Instructions."

"That's only if her in-court identification is believed beyond a reasonable doubt," Mac clarified. "And *that* is going to be the problem. It's 20 years later. He looks totally different now. He's gone from 17 years old to 37. Makayla is going to get killed on cross-examination. There is nothing that ties Stephens to the murder scene except for the testimony of a stoned, terrified woman, probably high on crack. I have nothing forensic. No fingerprints, no DNA, no confession. Nothing."

"That's not true!" Jo interjected sharply. "I'm reading the Court of Special Appeals decision right now," she continued, pointing at her iPad. "It says they recovered the handgun used at the scene inside one of this guy's *shoes* for God's sake. What more do you want?"

"Jo," Mac implored, "they seized *a* gun, not *the* gun. A cheap .22 Saturday-night special piece of junk. In those days, probably half of the people on Rotterdam Street had one tucked in their belts. And the investigators never conclusively matched the gun recovered at Stephens's house with the bullets taken from the scene."

Jo clicked her iPad off and said, "Well, that's a good enough link for me."

Mac tried again. "The crime scene techs couldn't recover any bullets at the scene usable for ballistics comparison. The bullets were hollow-point and shattered into a million fragments. The first shot, the one that grazed the dead guy's scalp, went through the drywall and hit a metal beam. It was completely deformed. Flat as a pancake. The second bullet, the one that hit the victim smack in the middle of his face? That bullet fragmented as it went through his skull. So, bottom line: we have no ballistics to match the bullets fired at the murder scene to Stephens's gun. Could be any .22 pistol out there, and there're *thousands* of them."

Ari was texting something on his cell phone and no longer listening.

Mac said, "They keep saying the gun was *consistent* with the type of bullets fired in the shooting. But not a match. Marcel St. Croix is going to make mincemeat out of that argument."

Jo said, "Well, it's consistent. That's good. At least it's not inconsistent."

"Yes, but that's definitely not going to be enough to prove this case beyond a reasonable doubt. Marcel—"

"Oh," Jo exclaimed. "So, your real worry is facing off against the great and powerful Wizard of Oz, also known as Marcel St. Croix? Is *that* what you're really afraid of? Losing to Marcel?"

Mac exhaled.

"I am OK with losing a trial," Mac replied. "I've won

enough jury trials over the years, so eventually I've got to lose a few. No, that's not it. What I'm concerned about is prosecuting a man who's been locked up for 20 years who is probably not even the right guy."

Ari spun around and said, "Just try the case, Mac! OK? If he refuses to take a plea, try the case! If we drop the case, I'll have the press hounding me about why, and I'm not getting involved in that shit, understand? If the jury acquits him, then it's not my problem. Don't you get it? I've got more important things to do than sit here and change your diaper. Try the fucking case!"

Jo stood up, snatched her iPad off the conference table, and tucked it under her arm.

Ari buttoned his suit jacket, opened the door, and walked out of his office.

Mac looked at Jo.

She said softly, "Like Ari said, just try the case. If the jury says he's not guilty, then I guess he's not guilty. It's up to them to decide. Not us. Pick a jury and let them decide. You're a very persuasive guy. Maybe they'll say he's guilty?"

CHAPTER 30

September 19, 2022
8:55 a.m.

"I'm picking the jury in five minutes," Mac said into his cell phone. He was standing in the hallway outside Judge Ryan's courtroom. "I've got to go back inside, Andre. The entire courtroom is filled with a huge jury pool. The judge is coming out of chambers any second. What's the emergency?"

"Well, I don't know if it's an *emergency*, Boss. But I went downstairs to the atrium to watch for Marcel St. Croix. He came through security about half an hour ago. He was carrying this, like, big chart exhibit. A photo blown up big and mounted on pressboard."

"Really? It's probably something he's got cooked up for his opening statement."

"You know how Frenchie is, always the showman."

Mac said, "We should have a jury selected by lunch. Then we go right into opening statements this afternoon."

"I tried to look at that photo."

"Well, could you see it?"

"Not really. Only part of it. I tried to get on the elevator with him so I could get a better look, but it was jammed, and I couldn't squeeze in without making it too obvious. But, Mac, he had those two Code 3 ladies with him. The old one had that big walking stick thing again."

"What was the part of the photo you could see?"

"It had a Christmas tree in the corner."

"A Christmas tree?"

Andre said, "Right. And we're in September. Hey, did you notice that old lady's cane? It has elephants and giraffes, and all these fucking zoo animals carved into it! I hope she's not a witch doctor, Mac! She might put a spell on your white ass!"

"Stop playing around. But that photograph—are you *sure* it was a Christmas tree?"

"All rise!" said Kristen. "Judge Roberta Ryan presiding. Please be seated."

Two hundred people stood up simultaneously, creating a rumbling sound that filled the courtroom. Mac rose from the prosecution table. Marcel stood at the defense table next to Eddie, who was not wearing the jail jumpsuit, but, instead, wore a pair of khaki slacks and a burgundy polo shirt. There was a strict rule that prisoners could not be observed wearing jail outfits in front of a jury. Eddie's mother Tamika—following Marcel's directions—had purchased the three new, colorful polo shirts and the slacks from Target, and Marcel had brought the new clothing down to the holding cells in the courthouse's basement. Eddie would wear the same brown slacks each day of the five-day trial, but he would rotate his three new shirts to create the illusion that he was wearing different outfits. Marcel preferred that the jury not know Eddie was incarcerated, so the rotating polo shirts was an attempt at misdirection, and, although Marcel was skeptical the jury would be fooled, the charade was worth the risk.

Judge Ryan assumed her position in her chair at the front of the courtroom. She was elevated, literally, over everyone in the room in deference to her position and authority. She took a quick look out over the crowded courtroom and then said, "Ms. Voice, will you please distribute the *voir dire* paperwork to Counsel?" Kristen took several steps across the well of the courtroom and handed Marcel a collated multiple-page document containing a list of the potential jurors. The list was a simple, basic, skeleton outline of each person called for jury duty, listing only their name, age, occupation, address, marital status and, if married, the occupation of their spouse. With just these basic clues, experienced attorneys like Marcel and Mac could intelligently guess which jurors might be sympathetic to their side, and which ones to avoid. But it was far, very far, from an exact science; jury selection was more of an art form, more like astrology and less like astronomy.

"Please stand and be sworn," Judge Ryan announced.

Everyone in the courtroom stood, creating a cacophony of human sounds—coughing, exclamations of "Excuse me"—mixed with the swooshing sound of 200 movie theater-type chairs flipping up.

Kristen spoke firmly to the entire assemblage, "Ladies and gentlemen of the jury *venire,* please raise your right hands. Do each of you solemnly swear or affirm that the answers you give shall be the truth, the whole truth, and nothing but the truth?"

Unsure, most of the jurors replied "Yes" or "I do" or didn't respond at all.

The judge then said, "Please be seated. You are now attending a session of the Circuit Court for Seneca County, Maryland. My name is Judge Roberta Ryan, and I will be presiding over this case. We are here to select a jury."

Mac turned his chair to face the large jury panel. He placed the outline on his lap. He wanted to match the names and occupations with the faces of each juror as Kristen did the roll call. Marcel, with his back to the audience, had a silver Mont Blanc pen in his hand and was already marking up his pages with plusses and minuses and arrows, an elaborate coded system he had developed over the years. Eddie sat next to him, looking alternately at Marcel's cryptic notes.

Twelve of these people could set Eddie free. Or send him back to Broad Run for decades. Eddie reached up and brushed a drop of sweat from his temple. He turned to look out into the gallery again and found his mother, Tamika, sitting next to Ophelia Jackson Katz in the very last row of the courtroom.

After all the jurors' numbers were announced, and everyone was inventoried, Judge Ryan said, "Thank you, ladies and gentlemen. Everyone seems to be accounted for. We are now at the point in the proceedings where we will select a jury. Let me explain: this is a two-step process. First, I will read some general questions to you as a whole to ascertain the acceptability of each juror. This process is called *voir dire*, which is a French term meaning, 'to speak the truth.' Then, after we have completed all of the court's general questions, the lawyers will have a chance to excuse or select a 12-person jury using their peremptory challenges. We will also seat two alternate jurors."

With that explanation, the judge announced, "This is the case of State of Maryland versus Edward DeLawrence Stephens. Mr. Stephens, will you please rise, sir?"

Eddie stood and turned to face the crowd. He stood tall and made eye contact with as many jurors as he could. His forehead was shiny, and large dark spots appeared on his shirt under his armpits and across his sternum, making his shirt a checkerboard pattern of burgundy and black.

"Does anyone in the jury panel know Mr. Stephens?"

There was silence in the gallery.

"Hearing no response, let the record reflect that none of the jurors has answered affirmatively." Judge Ryan said this out loud so the courtroom's recording system could capture each step of the process. Stenographers had become obsolete years earlier; now, everything was videotaped and carefully recorded.

She then asked if anyone knew Marcel or Mac. A woman in the back of the gallery raised her hand and said loudly, "I know Mr. MacIntyre. Or, I should say, I know *of* him."

Judge Ryan quickly interjected, "Please come forward, ma'am. Come up to the bench." The judge looked at Marcel and then to Mac and said, "Gentlemen?" Both Marcel and

Mac rose and walked to the front of the courtroom, standing like sentries on either side of the bench.

The woman was middle-aged and stocky. She was wearing yoga pants, Reebok running shoes, and a light blue nylon windbreaker, bearing a large bow-and-arrow logo on the back with lettering that read TUSCARORA ARCHERY. She walked up to the bench and smiled at Mac.

Judge Ryan activated a switch at the bench, and an obnoxious fizzy noise, sounding like static, emitted from the courtroom loudspeakers. The device creating the white noise was called a "husher," and it was designed to provide a masking sound to permit conversations at the bench to be confidential. When she was satisfied no one could hear their discussion in the gallery, the judge asked, "Ma'am, first of all, what is your juror number?"

The middle-aged woman said, "Um, my number? Oh, it's 18."

Both Mac and Marcel glanced at their paperwork to glean Juror 18's brief biographical information on the sheet.

Judge Ryan said, "So you said you knew the Assistant State's Attorney? How, and in what context, do you know Mr. MacIntyre?"

Juror 18 said, "Well, I don't know him actually myself, personally. But my husband is a cop. He's been a patrol officer here in Seneca County for 27 years. But he knows Mr. MacIntyre. I've heard him speak about Mac—I mean Mr. MacIntyre. Always said good things about him and that he was a great prosecutor."

"I understand," replied the judge. "Given that your

husband knows the prosecutor, ma'am, do you think your association with Mr. MacIntyre, or I should say, your knowledge of him—would that affect your ability in this case to be fair and impartial?"

The woman brushed her thin, suspiciously dark, jet-black hair back behind her ears as she pondered the meaning of this question and how she should answer it. Mac looked at Marcel, who was still looking down at this notes, scribbling some symbols like hieroglyphics.

After a pause, the woman said, "Well, like my husband always says, if Mr. MacIntyre is prosecuting someone, the guy's probably guilty. I'm just being honest, Your Honor."

"Thank you," said Judge Ryan. "You may have a seat back in the gallery."

The woman turned and walked back down the center aisle of the courtroom and reclaimed her seat.

At the bench, Judge Ryan asserted, "Gentlemen, she will be excused for cause. You may return to your seats."

When Marcel got back to the table, he leaned over and whispered to Eddie, "She knows the prosecutor. Her husband is a cop. The judge excused her. This is good for us."

Eddie responded, "Thank God. I didn't like her. She looked at me strange as she was walked up there. I've seen that look from white people before."

One by one, Judge Ryan asked the required preliminary *voir dire* questions. None of the jurors knew any of the anticipated witnesses, and everyone was pre-cleared for a five-day trial. After the judge finished with all the standard *voir dire* questions, the clerk called out the first dozen numbers.

Jurors One through Twelve, a wide assortment of humanity, arranged themselves in numerical order in the jury box.

When all 12 seats were occupied, the judge turned to the attorneys and said, "Mr. St. Croix, Mr. MacIntyre, are you prepared to use your preemptory strikes?"

"Yes, Judge," said Mac.

"Certainly," echoed Marcel.

CHAPTER 31

September 19, 2022
11:32 a.m.

This looks like a solid jury.

Mac subtly looked at the jurors one by one, methodically taking account of each person in this random collection of people. He knew they were all citizens of Seneca County and that they had all either voted, or had Maryland driver's licenses. The rest of what he knew was either gleaned from the clues in their brief biographical sketches, or was pure courtroom conjecture. Now that they were seated officially on the jury, each juror was now assigned new numbers corresponding with their designated seat: one, two, three, and so on, six in the front row and six in the back, with two alternates at the end of the jury box.

Juror One will follow me. He's on board for sure.

Juror One, by chance seated first and assigned the ministerial role as the Jury Foreman, was a young man, likely a student, with long brown hair, and thick eyebrows that converged into one fuzzy, horizontal line over his eyes. He was wearing Timberland boots and an olive-green, canvas military-style jacket, but he was definitely not a soldier.

That kid keeps staring right into my eyes. I like that. Good eye contact. He will be passive and will follow me. I can persuade him. Now, I need to figure out who are the strong personalities and leaders on this panel.

Mac pretended to read the printed outline for Juror Nine.

Not sure about this woman in the back row. I think she will bond with Makayla, and that's important, but she seems a little left politically. Wearing jeans to court?

He looked over at Juror Four, an elderly, nervous, Asian man seated in the center of the front row. He was wearing a mustard-colored flannel shirt with all of the buttons fastened, including the very top one by his throat. His light brown work pants were adorned with brass clasps connected to two vertical red suspenders looping over his shoulders.

Juror Four will do whatever I tell him to do. Chinese American man. He didn't raise his hand when Judge Ryan asked the whole venire if everyone spoke fluent English. Maybe he didn't even understand that question? I mean, if he doesn't speak English, how would he? I think he's safe for sure. He will go with the police witnesses and not create any waves in the Jury Room. Another follower. But who is going to lead this jury? Who is my ambassador? Who will argue my case for me once the Jury Room door is shut and I can't say anything else?

A large man in the last seat, Juror Twelve, was looking

at Judge Ryan and taking notes even though the trial had not yet started.

He's taking this seriously. Paying attention to everything.

Juror Twelve was a dark-skinned African American man dressed in a rumpled jacket and tie ensemble that was not quite a business suit, but yet he was more formally dressed than the rest of the jurors. He had thick eyeglasses and four pens clasped in his suit breast pocket. His profession was listed on the handout as "Therapist."

Therapist? What kind of therapist? Makayla did well with her drug treatment. This guy will like that. She'll be viewed as a success in this guy's eyes. He will believe her. But he's Black and Eddie is Black too. Will he feel a bond with Eddie, even on a subconscious level, or will he relate to Makayla more? I think he's good. Yes, that's my ambassador, Mr. Therapist. Don't let me down, OK?

After a back-and-forth process similar to a card game resembling human blackjack, both Mac and Marcel had used all of their strikes. When jury selection was completed, the jury was composed of eight men and four women. The two alternates were men.

Marcel took his pen and circled nine names. He passed the sheet of paper across the table to Eddie.

Marcel had circled the names of all the non-Caucasian jurors. There were five African American jurors, two Latinos, one Asian, and one East Indian. Eddie looked up into Marcel's eyes. Marcel winked.

"Mr. MacIntyre, you may address the jury," Judge Ryan said.

CHAPTER 32

September 19, 2022
1:36 p.m.

"Thank you, Your Honor. May it please the court," Mac replied, as he stood at the prosecution table. He reached down to the table and shifted a thick green book toward the edge. There was a small yellow sticky note protruding from the side of the book, marking a specific page.

"Ladies and gentlemen of the jury, at this time, it is my opportunity to present an opening statement to you. An opening statement is not evidence, but it is my chance to give you a brief roadmap of where I expect the testimony in this case will lead you. Evidence is comprised of the testimony of the witnesses and any tangible evidence or exhibits received by the court."

Mac shifted the green book to the edge of the table and then grasped it in his right hand. He picked it up and walked to the center of the courtroom. All the jurors were looking at the book by his side. It was a very simple technique to grab the jury's attention. Mac once used a newspaper for the same effect: a prop.

Holding it in front of the jury, Mac opened the book to the marked page and held it flat in his palm, like a waiter holding a tray. He read, "The identification of the Defendant by a single eyewitness, if believed beyond a reasonable doubt, can be enough evidence to convict the Defendant."

He snapped the book closed, creating a crisp clapping sound that echoed from the rear of the nearly empty courtroom. He scanned the entire jury box, looking for clues. "This is an open-and-shut case. It's as simple as that. But don't just take *my* word for it. What I've just read to you is from the Maryland Common Jury Instructions, specifically the definition of eyewitness identifications."

Mac held up the book again and said, "The Common Jury Instructions are the rules we use for all criminal trials everywhere across the State of Maryland—we use it every day in court. We use the exact same definitions in all cases to ensure uniformity and consistency. Fairness. I don't know what the verbatim testimony in this case will be, but I can guarantee you that, at the end of this trial, Judge Ryan will read you these words *exactly* as I've just articulated."

This was clever. Mac was bringing Judge Ryan into his presentation almost as a co-sponsor in support of his assertions and to give himself credibility before the jury. He walked back over to his table and softly put the book down and then patted it.

"This is a case about a murder, but it hinges on the direct

testimony of the person who actually saw the murder happen right before her very eyes."

Mac stepped out from behind his table again and held up three fingers on his left hand.

"Three people know who is guilty of committing that murder. Three people."

Eddie glanced up at Marcel. Marcel was looking down at his legal pad and taking notes of Mac's opening statement. Eddie saw Marcel jot down the words, "Three people?" Eddie turned quickly to make eye contact with his mother, who was again seated in the last row of the courtroom. Ophelia was next to her today, balancing the black African-themed cane between her legs with her eyes closed, rocking slightly in her seat.

"Three people: the first, unfortunately is deceased," Mac said. "His name was J'Mal Jefferson. He lived in a small apartment down near the border of Seneca County and Washington, D.C. Yes, we know he was a small-time drug dealer—I want to be totally upfront with you about that—and we will not sugarcoat anything in the presentation of this case. But, nevertheless, he did not deserve to be robbed and murdered. Unfortunately, Mr. Jefferson cannot speak for himself and point out his killer."

Mac paused. "But there is someone who can. And she will."

Mac looked at each of the jurors one by one.

"The eyewitness's name is Makayla O'Reilly. Ladies and gentlemen, please bear in mind that she was standing *in* the room when Mr. Jefferson was murdered. She was only a few feet away. She saw everything clearly." Mac paused between each word for emphasis as he spoke: she... saw... everything... clearly.

Two jurors looked at Eddie.

"Makayla O'Reilly saw *this* man," Mac said with a rising voice as he pointed at Eddie. "The Defendant—Eddie Stephens. She saw Eddie Stephens take a .22 caliber handgun out of his pocket and shoot Mr. Jefferson twice."

Tamika was coughing loudly in the back of the courtroom, and several jurors turned to glance out into the gallery.

"The first shot only caused a nonfatal wound down the center of Mr. Jefferson's scalp. However, the second shot *was* fatal, hitting him directly in his cheek. As Makayla watched this assassination unfold, Mr. Jefferson fell and crashed onto a glass coffee table in front of him."

Eddie reached up and wiped his nose on the back of his hand.

Mac continued, "After Mr. Jefferson shattered the table, in the final moments of his life, he bled out on the broken glass and died."

Mac took a quick inventory of everyone in the well of the courtroom to calculate if he was commanding the room's attention.

The jury's listening for sure. Marcel is taking notes, and Eddie's shirt is almost soaked.

Mac subtly looked slowly out into the gallery of the circular courtroom.

Eddie's mother and that other woman with the white hair

are getting agitated. That old lady is holding onto that big walking stick tightly.

Mac looked for a brief moment at the bench.

Judge Ryan is typing on her computer. Good. Must mean she is taking notes.

"After the Defendant had murdered Mr. Jefferson, he raced out through the door of the apartment and escaped. Makayla saw the entire episode. She saw it clearly and definitively. She is the eyewitness the Common Jury Instructions anticipates—a single eyewitness who is believable beyond a reasonable doubt. And that, Ladies and Gentlemen, is sufficient to arrive at a confident guilty verdict."

Marcel put his pen down and turned away from his desk. He touched the placard covered with paper behind him, the exhibit with the mysterious Christmas photograph. There was an improvised covering made of paper sheets taped together to conceal the enlarged photograph. The jury could not see what it portrayed. When Marcel turned around to touch it, several members of the jury watched him.

"In addition to Makayla's positive identification of Eddie Stephens as the shooter, you will also hear from the police officers who investigated this homicide, Assistant Chief of Police Sam Harper and retired Sergeant Rick York. These highly experienced law enforcement officers served a search warrant on the Defendant's home within days of the shooting and found a handgun that was completely consistent with the bullets used to kill Mr. Jefferson. This is an important fact that further links Eddie Stephens forensically to this murder."

Out of the corner of his eye, Mac could see Marcel furiously scribbling on his pad.

Mac summarized. "As I said, three people know who the murderer is. One of them, Mr. Jefferson, is dead and cannot tell us. The second one is Makayla O'Reilly, who is prepared to tell you firsthand what happened on July 5, 2002. The third person is sitting right here." Mac pointed with his left index finger at Eddie, extending his arm as far as he could in his direction.

Eddie looked directly at Mac and did not avert his gaze.

"Ladies and gentlemen, when you've heard all of the testimony, and seen all of the evidence, at the end of this case, we will be asking you to return a verdict of guilty on all counts. Thank you."

CHAPTER 33

September 19, 2022
2:30 p.m.

Mac took three steps toward his table and sat down. He leaned back in his chair and folded his hands in his lap. He pushed his legal pad and pen to the side of the table.

I'm not going to take any notes. Let the jury think none of what Marcel says is important. Not even worth jotting down. It probably won't matter since he's going to kick my ass in the next 60 minutes.

"Mr. St. Croix, you may give your opening statement," Judge Ryan calmly said.

Marcel rose slowly and involuntarily placed his hand in the small of his back. He grimaced slightly. With effort, he stepped into the center of the courtroom, turned to face the jurors, and said, "Eddie Stephens is not guilty. Completely not guilty. They have the wrong man."

Mac shut his eyes for a second.

Jesus, Marcel, that's a great opening line.

The jurors watched Marcel as he strolled back to Eddie and placed his hand on Eddie's shoulder. Marcel lowered his voice and said, "Eddie was never in that apartment in his life. And he definitely never shot anyone. He is 100 percent innocent."

Judge Ryan looked up from her laptop.

Marcel continued. "Ladies and gentlemen, as you've heard, my name is Marcel St. Croix, and I am proud to represent Eddie Stephens. At this time, it is our opportunity to present an opening statement. As Mr. MacIntyre said on behalf of the State, opening statements are *not* evidence. On that, I wholeheartedly agree with the prosecutor. So, he and I are in complete agreement that everything *he* just told you is not evidence. Everything he just said is his *theory* of what happened in a small apartment on Rotterdam Street in… *2002.*"

Marcel said the year "2002" very slowly and deliberately in five drawn-out syllables: "two-thousand-and-two," as if to emphasize how long ago it was. The rules of evidence would not permit the jury to know that Eddie had been previously convicted for this murder, and, years later, that his conviction was reversed on appeal. Marcel definitely did not want this jury knowing a previous jury had found him guilty. His purpose in drawing attention to the age of the case was to create mystery. He wanted each of the jurors wondering, "Why is this case so old?" Mystery, confusion, and unanswered questions: those were the tools an effective defense attorney used to construct reasonable doubt.

Jesus Christ, Marcel! Can you say 2002 any slower than that?

"Let me begin, ladies and gentlemen, by listing the many, many things that are *absent* from the State's case," Marcel stated. "First, there is no definitive forensic connection that conclusively connects Eddie to the crime scene. There are no fingerprints of my client taken from the murder scene. There is no DNA. No hair or fiber evidence. In this trial, you will hear about absolutely no type of forensic or scientific match. None."

Marcel held up his hands, palms forward, as he spoke, and then added, "The only so-called forensic connection the State mentioned was something vague and inconclusive about a handgun being *consistent* with the type of mutilated bullet fragments recovered from the crime scene. Consistent. I expect they will call a witness to testify that the handgun seized from Eddie's house was indeed *consistent* with those bullet fragments. But what does *that* prove? There are thousands of handguns—a .22 caliber handgun, to be precise—that are equally consistent. So that testimony is virtually meaningless."

Marcel pivoted and took two steps back toward his table.

"Think of it this way: if the prosecution told you the killer wore cowboy boots and then added that the police found a pair of cowboy boots in my client's house, that doesn't mean anything! It doesn't mean they are the *same* pair of boots! Just 'consistent.' That's not proof—that's speculation."

I have to interrupt Marcel. He just said the word 'consistent' five times in the last 20 seconds. This shit about the gun is killing me. But he shouldn't talk about it in his opening statement. I'll object to break his flow.

Mac stood and said with confidence, "Your Honor, objection. This is an argument better suited for closing, Judge. Not an opening statement. Counsel is being argumentative."

"Sustained," said Judge Ryan. "Mr. St. Croix, please confine your opening statement to the expected evidence in *this* case and please save the rest for your closing argument. The objection is sustained, and the jury will disregard Counsel's remarks."

Marcel faced the jury as the judge spoke. He did not turn. He was watching the faces of the jury.

"I apologize, Your Honor," Marcel said, still facing the jury.

"You may continue," Judge Ryan said.

"Thank you."

Marcel reached down and poured a glass of water from a shiny aluminum pitcher on his table. He took a small sip and said, "Now, let's talk about this supposed eyewitness, Makayla O'Reilly."

Mac shifted his feet so they were directly underneath his body in case he needed to stand up quickly and object again.

"As I understand, Makayla O'Reilly has undergone quite a transformation in the last 20 years, ladies and gentlemen. That's much to her credit, and we applaud her successful recovery from drug addiction. We expect the Makayla O'Reilly who takes the witness stand this week will be totally unrecognizable from the Makayla Schweitzer who allegedly saw a shooting back in 2002."

Mac pulled out a sheet of paper from his case file. It was a printout with computerized lettering.

Here come her prior convictions.

Marcel paused, and then added, "I expect the Makayla you will meet this week will be a poised, well-dressed, and well-rehearsed witness."

Marcel pointed at the courtroom's entrance, and said, "The Makayla from 20 years ago was a totally different person. Back then, she was suffering from a crippling crack cocaine addiction. Crack is a highly addictive substance. I'm sure the police officers who testify will agree with me on that. A crack addict will do just about anything to score another dose. You will further hear that Makayla has a conviction for a felony drug offense, Possession of CDS With Intent to Distribute."

Several jurors looked around the courtroom and up at Judge Ryan.

"You may be wondering what the term CDS means. In plain language, CDS means a controlled dangerous substance. That's what we call illegal drugs in court. In Makayla's instance, she was convicted of possessing crack cocaine in an amount large enough to show she had an intent to distribute it to others."

He said that just right! Damn. Marcel is good! He obviously knows he can't mention her prior misdemeanors and only the single felony she has on her record.

"You can rest assured that when I have the opportunity to cross-examine Ms. O'Reilly, I will ask her if she was under the influence of crack cocaine when this event occurred and if her ability to remember or perceive the event was impacted in any way, or even rendered useless, by any drug use on the night of this tragic incident.

"I will also have many questions for the two primary police officers who conducted the investigation in this case, Officer Harper and Sergeant York. I believe that they jumped to a conclusion in arresting my client, Eddie Stephens, and that the real shooter disappeared into the night on July 5, 2002.

"One more thing," Marcel said, as he walked back and picked up the mounted photograph leaning against the side of his table. He lifted the exhibit and removed the sheets of white construction paper that concealed the image. He brought it out into the center of the courtroom and turned to present it to the jury.

"See this enlarged photo? See the date here in the corner? This is a digital date imprinted on every photograph taken by this type of camera. The date is automatically recorded. Now, in today's world, some of you younger jurors, accustomed to how easily cell phones take photos, well, you may not realize how photos were created and printed back 20 or more years ago."

Mac was staring at the photo.

Marcel said, "In 2002, photographs were taken with a camera and a roll of film. Kodak used to be the name of a big film company. I'm not sure they even exist anymore. I certainly haven't heard anyone mention the word *Kodak* in years. However, in those days, you'd put a roll of film in a camera. Then, when you were done with the roll of exposures, you'd take it to a place like Fotomat. They used to have little kiosks in the mall parking lots. They're all gone now. Digital photography has rendered all of those kiosks extinct. As extinct as the dinosaurs."

What the hell is that picture? Marcel turned it around to show the jury, and I only got a glimpse of it. If I stand up and move to get a better look, I'll just draw attention to it. All I could see before he flipped it around was a bunch of people sitting in a living room with a Christmas tree in the background and dozens of wrapped gifts encircling the tree.

Marcel used his right index finger to point at the photo exhibit.

"See the date on the enlarged photo here? It says '12/25/2001.'"

The jurors in the front row leaned forward to confirm the numbers in the lower left-hand corner of the image.

"This is a photograph of the Stephens family on Christmas morning of 2001, approximately six months before the shooting in this case. Six months earlier! This photo was taken by Eddie's mother Tamika Stephens, and she is prepared to testify on behalf of the defense. She will tell you that this generic holiday photograph shows her family, her children, and her relatives simply celebrating Christmas in the privacy and safety of her own home."

So what?

Marcel dropped his voice a notch or two lower in volume, and said, "This is Eddie right here sitting on the sofa. See him?"

Now, all of the jurors were leaning forward.

"See Eddie here? See that he does *not* have dreadlocks?"
Oh shit. Eddie's hair is short.

Marcel whispered softly, "Eddie Stephens could not have

been the man with long dreadlocks that Makayla Schweitzer saw on July 5, 2002. That was less than six months after this photo was taken. He could not possibly have grown his hair that long in such a short period of time. That is impossible."

CHAPTER 34

September 19, 2022
5:33 p.m.

"'Impossible.' That's what Marcel said in his opening. His point about the dreadlocks is really concerning, Andre," Mac said.

Mac stood by his office window looking down on the Courthouse Square with his cell phone tightly pressed against his ear. The autumnal sun was shining brilliantly against the new District Court building across the street, and reflecting off the huge glass panels, creating a series of orange globes in mirror images. The SAO was quiet at this time of day, as ASAs were leaving early to fight the traffic home or hustling to get to outside events like softball games or barbecues with neighbors back in the suburbs.

"Wait," Andre said. "So the defense attorney, Frenchie, showed the jury a photo of the Defendant with short hair taken six months *before* the shooting? I gotta agree with him:

that's not possible. Takes a long time—two years at least—to grow natural dreads down your back like the shooter had back then. Also, I'm not believing that Eddie had the money for a weave to put fake ones in his hair. No way."

"I guess there are several possibilities," Mac replied. "One, it could be a fake photo. I mean, maybe the guy in the photo is a relative or someone who looks a lot like Eddie. A brother or a cousin maybe? Or two, is it possible that the date on the photograph is wrong? Or three: maybe Eddie came up with a way to pay for hair extensions? I remember reading an article once about how quickly human hair grows. It's approximately one inch per month, and those dreadlocks are like two feet long. Those are the only three possibilities I can think of."

Andre replied, "Yeah, I can think of a fourth possibility: he's innocent?"

"Well, the photo is not in evidence yet. It's a defense exhibit. It's not officially evidence until they lay a proper foundation and authenticate it. When they try to get it in, I'll have a chance to ask questions on cross about all of that. Eddie's mother is on the defense list of witnesses. I bet Marcel's calling her just to get that photo in."

"I like your fighting spirit, Mac, but sometimes you just need to know when to hold 'em and when to fold 'em. Can't you just drop this damn case?"

"The Fish and that annoying Jo Newgrange basically *ordered* me to try this case. I can't *nol pros* it now, or I'll probably get fired. I'm quoting The Fish exactly—he said, 'Just try the fucking case!'"

"I get that, Mac. But every day this case falls apart a little bit more. Remember what I said about a table with wobbly legs? Well, this shit is like some cheap-ass crap from IKEA. Feels like it's missing *three* legs now!"

Mac paused.

"Mac? You still there?"

"Yes, I'm here." After a few seconds of silence, Mac said, "Maybe I should resign? That might be the only way out of this trap."

"Get serious! You can't do that," Andre replied. "You always say no single case is worth losing your job over. Let's just put Makayla up on the witness stand and see if the jury believes her. And, by the way, what time should I get her here tomorrow? You said she's first up on the witness stand?"

Mac asked, "Can you go out there to Virginia really early and swing her back here to the courthouse by 8:30? Judge Ryan always takes the bench exactly at 9:30, so we can stash Makayla in the SAO conference room and let her chill out for a while. Get her some coffee and I'll text you when it's time to bring her up to the courtroom."

"Sure, Mac. No problem. You can add Uber driver and barista to the list of my credentials."

"Thanks. I'll give you a five-star review. But I can feel it coming, Andre. I think she's going to get mauled by Marcel."

CHAPTER 35

September 20, 2022
9:30 a.m.

"The State calls Makayla O'Reilly, Your Honor," Mac announced.

The jurors looked all around the courtroom, finally converging into a communal gaze at the courtroom's doors leading out to the hallway.

"Judge, may I step outside and get the witness? I believe she's just outside, Your Honor."

"Yes, of course."

Mac strolled down the aisle and pushed open the double doors.

"Makayla? We can go inside now. Just walk up to the witness stand and the clerk will swear you in."

Makayla was stylishly dressed in an eggshell-colored Alexander McQueen single-button blazer pantsuit. She was wearing a simple, white silk blouse accented with a modestly conservative silver necklace. She looked like a tall, thin confident executive, far from her streetwalker's appearance down on Rotterdam Street two decades earlier.

Makayla took one final deep breath and said, "Let's do this."

She marched down the center aisle, stepped into the witness stand, and shook her head, sending her blonde ponytail over her shoulder.

Judge Ryan said, "Good morning, ma'am. Please stand and be sworn in by our courtroom clerk."

The clerk stood and said, "Do you solemnly swear or affirm that the testimony you give shall be the truth, the whole truth, and nothing but the truth?"

"Yes, I do," said Makayla.

Judge Ryan instructed, "Please have a seat."

When Makayla was seated, Marcel said, "May we approach, Your Honor?"

"Yes, Mr. St. Croix. Certainly."

As Marcel walked up to the bench, Judge Ryan flipped the switch to turn on the husher device. Mac shifted over to create a private huddle at the bench.

Marcel said, "Judge, I've already discussed this issue with Mr. MacIntyre, but—as the Court knows—this witness is strictly prohibited from mentioning that this is a retrial. I'm sure all three of us can agree that it would be extremely prejudicial and immediate grounds for a mistrial if this jury learns that there was a prior guilty conviction rendered by a previous jury in this case."

Judge Ryan turned to Mac. "Mr. MacIntyre? Anything you wish to place on the record?"

"No, Judge. I agree and I have previously explained to this witness that she cannot, under any circumstances, mention the previous trial. She understands."

"Very well." Judge Ryan turned off the husher and said, "Mr. MacIntyre, you may inquire."

"Thank you, Your Honor," Mac replied, as Makayla sat down. She fiddled with the small microphone that snaked upward from the witness stand, and then folded her hands, resting her fists on the table.

"Please state your full name for the record, and if you would, please spell your last name, so the record is clear," Mac asked. He looked directly at Makayla, but with his peripheral vision noted how still and attentive the jury was. The room was quiet, except for the faint, intermittent clacking of Judge Ryan's fingernails on the keys to her laptop.

"My name is Makayla Schweitzer O'Reilly. That's O-R-E-I-L-L-Y."

"Thank you. And Ms. O'Reilly, I take it that Schweitzer is your maiden name?"

"Yes, that's correct. I got married in 2016. My husband's last name is O'Reilly."

"And, ma'am, can you tell us briefly a bit about yourself? Where do you reside—not your specific address—but generally where do you live?"

"I live with my husband in Ashton, Virginia. I'm a homemaker. My husband is in the retail automotive business there."

"Thank you," Mac responded. "Now, I'd like to focus your attention on events that happened on the date of July 5, 2002. Let me ask you some questions about what you witnessed on that date."

"Sure," said Makayla.

"Are you familiar with a location in Seneca County, Maryland called Rotterdam Street?"

"Yes. Although I haven't been there in many years. It's been maybe 15 years or more."

"Can you please tell the ladies and gentlemen of the jury what brought you to that neighborhood on that date?"

Makayla cleared her throat and reached behind her to tug at the matching white ribbon holding her ponytail, fidgeting with it. When she had arranged the knot to her satisfaction, she brought her hands back in front of her, clasped them together in the manner of someone at prayer, and said, "Well, it's been a very long time, but I do remember the night of July 5, 2002 very well. In those days... I was... Well, how should I say this? I was struggling. Both financially and with other personal matters. But I was on Rotterdam Street that night. It was just a regular, normal, muggy summer night. A lot of people were milling about. Hanging out. So, after it got dark—this was well after midnight, if I remember correctly—a guy came up to me. He was a young Black guy. He asked me if I knew of a place he could score—sorry, by score, I mean buy some drugs."

Mac was very still. He wanted the jury's full attention

directly on Makayla and not anyone else, not Marcel, not Eddie, not Judge Ryan, just Makayla.

"And did you know of a place where this man could buy some drugs?" Mac prompted her, trying to steer her narrative.

"Yes. Yes, I did."

"What did this man look like? Can you please describe his appearance for the jurors?"

"Yes, I can," responded Makayla. "Well, like I said, he was young. That's the first thing that popped out to me, how youthful he looked. Like a teenager, actually. And this was real late at night, so I remember thinking, 'Why is this kid still out in the streets?' But Rotterdam Street in summer was like a block party atmosphere. People all milling around on a hot night, if you can picture the scene."

"Let's focus on this teenager's appearance, OK? What else do you remember about how he *looked*?"

When Mac said this, several of the jurors glanced across the courtroom at Eddie, knowing that parts of Makayla's description should still logically match a younger version of the person sitting at the defense table.

"So, he was about 16 or 17 years old, I'd say. I remember seeing a little facial hair—just a little patch—on his chin, and I recall thinking that this guy couldn't even grow a proper beard yet. So, I do remember that detail."

Hearing that, Mac followed up, "What other details can you recall about his appearance? You mentioned his race..."

"Yes. He was an African American with a very light complexion, like he was mixed race."

Mac noticed several jurors swiveling their heads back

and forth between Makayla and Eddie as she spoke, a rapid switching like spectators at a tennis match following the ball as it traveled back and forth between two players.

Eddie's light complexion was exactly what Makayla was describing.

Mac, sensing progress, paused several beats for dramatic effect. He stood still, looking directly at Makayla, silent. After a moment, Judge Ryan interjected, "Mr. MacIntyre?"

Mac said, "So, Ms. O'Reilly, was there anything about this young, light-skinned teenager's hair that was memorable?"

"Oh, yes. There was. He had dreadlocks. Long ones. I don't know how else to describe them other than to say they were kind of like how Bob Marley's hair used to look. They reached below his collarbone and were hanging down his back, sticking out in all directions. His hair was actually the first thing I noticed about him when he walked up to me on the street. It was super distinctive."

"Do you recall what type of clothing was he wearing?"

"Um, let me think. Nothing jumps out. Just jeans and a baggy black T-shirt with a logo. Some sports team or a rap artist was on the front, I think. And he also had on some kind of flashy sneakers. I don't know all the brands, y'know, Nike, Adidas, Reebok, whatever. I'm not a sneaker person *per se*. But I do recall his shoes were some bright color, maybe like neon orange or bright red?"

"Thank you," Mac summarized. "Let's go back to when you were on the street, OK? First of all, what type of drug did the man ask you about, if you can recall?"

"Crack."

"Crack cocaine?"

"Yes," confirmed Makayla. "He simply walked up to me and said something about the weather. Just small talk. Like, we were all outside, and you could feel a summer thunderstorm coming on. You know how hot and humid it gets around here. He said, 'Hey, girl, rain's coming. Know anywhere I can get some rocks?' Which, I knew right away, meant he wanted to buy some crack. That's the code out there, or, I should say, how it used to be."

Mac continued leading her. "What was your response?"

"I said, yeah, I knew a guy who sold. This guy J'Mal. I had known J'Mal all summer as a guy with resources. So, I told the light-skinned guy I could take him across the street and up to a place where he might be able to get what he wanted."

"Was there any benefit to you for doing that? I mean, what incentive did you have to get involved in this transaction, Ms. O'Reilly?"

"Right. So, I said to the guy that I'd bring him to my source if he would tip me a rock for my own personal use. I admit that. I was in bad shape that summer."

Makayla looked down at the witness stand, bowing her head. "It's such a long time ago."

Mac knew it was better for him to bring out the flaws in Makayla's testimony before Marcel could, a courtroom technique known as "taking the wind out of their sails." But Mac did not want the jury to fixate on her weaknesses, so he decided not to emphasize them. He quickly steered her testimony back to the central issue of identification.

229

"Did you take the young man with the dreadlocks somewhere?"

"Yes. Up to J'Mal's apartment, which was literally across the street. I don't know the exact address, but it's right on Rotterdam across from the QuikStop convenience store. You walk up this flight of stairs to a landing, and then it splits into four apartments. J'Mal's door was to the far left once you got up that staircase."

Mac walked back to his table and reached down for a poster-sized chart mounted on cardboard. He picked up the exhibit and walked back across the courtroom to where an easel stood, like a tripod, ready to accept it. He arranged the chart vertically on the easel for everyone in the courtroom to see.

"So, Ms. O'Reilly, I've placed an exhibit here, as you can see. Do you recognize this diagram?"

"Yes. That appears to be a floorplan of J'Mal's apartment."

Mac turned to Judge Ryan and said, "Let the record reflect that I've marked this exhibit as State's Number One. I've shown it to Counsel pretrial, and he also received a copy of it in discovery."

"So noted," said the judge.

Mac, having been given clearance, turned to the chart and said, "Ms. O'Reilly, let me draw your attention to State's Number One. Does this exhibit fairly and accurately depict the floorplan and relative sizes of the rooms in the apartment in which this incident took place?"

Makayla peered at the chart and nodded her head. When she had reviewed it for a moment, she said, "Yes. That's it exactly. The entrance is at the top, and then it's just two very small rooms. The main room and a back room, I'm guessing a bedroom. That's it."

"Can you tell us what happened when you went into the victim's apartment?"

CHAPTER 36

September 20, 2022
10:29 a.m.

Makayla took a deep breath. She brushed a loose strand of nearly white hair from her eyes. She looked over at Eddie for a moment. All of the jurors were staring at her.

"So, I walked up the stairs with him and knocked on the door. I heard J'Mal speak through the doorway, and I could tell he was looking out through the peephole. He asked, 'Who's there?' and I said it was me, KayKay—that's what they used to call me, y'know, short for Makayla—and I said I had a friend with me. I didn't say specifically that the guy wanted to score something, but it was pretty obvious."

Mac asked, "Had you had any prior dealings with J'Mal? I mean, similar transactions?"

"Yes."

"Approximately how many times had you brought a customer up to J'Mal's apartment before this night?"

"Um, hard to say. A few times."

"So, I take it that J'Mal knew you and felt safe opening up the door?"

"Objection," said Marcel from his seated position. "Your Honor, unless this witness has the powers of telepathy, she wouldn't know what another person was thinking."

Judge Ryan said, "So, what is your objection, sir?"

"Calls for speculation," Marcel clarified, wrapping the proper legal language around his objection.

"Sustained. Ask another question, Mr. MacIntyre."

Mac reformulated the previous question to simply ask, "Did J'Mal open the door?"

"Yes," said Makayla.

"What happened next?"

"Well, we walked in. J'Mal stepped back as soon as we entered, and the light-skinned guy shut the door behind us and then stood near the door. I stepped into the apartment and took a couple of steps toward the corner of the room."

Mac walked up to the easel and pointed at the square on the exhibit marked "LIVING ROOM." He asked, "About here?" as he tapped on the chart.

"Yes," Makayla replied. "And then, J'Mal was, like, 'What's up?' and the guy said, 'Can I get a quarter ounce?' and then something to the effect of, 'I've got a roll,' because I remember he took out a thick wad of money and held it up. I remember there was a $100 bill wrapped around the outside. J'Mal said, 'OK, stay here.' And then he turned and went into the other room."

Mac pointed at a square on the chart labeled BEDROOM.

"Please continue," he said.

"OK, so then J'Mal came back out from the other room with a baggie in his hand. I should mention that there was a coffee table smack in the middle of the main room. It was made of wood and glass. Then, when J'Mal stepped forward to the edge of the coffee table, the light-skinned guy just pulled out a gun from under his shirt—I had no idea he had one!"

"Exactly where were you standing when you saw the gun?"

Makayla turned to look at the chart and said, "Over toward that corner, but still in the room. I mean, this is a pretty small apartment. I was only like six feet at most from him."

"Then what happened?" Mac asked.

"He just shot him. It was shocking. I couldn't believe what was happening. I saw him hold this shiny little gun up—I guess he pulled it out from his waistband because he wasn't wearing a jacket or anything. Just a floppy T-shirt. The first shot went right over J'Mal's head or maybe grazed the top of his head, I think."

She made a swiping motion with her hand to simulate a bullet flying across the top of her hair.

"The sound of the shot was ear-piercing! I'm not a gun person *per se*, and I've only shot a gun a few times in my whole life, and both times, we were outdoors in a country setting, not indoors. The sound was so loud! I remember my ears buzzing, and I turned to face the corner. I was so scared. I think I was in shock, actually."

Mac said, "What happened after the first shot?"

"There was immediately a second shot. It's was like 'Boom!' 'Boom!' Two shots fired in rapid succession. Like I said, I was curled up in the corner of the room facing away so I didn't actually see the second shot hit J'Mal, but I *heard* him crash down and break the coffee table. When I heard the glass shattering, I turned to look, because I didn't know what was happening."

"When you turned back, what did you see?"

Makayla froze. She reached behind her and pulled her ponytail around to the front of her shoulder. Her eyes were glistening with fluid, and the corner of her mouth twitched almost imperceptibly.

After a few seconds, she answered. "J'Mal lying on top of the crashed table. There was a lot of blood pouring out of his head. Both in front and especially in the back. It was like spurting out of the back of his head. I've never seen anything like that in my whole life." She reached for the box of tissue, grabbed two, and crumpled them into a ball. She blew her nose.

Mac asked, "Where was the light-skinned man at that point in time?"

"He quickly stepped across to where J'Mal was lying and snatched up the small plastic baggie filled with crack. He grabbed it real quick and then dashed out of the apartment. I was just praying he didn't shoot me too since I was a witness or something."

"Ma'am, do you see the man you have just described as the shooter anywhere in this courtroom right now?"

There was a significant pause. Makayla looked directly into Mac's eyes.

"Yes. I see him."

Mac turned toward the defense table.

She said, "That's him, sitting there. Of course, he's older. But that's definitely the same man. That's him." Makayla pointed her left index finger at Eddie Stephens.

Mac turned to look at Eddie, who sat silently with wide-open eyes.

Mac asked, "Ms. O'Reilly, let me ask you this: how *certain* are you that the man sitting here today is the same man you saw on July 5, 2002 shoot J'Mal Jefferson and kill him?"

"I'm 100 percent certain. I will never forget his face. It sticks out in my mind like a photograph. That's him. Definitely."

Mac turned toward Judge Ryan and asked, "May the record reflect that the witness has identified the Defendant, Edward DeLawrence Stephens, who is sitting at the defense table?"

"So noted," responded the judge.

CHAPTER 37

September 20, 2022
1:20 p.m.

"How did she do?" Andre asked as he stepped into Mac's office, holding two cups of coffee.

Mac said, "I have to get upstairs. The lunch break is almost over, and Judge Ryan will be taking the bench in 10 minutes. She was not too bad, actually. Much better than I thought she'd be. First of all, she looked perfect. Very professional. Dressed beautifully. She had an elegant demeanor and sounded sharp. I think the jury was impressed."

"But what about her ID of Stephens? Was she solid, or did she cave in?"

"Well, on direct, she was good. She said she was 100 percent certain Stephens was the guy who did the shooting. What more can I ask for?"

"Awesome, man, that's great!" Andre replied.

Mac gave one last look around his office, picked up a

cardboard box that said EVIDENCE STEPHENS written in Magic Marker in large letters on the side, and said, "I have to move fast, Andre. Did you see York or Chief Harper anywhere? They are scheduled to testify after Makayla's done. Should get through both of them today."

"Yeah, I was going to tell you, I saw Harper downstairs in the cafeteria. He was at a table with, like, four other cops. All in uniform. He was at the head of the table talking up a storm. I mean, what? He was named the new Chief like three weeks ago, and he's already got all these other mofos kissing his ass already. It's disgusting."

"OK. What about York? See him around anywhere?"

"I have no idea what that guy looks like, so I don't know. There was one guy at the table who wasn't in a uniform, but that can't be him."

"Why do you say that?"

"Because that guy looked like a junkie or a homeless man. He was completely bald up top, but he also had a long ponytail down the back. I hate that look. Only white people got that redneck look. I say just shave it all off, dude. And he was wearing cargo shorts. I mean, only an idiot would come to court to testify dressed like that."

"Oh, Jesus," said Mac.

Andre asked, "What's next? Who's testifying now? Has Frenchie squared off with our girl yet?"

"I'm finished with my direct of Makayla. Now, it's Marcel's turn to cross-examine her."

Mac's cell phone rang. He lifted it out of his suit pocket and said, "Hello? Mac MacIntyre." There was no answer. He looked at the screen, and it said UNKNOWN. He clicked the phone off and said, "Andre, it's another one of those hang-up calls. They've got my cell phone number now."

Andre said, "Oh damn. Did you hear that weird breathing noise again?"

"Shit. I hung up fast. I wasn't thinking. I should have put it on speaker so you could hear."

"Now, it's your cell phone." Andre paused, thinking. "Whoever it is has your private number now. Did you give it out to the witnesses so they could reach you in an emergency?"

"Yes, I always do that. And Marcel knows it, too. He may have given it out, too. I have no idea."

Andre said, "It could be anyone. That's fucked up. Be careful, Mac. I'm worried about those calls, man."

"Mr. St. Croix? Any cross-examination, sir?" Judge Ryan asked.

The jurors were settled into their assigned seats. As a group, they had been escorted by three sheriff's deputies down to the cafeteria in the basement level of the Judicial Center. The judge had instructed them not to discuss the case until all of the evidence had been received. So, awkwardly carrying plastic trays, they filed through the cafeteria line chaperoned by the three burly deputies, who directed them to all eat at a designated table in the far corner of the large, expansive dining hall.

Makayla had been stashed in the SAO conference

room—the exact spot where she had been interviewed by Mac and Andre months earlier—where she nibbled on an egg salad sandwich and an iced tea which Andre had brought up from the cafeteria for her. Now, she was back on the witness stand, ready to answer more questions.

Marcel stood up, patted Eddie's large shoulder, and gently squeezed his prominent trapezius muscle.

"Thank you, Judge Ryan," Marcel said, as he stepped into the center of the courtroom without any notes in his hand. He had the expression of a famished man about to feast.

Mac leaned forward, placing his elbows on the prosecution table. He shifted a new, blank legal pad in front of him and plucked his customary red felt-tip pen from the interior breast pocket of his jacket and wrote CROSS on the top of the first page.

Marcel began, "Ms. O'Reilly, let me begin by asking you about this startling incident that occurred while you were in Mr. Jefferson's apartment..." It was a clever technique for Marcel to begin his cross-examination out of sequence, in the middle of Makayla's story, not at the beginning. If she lied or embellished the facts, Marcel would ask questions out of chronological order. By asking questions that jumped back and forth in time between several topics, he could more effectively root out the truth.

Marcel asked, "You testified on direct examination that the firing of a handgun in your presence was—I think the word you used was 'shocking'—is that correct?"

Makayla answered, "Yes. It was very shocking. I've never seen someone murdered before my eyes."

"And you said you 'turned away' and that you 'faced the wall,' didn't you?"

"Yes."

"As I recall your testimony before lunch today, Ms. O'Reilly, you said your 'ears were ringing,' correct?"

Makayla confirmed, "Yes." Marcel was leading her exactly where he needed her to go. That was the biggest difference between direct examination and cross-examination. On direct examination, the attorneys had to ask open-ended questions and let the witness describe what happened. But on cross-examination, the attorney was, in a way, the person who was actually testifying. A good cross-examiner made statements he wanted the jury to hear in the form of a question, and then asked the witness to confirm or agree with the attorney's assertions.

Marcel hammered home his point, "So, being in shock, and with your ears ringing, and facing *away* from the shooting, it would be fair to say, ma'am, that you did not actually *see* the shooting occur, isn't that correct?"

Makayla paused and looked up at the ceiling for a moment before answering, "Well, I did see the first shot, which, as I said, missed J'Mal and flew right over the top of his head. I think I said it grazed him. But you are right: I didn't see the second shot as it was fired. I sure *heard* it, though."

"You heard it? And you heard the first shot too? Is that right?"

"That's true."

Marcel clarified, "So, the *first* shot was the sound that

began making your ears ring, and the second shot amplified the ringing sensation even more, correct?"

"Yes."

"And while you were in shock, with your ears ringing, and with your face turned away from the shooting, you weren't looking at the man with the gun *at all* when the second shot was fired, isn't that correct?"

"Um... I didn't see the second shot, as I said. But, as I testified, I had already spent time talking with him down in the street."

"We will get to that in a minute, ma'am. But, for the sake of answering my question, can we agree that, while you were briefly inside the apartment, your focus was not on the gunman's face?"

Makayla didn't answer and crinkled her brow.

Mac wrote on his legal pad: **DIDN'T SEE FACE CLEARLY WHILE IN APT.**

"Well, what is your answer, Ms. O'Reilly?" Marcel repeated.

"I agree that I was in shock, and I agree that I turned away from him while we were inside the apartment," she answered.

"Well, let's back up a bit in your story. Before you climbed the steps to the landing where the apartment was, you were outside in the street, and you talked for a moment to a young man—I'll just use the term 'the light-skinned man,' since that's what you called him. When you were outside in the street talking to the light-skinned man, was it raining?"

Makayla's skin was pink and turning a darker shade of

red with every question. Matching red blotches appeared on her face, one on each cheek.

"No, I'm sure it wasn't raining yet. I didn't notice that it was raining until later, after the shooting, when I was leaving the apartment."

Marcel followed up, "Yes. But, Ms. O'Reilly, it was actually more like a heavy thunderstorm with lightning strikes, correct?"

"Yes. I agree with that. But, as I said, that was later. Not when I first met the light-skinned man by the curb."

"I see," Marcel said, wrapping up his point. "So, if it wasn't raining when you *entered* the apartment, but then it was raining heavily as you were leaving, it only makes logical sense that the thunderstorm *began while you were inside* Mr. Jefferson's apartment? Correct?"

"I guess I agree with that," Makayla said.

Mac jotted down a note: **COULDN'T SEE, COULDN'T HEAR, COULDN'T THINK STRAIGHT. DISORIENTED. IN SHOCK. UNRELIABLE WITNESS?**

CHAPTER 38

September 20, 2022
2:27 p.m.

"Ms. O'Reilly, I'd like to move to a different point in time for my next series of questions, OK? Let me ask you about what happened directly after the shooting."

"That's fine," said Makayla.

Continuing his cross-examination, Marcel slowly stepped to the center of the courtroom and asked, "So, did you call 911? Even though you did not have a cell phone of your own?"

"You're right. I didn't have a phone. If I remember correctly, I didn't get a cell phone until maybe a few years after this all happened. But, yes, right after your client shot J'Mal in the face, I notified the authorities."

Marcel glanced at the jury. The elderly Chinese American juror in the front row cupped his ear. Marcel pounced. "But if you didn't have a cell phone, how did you call 911?"

"Well, after the shooting," Makayla rambled. "I ran out

of the apartment to the little landing area. Then I ran down the stairs to the street. At first, I didn't even notice it was raining—that's how much in shock I was. But as I got down to the sidewalk, I felt rain splashing on me, and I remember looking down at my shirt and it was getting soaked."

"Ma'am, can you please answer my question? Where did you place the 911 call from?"

All of the jurors were listening intently. Mac was looking down at his legal pad. Eddie was animated, shifting back and forth in his chair.

Makayla said, "I went into the store on the corner. It's a little all-night convenience store. I'd been in there a million times before to use the ladies' room and sometimes to buy food. There was this Spanish woman I knew. Her name was Ana. I asked her if I could borrow her cell phone. And then I called... I didn't literally call 911. But I did basically the same thing. I immediately contacted Officer Harper who I knew from previous... previous... I knew him from working with him before."

Marcel spun quickly towards the witness stand and raised his voice. "*Working* with him? Whatever do you mean? Were you a Seneca County police officer on July 5, 2002?"

"No. But I worked with Harp—that was what I called him, Harp—I helped him with stuff happening in the street."

"In what capacity did you *work* with him?"

"I guess you could say I helped with investigations around the Rotterdam Street area. I gave him tips and stuff like that. Told him about things that were going on."

"I see," Marcel simply responded as he stood motionless

looking at Makayla. He did not ask any follow-up questions. He intentionally waited.

Makayla waited, too. But after a long, awkward silence in the courtroom, she continued, "I had been working with Harp and his partner for a couple of months, maybe half a year. I can't remember exactly. It was confidential, and no one knew on the outside."

"And, Ms. O'Reilly, for giving information to these two police officers, what was in it for you? What compensation did *you* receive for your help as a confidential informant?"

"I was paid. If I told them about something, I'd get a fee. So, over time, I earned several fees. They'd add the fees up, and then they'd pay me what they owed me in a batch for several jobs I'd done. Also, when you say compensation, I guess I should say that Harp agreed not to file any charges against me for what happened to J'Mal."

Marcel paused. He turned to scan the jury box, making eye contact with all twelve jurors, and said, "What was the monetary compensation you received for your services? How much were you paid?"

"Well, it was different amounts for different things. But the payments were a couple hundred dollars each. Sometimes more, sometimes less."

Marcel slowly walked back to the defense table, taking his time to plod across the courtroom. He wanted these revelations to sink in the jurors' minds and marinate. When he reached the table, he turned to Judge Ryan and said, "Court's indulgence, please." He leaned over to whisper something in Eddie's ear and then straightened his posture to stand fully erect.

"Did the Seneca County police respond to your call?"

"Yes. In the QuikStop. I remember being really afraid and not thinking clearly. I remember sitting down on the floor actually. I was drenched too. But soon the two officers came in the store and got me. Wait. No, I went outside and met them on the curb, not inside the store."

"You said 'two officers.' Do you recall who the second officer was? The one who accompanied Officer Harper?"

"His name was Ricky. He was the sergeant. Like, Harp's partner or maybe his supervisor even. But Ricky was there too. I'm sure about that."

"What happened after the two officers arrived?"

"Well, I got inside their car. It wasn't a marked police car. Not a cruiser. Just a regular, beat-up old car. I think they got it in a vehicle forfeiture or something. But it was set up like a cop car and had all the equipment. We sat in there. I sat in the back, and Ricky and Harp were up front."

"What happened next? Did you talk with them?"

"Yes. First of all, they asked me if I was hurt or something like that. Then Harp said—"

"Objection!" Mac asserted loudly. "Calls for hearsay, Judge. She can't testify to what Officer Harper said."

"Sustained," said Judge Ryan. "Ask your next question, Mr. St. Croix."

Marcel explained, "Ms. O'Reilly, you are not allowed to tell us what other people said. Just what you said. Let me ask you this: how long were you discussing the events with the officers?"

"Just a few minutes, I mean, literally within like two

minutes, the street filled up with cop cars and an ambulance, and it was very chaotic. So, I just stayed in their car. They gave me a blanket since I was soaked, and I just curled up in the backseat."

Marcel asked, "What do you remember next?"

"I must've crashed—I mean, I fell asleep. The next thing I remember is the car moving, and I woke up. It was sunrise. The street was empty by then. I guess they'd taken J'Mal out of the apartment on a stretcher or whatever they do. I don't know. I think my body and my mind just shut down."

"You said you were in the car, and the car was moving; where did you go?"

"Harp was driving at that point, and Ricky was up front with him. I remember I had to pee real bad. So, they stopped at this Exxon station, and I used the bathroom. When I came back out to the car, Harp had a big cup of hot coffee and a corn muffin for me. I was starving, so I ate it, and then they said they had to go back to Headquarters."

"Did they leave you there at the gas station?"

"Yes. But they asked me to meet them for dinner to discuss the next steps and said they'd treat me to a nice meal."

"And where did that rendezvous take place?"

"Some French restaurant. I remember it pretty well."

"Did you subsequently meet them for dinner at this French restaurant?"

"Yes. I think it was like a couple of nights after the shooting. They took me to this fancy place. I'd never been to an expensive restaurant like that before. I remember it had tablecloths on the table. It also had a menu I couldn't read since it was in French. For some reason, I recall they had pieces of bread in a basket but no butter. You had to dip them into oil on a saucer. I'd never seen that before either."

"What was the purpose of you meeting them there?"

"They wanted to talk about J'Mal and the light-skinned guy who shot him. Like, interview me. And to be totally honest, I was hungry. So, I agreed to go there with them, and I figured at least I'd get a good hot meal for free."

"So, it was the three of you at the restaurant, right? You and Harp and Ricky?"

Makayla hesitated and placed her hands in her lap. She reached for the microphone in front of her and twisted it. After a moment, she said, "There was a fourth person."

Marcel spun around with newfound dexterity and said, "A *fourth* person? Who was that?"

Makayla said, "That's when I met the prosecutor assigned to the case. He had dinner with us, too. He's a judge now. His name was Daniel Bennington."

CHAPTER 39

September 20, 2022
5:55 p.m.

Mac sat on a park bench in a shady spot in the far corner of the Courthouse Square. He had a thin manila envelope in his hand. Andre stood and paced back and forth between the Old Colonial Courthouse and the Circuit Court, keeping an eye on the front doors to the courthouse. The sun had begun its inevitable descent to the west, dripping down orange light over the whole Judicial Center complex. Any moment now, Marcel would exit the building, and Andre would flag him down.

Andre waved at Mac and gestured toward the courthouse. Marcel, carrying his trademark wooden briefcase, left the building, stopped, and looked around the park. He reached into his jacket, took out a small case, and placed his designer sunglasses on the bridge of his nose to shield the brightness of the summer sunset. Marcel looked up and saw Andre waving and nodded his head. Mac shifted his weight on the bench and glanced around the Courthouse Square to scan all the people in his range of vision: other lawyers were heading back to their offices to decompress after difficult days in court; witnesses, cops in uniform, and clusters of miscellaneous people were milling around in front of the courthouse doors, congregating and discussing what had happened in their cases earlier in the day. There was a steady stream of courthouse employees pouring out of the four buildings in the Square—dozens of hanging ID tags earmarked them—and now they were heading home, up the Interstate, now congested and tangled with rush-hour traffic.

Marcel walked to Andre, and they shook hands.

"You said Mac wanted to meet?" Marcel asked.

"Yes, Mr. St. Croix..." Andre started to say, but Marcel cut him off and interjected, "Please, just call me Marcel. No need for formalities."

"OK, cool," Andre replied. "Mac's over there." He pointed across the lawn.

"I like his office. Gets plenty of natural light, I see," Marcel joked.

They walked briskly across the small park, and Mac stood up when Marcel was within a few feet. They, too, shook hands.

Marcel said, "You wanted to meet?"

"Yes," Mac replied. "Please let's sit. I've got something I need to talk to you about."

Andre did not sit. He gave the park bench to Mac and Marcel and stood, protectively watching in all directions. No one was within 30 yards.

Mac said, "Marcel, so we talked to Makayla O'Reilly after court late this afternoon. Your cross raised some questions—well, at least, I should say, it raised some concerns in my mind, and I wanted to discuss them with you before we called our next witness."

Marcel asked, "And who exactly is next in your batting order? You've got Chief Harper next, right? And then that other cop York and... Have you decided to call Judge Bennington as a witness or not?"

"Marcel, let me explain. So, we just talked to Makayla. That restaurant meeting? It was the first we'd ever heard of it, I swear. She never mentioned anything about a meeting in a French restaurant before. I mean, you know how it is, Marcel. Sometimes witnesses are unpredictable. But this is more serious than the usual screw-up by a nervous witness. We may have stumbled on some *Brady* material."

"I'm all ears," Marcel said succinctly.

Mac continued, "So, after your cross today, we sat down with Makayla in my office. Andre was supposed to drive her home, but we paid for an Uber and sent her on her way instead."

"Quiet, Mac," Andre said sharply and tipped his head toward the front door of the courthouse where Kristen, the judge's clerk, emerged from the building. Mac looked across the lawn and saw her; she was staring at them, squinting, from about a block away. After a moment, she took two steps toward them and then stopped. Abruptly, she turned and walked back inside the courthouse.

Mac lowered his voice and said, "So, Marcel. We found a

note in the original evidence box. It is marked 'work product,' but we don't know who wrote it. I have a good guess who, but I don't know for certain."

"I'm guessing Judge Bennington," said Marcel. "He was the original ASA on the case, so it's likely his note. The term 'work product' is not a term or expression that police officers use, generally."

"I'm keeping my mind open," Mac replied. "But obviously, if it's exculpatory, I'm obligated to share it with you. We couldn't decipher it, but based on what Makayla just disclosed, well, I think you should see this."

Mac handed Marcel the manila envelope. Marcel unclasped it, unwilling to let his curiosity rage for even a moment longer, and slid out a photocopy of the note.

"What in God's green Earth is this?" he said.

Mac pointed at the sheet of paper and said, "See? The first line has water damage, but those words don't look like an English phrase. Is that French?"

Marcel looked intently at the letters: **BU NA SERA**. After a moment deep in thought, he said, "That's not French. I speak French, remember? That's Italian. *Buona sera*. It means good evening in Italian."

"Oh, Jesus!" Andre exclaimed. "That's the name of an Italian restaurant a few blocks from Rotterdam Street."

CHAPTER 40

September 21, 2022
10:33 a.m.

Judge Ryan said, "Mr. St. Croix, is the defense ready for cross-examination of this witness?"

"Yes, Judge," Marcel confidently replied.

He took two steps around the edge of the table, leaving his notes behind him. Mac sat calmly at the prosecution table and picked up his felt-tip pen. The jurors were shifting in their seats and rustling around, as if to prepare for a whirlwind of questions from Marcel, like a tornado approaching on the horizon. Judge Ryan subtly slid her laptop a few inches to her side so she could have an unobstructed view of Rick York, who was sitting stiffly in the witness stand.

"So, Mr. York, let me ask you some questions based on what Mr. MacIntyre just established with you on direct examination," Marcel began.

"No problem, man," York responded.

"First of all, I mean no disrespect when I refer to you as 'Mister' York. But you are no longer a Seneca County police officer, is that correct?"

"That's true. I retired about 15 or 16 years ago. I moved to Colorado, where I now reside."

Marcel followed up, "And are you employed there, Mr. York?"

"No, sir. I am retired, like I said. I also get some disability benefits from a neck injury I got serving a search warrant before I retired. We were searching this house, and I accidentally jammed my head into a beam."

"Let me ask you about the events surrounding a homicide that occurred here in Seneca County on July 5, 2002. Do you recall that episode?"

"Um, not really. Well, I mean, yes. I do remember it vaguely, but it's been a long, long time, to be honest."

"I want you to be honest, Mr. York," Marcel countered.

"OK, of course," York said with a nervous short laugh. "I mean, it's just a saying, 'to be honest.' I didn't mean anything sarcastic by it, y'know."

"Understood. Let me ask you about that homicide. You were working for the Seneca County Police Department on that date, correct?"

"Yes."

"And in what capacity?" Marcel said.

"I was the Sergeant working Vice at that time. We were working the Charlie 6 sector at that time."

"This would include the Rotterdam Street area, is that right?" Marcel confirmed.

"Yes. Rotterdam back in the day was a real hot spot. We had a lot of prostitution and street dealers and what they called quality-of-life crimes. Like, breaking into vehicles and some street robberies and, generally, stuff like that. But a ton of CDS cases, too."

"And, Mr. York, when you use the expression CDS, let's just clarify for the benefit of the jurors—you are referring to the acronym for controlled dangerous substances, is that correct?"

"Yes, CDS means, basically, drugs. Marijuana, crack, hallucinogenic stuff like LSD, pills. This was back in the time when crack cocaine was real bad and a major problem for us."

"By 'us,' you mean the police?" Marcel said.

"Yes. A big problem."

"So, how did you first become aware of a homicide of a victim named J'Mal Jefferson on July 5, 2002?"

"Um, well, I was sitting in my unmarked vehicle—it was an old car we had acquired in a seizure and converted into a U/C vehicle. I was with another officer on my shift. His name was Sam Harper."

Marcel asked, "Sir, when you use the expression 'U/C,' that is an abbreviation for undercover, correct?"

"Yes. Undercover. Meaning the vehicle was unmarked, but it was fully equipped with police equipment like lights and siren, but they were hidden. It looked just like an old, battered-up, regular car. Not like a police cruiser."

Marcel took that information and built on it. "And you, sir, were not wearing a police uniform, isn't that true?"

"Right. We were in civilian clothes, and both of us had full beards and were trying not to look like cops. That didn't always work, but we tried not to stick out on Rotterdam Street. Me and Harp were trying to blend in as best we could."

Marcel asked, "Where were you, to the best of your recollection, when you first became aware that there had been a shooting?"

"I was, like I said, in the unmarked car with Officer Harper. He got a call on his cell phone. As undercover officers working Vice, we had just been issued Department cell phones, and I don't remember if I even had a pager at that time anymore. But, to answer your question, I was sitting in the front passenger seat, and Officer Harper was behind the wheel. And then he got a call saying there had been a shooting nearby."

"Who called with that information?"

York said, "This girl named Makayla. Some of the people on the street called her KayKay, if I remember right."

"Who was Makayla? How did you know her?"

"She was a confidential informant—or CI—who had been working the street for us. I'm not going to say she was a prostitute or a drug addict or whatever, but I'll just say she helped me and Harp with tips from time to time. And she was extremely reliable—I definitely remember that."

Marcel asked, "What do you mean by reliable?"

York explained, "Well, Makayla almost always had good information. She was valuable. She told us who was selling and who was buying all up and down the street. And she was almost always right."

Marcel continued, "So, when Makayla called Officer Harper, could you hear the conversation?"

"Objection," Mac said. "Calls for hearsay."

Judge Ryan turned to Marcel with a quizzical expression.

Marcel said, "Your Honor, I am not offering it for the truth of the matter asserted, but rather for the witness's state of mind. Her statement would also qualify as an excited utterance exception to the hearsay rule."

"Overruled," said the judge.

York looked back and forth between Judge Ryan and Marcel. Marcel said, "The objection is overruled. You may answer."

York said, "Yes, I could definitely hear her and Officer Harper talking on the phone. I mean, he was next to me in the front seat of the car. I could hear Makayla through the speaker. She was distraught. Crying. She was very upset. That much was very clear."

"What did you hear her say?"

York answered, "She said a guy—a dealer—had just been shot. We were only around the corner basically, so I knew it was real close. She said she was in the QuikStop. So we went there fast."

"Do you recall the weather at that point in time?"

"Oh, right. Yes, I do. It was raining real hard, like a storm passing through. Typical for a July around here. When I think back on this, I can see the windshield wipers slapping back and forth in my mind."

"What, if anything, did you do in response to Makayla's call?"

"We drove over fast and there she was. Soaked. She was very upset. When she calmed down, she told us she had brought this guy up to the dealer's apartment, and then, when she got there, the buyer just shot the seller in the face and stole his bag of crack. That's what she said."

"Did she describe the shooter?"

"Oh, yeah. She said he was a real young guy, an African American guy. And she said he had long dreadlocks in his hair. I clearly remember that. She said his name was 'Eddie,' and we knew immediately who she meant, based on that description."

Marcel interjected. "Are you sure she said 'Eddie,' and not 'Freddie,' or even the nickname, 'E-Z?' People used nicknames on the street, right? Not their actual names. Correct?"

York responded, "E-Z? There was another kid who used that name, I think. But I'm pretty sure she said 'Eddie.'"

"And—based on that description—did your investigation narrow to one specific individual?"

"Yes. We applied for a search warrant for your client's house. Eddie Stephens."

"Let me get back to Makayla, if I may. Did you subsequently meet with Makayla to interview her?"

"Yes. We stayed with her all night, if I remember correctly. It was definitely light outside when we dropped her off at a gas station, so it must've been like around 6:30 or 7:00 the next morning. But Officer Harper asked her to meet with us again—I think it was the next evening—and we said we'd pick her up at the same Exxon station and take her out for a good meal, since she was pretty broke in those days."

Marcel asked, "And what was the name of the restaurant you took Makayla to?"

"Some Italian place, I forget the name. About three

blocks off Rotterdam, in the Little Italy section, although it's almost all Asian these days. Back around 15 or 20 years ago, that whole side street was filled with Italian restaurants and pizza places. Now, it's all Vietnamese and, I think, Korean."

"Does the name 'Buona Sera' sound familiar?"

"I think that's it. Right. It was right on Brewer Street, like I said, about two blocks down from Rotterdam."

"Who was at the dinner at the Buona Sera restaurant?"

York replied, "Well, it was me and Officer Harper and Makayla. And then the ASA joined us. Danny Bennington. He showed up separate."

"ASA stands for Assistant State's Attorney?"

"Right."

"What was your purpose in meeting with Makayla?"

"Well, to introduce her to the prosecutor, number one. But more importantly, to ask her some more questions and get details about the shooting and her interaction with Eddie Stephens."

"What else happened at this meeting?"

"Well," York continued, "we all ordered food. Can't remember what. Something Italian of course. But I remember this girl Makayla eating. She must've been starving. She ate like six pieces of Italian bread before the main meal even came. I can see that in my mind right now: she was sopping up the olive oil with the bread and eating one piece after another."

"Aside from the meal, what else happened?"

"Objection," said Mac. "This clearly calls for hearsay, Judge Ryan."

"Sustained," replied the judge. "Mr. St. Croix, we are

well past any state-of-mind exception. So I will sustain the State's objection."

"Thank you, Your Honor." Marcel turned toward his table and lifted a sheet of paper.

"Mr. York, did you take any contemporaneous notes while at this dinner with Officer Harper, ASA Bennington, and Makayla?"

"I can't remember."

Marcel reached down to the table and picked up a small blue sticker that had the words 'Defendant's exhibit' stamped on it. He peeled off a small, rectangular sticker and stuck it on the back of the sheet of paper.

"May I approach?" Marcel asked Judge Ryan.

"Yes, sir."

Marcel walked up to the witness stand and placed the sheet of paper down on the witness stand in front of York.

"I have marked this single sheet of paper as Defendant's Number One."

He pointed at it and said, "Mr. York, let me draw your attention to Defendant's Number One. Do you recognize the handwriting?"

York picked up the paper and held it directly in front of his face, studying it.

"This is my handwriting."

CHAPTER 41

September 21, 2022
11:31 a.m.

Marcel said, "So, you can confirm that you wrote this note, Mr. York?"

"Well, it's my handwriting, so, yes, I must have written this note. But I don't recognize the content. It's all scrambled up and looks damaged, so I can't read it. But I must have given this note to Harper after the meeting. That's how we did interviews. One of us would conduct the interview, and the other would take notes. Some of what I wrote has been erased. Looks like it's gotten wet 'cause a lot of the ink is blurred and some of the words are missing letters."

Marcel pounced. "But, sir, you will confirm that the portions of the note that remain undamaged are definitely your handwriting? *You* took these notes, correct?"

"I'm going to have to say yes. But I'm looking for my

signature or at least my initials, and I don't see them anywhere on this."

Marcel asked, "First of all, do you see the name of the restaurant, *Buona Sera*, right there at the top of the page?"

York said, "Well, some of the lettering is messed up. But, yeah, I can see a partial name."

Marcel followed up. "And to the right of the name of the restaurant, there appear to be three letters—not full initials with a first name and a last name—but single letters."

Marcel pointed to the letters in the corner of the page and said, "Do you see them here?"

"Yes. There's an H and a R. And then there's a B. And then there's an 'and' symbol thing. Then it gets all faded or waterlogged after that."

Marcel now took control of the cross-examination like a jockey pulling the reins on a racehorse. He now switched his tone and began using all leading questions designed to draw a simple 'yes' or 'no' answer.

"This first initial is the letter 'H,' correct?"

"Yes," said York.

"H would stand for 'Harper,' right?"

"Yes."

"And R would stand for you, sir, isn't that correct? R being the first letter of your first name, Rick. Isn't that true?"

"Um, yes. R would be me."

Marcel continued, "And then we have the letter B. That would be short for Bennington, wouldn't it?"

"Bennington. Yes. He was sitting right there in the booth with us."

"And then you have the ampersand, which is the symbol for the word 'and.' Do you see that?"

"Yes, Mr. St. Croix. So, that means that the last person at the meeting's name has been erased by this apparent water leakage."

"The fourth person at the table was Makayla, isn't that correct?"

York replied, "Yes. She was there."

Marcel pointed down at the paper again. York had placed it flat on the witness stand.

"I see two entries below that, Mr. York. I see the notation '$750' twice. It appears once with the letters 'GJT.' Then, it appears a second time with the notation 'T' after it. Do you see what I am indicating?"

"I see the note, yes."

"Mr. York, the note refers to payments that you made to Makayla to testify, isn't that right? Once—for $750 to testify to the Grand Jury, and then a second payment of $750 to testify at the trial of Eddie Stephens. The jury trial. Isn't that correct?"

"Yes. We paid her. But not to testify! We paid her money she was owed for previous information she'd already given us. When we were at the dinner in the restaurant, Makayla told us all about the shooting. But then she asked to get her fees for previous work she'd done for us earlier that summer. So, Harp paid her. But it wasn't for anything to do with Eddie Stephens's case. They were totally unrelated payments, I swear."

Marcel stood in front of the defense table and did not respond. He turned toward the jury and looked at each juror slowly. Some were smirking. Some were shaking their heads. Some were looking down at the floor.

After a few moments of silence, Marcel asked, "Below the notes listing the payments, there appears a phrase, 'For vices ended.' Do you see that, sir?"

"That's not 'for vices ended.' That's missing some letters. If you put the missing letters back in, the note says, 'For services rendered.'"

Marcel said, "And the 'services rendered' would be for Makayla to testify against Eddie Stephens! To testify before the Grand Jury and at his jury trial for murder, isn't that so?!"

York said, "No, sir. That's incorrect."

"Let me ask you about another area of questioning. You and other police officers searched the apartment for evidence, I assume?"

"Of course."

"And, since none of the police reports written at the time make mention of any drugs seized from the apartment, I take it that no contraband was discovered inside Mr. Jefferson's residence, correct?"

"What do you mean by contraband?" York asked.

"I mean illegal drugs. Crack cocaine, for example."

"No, nothing was found of that nature."

Marcel doggedly followed up. "Did you search Makayla? Did she have any CDS in her possession?"

"Well, I do recall Harp—I mean, Chief Harper—patting her down outside the QuikStop. That's normal procedure. You can't let anyone get inside a police car without first searching them. There was nothing on her."

"How do you know that Makayla didn't take any drugs from the apartment and keep them for herself? Maybe she hid them somewhere?"

Mac jumped up and exclaimed, "Objection, Your Honor! Calls for speculation."

Judge Ryan responded, "Overruled. The witness may answer if he knows."

York took a moment to digest the rapid-fire questions and then replied, "She wouldn't do that! She would never lie to us. No way."

CHAPTER 42

September 21, 2022
6:13 p.m.

Andre caught the ball under the hoop and turned to look up court. Seeing none of the other players open, he dribbled across half-court and waved the other guys on his pickup team away; he wanted as much space as possible to go one-on-one.

The big guy, the new transfer officer from the Maryland State Police, clogged the middle of the paint, so Andre kept his dribble alive and, again, shooed all of the other cops on his team to the weak side of the court. Once he was safely isolated, Andre took control. Cruising down the right of the lane, he came to a jump stop and faked a shot with both hands jerking upward, and when the tall state trooper left his feet for the pump fake, Andre slithered underneath him and scooped the basketball off the fiberglass backboard and through the net.

"Game!" he said. "That's 21. We win."

The Police Academy had a well-supplied gym, since, after all, it was a good idea to keep Seneca County's police officers in athletic shape. The main gymnasium had a full-sized basketball court, a large weight room, a hot tub, and a sauna. All cops and other law enforcement employees had free rein.

"Yo, Chief," a young, rookie officer said to Andre. "Nice move, bro."

"Thanks."

Andre slapped hands with his teammates and made small talk with the players on the other pickup team, one of whom asked, "Who's got next? Okoye, you gonna run it back?"

"No, man. I'm done."

Andre walked back to the locker room as the players dispersed. He got to his locker, unclasped the combination lock, took out a large white towel, and stripped off his soaked workout clothes. He walked naked across the men's locker room and went into the sauna. It was filled with three other men. Two were seated on the lower of the split-level wooden benches, and a large heavyset man was sprawled out across the top bench like a sweaty beached whale. When Andre entered the broiling-hot sauna, the dripping, heavyset man sat up from his prone position to give him a wet space to sit in.

"Sorry, man. Here you go," the man said, offering room for Andre.

It was so hot, the cedar-wood bench where the sweaty man had lain was already almost dry.

Andre took his towel and draped it over his head. He leaned into the corner space, careful not to touch the wooden walls, and started to drift asleep. Perspiration ran anew down his forehead and began dripping into his lap. One of the other men said, "Hey, Marquis, did you hear about Harper testifying today in that old murder case? I hear he got totally fucked up by the defense attorney."

Under the towel, Andre's eyes snapped wide open. He slowly reached up and arranged the towel so it covered his whole head, and then he slumped against the wall and let his head hang in the corner. He softly made snoring sounds and pretended to be asleep.

"Yeah, dude. Finally got named Chief after all these years of politicking. I only met him a couple of times, but he seems like a redneck to me. He came to speak to my class when we graduated from the Academy, and, honestly, he sounded dumb as shit. He was saying we didn't need training on profile stops because, in his opinion, none of the cops in Seneca County were racist. But, anyway, what's the murder trial about?"

"It's way old. Back from when Harper was on Vice down on Rotterdam Street. Apparently, some dealer got shot and killed and robbed in a drug rip and—what I'm hearing—is that Harper and this other burned out sergeant on his shift set some kid up they didn't like to take the fall. Framed him. And the kid got convicted, and some hardcore judge crushed him at sentencing. Gave him life. Kid's been at Broad Run for 20 years."

"Yeah, but why is the case back again in court?"

"Because the PD who represented him sucked. Like, really bad. And the appeals court reversed it for non-effective counsel, or whatever it's exactly called."

"Wow. That's wild. So, they have to do the trial all over

again? Why don't they just let the kid go? I mean, he shot a drug dealer. So, fucking what? You could call that community service for Christ's sake."

"I hear you, bro. But I hear Chief Harper was just ripped to shreds when he testified today. He pretended like he didn't remember anything. Kept saying 'I can't recall' over and over and shit like that."

"Well, it's been 20 years. Maybe he can't recall?"

"Dude, it was an 0100. You don't forget those cases. You only get one or two or maybe three murder cases at most in a whole career."

"Yeah, I guess you're right."

"This girl testified that the Defendant was definitely the guy who did the shooting, but her testimony was shaky too, I hear. And then it came out that they paid her ass to testify!"

"No! No way. Paid her? No, I don't believe that. No cop would be that stupid."

"Well, this guy Harper said, yes, she did get paid, but that it wasn't for testifying about the dead dealer but for her earlier work as an informant. He tried to justify it. But, man, that sure looks bad. Real bad."

"Oh my God. Even if they paid the girl for old work, that looks super suspicious. You don't do that."

Andre listened intently with the towel over his head and kept making snoring sounds until the two other cops left the sauna.

Oh man, Mac must be dying right now.

CHAPTER 43

September 21, 2022
7:11 p.m.

Ari Fischbein slammed his fist down on his desk and said, "Jesus fucking Christ, Mac!" Ari picked up his landline phone and pressed one of the autodial buttons. "Jo, get in here now," he yelled. "Mac wants to quit this trial. Can you believe that?!"

Mac leaned back in the plush office chair.

Jo popped into the office and glanced back down the hallway behind her. There was no one in the SAO this late at night except the three of them.

"Jo, can you straighten this guy out, please?" Ari said, tilting his head toward Mac. Mac loosened the knot on his tie and tried to control his racing heartbeat.

Jo said, "What's going on?"

Ari turned his face to stare at Mac. Mac said calmly, "I

was just bringing Ari up to speed with the Stephens trial. Honestly, it's not going very well. I thought you should know."

"What do you mean?" Jo asked. "Isn't Judge Bennington set to testify tomorrow? He will be great in front of the jury. Can't ask for a more professional witness than a sitting judge. They'll believe whatever he says."

"Perhaps," Mac replied. "But I really don't know if we—meaning 'we' as an office—should go forward with the case. It's falling apart fast. I'm thinking it might be better to concede and *nolle* it. Better than having all this cover-up stuff come out publicly. Don Morris is in the courtroom every day, and Judge Bennington, not to mention the police *and* our office, are all going to be massacred in the news."

Ari stood up. "I'm late. I'm giving a speech on 'sensitivity training' in 45 minutes. I've heard enough. Mac, how many times do I have to explain to you that it's better to lose this fucking trial than to drop it? If we *nolle* it, then it's *our* decision to can this case. If the jury comes back not guilty, then we just blame them for being stupid. So, just finish the trial and stop overthinking all of this shit."

Ari reached for his suit jacket which was neatly hanging from a wooden hanger behind the door to his office. He put the jacket on and grabbed his briefcase. "Jo, explain how this works, OK? And also explain to him that if he doesn't want to do the heavy lifting in the office anymore, well, maybe it's time for him to cash in his chips and find another less demanding job. It's up to him. Later." He left the office and walked down the hall, then disappeared around the corner toward the front reception area.

Jo said, "Tell me—what's going on, Mac?"

Mac slumped down in the chair. He said, "It's a total mess. Not only are we very likely going to lose this trial, but I'm worried this guy Stephens isn't even the killer. If he's not the killer—or I should say, if I have a reasonable doubt myself—then I'm ethically obligated as a prosecutor to halt the case. Right? Maybe Ari skipped over that part—y'know, ethics class, in law school?"

Jo reached behind her for one of the chairs at the conference table and spun it around. She sat down, tossed her hair extensions over her shoulder, crossed her legs, and said, "Mac, you have a direct eyewitness to the murder. That's the best possible evidence you could ever have in a trial like this. Remember, it's your job to *present* the case, not *decide* it. That's up to the jury. Not you."

"But, Jo, I have sworn obligations. I took an oath as a prosecutor. I can't just ignore that! This eyewitness's testimony is so flawed. First of all, she was probably high out of her mind on crack when this shooting happened. Second, she only got a brief moment to see the guy who shot the victim. Third, her ID is so flimsy. She said a young, light-skinned Black guy with dreadlocks was the shooter. I mean, that description could've applied to probably 50 guys hanging out on a summer night on Rotterdam Street in 2002."

"But she saw him! That's direct evidence. And then she promptly picked him out of a photo array, right?"

"Yes, but the jury won't hear about the photo array. That was suppressed because these idiot cops screwed that all up."

"But," Jo said, "still, the fact is that she *did* identify him in a photo array. Knowing that should make you feel more confident in her identification!"

"Well, what ruins my confidence is the fact that it's possible she was *paid* to testify before the Grand Jury. And then she may have been paid a second time to testify in the actual jury trial itself. That just came out on cross-examination about three hours ago! This moron retired cop, York, says, 'Oh no. She wasn't paid to testify. She was just given money we owed her for being an informant on prior occasions.' I mean, please. The jury was literally shaking their heads when he said that. I've done a lot of trials, Jo. I watch the jury for clues. This guy York just destroyed any credibility Makayla had left. And it also destroyed *my* credibility. Jo, the cops paid her!"

Jo did not respond. She squinted, and her nostrils flared subtly.

Mac continued, "And that's not the end of it, Jo. Get this: Judge Bennington—well, he wasn't a judge at the time, but he was the ASA who handled the first trial—Bennington was *there* when she got paid! He witnessed that! He never questioned the payment. Never reported it. Didn't tell the original defense attorney. I mean, Jo. That's such obvious *Brady* material. He withheld it. That's terrible."

"I'm sure he won't say all of that when he testifies."

"Jo, there is a note confirming it. And Makayla testified to meeting Bennington at a restaurant where she was compensated. Chief Harper, this dumbass cop York, and our own State's Attorney's Office alumni, Judge Bennington, were all at this meeting in the restaurant with Makayla. We can't get around that fact now. Marcel entered the note into evidence as a defense exhibit. Jo, let me say this in an official, legal way: we are totally fucked."

Jo asked, "Who wrote the note?"

"The brain-dead cop, York."

"Did Judge Bennington sign it?"

"No."

"OK, so he can say he didn't realize what any payments were for. Stick with that. He can just deny it. The jury will believe a judge over some senile retired cop. Say the payments were for earlier work as an informant. For undercover tips. She had been providing information to these cops long before the drug dealer guy was killed, right?"

"Yes, Jo. But even if she *wasn't* actually getting paid for testifying, it just looks awful. I think it's a fatal blow. I think we should take the high road and just drop the case. Cut our losses before all this shit comes out tomorrow and shows up in the *Journal*. Don Morris is sitting there all day writing on his little reporter's pad. Stephens already did 20 years on this case. And he might not even be the right guy! Why can't we just let this go and be done with it?"

"We can't. You heard what Ari said. If we drop the case, that will make Judge Bennington look even worse. Like we are covering up for him. And we definitely can't have that. Every judge in this courthouse will hate us. That will cause all kinds of problems for us. Mac, you have to look at these things with a political filter sometimes! No, I agree with Ari: we can't drop this case."

"A political filter? Politics? Jesus, Jo, I didn't go to law school to be a politician. I'm just trying to do what's right here, and going forward with this trial is not right."

Mac looked at the ceiling, his mind racing in a swirling kaleidoscope of thoughts.

Marcel's sleek wooden briefcase, Ophelia's X-shaped braids on the top of her head, Eddie's massive trapezius muscles, Judge Ryan's hidden hand, Kristen's cherry-red lipstick, the eyes of jurors shooting back and forth, Makayla's blonde hair dripping down her back.

"So, Jo, let me make sure I understand you completely. You're saying I can't drop this case under any circumstances? Even if Stephens might be innocent and the first trial was horribly tainted? Just keep going forward?"

"Exactly. Just finish up. Stephens—and Marcel St. Croix, by extension—are both fools for not taking a time-served plea. That was their decision. They were bluffing that we'd *nolle* it. But we can't do that. So, finish the trial and let the jury decide. Then, if they say he's guilty, great. If they say he's not guilty, we can smooth that out easily. Just give the best closing argument you can whip up and let the chips fall where they may. Who is your next witness tomorrow?"

"Your pal, Judge Bennington."

CHAPTER 44

September 22, 2022
9:09 a.m.

"Daniel Wright Bennington."

Mac said, "Thank you, sir. And can you please spell your last name so the record is clear?"

Mac glanced around, mentally taking account of everyone in the courtroom. First, he looked at the jurors. They were sitting in their assigned seats in the jury box, settling in for a long day of testimony. The elderly Asian man in the front row was gripping his pad so tightly the pages were curling up in his fist. The younger man with the military-style jacket, poised in the posture of a secretary, was carefully taking notes.

As Bennington began spelling his name, Mac rotated his vision and spied Eddie and Marcel at the defense table. Eddie poured a cup of water from the pitcher into a white Styrofoam cup. Marcel was rustling through his notes, pen in hand, ready to make amendments to his prepared outline. Mac quickly glanced into the gallery. Eddie's mother, Tamika, was sitting in her preferred seat in the last row. Today, Ophelia Jackson Katz sat next to her, holding Tamika's hand. The reporter for the *Seneca Journal*, Don Morris, was slumped down on the other side of the courtroom, furtively clicking on his muted cell phone. A cluster of younger visitors—perhaps law students or interns—were sitting in the front row as if they were at the movies, ready for the spectacle of seeing a sitting judge testify in a first-degree murder trial.

"B-E-N-N-I-N-G-T-O-N."

Judge Bennington was not wearing his usual black robe. Today, he was simply another witness in the case. As such, he was not afforded any special considerations and was sworn in by the courtroom clerk in a perfunctory manner. However, it was not lost on anyone in the courtroom, including Judge Bennington himself, that it was extremely rare for one judge to be testifying in front of another judge.

Mac turned to the witness and said, "Sir, what is your occupation?"

"I am a Circuit Court judge for Seneca County, Maryland. I preside over my courtroom on the seventh floor of this building right here in the Judicial Center. I handle a variety of matters, including civil cases, family law matters and criminal trials. I have been a judge for more than 15 years."

"Before you were appointed to serve in your current capacity, sir, what was your previous employment?"

"Before I became a judge, I was an Assistant State's Attorney, also here in Seneca County. Well, let me clarify: when I first started my career as a prosecutor, I was an Assistant

State's Attorney, but I was subsequently promoted to the position of Senior Assistant State's Attorney. I worked in your office, Mr. MacIntyre, for—let me see—I believe it was seven or eight years before being nominated to become a judge."

Mac followed up. "On the date of July 5, 2002, were you employed in the capacity as a Senior Assistant State's Attorney?"

"Yes." Bennington did not look at the jury. He kept his posture and his head completely still, and his eyes were locked with Mac's. The room was completely silent except for a slight buzzing noise, like a pesky mosquito, emanating from the overhead fluorescent lights and the staccato tapping of someone's foot in the jury box.

Eddie pointed at the notepad in front of Marcel and nudged his elbow. Marcel picked up his pen and made a check mark next to his list of prepared cross-examination questions. Judge Ryan looked up from her laptop.

Mac said, "Now, focusing your attention on that date in the summer of 2002, do you recall the events of that evening?"

"Yes. Yes, I do," replied Bennington.

"Did you become aware of a homicide that had occurred in the Rotterdam Street neighborhood of Seneca County, Maryland?"

"Yes. I first became aware of it while I was at home with my family. Everyone was asleep. I recall getting paged on my office pager very late at night, or, I should say, very early in the morning. I believe it was around 3:30 a.m. We had pagers back in those days. As soon as my pager beeped, I knew that something urgent had happened. Something was amiss."

"What was your position within the State's Attorney's

Office at that time? Not your title, but which unit or division within the office were you assigned to then?"

"I was on the Major Crimes Unit. We handled all the serious cases countywide. In those days, Seneca County might have had approximately a dozen or so homicides in a calendar year, so each member of Major Crimes would be assigned perhaps two a year. So, when my pager went off so early that morning, I had an inkling that I was about to be assigned the next murder. And that's exactly what happened."

"As a result of getting paged, did you leave your house and go somewhere?"

"Yes. As was the protocol at the time, I was tasked with driving down to the crime scene in the event any legal issues cropped up. I was there to consult with the police if necessary. Things like how to advise a suspect of their Constitutional rights, or, perhaps, the necessity to apply for a search warrant."

Mac asked, "And your goal at that time was to follow the protocols?"

"Yes. I was just the next man up, so to speak."

"Understood. So, after you were alerted via pager, where did you go?"

"I went down to Rotterdam Street, which is all the way over on the other side of Seneca County from where I lived. But traffic was extremely light—I think it was almost 4:00 a.m. at that point in time—so I got there relatively quickly."

"When you got to the location of the homicide on Rotterdam Street, what was going on?"

"Well, it was an active crime scene. The shooting had occurred in a walk-up apartment and the whole area was marked off with yellow tape. The decedent's body had already been transported away. They would have taken the body to the Medical Examiner's Office in Baltimore. I remember the room where the shooting occurred. Even after all these years, I can see it clearly in my mind. There was a broken glass table shattered in the center of the room and a very large amount of blood on the floor. There was at least one bullet hole in the wall. There were police officers milling about outside the apartment and down on the street, but inside were just the primary investigators and the crime scene techs. They were already processing the apartment."

Mac flipped a page in the three-ring binder on his table to the page with the old Statement of Charges. He looked up at Judge Ryan. She was staring at her laptop and tapping the keys on her computer.

"Do you remember the names of the police officers you spoke to that night? The ones inside the apartment. Who was in charge of the investigation, if you recall?"

"Yes. Chief Harper was there. Sam Harper. He seemed to be the one in charge. He was a patrol officer back then—no, sorry—I mean he was on the Vice Team. Or maybe it was the Vice Squad. I forget exactly how that unit was called. But he was not in uniform, so he must've been working in an undercover capacity that night. He wasn't Chief of Police then, of course. Back then, he was simply Officer Harper. But he was there. That I am certain of."

Mac said, "Anyone else?"

"Yes. His sergeant was there as well. I believe his name

was York. But he retired later that year, after the trial, and I never spoke with him again."

"But on July 5, 2002, did you speak with both Officer Harper and Sergeant York?"

"Yes."

"Without telling us what they said—that would be hearsay—what was the context of the conversation?"

"Well, we discussed what they believed had happened concerning the shooting. They were filling me in because it was going to be my case."

Mac dug deeper. "As a result of that initial debriefing from Officer Harper and Sergeant York, did you subsequently meet with anyone else? Someone who was a witness to the shooting?"

"Yes. They set up a meeting the next evening—or shortly thereafter. But, yes, I *did* meet with a young woman who had been inside the apartment at the time of the shooting. I was told she had actually witnessed the event."

Mac glanced at the jury. They were all listening attentively.

"Please continue."

Bennington said, "The four of us—that would be me, the female eyewitness, and the two police officers—we met at a restaurant nearby. I honestly can't remember which one. It's been 20 years or so."

"Please tell the jury what you remember about this female witness."

"Well, I've since been reminded of her name. It was Makayla Schweitzer at the time. On the witness list for this trial, she's listed by her married name, Makayla O'Reilly. Can I call her Makayla just to be clear?"

"Yes. We will call her Makayla for clarity. Again, I'm not asking you to tell the jury who said what, but let me ask you this," Mac said.

He paused.

I hate to do this, but I've just got to take the risk. Better for me to mention this shit before Marcel does. Take the wind out of their sails. Maybe the jury will get confused if I'm the one who brings this up first.

Mac said, with no particular emphasis, "While you were at this restaurant, did any money exchange hands that you yourself saw with your own eyes?"

A juror in the front row, the elderly Asian man, leaned forward and cupped his ear.

"Yes. One of the cops—I can't remember if it was Officer Harper or Sergeant York, but I clearly recall one of the two—gave Makayla some money discreetly. Not exactly under the table, but also not out in the open either. It was cash. Folded up. From where I was seated next to Makayla, I could see a $100 bill on the exterior of the money fold, so it was probably a few hundred dollars. They said it was for a previous job she'd worked for them."

"Objection!" said Marcel without standing. "Calls for hearsay, Your Honor. He can testify what he *saw*, but not what he *heard*, Judge. We ask that the last sentence be stricken."

"Sustained," Judge Ryan quickly interjected. "The jury will disregard the witness's last statement."

Mac clarified, "Judge Bennington, I am not asking you

to tell us what you heard, just what you saw. Did you actually *see* the money change hands?"

"Yes, Mr. MacIntyre. I did. Makayla took the fold of money and put it into the front pocket of her jeans. I remember that clearly."

Mac asked, "Do you recall, Judge Bennington, if anyone at the table was taking notes or writing on a sheet of paper?"

"Well, *I* didn't take any notes, that's for sure. But I do seem to recall that one of the police officers—I honestly can't remember which one it was—but one of them was jotting notes down. I can't remember if one of them gave it to me or not. But, if one of them gave me any notes, I would have considered that to be work product, and if that happened, I am sure I would have put it in my case file along with all of the other paperwork associated with the investigation."

Five of the jurors scribbled on their pads. Eddie turned to look back at Tamika and Ophelia.

"Let me ask you this, Judge Bennington: was the restaurant an Italian restaurant?"

There was a noticeable pause. Bennington looked up at the ceiling for a moment. "Let me think," he mused. Then he said, "Yes. Yes, it was. A nice place a few blocks away."

"Was the restaurant called Buona Sera?"

"Yes. Now that you mention it, that's correct."

CHAPTER 45

September 22, 2022
11:00 a.m.

Judge Ryan said, "Mr. St. Croix? Cross-examination?"

Marcel stood and replied, "Thank you, Your Honor." He buttoned his suit jacket, moved slowly around the defense table, and positioned himself in the open space of the courtroom, preferring to have no barriers, not even a table, between himself and the jury. He now commanded center stage. His performance was about to begin. The curtain was rising.

The jurors were attentive. Their eyes followed Marcel as he approached the witness stand where Judge Bennington sat. Eddie leaned forward in his seat, and his foot shook back and forth like a metronome clicking a fast tempo.

"Sir, I'd like to ask you a few follow-up questions, if I may?"

Bennington then turned, for the first time since entering the courtroom, to look at Marcel, but did not look toward the jury box. He assiduously avoided looking at Eddie, as if he was a horse with blinders on. Bennington had a blank expression on his face, the result of years of practiced neutrality as a judge himself, but his deliberate placidity was betrayed by a large vein in the center of his forehead noticeably throbbing, like a pink worm scuttling toward his scalp as if to seek refuge in his thick grey hair.

He did not reply to Marcel's question.

Marcel paused and leaned back against the defense table for support. He had no notes in his hand, as if to signal to the jury how unnecessary they were. He crossed his arms across his chest.

"Let me start where Mr. MacIntyre just ended. You mentioned someone was jotting down notes on a pad. That pad was a standard legal pad, isn't that so?"

Marcel walked two steps toward the prosecution table where Mac sat and pointed down.

Judge Bennington did not answer.

Marcel exclaimed, "A yellow legal pad? Like *this one* on the State's Attorney's table? One of the cops had a *legal pad* with him that night?"

"Objection," Mac said, standing quickly. "That's a compound question. It's actually three questions."

Judge Ryan said, "Mr. St. Croix?"

Before Marcel could rephrase his question, Judge Bennington jumped in.

"It's been 20 years. I can't recall that type of detail after all this time."

Marcel, knowing he had effectively set his trap, simply said, "We will return to this topic in a bit." Quickly changing his line of cross-examination, Marcel switched directions and asked, "buona sera means 'good evening' in Italian, does it not?" Marcel asked.

"I'll have to take your word for that, Mr. St. Croix, but I don't dispute that."

The pink worm started crawling again

"So, let me see if I've got this straight," Marcel continued. "At this fancy restaurant—they had tablecloths on the tables, right? You sat in a booth with then-Officer *Harper* and Sergeant *Rick* York, isn't that true?" Marcel placed disproportionate emphasis on the words "Harper" and "Rick."

Bennington answered, "Yes, that's correct. Harper and York."

"Yes. And there was a third participant in this conspiracy, wasn't there? A young woman named Makayla who was snuggled up right next to you, Judge. Right?"

"Objection!" said Mac.

"Sustained. Please rephrase," said Judge Ryan.

Marcel said, "Was Makayla in the booth with you?"

Judge Bennington answered, "Well, I wouldn't say 'snuggled,' but, yes, she sat next to me, the four of us together around the table."

"Right," said Marcel. He paused and took a few steps towards the edge of the jury box, hoping to draw Bennington's gaze toward the jurors, forcing him to turn his head 45 degrees. "Had you ever met Makayla before that moment?"

"No."

"Did you know who she was—well, strike that—did you know *why* she was joining you and the two police officers for dinner at a pricey restaurant?"

"Objection!" Mac said. "Calls for hearsay."

"No," Judge Ryan officiated. "It goes to the witness's state of mind. I'll allow it."

Bennington answered, "I had been told she was a direct eyewitness to the murder. And I was asked to join them so I could meet her and see if I could answer any questions she might have. An Assistant State's Attorney would do that in every case. Try to help a key witness understand the process and prepare for trial."

Marcel turned his entire body to face the jury, turning his back on the witness stand. He said, "In every case? An Assistant State's Attorney would have dinner with a witness and the police officers on the case? You're kidding, right?"

"Objection!"

"Sustained. Please, Mr. St. Croix, try not to be argumentative with the witness."

Marcel was facing the jurors. He had a wry, crooked smile on his face. He waited a few beats and then asked, "Well, what else did you discuss with Makayla?"

"I think we discussed, generally, how the criminal justice system would unfold. I'm pretty sure that I mentioned that she would have to appear before the Grand Jury to testify to them first, and how the Grand Jury was just a preliminary step which led to an indictment. Then, I explained that later she would also have to testify in the actual trial, but that it was a two-step process: first the Grand Jury, and then the 12-person jury trial. I also wanted to *bond* with her—again, as I would with any witness to prepare for any trial—since she was essential to proving that your client, Mr. Stephens, shot and killed the victim."

Bennington looked at Eddie for the first time.

Tamika, in the last row, was wheezing. Ophelia reached down to her shoulder bag to get a fresh packet of tissues.

Mac sat still at the State's table, bracing for what felt like a large oncoming wave about to crash into him.

Marcel smiled, and his eyes brightened with a sadistic glint, like a cat holding down an injured sparrow.

"Judge Bennington, well, well. Did you *bond* with Makayla? As planned?"

"I'm not sure I understand the question, Mr. St. Croix."

"Let me ask it this way: did Makayla *bond* with you? I mean, when you *paid her to testify*?"

"Objection! May we approach?!" Mac said to Judge Ryan.

CHAPTER 46

September 22, 2022
11:47 a.m.

Judge Ryan waved to both Marcel and Mac to come up to the bench. She turned on the husher device, releasing the obnoxious, swishing white noise into the courtroom. She abruptly switched it off, looked over at the jury box, and said, "Ladies and gentlemen, it's almost time for the midday luncheon recess. I will therefore ask you to return to the Jury Room and collect your belongings. I have a legal matter to discuss with counsel, so this would be an appropriate time to break." She looked at the two sheriff's deputies in the courtroom and added, "The deputies will escort you down to the cafeteria. I remind you to please stay together as a group and remember—do not discuss the case. Unfortunately, we will have to retain possession of your cell phones here in the courtroom, but I assure you they will be secured. Deputies, you may take them down."

She turned to Judge Bennington and said, "Sir, you may step down. Please be here at 1:30." Bennington walked out of the courtroom.

Collectively, the jurors rose and began to make their way back to the Jury Room with an assortment of polite exclamations. It was typical for a jury of ordinary citizens, faced with the unusual task of sitting in judgment of another, to relieve the stress of jury duty by engaging in small talk, as they would in their normal lives. Jury duty forced them to listen all day and remain speechless, a very unnatural change to their daily existence.

After someone said "Excuse me," and another replied, "You're good," a middle-aged female juror, with suspiciously platinum blonde hair and wearing a business suit, asked, "You said we couldn't take our phones with us? I have to call the babysitter."

Judge Ryan replied, "Ms. Voice, my law clerk, will assist you with all housekeeping matters. Please direct your questions to her."

At the sound of Judge Ryan saying her name, Kristen jumped up from her chair and she began hustling the jurors into the Jury Room to collect their belongings to bring to the cafeteria. Kristen had her hands outstretched to sweep the jurors into a manageable formation, in the manner of a determined dog herding wayward sheep.

One of the two deputies held the courtroom door open as the jurors filed out. The other deputy remained behind Eddie at the defense table.

Another juror, the young woman with the pierced

eyebrow, was wearing a rainbow-themed T-shirt today. She asked the deputy at the door, "Do they have any vegan options down there in the cafeteria?"

The deputy did not answer and shooed her through the door, saying, "C'mon, c'mon, let's go."

When the courtroom was cleared of all jurors, Marcel and Mac both stepped up to the bench. Judge Ryan said, "Mr. St. Croix, I know you enjoy a dramatic monologue in the spotlight, but can you please take it down a notch? Your last set of questions was a bit over the top."

"Yes, Your Honor, I apologize."

Mac jumped in. "Judge, first of all, I object to the use of the word 'conspiracy' because, obviously, it has legal significance. In fact, as we all know, conspiracy is a crime. So, I object to Mr. St. Croix throwing that word out there before the jury."

"I already sustained your objection on that point," replied Judge Ryan.

"Well, additionally, Judge, I object to his last question, which was something to the effect that *the witness* paid her to testify. There has been no testimony thus far that Judge Bennington paid anyone to do anything. So, my objection would be that no proper foundation has been laid."

Judge Ryan said, "Mr. St. Croix? Any response?"

"Yes, Your Honor," Marcel began. "It *has* been established, through the testimony of both Officer Harper and Sergeant York, that the three of them—that is, the two officers and the witness, Judge Bennington—all three met together with the eyewitness Makayla. So, actually, we have heard testimony from *four* people describing this clandestine meeting at the Italian restaurant."

Judge Ryan had heard enough. She said, "I agree that it has been established by multiple witnesses of the existence of this meeting, but your last question, Mr. St. Croix, referenced Judge Bennington himself *paying* the witness to testify. That is where the problem lies."

"Exactly," Marcel said. "It is a terrible problem."

Judge Ryan gritted her teeth. She expounded further. "You asked the witness if *he* paid her. And it has not been clearly established that he did. In fact, he *denied* paying her. He testified that he observed one of the two police officers exchanging money. It doesn't really matter who that was. So, Mr. St. Croix, you may draw any inferences you wish—and I don't need to tell you, sir, with all of your courtroom experience, how to incorporate those inferences into your closing argument. But, at this stage, I will sustain the State's objection, and I will strike your question from the record, and I will also ask the jury to disregard it when they return from lunch. Understood?"

Marcel bowed his head respectfully and said, "Yes, Your Honor."

Mac didn't smile. The question itself, even unanswered, had achieved its goal.

Judge Ryan continued, "We will resume with the cross of Judge Bennington at 1:30. Gentlemen, have a nice lunch."

Kristen said, "All rise!" with an unnecessarily loud tone since there were only a handful of people in the courtroom.

Eddie stood up, and the deputy behind him shackled his

wrists behind his back. Tamika emitted a short exclamatory wail as she heard the metal handcuffs clicking shut. Ophelia said, "Now, now. This ain't the first time you've seen him like that, for God's sake, Tamika!"

Mac turned to Marcel and said, "See you after lunch." He turned and briskly left the courtroom.

Marcel gathered his notes, turned, and ushered Tamika and Ophelia out through the doors, saying, "I'm going to go down to lockup to talk to Eddie. I'll skip lunch. I'm not very hungry."

The lone remaining deputy escorted Eddie out through the side door. A loud clank ricocheted through the courtroom as the door slammed shut.

In the hallway, Tamika said to Ophelia, "That Bennington judge is a liar! He knows he did my boy wrong. I bet that's what Mr. St. Croix is going to talk with Eddie about downstairs!"

CHAPTER 47

September 22, 2022
12:21 p.m.

"I can't eat this shit!" Eddie exclaimed as he grabbed the receiver from the cracked plastic telephone mounted to the wall inside the small cell-like room in the courthouse's basement lockup area where he was meeting with Marcel. Eddie gestured for Marcel to pick up the telephone on his side of the thick glass partition that separated them. Marcel took off his tailored Emporio Armani black wool suit jacket and folded it across his lap as he sat down on a grimy, white plastic folding chair. He lifted the telephone receiver from its position mounted on the wall to his side, wiped it with his handkerchief, and put it up to his ear to talk to Eddie.

Eddie was holding an apple and had a white Styrofoam box opened on his lap. He took a bite from the apple and said into the receiver, "Damn apple is the only thing this jail can't ruin. See this damn cheese sandwich? I've been eating this garbage for half my damn life. These little slices of orange shit. Not sure it's even cheese. Seems more like plastic. When I get outta here, I'm gonna eat some real cheese! Some Gouda or Swiss or even a melted cheese fondue. You must've had that, Marcel, you being French and all. Hell, I might eat a whole damn pizza, man. With pepperoni and *extra* cheese!"

"Well," Marcel said. "Don't call Domino's just yet. We still have a ways to go before winning this case." Marcel wiped his hands on his handkerchief and carefully folded it into squares. "Lord, this place is dirty," he remarked.

"That Bennington is lying! I can feel it in my bones, Mr. St. Croix. You don't survive 20 years at Broad Run and not develop a sense of who's lying and who's telling the truth. You live with scammers and killers and con men all packed in like sardines, and you can spot 'em a mile off. That judge is a fucking liar!"

"Well, I would have to agree with you, Eddie, on that point, although I might express it a bit differently. But here's the thing: it doesn't really matter *who* paid that woman Makayla to testify. The point is one of them did. Either Harper, or York, *or* Bennington. They were all working together toward the same purpose. So, while technically it may not be a conspiracy in the legal definition of the word, the jury has taken the point well. And that's good. It's very damaging to their case. Very damaging."

"I can't eat this shit," the woman with the rainbow T-shirt said as she observed the hot food choices in the Judicial Center's basement cafeteria. She was speaking to Juror One, the scruffy young man with long hair, earrings, and the spectacular unibrow. She said, "The choice is some kind of meat in brown gravy—what is that? Or fried chicken? God, don't they even have a salad bar here?"

"I don't know. First time on jury duty for me," said the young man. "I just voted on Election Day for the first time last year. What's your name?"

"Hi, I'm Carolyn. Well, you can call me Cary. Nice to meet you."

"I'm Julian. We must be the only two people on this jury who aren't Boomers, right?"

"I know! Hey, I'm just going to grab a cup of coffee from the machine up there past the registers. I'll meet you at the table. We're all supposed to sit together. All these rules are driving me crazy! I hate being confined like this. You'd think *we* were the prisoners instead of that poor Eddie guy. Have you seen how scared he looks?"

Julian quickly looked over his shoulder and responded, "Keep it down. We're not supposed to be talking about the case. That's what the judge said."

"Oh, right," Cary replied. "I'll see you at the table."

Cary started to cut to the front of the line and leave, but the deputy was watching and stepped forward. He reminded her, "Hey, ma'am! Stay together as a group. If you don't want to eat, that's fine. But stay here as a group until everyone else has gotten their food, OK? We don't allow the jurors to split up and wander all over the cafeteria."

She looked at him and gave a salute, as if acknowledging orders from a military superior. When the deputy moved to the back of the line, she said to Julian, "God, I hate these cops! Always telling you what to do. Disgusting, these tyrants. Can't wait for this trial to be done. And I'm ready to vote not guilty anyway."

"Hey," Julian whispered. "Quiet! Please, I don't want to get in trouble and get held in—what's it called?"

"Contempt. Contempt of court."

"Right. That."

"You can't possibly think this guy is actually guilty, can you?" Cary asked.

Julian said, "They found a gun in his sneaker. I don't have any guns in any of my sneakers hidden under *my* bed. I hope the lawyers talk more about that. Honestly, that bothers me a whole lot."

"Seems like everyone in America has a gun. It's not illegal, y'know."

Julian said, "I have to think about that."

"But here's the thing," Cary said. "That Judge Bennington should be held in contempt! I wonder if you can do that. One judge hold another in contempt. But he was totally lying through his teeth."

Julian glanced back behind him.

Cary said, "That defense lawyer is destroying him. He got Bennington to admit he saw the cops *pay* that woman to testify! You can't do that! Jesus, how corrupt. How did that guy ever get appointed to be a judge?"

Judge Bennington sat at his desk in his chambers with his golf club splayed horizontally across his lap. He spun it faster and faster.

His law clerk, Melody, called out from her small adjoining office, "Judge, would you like me to go downstairs and grab a grilled cheese sandwich for you? A cup of coffee?"

"No, that's OK, Mel. I'm not hungry. I've got to be back in Judge Ryan's courtroom at 1:30. I'll eat something later. I'm still testifying in that case that was reversed, y'know, that Stephens murder case."

"Right," she replied. "How's it going? Are you almost done with cross? Is Mr. St. Croix being all flashy and show-off-y like he usually is?"

"Yes. But I don't think he's laid a glove on me yet. He doesn't seem to really get the point. No one cares if this eyewitness—this woman named Makayla—received her pay for previously helping the police. No one cares about that, and he keeps going on and on about it. Such a waste of time."

"She was paid? You mean, money?"

"Yes, but not for doing anything in my case. For some unrelated work she'd previously done for the police in an undercover capacity. Trust me, that's how it works. I think the jury can tell St. Croix is trying to trick them. I've been watching them pretty closely. They don't seem too impressed with all of his antics. I think his act is wearing thin."

"OK, Judge. Well, you're the expert. Are you sure you don't want something to tide you over? I can get something out of the vending machines on the third floor."

"No, that's fine, but thanks. I just want this case to be over so I can return to my normal dockets."

Melody turned and walked toward the door. Judge Bennington momentarily stopped spinning his golf club, lowered his perspective, and watched her as she walked all the way across chambers and left.

"I'm starving," said Mac. Andre sat down on the couch in Mac's office and, with some extra flair, unpacked the takeout plastic bag from Sushi Queen.

"Here's two California rolls and six pieces of salmon. What do you call salmon again?" said Andre.

"*Sake*. Did you remember to get soy sauce too?"

"Yup. Of course. How many times have I delivered this shit to you? Like 10 million? Here we go: here's the chopsticks and the ginger and the wasabi in the little packet thing. And here's the soy sauce," he added, handing Mac a small shot-glass-sized container.

"Thanks, brother."

"So, what's happening upstairs? Did Judge Bennington get his ass kicked?"

"Oh my God, Andre. It was embarrassing. He got

decimated. And we aren't done yet. Marcel's continuing with his cross in half an hour. All I can do is sit there and try not to react. But I'm watching the jurors, and they can see what a disaster this is. Dude, they paid this chick Makayla to testify and not only before the Grand Jury, but also for the fucking trial!"

"Yeah, well, we knew that."

"True. But it's all coming out in the open! Bennington wouldn't admit that he himself paid her ass, but it doesn't really matter. He acknowledged that he *saw* her get paid and didn't object or stop it or report it. He just went along with it! I mean, where is this guy's brain?!"

"Are you going to eat both of those California rolls?" Andre inquired.

"Damn straight."

"So what's coming up after lunch? Think Frenchie's got some more shit to lay on our good Honorable Judge Bennington?"

"Yes. The big wave is coming. About to smack all of us in the face. Marcel's had that crazy note laying out on his table in front of him all morning. I have a feeling it's about to be used like a hammer to hit that Bennington dope right on the head."

"Oh my God. The note with all the missing letters?"

"Pompous, smug Judge Bennington's about to get his bell rung."

CHAPTER 48

September 22, 2022
1:28 p.m.

Mac was standing in the hallway outside Judge Ryan's courtroom when the deputies walked up to the door and unlocked it. As instructed, the jurors waited at the far end of the hallway. Some were lounging on the sofa, others were focused on their cell phones, and some were looking out of the large picture windows overlooking the Courthouse Square. Nine flights below, the lunch hour crowds were beginning to disperse and head back inside one of the four courthouses anchoring the rectangular park.

Mac's cell phone buzzed in his pocket. He pulled it out and glanced at the Caller ID. It said BLOCKED. He said, "Hello, it's Mac MacIntyre." There was no response, although Mac could hear the same muffled, faint breathing, as if someone had their hand over the speaker at the other end of the call. He repeated, "Good afternoon. This is Mac MacIntyre. Is anyone there?" Again, no response. Mac hung up.

He looked down at the far end of the hallway again. He counted all 14 jurors: the 12 seated in the jury box, and the two alternates. He examined them carefully. Eight jurors were holding cell phones up to their faces, five were looking out of the windows, and one was asleep on the couch, slumped over with his head reclined on the armrest. The female juror, the one with the rainbow shirt, was staring at Mac and holding her cell phone up to her ear, but, as his eyes met hers, she quickly turned and slid her cell phone into her back jeans pocket.

Kristen broke his concentration as she stepped through the unlocked courtroom doors and looked at him. She smiled and said, "Judge Ryan told me to assemble the jury. She's ready to start. Have you seen Judge Bennington?"

"No," said Mac.

Kristen went down to the far end of the hallway and began gathering up the jurors with big sweeping gestures of her arms, like a workman on an airport tarmac directing a plane which gate to go to. Just as the jurors filed back into the courtroom, Judge Bennington stepped off the elevator, turned, and walked towards the courtroom. A moment later, Marcel, Ophelia, and Tamika appeared from another of the six elevators.

Mac went into the courtroom. Eddie was already sitting at the defense table with two deputies behind him.

Marcel came in and sat down next to Eddie and immediately began whispering in his ear. He unclasped his wooden briefcase, reached in, and slid out one page of paper.

He placed it on the table in front of his seat. Ophelia and Tamika sat down in the last row of the gallery.

"All rise! The Circuit Court for Seneca County is now in session. Judge Roberta Ryan presiding," Kristen announced.

Judge Ryan walked three steps from the door to chambers and alighted the stairs to her elevated bench.

"Good afternoon. Please be seated."

The jury sat. Ophelia and Tamika sat. Mac sat. Marcel remained standing, and Judge Bennington stood all the way in the rear of the courtroom, also standing.

"Are all parties ready to proceed?" the judge asked perfunctorily.

"Yes, Judge Ryan," Mac stated.

"Absolutely, Your Honor," Marcel said, with an anticipatory tone.

Eddie tugged at his polo shirt and shot a quick look back at Tamika and smiled.

"Judge Bennington, please resume the witness stand," Judge Ryan said.

"Yes, ma'am," Bennington said, as he walked confidently down the center aisle as if he were approaching the 18th hole of a golf course at the most exclusive country club in Seneca County.

Bennington stood over the witness box, and Judge Ryan stated, "Sir, I remind you that you are still under oath. Please be seated. Mr. St. Croix? You may inquire."

Marcel said, "Thank you, Judge," and paused to let everyone on the jury watch him pick up the single sheet of paper on his table. He picked it up with two fingers like pincers and rattled it to draw even more attention to it.

Bennington sat down and crinkled the corners of his mouth into a forced smile. The jurors shifted their gaze from Marcel's rippling paper to look intently at the witness. Mac leaned back and slipped his pen into the top breast pocket of his jacket.

Mac reached down and felt his phone in his suit jacket.

I wonder who was calling me. It couldn't possibly have been one of the jurors. If one of them called, it wouldn't have said BLOCKED on the Caller ID. It's got to be someone inside the courthouse using a landline. Andre said cell phone calls from outside would say UNKNOWN. He's got to know that stuff better than me.

Marcel broke his train of thought by saying, "Now, sir, let me ask you some questions about this document I've had marked as Defense Exhibit Number One."

He hasn't called Bennington "Judge" once. I wonder if the jury has noticed.

Marcel said, "Let me show you Defense Number One." He walked slowly three steps to the witness stand and offered the single page to Bennington, who took it and held it aloft in front of his face.

He's holding it like a handheld mirror. Take a good look at yourself, Judge Bennington.

"First of all, this sheet of paper is from a standard yellow legal pad, correct?"

"Yes, Mr. St. Croix, it appears so, but this page is very old and is damaged, so I can't be completely sure."

"Sir, let me direct your attention to the top line of the document," said Marcel. "When accounting for the missing letters, it reads Buona Sera. Is that correct?"

"I would say yes," said Bennington. "That's the name of the Italian restaurant we've already discussed at some length repeatedly."

"Well, let's repeat it a bit more, if you don't mind, sir. OK?"

Bennington did not respond.

Marcel asked, "So, you agree that you attended a dinner meeting at this restaurant, yes?"

"Yes. I think I've said that like six times by now, Mr. St. Croix."

"Seven."

"Objection!" said Mac. "Judge, this is argumentative, asked-and-answered and repetitive."

"I'll allow it, but Mr. St. Croix, let's move along."

"I apologize to the Court, ma'am."

Jesus, Marcel! Stop being so obsequious!

Marcel said, "These letters on the top line at the right edge of the page. Can you see them sufficiently?"

Bennington said, "Yes. I make out an 'H' and an 'R' and a 'B' and then the symbol for the word 'and.'"

"Ampersand?" asked Marcel.

"Is that what it's called? I'll take your word for that."

Marcel turned, took two steps, glanced up at Eddie, and then spun back around toward Bennington.

"H? The investigating officer was *Harper*, correct? And he went by Harp, right?"

"Correct."

"R? His partner was *Rick*, isn't that so?"

"Yes."

"Your name is Bennington? And that begins with a '*B*,' does it not?"

"That's two questions, Mr. St. Croix. But, yes, my name is Bennington. And, yes, that starts with a B."

"The ampersand indicates that there was a fourth person at the meeting, does it not?"

"Yes. Like I said, that would be Makayla."

"Ah, Makayla. See the next line down on the note? It says '$750.' Then there is a dash. And then it has three initials, 'GJT.' Do you see that?"

"Yes. I do."

Marcel asked, "And 'GJT' stands for 'Grand Jury testimony,' correct?"

Bennington paused. He looked up at the ceiling of the courtroom for a moment and then brought his gaze back down to the paper marked Defense Exhibit Number One.

Marcel said, "Sir, are you trying to think of something else that has the initials 'GJT' that is *not* Grand Jury testimony?"

Mac shifted his body weight, leaned forward, but decided not to object.

Judge Ryan looked at Mac, poised.

Mac leaned back in his chair.

Marcel said, "Sir? Can you answer my question, please?"

Bennington responded, "It could mean a lot of things, I suppose."

"Yes," Marcel quickly replied. "But as you sit here

today—testifying before this jury under oath—you can't think of anything else *other* than Grand Jury testimony that starts with the letters GJT, can you?"

Judge Ryan interjected, "Counsel, let's move on to another line of questioning, please."

"Yes, Judge Ryan. I shall," replied Marcel. He looked at the witness intently and said, "Let me ask you about the next line on Defense Exhibit One. See it, sir?"

"Yes," said Bennington.

'It also says '$750.' And it has a 'T' after it. Is that correct?"

"Correct."

"The word *trial* begins with the letter 'T.' Can we at least agree on that?"

"Yes, Mr. St. Croix. The word trial begins with the letter 'T.'"

"Let's move to this next line. At first glance, it *appears* to say 'For vices ended.' But, sir, is it fair to say that there is sufficient space in the sentence for missing letters to be filled in so it would read '*For services rendered?*'"

Bennington picked up the exhibit.

Jesus, answer the question, you dope, and stop thinking so much. Just answer the questions naturally! This is torture!

Mac looked at the jury. The woman in the rainbow-themed T-shirt was shaking her head from side to side. The young man with the earrings seated in the first chair was looking down at the floor. The elderly Asian man was scribbling quickly on his notepad.

Bennington said, "Mr. St. Croix, it says, 'For vices ended,' but I agree there are some missing spaces between the letters, and, I might add again, the paper is very deteriorated for some reason, so I just can't testify one way or the other. It's open to interpretation, I'd say. It's not up to me to decide."

Marcel listened to his answer and slowly nodded his head. He paused for several moments. Judge Ryan looked up. Mac looked down at his table. Marcel said, "You, sir, are correct: it's *not* up to *you* to decide." He took another step towards his table, turned back to Bennington, and said, "We will let the jury decide."

Judge Ryan again spun her head expectantly toward Mac. Mac remained motionless.

Marcel asked, "This next line says, 'B: Mark work prod.' Then, there are several missing spaces where it appears other letters have faded. And then the numbers '911' are at the end of the sentence with an asterisk to designate something. Have I stated what this line on Exhibit Number One looks like accurately?"

"Yes," said Bennington.

"The 'B' is you. 'B' for Bennington?"

"Yes. I have said many times that I was at this meeting."

"It says, 'Mark work product,'" Marcel noted. "Work product is a designation that attorneys use to classify documents as privileged or confidential, right?"

"Yes."

"The term work product is something lawyers use, isn't that so?"

"I agree."

Marcel asked, "Then why, sir, would you ask the police officers to mark *their* note as *your* work product?"

"I'm not sure. This happened 20 years ago. I don't have an answer."

"Oh, no answer," said Marcel. He nodded his head again. "Well, Judge Bennington, we need answers. My client has been locked up at Broad Run for the last 20 years. In fact, he was arrested shortly after you had this dinner with the eyewitness and observed her being paid cash money by the police. And then you advised them to mask the payment as 'services rendered,' isn't that true?"

Mac quickly rose and said, "I object, Your Honor."

"Sustained," said Judge Ryan.

"I have no further questions," said Marcel.

CHAPTER 49

September 22, 2022
5:18 p.m.

Yo, Dog, text me. Can't talk now. At HQ.
Boring training class. This Speaker was
supposed to stop at 5 and it's way passed.
How did Ct go with Benn on stand?

> Terrible. Bennington was ripped by
> Marcel St. C. It was a disaster. Then
> Judge Ryan asks me "Do you rest your
> case, Mr. MacIntyre?" I said yes, and it
> was embarrassing as hell.

Did Frenchie ask for MJOA?

> Yes. But she denied his Motion for
> Judgment of Acquittal. But barely.

No shit. What happed?

> Well, a judge almost never grants an MJOA unless the case is complete BS. Here, with Makayla saying she saw the 0100 directly, there's no way Ryan would grant an acquittal half way thru the trial. But this case is crumbling fast.

What now? Just keep going?

> We have no other choice.

Can I do anything to help?

> Bring me some Starbucks when your training is done, haha? I'm staying here in the ofc for a while to get ready for tomorrow.

What's happning tmrow?

> Well, Ryan denied the Motion for Acquittal, so we start with the defense case.

 DOUBLE BLIND

Who is their 1st witness? Can I do any background checks? I can do that on my phone here. This speaker is so bad. Talking about profile stops and how patrol can't do them when all of us know they do that shit literally every day.

> Right. Well, good to get that training I guess. Profile stops are illegal now.

It's completely pointless. Cops will just keep on doing them. We all know that.

> Sad.

So hey, do you need me to look at Case Search and see if the D witnesses have any priors?

> No. It won't make a diff. But thanks.

What is the name of the first defense witness tomorrow?

> The Defendant's mother.
> Tamika Stephens.

CHAPTER 50

September 23, 2022
9:01 a.m.

"Tamika Stephens. Spelled S-T-E-P-H-E-N-S."

"Thank you, ma'am," said Marcel. "And what is your relationship to the Defendant, Eddie Stephens?"

"He's my son."

Tamika was dressed in a multicolored skirt with floral designs. She wore a tight, cloth jacket wrapped around her broad, sturdy shoulders. Her salt-and-pepper hair was freshly styled with a shorn patch at each temple and a ridge of puffiness down the center of her scalp in a faux Mohawk style. She wore two extra-large silver hoop earrings that bounced off her shoulders as she spoke. Her light brown, café-au-lait-colored skin glistened in the harsh courtroom fluorescent light. She projected a noble, strong presence and had the gravitas of a monarch.

She glanced toward the back of the courtroom and caught

the eye of Ophelia Jackson Katz huddled up in her chair in the last row. Ophelia looked, in comparison to Tamika, to be small and frail, with a crumpled, concave posture. Her whole body seemed tiny and cadaverous, yet her eyes burned brightly as they dashed around the courtroom following the action.

Mac followed Tamika's eyes and saw Ophelia scrunched up in her chair. He then turned to watch Eddie, who was calm and still, as his mother sat across the courtroom on the witness stand. It was the closest Eddie had physically been to his mother in 20 years without a protective barrier or sheet of glass between them.

Marcel stood up.

"You may question the witness," said Judge Ryan, who pushed down the sleeves of her black robe before she lifted her right hand up to adjust the lid of her laptop so she could peer out and see the entire courtroom unobstructed.

"Thank you, Judge," said Marcel. He took a step toward the center of the courtroom, then stopped and turned back to make sure his poster-sized pressboard exhibit—the large photograph—was within reach as it lay on its side between Marcel's table and Mac's. He unclasped the two alligator clips holding the paper covering draped on the photograph, readying it to be displayed. He put both clips in his jacket pocket so they wouldn't rattle on his table, or get knocked to the floor and become a distraction.

"Mrs. Stephens," he began. "I'd like to show you an exhibit that has previously been marked Defense Number Two." He slid the large photo from between the two tables and carried it to the easel set up next to the witness stand.

All eyes in the courtroom followed him.

"Now, Mrs. Stephens," Marcel said, pointing back toward the easel. "Can you see this clearly?"

"Yes, sir. I sure can. That's a photo..."

Marcel interrupted her, knowing her propensity to get carried away with emotion could make her testimony unpredictable, like a lone sheet of loose newspaper swishing down the street on a windy day.

"Let me ask you another question," he began. "Let's take this slowly, Mrs. Stephens."

"OK," said Tamika.

"Is this a photograph?"

"Sure is."

"And ma'am, do you recognize what is depicted in Defense Number Two?"

"Yes. I do. That's my family at Christmas, Mr. St. Croix. That's the living room in my apartment. I still live there, so it hasn't changed much. You can see all the family photos on the wall. See 'em? That's my husband Emerson, God rest his soul."

Judge Ryan jumped in, "Ask another question, Counsel."

"Is Defense Exhibit Number Two a fair and accurate depiction of the way your living room looked Christmas morning on December 25, 2001? And, secondly, are the individual people in the photo also shown accurately?"

"You mean is it a good photo? Yes! It sure is."

Marcel turned to the bench and said, "Judge Ryan, having established the proper foundation, I would move into evidence Defense Number Two."

Judge Ryan said, "Mr. MacIntyre? Any objection?"

Mac quickly stood and replied, "No objection at this time, Your Honor, subject to cross." He sat down.

Judge Ryan announced, "It will be received. Mr. St. Croix, you may continue."

"Thank you," said Marcel, turning to face Tamika. "Please describe to the jury, ma'am, what this is a photograph of."

"It's a picture of my family, like I said, in my apartment on Christmas morning many years ago. Like 20 years, for real. See there? On the floor in front of the tree? That's my three grandkids. The little boys are Marquis and Craigrick. They're both graduated from college now. See that baby in the car seat on the floor? Her name is Marielsa. That's a Spanish name, 'cause her father is Spanish."

Marcel crossed the well of the courtroom and picked up a long pointer from the clerk's table where Kristen was sitting. Grasping the pointer, Marcel marched back to the easel and used the long, thin stick to point to a portion of the photograph where two young men were seated on a couch.

"And who are these two individuals?"

Tamika replied, "That's Marquis's father, Toby." She paused and raised her fist to her mouth. Her voice quivered as she said, "And that's my son Eddie sitting right next to him. Eddie's holding a football, which was given as a present to one of the kids. See?"

"Thank you," said Marcel. "So, you just mentioned a present. Are you absolutely certain this photograph is a picture of Christmas morning?"

"Well, yes! It sure is! See the Christmas tree back there with lights on and all that tinsel? And see all that wrapping paper on the floor? There's no doubt. What other day could it be? And it was the year 2001. See the marking there in the corner? That's the date right there. December 25, 2001."

Marcel did not answer her question. He took the long pointer and held it vertically to his side like a soldier with a rifle at attention.

He said, "Let the record reflect that the witness has indicated a series of numbers which are depicted on Defense Exhibit Two as red, digital numerals in the lower left-hand corner of the photograph. They bear the numbers: one, two—then a slash symbol—then a two and a five—and another slash—then the year 2001."

Judge Ryan paused, looked at Mac, paused again, and hearing no objection, said, "So noted."

"Now, Mrs. Stephens," Marcel continued. "Take a good look at your son Eddie seated on the couch here in the photo." He took the pointer and tapped on the exhibit. A tear ran down Tamika's cheek. She did not wipe it away. She turned to look at the jurors. All of them were watching her closely. The elderly Asian man had a hand over his mouth. The woman with the rainbow shirt leaned back with her arms folded defensively across her chest. The young man with the long hair was drawing a small copy of the photograph on his notepad, sketching quickly and making scratching noises as his ballpoint pen scraped across the paper.

"That's my boy, Eddie! He's been locked up for 20 years for doin' nothing! Those damn cops lied on him!"

Mac shifted his feet beneath him, and his quadriceps flexed involuntarily as he automatically began to rise to pose an objection. No witness was allowed to comment on the credibility of another witness. Despite that, Mac instantly changed his mind, and remained perfectly still in his seat.

Tamika reached up and wiped her nose with the back of her hand, leaving a wet trail from her wrist to her knuckles. She started crying.

Judge Ryan interjected, "Mr. St. Croix, would this be a good time for a recess?"

Before Marcel could answer, Tamika sharply exclaimed, "No. I'm OK. I want to continue." She sniffled, shifted her weight in her chair, and leaned forward. "I'm ready."

"Thank you," said Marcel. "I'm almost done."

"Oh, I'm ready. Been waiting a long time for this. Go ahead."

"Mrs. Stephens, I'd like you to focus on Eddie's appearance in this photograph." He tapped again on the exhibit with the pointer. "Is this *exactly* the way Eddie's hairstyle was on Christmas morning of 2001?"

Tamika said, "Yes, sir. You see he ain't got no braids. He had cut 'em all off at Thanksgiving of that year. I remember that clearly, because we always have a big family football game on Thanksgiving, and Eddie said he couldn't play good with those long dreads. He cut 'em all off. By Christmas, they'd been gone for a month, and that's how he looked. Close cropped. I'm sure of it, and, well, y'all can see it in the picture for yourself. His hair is real short. See?"

CHAPTER 51

September 23, 2022
6:38 p.m.

Mac walked across his studio apartment and stepped into the tiny kitchenette. He looked down at the black granite counter where a white, hockey puck-sized Amazon Echo device sat next to his Keurig coffeemaker. He asked, "Hey, Alexa. What time is it?"

"It's 6:38 p.m. Would you like to hear about your upcoming events?"

"No."

He opened his refrigerator and saw absolutely nothing appetizing to eat inside. The bottom two shelves were weighed down by two cases of Nestlé Pure Life Purified Water, and the upper rack had nothing but a mysterious, large stain and two waxy, eggshell-colored takeout containers from the Chun Cha Fu restaurant down the street.

"Alexa, how long does Chinese food last in a refrigerator?"

"Chinese food will last up to two or three days with proper refrigeration."

Mac gingerly lifted one of the boxes out, opened it, and immediately recoiled from the stench. He looked down into the container and saw fuzzy green mold creeping up the inside of the box like ivy climbing up a brick wall. He flipped the lid on the garbage can open with his foot and tossed the offending box away. He didn't even open up the second box, and tossed it after its twin where it made a plunking sound as it hit the bottom of the trash.

"Alexa, what time is it?"

"It's 6:39 p.m. Would you like to hear about your upcoming events?"

"No! And fuck you Alexa, OK?"

"I'm sorry. I didn't understand your last question."

"Never mind."

Mac stepped out of the kitchenette, walked across the small living room, and unplugged his cell phone from the charging station on a small, scratched end table next to the couch. He autodialed Andre.

"Hey, Mac. What's up, boss?"

"Andre, are you hungry? Do you want to get something to eat? I'm starving, and I literally have nothing here in my apartment. I just threw out some old takeout from the Chun Cha Fu."

"Not that shit we ordered last month?"

"I don't know. Want to meet up?"

"I'm leaving the Academy. Just got finished with my jujitsu class, bro, and I'm heading out of the parking lot. I think I pulled my rotator cuff. Now that you mentioned the Chun Cha Fu, I could eat some Chinese food right about now. I can pick up some takeout and meet you down at The Waiting Room in about 45 minutes? It's nice out tonight, and I've been indoors all day. Sound good?"

Mac replied, "10-4. But hang on."

He turned to face the kitchen area and said, "Hey, Alexa. What's the weather right now? Any rain forecast?"

"The temperature in Seneca County is 74 degrees with clear skies. Rain is not expected tonight."

Mac spoke into his cell phone. "That sounds great. Meet me at 7:15. Get me some shredded pork with dry bean curd, OK? And a small order of shrimp fried rice. Been a rough day in court."

Andre said, "I'm coming down the highway already. Talk to me as I'm driving. Who testified today?"

"That old lady Ophelia Jackson Katz. She was devastating."

"No shit?"

"Tiny little woman about 100 years old. I mean, the Defendant's mother completely destroyed our whole case with that Christmas photo. Then Marcel put on like four other family members to swear that it was Eddie in the Christmas photo as corroboration. Now, this lady today. Andre, this case is worse than a disaster. I've lost cases before, and it always stings, but this is different—this one is humiliating."

"What could *she* possible say? I mean, she wasn't there in the apartment when that J'Mal guy got lit up. So, what's that old woman got to say that counts for anything?"

"Character witness testimony. It's admissible under

Maryland law. It was *very* powerful. That lady is an excellent public speaker. She's ancient for sure, but, man, she was commanding and strong on the witness stand. I was watching the jury. They absolutely loved her."

"Character witness? She can talk about Eddie Stephens when she probably hasn't seen him in, what, 20 years?"

Mac put his phone on speaker and walked into his small bedroom. He placed the phone down on his unmade bed and crossed the room to grab a pair of jeans that were hanging from the swivel chair by his desktop computer.

"Well, you might be surprised," Mac said. "She's been to see Eddie like 50 times over the years up at Broad Run. I wasn't expecting to hear that. But she kept saying what an angel he was as a kid when he attended the Miles Davis School. She even said he was bullied a lot when he was in high school. Maybe they're laying the foundation for why he had a gun in his sneaker—I don't know."

"Mac, I'm pulling up to the Chun Cha Fu. Meet you at The Waiting Room in 20 minutes," Andre's voice came through the phone's tiny speaker. "I want to hear all about that old voodoo lady, OK?"

"Right, I'm heading out now. See you soon. But I'll tell you this: that old voodoo lady just cast a spell on our asses, Chief."

Mac pulled on his old Tony Lama cowboy boots, zipped up his jeans, and snatched the black hoodie from the hook behind his closet door. Grabbing his keys and wallet, he picked up his cell phone exactly at the moment it rang.

The Caller ID said UNKNOWN.

"This is Mac MacIntyre."

There was a pause.

"*Hvala vam.*"

"Zaria! My special secret. Are you OK?"

"Yes. I just wanted to hear your voice."

"Aw, that's sweet. You are definitely the sexiest Yugoslavian I know."

"That's because there are no more Yugoslavians left!"

"I should be more precise: the sexiest Slovenian since 1992 when your former country broke up into six new countries."

"When can I see you again?"

"As soon as this trial is done. Can't wait, Z."

"I can't wait that long."

"Won't be long. Hey, I'm running out to meet up with Andre. I'll call you soon."

"I miss you."

"Miss you too, Z. Bye."

CHAPTER 52

September 23, 2022
7:31 p.m.

When Mac pulled into the empty parking lot of Lock #18 on the river, Andre was already sitting at the picnic table in the far corner. The air was warm and thick, dense with humidity, and the smell of cut grass was mixed with the crisp, salty scent wafting from the water's edge. The roiling sound of the rumbling rapids drowned out the occasional bark of a dog somewhere down on the walking path. Mac stepped out of his yellow Jeep and strolled across the blacktop, waving to Andre as he walked toward him.

"Hey, man," he said. "Thanks for picking up the takeout. How much do I owe you?"

Andre replied, "I got you, boss. You catch the next one." Opening up the white plastic carryout bag, Andre said, "Got you that disgusting bean curd shit and here's the fried rice. Take these soy sauce packets and chopsticks."

"Awesome," said Mac as he straddled the bench at the picnic table.

Andre said, "Ah, The Waiting Room. How long have we been calling this place that?"

"Good question. I mean, we've met here countless times. Like you said, it's perfect: no people, no possible listening devices, completely private. Hey, I'm not as paranoid as you, Mr. Special Assignment Team undercover man, but I agree it's the ideal private place to meet. How did we start calling it The Waiting Room? I think you came up with that."

"If *I* came up with that nickname, then I like it even more!"

Mac said, "You heard about the Big Algonkian Tree?" as he nodded toward an enormous, majestic white oak on a small knoll about 50 yards upriver. "It was in the *Journal* the other day."

"What about it? I love that tree! Imagine what it's seen—I mean, going way back to Indian days. Before any white man saw it, or Black man too, for that matter."

"It's dead," said Mac.

"No way! Dead?"

"Yes. The paper said the Seneca County Historic Preservation Commission voted to have it cut down before it fell over and crushed someone. It's almost 300 years old."

"That's old, man."

Mac continued, "They estimate it was a seedling in 1732. That's the same year George Washington was born. Climate issues burning up this whole planet, Chief. We'll all be dead one day soon, I guess."

"All of us are terminal, Mac."

Mac paused to consider the absolute logic of that statement while Andre distributed the four white cubic boxes of Chinese food, giving two to Mac, and then he reached into the bag and lifted out a large 20-ounce bottle of Diet Mountain Dew and unscrewed the cap.

"How can you drink that?" Mac asked.

"What do you mean? This is the elixir of the Gods."

"That crap is so bad for you, man. Talk about unhealthy. That stuff is like a laboratory experiment. All chemicals and fake coloring, not to mention that sugar substitute which is literally all artificial. That poison will kill you long before global warming does."

Taking a long swig from the bottle, Andre said, "I live dangerously."

After a pause to devour a boiled dumpling, he added, "Can I ask you a question?"

Mac replied, "You just did."

"What?"

"You said, 'Can I ask you a question?' That's a question."

"Oh, Jesus, do you have to be so literal? So, everyone says you have a legit photographic memory. Is that true?"

"Well, I don't know. I just remember things. It's been like that my whole life, Andre. But I don't have what's called an eidetic memory."

"Wait. How do you say that word?"

"Like 'eye-det-ic.' That's when someone can memorize data and numbers perfectly, like the whole phone book. That's different from how my memory works. Mine is called 'heightened episodic' memory, meaning I can remember just about everything that's ever happened to *me* in my life. I can just 'see' things—my own life experiences—replay in my mind. But it's not a perfect memory, like a photograph. Also, if I read something, Andre, it sticks in my mind forever. I can't explain it."

"That would really come in handy, to have a memory like that," Andre said.

"Well, it sure as hell helped me in law school, but people with so-called photographic memories are closely related to savants or people with autism or Asperger's Syndrome, so it's not all it's cracked up to be, honestly. It's a blessing and a curse, and you can never turn it off."

"Maybe that's why you can never keep a girlfriend for more than five minutes."

Mac paused and looked down the river at the dying tree. "I wish you had met Celine. Just once."

Andre quickly looked up at Mac's face and then immediately looked down at the picnic table. Softly, Andre said, "Sorry, man. I didn't mean to..."

"It's OK. She was more than a girlfriend, you know." Mac paused two beats and added, "Well, now you know why I hate all that God shit and, in particular, that stupid cliché expression, 'everything happens for a reason.' There was no reason for what happened in Amsterdam."

Andre stopped eating and froze still, but he couldn't think of any appropriate words to say.

After a pause, Mac turned to face Andre and said, "It is what it is."

Taking the opportunity to distract Mac, Andre said, "No! Not 'it is what it is!' That's your worst cliché of all time. I know you *hate* that saying!"

"It's so stupid, Andre. You could say that about anything. *Everything* is what it is!"

Andre asked, "What's the earliest memory you have, Mac?"

"I remember being at the beach when I was three. My father hoisted me up on his shoulders and stepped out into the ocean. He was a big man, too. Stood six-foot-four, so up on his shoulders like that, I felt like I was 10 feet high. But I was really terrified of the waves and the water. The ocean seemed so incredibly big."

"You remember something when you were *three*? Really?"

"Yes. I can see it in my mind perfectly even now. Most people's memories start at around age five or six, but—I've checked—I was only three when this happened."

"What happened?"

"Well, like I said, I was really scared. So, my father walks out with me on his shoulders until he's up to his waist. I guess he was trying to show me it was safe. And then—all of a sudden—with no warning, he just flips me off his shoulders and throws me in the water! I'll never forget that. I was crying and freaking out and felt like I was drowning, and then he picked me back up. I was gasping for air and clinging on to him. I have never forgotten that incident."

"Sink or swim," said Andre. "That's what they say."

"Yeah. True. Well, I was sinking, that's for sure. I never really trusted my dad again after that."

A minute went by as they ate, and then Andre asked, "So, tell me about this Rosa Parks lady today in court. What's her story?"

Mac worked expertly with his wooden chopsticks, as if he was a surgeon operating with two scalpels, and began excavating the assemblage of food arrayed before him. He swirled the dry bean curd into the shape of a nest in the bottom of the box and then lifted it out in dripping strands, shiny with sesame oil.

Without looking up, Mac said, "Jesus, what a life that woman had. It sure sounded like she was right there in the middle of the Civil Rights Movement. She worked with all of those iconic people that you always hear about. John Lewis, probably MLK himself. Not Rosa Parks, but close. Check this out: Ophelia Jackson Katz was the youngest of 21 children, can you believe that?"

"That's one short of a whole football team. Damn. Parents were busy," Andre remarked.

"So, her family was originally from a place called Belzoni, Mississippi. Sharecroppers. By 13 years old, she said she was picking 100 pounds of cotton a day. That kind of sounded like an exaggeration, but I sure as hell wasn't going to challenge her on something like that in front of the jury, for Christ's sake. They were digging her story big time."

"How the hell is picking cotton a century ago relevant to Eddie Stephens shooting someone on fucking Rotterdam Street?"

"It's not, really."

"Why didn't you object to it then? I've heard you say 'Objection! Irrelevant, Your Honor' a million times."

"I had to hear the rest of her life story. It was pretty interesting."

"You never could resist a little drama," said Andre, smiling.

"So," Mac continued between bites. "In 1963—she was a young, single woman then, a few years graduated from high school—she wanted to vote. They wouldn't let her down in Mississippi, of course. Made her take some ridiculous literary test. Then, when she aced the reading test, they said it cost money to vote. A poll tax. So, she joined this Civil Rights group of college students trying to help Black citizens vote, and, of course, all sorts of blatant racism and violence by the Ku Klux Klan erupted. When her house got all shot up in a drive-by, she left town all by herself and took the train to Washington, D.C."

"Man, that's rough. My people were probably still in Nigeria then. This was in 1963?"

"Yeah, but once she got up North, I guess things got better," Mac noted.

"North. South. It's all America. It's all basically racist," Andre stated. "This whole country is *founded* on racism, Mac. See that big Algonkian Tree? Betcha some poor guy got lynched on that thing at some point."

"Well, at least Ophelia Jackson got away from Mississippi and could attend college up here. Turns out, she was sort of an academic genius, at least that's how she sounded telling her life story. Scholarships, awards. First this, first that. She went to Georgetown. She was going to go to law school too—she said they had zero African American women in her entry class. But just as she was about to enter law school, she met her husband at a political rally and decided not to go. He was this Jewish guy, Katz. Real smart. She said he was a student-leader type who later was big on protesting against the Vietnam War and Nixon and all that stuff. You know, Watergate times. But then, after that, he made millions as a top attorney in D.C."

"She gave up a scholarship to law school?"

"That's what she said. But with all this extra money Mr. Katz made, they opened up the Miles Davis School for the Arts, and that's where Ophelia really made her mark."

"I've heard of that school. A lot of Black performers graduated from there. What's the name of that comedian who went there? You know who I mean—he's doing movies in Hollywood now."

"So, that's where she met Eddie Stephens. He was, apparently, at least according to Ophelia Jackson Katz, a musical prodigy. Super talented. Could play multiple instruments. She said he was offered a scholarship to Julliard in New York City. You ever heard of Julliard?"

"No."

"Well, take my word for it—it's like the best music school in the country."

Andre was finished eating and put his chopsticks, napkin, and unused packets of soy sauce inside his box and shut it. "Are you done eating?"

"Almost."

"What's all of that background stuff got to do with Eddie

Stephens and if he did or did not shoot a guy in Seneca County in 2002?"

"Like I said, she's allowed as a character witness under the Maryland rules to say he's not violent and has a reputation for peacefulness. But the real reason Marcel probably called her as a witness was to bond with all the Black jurors. Smart move. And she bonded with *all* the jurors, not just the Black ones."

"How did the jury react to her?"

"Loved her. Absolutely fell in love with her. That's why I said we are totally fucked, Andre. It would have been less painful if she had just walked across the courtroom and hit me in the head with that big-ass walking stick."

Andre scooped up the remains of their meal, stuffed both boxes into the white plastic bag, and walked to a large metal barrel in the corner of the parking lot. Mac stood and stretched.

Andre strolled back and said, "What's happening with the trial tomorrow?"

"Marcel rested his case late this afternoon. Monday, we have jury instructions in the morning, and then, after lunch, we'll do our closing arguments."

"Well, you got the rest of the weekend to get that shit ready."

"Thing is," Mac replied, "I have nothing to say."

"What do you mean?"

"How can I argue to this jury that Eddie Stephens is guilty when even *I* don't think he did it?"

CHAPTER 53

September 26, 2022
3:44 a.m.

Mac's cell phone rang. That wasn't usually a good sign at 3:44 in the morning.

He looked at his all-white cat, Iago, who was curled up in his customary spot against the windowsill. Iago sighed, licked his paw, and went back to sleep.

He glanced at the cherry-red numbers beaming from the digital alarm clock positioned on his nightstand, and shook his head to clear his mind.

Is this a dream or real?

Quickly realizing he was awake and not dreaming, he reached for his phone and picked it up from the nightstand. He clicked the phone to receive the call and said, "Hello?"

There was no answer.

He heard a faint wheezing sound coming through the

small speaker at the bottom edge of his cell phone, unsure if it was an electronic noise or someone breathing erratically.

"Who is this?" he asked.

The phone clicked and then disconnected.

He checked to see how much battery power his phone contained. It was at 92 percent. He reached for the charger and plugged it in.

Who the fuck is calling me? Trying to disrupt my sleep knowing I've got a big closing argument this morning? Maybe it was just a wrong number?

He lay back on his pillow and fell asleep. He woke up again and had no idea how long he'd been sleeping. It could have been two minutes or two hours. He stared at the ceiling. Sleep didn't come easy to Mac. His brain was always swirling around with thoughts conflicting with each other, some positive, some negative, always contesting which was more powerful, like the wind competing with the rain in a hurricane to see which was stronger.

He gave up trying to sleep. The sun was just beginning to pour through the blinds on his bedroom window.

Getting out of bed, he walked to the kitchen and flipped open the Keurig coffeemaker's lid and inserted a pod of premium Starbucks Dark Roast Breakfast Blend into the most important machine he owned.

Might as well just get up. I'll never fall asleep again now. Damn insomnia torturing me.

He watched the stream of black fluid sluice into his mug, and then he shook his head to try to clear his mind for the approaching day. That closing argument was coming as sure as the sunrise, inevitably and unstoppably.

What the fuck am I going to say about Eddie Stephens? I've got to say something. But what? Maybe a cup of coffee will help me focus. Make a mental outline. List every reason he might be guilty and just roll with that?

Iago appeared at Mac's feet, briefly rubbed against his ankle, then flopped on his side on the kitchen floor and stretched magnificently.

"I guess you can get breakfast early, too."

Iago rolled over and looked up plaintively with his smoky-grey eyes.

"You're not much of a talker, Iago, but you're one hell of a good listener."

Mac reached into the kitchen cabinet, pulled out the laminated paper bag of dry Purina cat food, and poured a half-cup full of asterisk-shaped morsels into the small china bowl in the corner. Iago lumbered over and began eating, making a crunching sound.

"Same thing every day," Mac said. "It's a miracle you never get sick of it."

Just as Mac lifted his coffee mug to his lips to get his first jolt of the hot, black, caffeine-laced brew, his cell phone rang again.

Mac crossed back into his bedroom, reached down to the charging station on the chair beside his bed, and unplugged his cell phone. He decided to let it ring three times before answering. The Caller ID said UNKNOWN.

"Hello, this is Mac MacIntyre."

A man's voice that he recognized but couldn't place said, "Hey, Counselor, how're you doing this beautiful blessed day?"

"Who is this?"

"This is Alonzo Randall-El. I'm calling, Mr. MacIntyre, because I wanted to catch you before you left for work."

Mac's brain started swirling like a kaleidoscope again: positive thoughts fighting against negative ones. The negative thoughts won this round.

Randall-El? I've seen that guy before on TV. He's on CNN all the time. Kind of a jive-ass attorney. Always wearing brightly colored three-piece suits, with the vest and all. He's that self-promoting loudmouth they use to comment on criminal cases. Biggest ego imaginable. And he always spins any question back to who he is and what he does.

"Mr. Randall-El, it's like 5:30 in the morning."

"You're correct. Please call me Zo. No need to stand on formalities. Like I said, I wanted to catch you before you left for work. Early to bed and early to rise makes a man healthy, wealthy, and wise!"

That cliché clanged against Mac's brain, waking him up a bit more.

Mac said, "That's a Benjamin Franklin quote."

"Really? I never knew that, Counselor. Anyway, so I hear you have a big closing argument in the Eddie Stephens case today," Zo said.

Mac paused, digesting this comment, suspiciously unsure of its potential motive.

"Yes, that's true. I presume Zo is short for Alonzo. Do you have some interest in the Stephens case?"

DOUBLE BLIND

Mac took a large gulp of his coffee, hoping it would sharpen his survival instincts, although it was unnecessary because his mind was already set on high alert.

"I got your number from Marcel St. Croix. He's an old friend of mine. And Ophelia—Ms. Ophelia Jackson Katz—I've known her for decades."

Mac said, "Why are you calling *me*? Let me ask again: do you have an interest in the Stephens case? Are you joining his defense team or calling me for another, unrelated reason? Can you answer that question first before we continue this conversation, please?"

"Absolutely! No problem. Can I ask you a question?"

"You just did. Never mind. But Zo, let me ask *you* for the third and final time: what is the purpose of your call?"

"Well, yes, I *am* calling you for a totally unrelated reason. So, I know you're busy with a big trial, and, trust me, I've done quite a few myself. Maybe you've seen me on the news from time to time, or maybe you've listened to my podcast?"

Mac didn't answer. There was a brief pause.

"Well, Mac, the reason for my call is to see if you'd be interested in meeting with me sometime to discuss the possibility of you joining forces with me? I mean, everyone downtown knows you're one hell of a great trial lawyer and—just Google me and my law firm—I have a *very* lucrative practice on K Street. We could always use a great litigator like you to team up with. Randall-El and MacIntyre. How does that sound?"

Mac was pacing across his tiny apartment. He strolled to the window, where he quickly glanced to see if the sun was rising over the buildings in the Courthouse Square. He turned and walked back to the kitchenette.

"Are you still there?" Zo said.

"Yes, I am. Sorry."

"So, Mac, I run one of the top civil P/I firms in D.C. We handle both State and Federal cases, exclusively multimillion-dollar claims. We specialize in cases of police brutality and civil rights violations. My firm represents families who've suffered wrongful death cases involving their loved ones. You know the George Floyd case? We do those kinds of lawsuits all over the country, and, as you know, we get a 40 percent contingency fee of any award we negotiate or settle for."

Jesus, those guys make millions a year. I can't even imagine how rich I'd be.

"Of course I've heard of George Floyd, Zo. I've been a prosecutor for more than 20 years. And I actually do watch CNN sometimes."

Zo laughed and said, "Well then, you know what I'm talking about! I could use a guy with your deep experience and familiarity with police procedures. We want to expand from D.C. into Maryland. Lot of cases coming out of Baltimore now. We need someone with your skill at persuasion in front of a jury. Imagine if—instead of getting a guilty conviction in each murder trial you did—you got a multimillion-dollar judgment? You'd be a wealthy man, Mac. And I'm not just talking wealth. I'm talking *generational* wealth. Are you interested now?"

"You've got my attention. But why are you calling me today? I find the timing curious. Are you telling me you have no interest in the case I'm doing a closing argument in today?"

"Not really, man. You do your thing. I was just talking to Ms. Jackson Katz about a different matter, and your name came up. She suggested I call you. She thinks you're a great lawyer, and, well, I guess she thought we might make a damn good team."

"I appreciate the call. Let me think about it, OK? I've got to get ready for work now, but I'll get back to you once this case is done. But I can tell you one thing right now: I like the sound of MacIntyre and Randall-El better."

Zo laughed and said, "One way or the other. Oh, and Mac, good luck with your closing argument today."

"Thank you. Bye."

CHAPTER 54

September 26, 2022
6:15 a.m.

When Mac got out of the shower, he couldn't wait any longer, and, with a towel wrapped around his waist, he texted Andre:

> Chief, you won't believe this, but that downtown D.C. attorney Alonzo Randall-El called me at sunrise today. Are you up?

He looked down at his phone. The text was marked with the word "received," but next to it was a little half-moon icon, indicating that Andre had silenced his phone.

Iago was back in his spot by the window, looking out on the Courthouse Square. There was almost no activity in the park or surrounding streets this early in the morning, except for a lonely delivery truck parked in front of the Judicial Center.

In the far corner of the park, adjacent to the Old Colonial Courthouse, a utility vehicle marked "Maryland Pepco" was parked beside an uncovered manhole. An obnoxious electronic beeping sound echoed across the Square, and a workman in stained overalls was placing neon-orange cones around the manhole. The first beams of sunlight were piercing the irregular skyline of the downtown area, slashing down to the ground like sunshine peering through the slats of gigantic, imaginary Venetian blinds.

Iago's pink, opaque, triangular-shaped ear turned instinctively with each distant beep of the utility vehicle.

"See anything interesting down there?" Mac said to Iago, who didn't respond.

Mac stepped into his closet. It wasn't quite a walk-in closet, but more of a walk-through closet, forming a bridge from his tiny bedroom to the studio apartment's bathroom. On the left side, he had a rack of at least 25 assorted dress shirts for court. Assiduously arranged next to the shirts, there was a row of 12 nearly identical suits. His suits—actually, more like his uniforms—were all sized "38 Long" and lay like soldiers in formation, a series of muted, inconspicuous blue, brown, grey, and black fabrics neatly lined up on wooden hangers. He decided to wear a light blue shirt with his best Navy blue Hugo Boss suit from Nordstrom.

Black shoes or brown? I hate getting all dressed up. If I could, I'd wear sweatpants and a T-shirt to court. These suits are just my costumes.

His phone pinged.

DOUBLE BLIND

Andre's text read:

That dude Alonzo is the bomb, man! Seen his ass on TV all the time. Why is he calling you?

Mac laid his suit on his bed and draped the shirt over it, making layers of clothing to simulate how they would look upon him once dressed. He stepped back into his closet and selected a subtle, pinstriped, sky-blue necktie from the rack mounted on the wall. He crossed back to his bed and placed the tie vertically down the center of the shirt.

"Now, don't walk on my clothes, OK?" he said to the cat.

Satisfied, he picked up his phone. He texted:

Offering me a job! Says I can make millions in lawsuits against corrupt police. Guess I know something about that, right?

Mac stepped into his bathroom and picked up his electric shaver.

His phone pinged again. Andre's text read:

Careful. Sounds like a trap. BTW, why does that guy have that damn "El" after his name anyway?

Mac texted:

"El" after a name means they might belong to the Moorish Science Temple of America or another Black nationalist or Black Muslim group.

Andre's text read:

How do you know more about being Black than me?

Mac smiled into the mirror.
A follow-up text arrived:

Don't trust him!

Finished shaving, Mac walked back into the bedroom and began dressing.

"Hey, Iago, can I ask you a question?"

The cat looked up at the sound of his name.

"What the hell am I going to say in my closing argument today?"

Iago yawned and turned to look out of the window at the workman five flights below who was making a scraping sound as he arranged the orange traffic cones.

"What am I going to say? I can do a killer closing argument in my sleep, Iago. I've done a million in my career and I'm damn good in front of a jury. But I keep thinking of Eddie Stephens being in jail for 20 years because of this crazy case. It's not right. I can't say—in good conscience—that he's guilty of shooting a man to death when even *I* am not convinced he did it. I took a damn *oath* to do the right thing in these cases, and telling the jury an innocent man is guilty? I just can't do that."

Mac buckled his belt and picked up the blue striped necktie. He wrapped it around his neck and flipped the collar down over it.

"And I can't waive my closing argument and make it obvious I'm tossing in the towel. I'll get fired, and I don't want that either. The Fish and Jo will go crazy. And that damn Chief Harper. He will make my life a nightmare with every new case I get. He can turn the whole police department against me. You know how all that blue brotherhood bullshit among cops goes."

Mac crossed back into the bathroom and gazed at himself in the mirror.

"Not to mention that liar, Judge Bennington, Iago. Are you listening to me? This is important." Iago rose, arched his back, kneaded the bed several times, and then plopped down in the exact same spot as before.

"A Circuit Court judge can wreck my career inside the courthouse. And if the Fish doesn't outright fire me, he'll do something devious like reassign me to traffic court to intentionally humiliate me. If he did that, I'd *have* to quit. Then I lose all my benefits and healthcare. I can't do that either. Andre is right: this *is* a trap."

He knotted the tie, checked its geometrical symmetry in the mirror, and slipped on his suit jacket.

"But I just can't get up in front of this jury and use my skill to persuade them to come back with a guilty verdict. I mean, who knows? Maybe they will convict Eddie *again*? That's a nightmare I can't live with."

The hurricane in his mind returned.

Makayla with her blonde ponytail swishing behind her as she walked up to the witness stand, Tamika gasping for air and crumpling up a frayed tissue against her nose, Marcel holding up the Christmas photo, Judge Ryan dipping her left hand below the bench, Kristen raking her hair backwards with her fingers over and over, that idiot York yawning on the witness stand between questions, his clothes reeking of weed, a pair of bicycle wheels spinning haphazardly.

"Are you paying attention, Iago? What am I going to do?!"

The cat curled up into a white spiral, closed his eyes, and sighed.

CHAPTER 55

September 26, 2022
9:01 a.m.

MCJI Cr 3:30

MARYLAND COMMON JURY INSTRUCTIONS

The burden is on the State to prove beyond a reasonable doubt that a) the offense was committed and that b) the Defendant was the person who committed it.

You have heard evidence regarding the identification of the Defendant, Edward DeLawrence Stephens, as the person who committed the crime. In considering the accuracy of this identification, you should consider:

1. The witness's opportunity to observe the person committing the crime;

2. The length of time the witness had to observe the person committing the crime;

3. The witness's state of mind, and any other cir-

cumstance surrounding the event.

You should also consider the witness's certainty or lack of certainty, and the witness's credibility, as well as any other factor surrounding the identification.

The identification of the Defendant by a single eyewitness, if believed beyond a reasonable doubt, can be enough evidence to convict the Defendant. However, you should examine the identification of the Defendant with great care.

CHAPTER 56

September 26, 2022
9:02 a.m.

"Mr. MacIntyre, is the State ready to proceed with closing argument?" Judge Ryan asked, peering out from the top of her laptop.

Mac slowly rose from his chair and replied flatly, "Yes, Your Honor."

He flashed a glance at the large clock on the wall behind the judge. It was 9:03.

The courtroom was more crowded than it had been all week. There was a group of about a dozen law students hovering in a cluster behind Marcel and Eddie's table. The students were looking all around the room, in the manner of guests invited to a matinee performance with the curtain about to rise. Tamika and Ophelia were in their customary seats, but leaning forward with expectation, Tamika's elbows braced on the seat before her. The reporter for the *Seneca*

Journal was also slumped down in the last row, scribbling on a small notepad. Even the two sheriff's deputies were listening, not daydreaming as usual, as they sat in their usual positions behind Eddie.

The jurors sat still, holding their small pads and pens, but not writing anything down. The elderly Asian man in the front row shifted his gaze back and forth from Marcel to Mac and then up to Judge Ryan on the bench.

Kristen was leaning forward in her chair, ready to respond to any question Judge Ryan may have. She reached up and unbuttoned her shirt's topmost button and tugged at the silver chain that circumnavigated her long, thin neck.

Mac turned his head slightly and with his peripheral vision caught a motion coming from the courtroom door.

The Fish entered the courtroom. Jo trailed him. They sat in the very last row in seats near the door.

Oh Jesus! They came to see if I waived my closing! Oh my God.

Mac shifted his papers on the prosecution table.

"Mr. MacIntyre?" Judge Ryan asked. "Is the State ready to proceed?"

"Yes, Judge. Thank you."

Can't go forward. Can't go backward. Can't go sideways. Can't go around.

Andre entered the courtroom and walked confidently past The Fish and Jo and took a seat right behind Mac in the front row. The jurors' eyes followed him as he walked down the center aisle, wearing his black, motorcycle jacket, Jordan 5s, and tight, black jeans. He was not wearing his business suit.

Mac glanced at Andre, and a rush of soothing calmness washed over him. Steeled by Andre's charismatic presence, Mac walked to the exact center of the courtroom, turned, and said confidently, "Ladies and gentlemen of the jury..."

At that moment, Mac had pulled the energy of the entire courtroom to him, like a vortex. Center stage, he sensed the collective focus of his audience.

"Now is my opportunity to present a closing argument to you. Closing arguments are based on the evidence and testimony from the witness stand that has been admitted by Judge Ryan in this case."

So far I haven't said anything. That's it! That is the only way out of this trap! I'll talk and talk and talk and say nothing!

"Evidence isn't guesswork or speculation or conjecture. Evidence is comprised of facts—proven facts."

If I keep talking, The Fish and Jo can't say I didn't try. But if I ramble on and on and don't really say anything substantive, I can let Marcel win this case and set Eddie free!

"Let's discuss the evidence in this case."

The Asian juror flipped over a page in his notepad, ready to take notes of the important things Mac was about to say. So far, he had written nothing.

"First of all, you heard Judge Ryan explain what eyewitness testimony involves. You heard her read the Maryland Common Jury Instruction which guides us what to look for in cases involving eyewitnesses. The jury instruction will show you what elements to consider as you seek to arrive at your verdict. 'Elements,' I say. That means the ingredients that the law in Maryland has determined jurors should account for in a criminal case like this one."

The young woman with the tattoo on her neck—she wasn't wearing the rainbow-themed T-shirt today—leaned back and looked at the ceiling.

She understands. She knows what I'm doing.

"So, if you read the Jury Instruction—and you will have a copy of it with you in the Jury Room as you deliberate—you will note there are a couple of factors to consider when evaluating the eyewitness testimony of Makayla Schweitzer O'Reilly in this case."

The Fish glanced at his watch and tapped Jo on her shoulder.

Mac looked back at the large clock. It was 9:14. The Fish had lasted 11 minutes.

Jo shuffled her knees sideways in the aisle, and The Fish stood up and wriggled past her. He squeezed by, turned, and exited the courtroom.

That dude has the attention span of a three-year-old. One down, one to go.

Jo pursed her lips and gripped her cell phone tightly. She began tapping on it furiously with both thumbs, a blur of moving digits, as Ari Fischbein disappeared out of the courtroom.

Mac continued, "The first factor—the first element—is opportunity. Opportunity to observe the crime. Well, in this case, it is uncontroverted that Makayla saw exactly what happened when an assailant accompanied her into the victim's apartment to make a purchase of illegal drugs. She was right there. She was in the best position to see the event unfold and, more importantly, the man who did the shooting.

"She described the shooter as a young, slightly built African American man with a light complexion."

The Asian man looked at Eddie for a moment, and then wrote something down on his pad.

Mac said, "A man with long braids. With his hair in dreadlocks or plaits or braids—I think we can use these terms interchangeably."

The female juror with the tattoo on her neck shook her head and crossed her arms tightly across her chest.

"And," Mac continued, "we heard from two Seneca County Police Department officers—Chief Harper and retired Sergeant York—that Eddie Stephens had a hairstyle exactly like that prior to the shooting.

"Makayla had both the opportunity and the time to identify Eddie Stephens as the assailant. So, both of those elements are satisfied according to the Maryland Common Jury Instruction on the reliability of an eyewitness identification. But there is more: she has the *certainty* as well. You heard her testify: she testified that she was 100 percent certain. *100 percent.* A witness cannot be more certain than that."

Tamika bent over, coughed, and stared at the floor.

"Ladies and gentlemen, I ask you to focus your attention on this final element of the Jury Instruction: 'a single eyewitness if believed beyond a reasonable doubt' is totally sufficient to convict the Defendant of this offense. And that is exactly what this case presents: a single eyewitness in Makayla who is certain to an absolute degree. The law says that *alone* is sufficient to render a guilty verdict."

Mac spoke passionately for the next 60 minutes using a mix of platitudes and canned, generic comments usable for any case: what proof beyond a reasonable doubt meant, how the presumption of innocence had to be overcome by the strength of the State's case, and then he ended his closing argument by fawningly thanking the jury for their service. He said a lot. He said nothing.

That should be enough to cover my ass.

"Therefore, on behalf of the State of Maryland, we ask that you find the Defendant, Edward Stephens, guilty of Murder in the First Degree. Thank you."

CHAPTER 57

September 26, 2022
1:30 p.m.

"Mr. St. Croix, you may address the jury," said Judge Ryan from behind her bench.

Marcel paused a beat, then another, until he felt he had drawn the eyes of the jury upon him. He exaggerated the difficulty for him to rise from his seat, struggling to unfold his body slowly, the way a construction crane, hinged in the middle, labors to straighten fully erect. Mac couldn't suppress a very subtle grin. He appreciated what Marcel was doing.

Oh, Jesus, Marcel! Cut the obvious theatrics already! Trying to win an Oscar as the Best Performance by an Attorney in a Lead Role?

The courtroom was full now. It was fascinating how word spread in the busy Seneca County Courthouse over lunch. Myriad conversations, exclamations, and cell phone clicks all swirled around the building when something interesting was unfolding in one of the courtrooms. Hundreds, if not thousands, of assorted people cruised through the public courthouse each day: a typhoon of activity, with people having civil cases resolved—divorces, adoptions, lawsuits involving various degrees of negligence and recklessness—and criminal cases, each one with witnesses, police officers, and attorneys. The regular cast of characters—the employees who worked inside the complex—the prosecutors, public defenders, clerks, sheriff's deputies, and judges, none of them were immune from petty gossiping and swirling rumors. Additionally, since it was a municipal building open to anyone, it also inevitably attracted the detritus of the community: homeless people seeking shelter or air conditioning on a broiling-hot day, retirees looking for free entertainment or groups of school kids on tours being exposed to the vagaries of justice.

Tamika and Ophelia Jackson Katz commanded their usual spots in the last row behind Marcel and Eddie's defense table. Today, Tamika was not wearing one of her usual colorful tracksuits, but, instead was dressed in a flowing, bright Creamsicle-colored, orange cape, with a matching hat, as if she was attending Easter services at her Baptist church. Ophelia sat next to her, rocking slightly back and forth, a hostage doomed to her advancing Parkinson's. Two full rows of the courtroom gallery were now occupied by a phalanx of chattering, noisy law students and interns, all of whom had come to be entertained by watching the great courtroom magician, Marcel St. Croix, perform. Perhaps Marcel could wave his hands and make the State's case disappear?

Mac glanced around the crowded courtroom.

This is torture. I don't mind losing a case, particularly THIS case, but Lord, please, can we make this fast?

Marcel began his closing argument with the classical, old-fashioned format. "Thank you, Judge Ryan. May it please the Court? Ladies and gentlemen of the jury..." When he felt all of the courtroom's attention centered on him as if he were an actor alone on stage in a spotlight, he said, "In my opening statement, I *promised* you one thing: that Eddie Stephens was 100 percent innocent. Today, at the end of the trial, I stand fully invested in that proclamation."

He stood in the center of the courtroom. With a dramatic sweeping motion, he gestured towards Eddie at the defense table and said, "And I was 100 percent correct, because Eddie *is* 100 percent not guilty!"

Marcel, did you really use the phrase "100 percent" three times in 30 seconds?

Mac shifted his weight to object, knowing that it was improper for an attorney to inject his own credibility into a closing argument. The rules of evidence precluded Marcel from telling the jury *he himself* thought Eddie was innocent any more than Mac was allowed to could tell them he believed Eddie was, in his personal opinion, guilty. That determination of guilt or innocence was called "the ultimate issue" in the law, and that decision was strictly for the jury alone to decide.

I'll let that slide.

Mac didn't object.

Marcel continued, "Let's examine the State's many failures to meet their burden of proof. Let me remind you, ladies and gentlemen, what Judge Ryan instructed you just before lunch about the requirement that Mr. MacIntyre is obligated to meet: he must prove to you beyond a reasonable doubt that Eddie is guilty of each and every element of the offense."

Marcel? You have to bring my actual name into this? Can't you just say the State or the prosecution? Don't make this personal, please. I hate when defense attorneys do that shit.

"Mr. MacIntyre, the Senior Assistant State's Attorney sitting here at the prosecution table, must prove this case to your satisfaction. We, the defense, are under no obligation to prove anything. I submit to you that the State's case has been a complete failure, if not a totally unmitigated disaster. However, not only has the State failed to prove Eddie's guilt—they have actually helped to prove his *innocence*. And in almost 50 years of trying cases here in Seneca County—in half a century—I don't believe I've ever seen *that* done before."

Mac shifted his weight again, and his chair squeaked, drawing the attention of several jurors. He did not stand up.

Judge Ryan swiveled her head to stare at Mac.

Marcel continued, "All of the State's witnesses might as well have testified for the defense."

Marcel turned his head towards Mac and paused. When it was clear to everyone that Mac was not going to object, Marcel continued, "Let us discuss the many significant ways the evidence demands a not-guilty verdict."

Here we go. Fasten your seatbelts.

"First of all, let us be very clear about what we *know* happened on July 5, 2002." Marcel again elongated his pronunciation of the year into five syllables: two-thou-sand-and-two, dragging it out to emphasize how old the case was.

"That was a very long time ago. Do you remember what *you* were doing on July 5, 2002? Of course you don't. Human memory doesn't work so infallibly. Let me ask you: who was the President of the United States in 2002? You'd be correct if you said George W. Bush. Remember back to those days? 9/11 had happened less than a year earlier.

"What else happened that year? Well, the Fujitsu Company invented a device called an iPad. Michael Jackson dangled his baby from a hotel balcony. The Winter Olympics were held in Salt Lake City. Tiger Woods won the U.S. Open. And who won the NCAA basketball tournament?"

A voice, barely audible, seeped out from the gallery, "We did."

"Yes!" said Marcel. "You're right: Maryland won the Final Four. Sure seems like a lifetime ago, doesn't it?"

The jurors looked around, trying to ascertain who had spoken.

"Let us just say that it's been a long, long time," Marcel reinforced. "But, despite that, we know that on July 5, 2002, a young man named J'Mal Jefferson was robbed and shot to death. Well, we know *someone* killed him. Someone who was identified—and let me underscore this salient point—the killer has only been identified by *one* person. Makayla Schweitzer O'Reilly. It bears emphasizing that the reliability of the State's identification rests on just one person. And that singular person is a completely *unreliable* witness. Makayla cannot be believed or trusted.

"Without Makayla, there is no case. I'm sure you've noticed—as have I—that there is absolutely no forensic evidence conclusively linking Eddie to this crime scene. No DNA sample left anywhere in the apartment. No fingerprints on a doorknob, for example. No random loose hair collected from the floor. No confession. No nothing. Oh, yes, there was something mentioned about a handgun, wasn't there? I didn't hear Mr. MacIntyre mention it much in his closing, did you? I'll get back to that in a minute.

"So I ask you to examine Makayla's testimony with great care. Remember when she testified that she was heavily addicted to crack cocaine at the time of the shooting? Did she snort or inject drugs before this event occurred? Possibly. Were her perceptions altered or affected because of that? Possibly. Did she confuse Eddie with one of dozens of people who were hanging around Rotterdam Street on that stormy, rainy night 20 years ago? Most likely.

"Let's examine how she described this assailant. She told you he was a young, African American man, thin in build, with a light complexion." Several jurors quickly glanced at Eddie sitting at the defense table. He was no longer young. His body was thick from years of push-ups and bench-presses and was now powerfully constructed. Inestimable repetitive weightlifting in prison had completely altered his physique.

"And now we get to Makayla's description of the assailant's hairstyle. This is critical. I'm sure many of you recall that description. Perhaps some of you took notes about the assailant's hairstyle."

As Marcel spoke, he walked back to the defense table and grabbed the corner of the poster-sized Christmas photo mounted on cardboard. He picked it up, walked with it back to the far back wall of the courtroom, and placed it on the easel. Turning, he said, "Ladies and gentlemen, what do you see here?"

Marcel pointed to the exhibit, saying, "No one in this photo has long hair, dreadlocks, braids, whatever you'd like to call them. See Eddie sitting on the couch on Christmas morning with his loving family?" Marcel tapped with his index finger on the exhibit. "Eddie is the one holding a football. A photo freezes a moment in time. Note these digital red numbers down here in the corner of the photograph. The date of this photo is December 25, 2001! Approximately six months before the shooting. Does the State actually want you to believe that Eddie's hair grew something like 24 inches in the next six months? That's physically impossible."

There was a buzzing of human sounds percolating from the gallery: whispers, scratching of pens on paper, scraping of shoes on the floor. Mac turned his head to look. He didn't want to make eye contact with anyone but could feel dozens of eyes bearing into his face as he rotated his head. He wanted to check one thing.

Jo left too.

"So, ladies and gentlemen, I ask you: is Makayla's identification just a faulty mistake? Or did she have a more sinister, ulterior motive to pick Eddie out for the cops as the mysterious gunman who shot Mr. Jefferson? Let's talk about that..."

CHAPTER 58

September 26, 2022
2:24 p.m.

Marcel walked back to the defense table and pointed to a thick, black oversized Magic Marker lying ominously against his notepad. Eddie picked up the marker, handed it to Marcel, and then turned to glance at Tamika, who was leaning forward against the seat in front of her, rubbing her hands together. Marcel walked across the courtroom and took the Christmas photo down from the easel, propping it upright against the wall so it could still be clearly seen. With his marker, Marcel drew an enormous question mark against the white paper pad: **?**

"Reasonable doubt," he said, pausing. He clicked the top shut on the marker and laid it down on the small, wooden groove on the easel.

"It is not a 'fanciful' doubt. It is not a 'whimsical' doubt," he said, using the exact words of the Maryland Common Jury

Instruction. "It is a doubt founded upon reason. Ladies and gentlemen, this case is riddled with flaws, mistakes, missing pieces and, well, how should I say this? It has a dark aspect to it—a corrupt aspect, something rotten—that needs to be questioned." He tapped with his finger on the huge question mark. He tapped 12 times. "There is a reasonable doubt for each of you jurors.

"*Buona sera.* It means good evening in the Italian language. And it was the name of a restaurant near to the location where this tragic event unfolded. *Buona sera.* Yes, it was a good evening for Makayla Schweitzer because she was given an opportunity to cash in on what had previously been a nightmare in her life. But once she got to the Italian restaurant, profit and monetary gains were on the tablecloth as much as fresh bread and olive oil.

"There were four people sitting around that table on that fateful night, ladies and gentlemen: Makayla, Officer Harper, Sergeant York, and—this is quite peculiar—the Assistant State's Attorney assigned to prosecute the Jefferson homicide. Each had a motive, and none of them was pure. Deceit, dishonesty, and corruption were present on that table as much as the linen tablecloth."

Marcel quickly turned back to the large question mark he had sketched on the big notepad propped up on the easel and began methodically tapping on the pad. Spinning back to face the jury, he explained, "Makayla's motives were several, but all of them selfish and without regard to the damage she would cause. Addiction is a terrible thing. Almost everyone these days has some experience—either personal experience or with family members or friends who have suffered battling the demons of substance abuse. Alcohol. Opioids. Even nicotine in cigarettes. All of these substances are addictive. But crack cocaine, ladies and gentlemen, is one of the most sinister, toxic poisons ever known to man. And we know from Makayla's own testimony that she was fiercely struggling like a junkie on the night of this shooting. Such an addiction is costly. It needs to be fed. It's an expensive habit. And Makayla, trapped in this horrible cycle, saw a way to cash in: all she had to do was say what the cops wanted. And what did the cops want? They wanted to close out a murder case. And who came to mind? Eddie Stephens. So all Makayla had to say was that Eddie was the man in the apartment who committed this murder. So, she said it. And then she got paid. And then she got high smoking crack.

"There were two police officers at the table. First, we have the ambitious, career-focused Officer Harper. They called him Harp. Well, 20 years later, we see that young Officer Harper has achieved great career advancement within the police department. That young, aggressive officer is now Chief of Police Harper. Cream always rises to the top, I guess."

Mac stood to object. "Your Honor, that last comment is sarcastic and is not a proper statement for closing argument."

"Sustained. Move on, Mr. St. Croix," Judge Ryan robotically said.

"Harp and Sergeant York wanted to do two things: a) close out the Jefferson homicide quickly with an arrest; and b) simultaneously target a young man who they believe had pulled a prank on them earlier that summer by allegedly throwing paint on their undercover, unmarked police cruiser. No one was ever charged with that misdemeanor vandalism, by the way. The officers suspected it was Eddie, but they probably also misidentified whoever did that, too."

Marcel walked back to the defense table, slid behind it, and stood directly behind Eddie. He placed both of his hands on Eddie's shoulders and said, "Ladies and gentlemen, don't let them get away with it. Eddie Stephens is 100 percent not guilty."

Marcel waited until he sensed the room focus on Eddie, who reached up and wiped his forehead with a paper towel. After a beat, Marcel walked around the table and stood back in the center of the courtroom.

"And I would be remiss if I didn't say something about Judge Daniel Bennington."

Mac shut his eyes. *Oh shit.*

Marcel lowered his voice. "I have great respect for the bench." He turned his head toward Judge Ryan and subtly dipped his head, as if bowing towards her. "Mr. MacIntyre and I are members of the Bar and, as attorneys, we have both taken an oath to be faithful to the laws and the Constitution of the State of Maryland."

Here it comes.

"But, Judge Bennington," Marcel again lowered his volume, "his actions on this night at the Buona Sera restaurant were disgraceful. I hesitate to say this, but it is my duty to zealously defend an innocent man. What then Assistant State's Attorney Bennington did was much more than lazy, or negligent or sloppy. He saw money exchange hands. He saw Makayla—the State's key eyewitness—accept cash money from the police! That's *obviously* wrong! And then he told no one? And then he did nothing about it? At the very least, it was clearly a dereliction of his duty as a prosecutor. I will leave it to others to decide if it was, in fact, a criminal conspiracy or deprivation of my client's civil rights. We, alas, are not here today to decide those issues, but, as Eddie's lawyer, I am *obligated* to point these things out to you."

The swirling of noise from the gallery was appreciably louder as Marcel finished speaking. Mac clearly heard a young voice say, "Wait, Judge Bennington did what?"

Marcel crossed back to the defense table and lifted a single sheet of paper. "Oh, well, I stand corrected: Judge Bennington actually *did* do something. He kept this note. Oh yes, he buried it inside hundreds of pages of evidence and documents. But this note, this one page, *recorded* the corrupt transaction with Makayla. It doesn't matter one iota if he wrote it himself. He saved it. What is most curious to me is the unorthodox use of the phrase 'work product' on this note. That is not normally an expression used by police officers. That is an attorney's voice. So, by not disclosing the contents of this single page, Bennington hoped that this secret meeting would never come to light. Ladies and gentlemen, this thin sheet of paper is all that you need to find Eddie Stephens not guilty."

There was another rumbling in the gallery, like the aftershock of an earthquake.

"Oh, yes. The handgun. I wanted to ask Mr. MacIntyre about that before I sat down." Marcel turned to look directly at Mac, who met his gaze placidly. Marcel turned back to the jury.

"Has there been *any* testimony directly tying Eddie Stephens to the crime scene? Certainly not the gun that we've heard that was seized from Eddie's residence. First of all, there are millions of similar handguns legitimately owned by citizens under the Second Amendment. Eddie's gun—which is not illegal to possess under Maryland law—has thus far not been shown to have any actual forensic link *whatsoever* to this case. Did you hear any ballistics expert testify that the exact same gun taken from Eddie's house matched the bullets at the crime scene? I didn't."

Marcel turned and glanced over his shoulder to speak to Mac. "Will Mr. MacIntyre say anything about this gun when he stands up to address you after I conclude speaking? I'm curious to see what he says. Of course, if he doesn't say anything at all about the gun, well..." His voice trailed off to silence.

After a few beats to let that challenge sink it, Marcel concluded with, "Therefore, ladies and gentlemen of the jury, we ask that you return with a verdict of not guilty. Thank you."

CHAPTER 59

September 26, 2022
6:17 p.m.

"She said she'd hold the jury until 8:00 tonight. That's the latest she will go before excusing them," said Marcel to Mac as they stood in the vast hallway outside Judge Ryan's courtroom. Tamika and Ophelia were the only people in the entire space, sitting on the sofa at the far end with a large takeout bag from Panera Bread. Ophelia was leaning back with her chin up, either asleep or resting, while Tamika was spreading napkins across the small table in front of them and arraying the cylindrical, wrapped sandwiches in front of them, like a picnic.

Marcel said, "Mac, would you like to have dinner at Avery Country Club? My treat. It's just down Seneca Pike two miles."

"Yes, I know where it is, Marcel, but I've actually never been inside there."

"Well, there's a first time for everything. C'mon, we

can get there and back easily before 8:00. What do you say, Counselor?"

Mac looked around and noted that Ophelia was now lying down across the sofa. Tamika was eating a sandwich and looking intently at her cell phone.

Marcel turned his head to let his gaze follow Mac's eyes down the hallway and then said, "Oh, they'll be alright. If anything happens with the jury, someone will call both of us. Let's go. I'm famished."

"OK," said Mac. "But first let me tell Judge Ryan's law clerk that we'll be stepping out of the courthouse and getting something to eat. She can call if anything crazy happens with the jury." He looked at his watch. "I'll be right back."

Mac stepped back into the empty courtroom and dropped his box of files on the prosecution table. He knocked on the door to Judge Ryan's chambers.

"Oh, hi, Mac!" said Kristen, who opened the door but did not step out. "Your closing was so good. I loved it."

"Thanks. Hey, Mr. St. Croix and I are going to grab some dinner down the road. We won't be far, so if Judge Ryan needs us, here's my cell number." He jotted the number down on a legal pad and ripped off the yellow page.

Kristen took it, folded it, and said, "Wait. You're going out to dinner with your opponent? Is that normal?"

"Yeah, of course. We fight hard and sometimes throw elbows around when we are litigating, but those are just the roles we play. It's not personal. Marcel and I are friends, actually."

"Oh. Weird. Well, I've got a lot to learn."

Mac turned to leave, smiled, and said, "Tell Judge Ryan we are not far away. Call me if you need us."

He left the courtroom hurriedly and stepped out into the hallway. Marcel was all the way down at the far end and had parked his rolling suitcase behind Tamika's chair. Mac ignored them and turned the corner to the bank of elevators.

Marcel said to Tamika, who still had her cell phone pressed against her ear, "I'll be back. I'm going to talk to Mr. MacIntyre about some legal issues we haven't sorted out yet." Getting no response from Tamika, he walked around the corner and gave a thumbs-up signal to Mac.

They got on the elevator and took it down to the public parking garage.

In minutes, Marcel's vintage, orange 1978 Datsun 240Z pulled up in front of Avery Country Club, where a valet came out and helped Marcel out of the driver's seat.

He was a young man with a long, black ponytail wearing a white outfit with a red vest over his shirt which had a nametag saying Norton. He tossed a cigarette into the bushes and said, "Good evening, Mr. St. Croix. Will you be needing your vehicle soon or should I park it in the far lot?"

"Thank you, Michael," said Marcel. "We will only be here about an hour, so if you could keep it right up here, I'd appreciate it." He handed the valet a $20 bill.

"Thank you, Mr. St. Croix. You betcha!"

Marcel guided Mac down an ornate hallway filled with framed mementos of prior golf tournaments and fundraisers and old black-and-white photos of long-since-dead prominent citizens of Seneca County. There were no women or Black men in the rows of head shots. As they got down the carpeted hallway, Marcel directed Mac into a large dining room, which was mostly filled with diners. They sat down, and a waiter came to the table and said, "Mr. St. Croix, good evening. The usual?"

"Yes, thank you, Aaron. I'll have cottage cheese—can you bring it with French dressing on the side?" Marcel asked. "And I'll also have a side order of sliced avocado. Just ice water with lemon, too. Thank you very much."

Mac said, "Can I order something from the lunch menu?"

"Certainly, sir."

"OK. I'll have a grilled cheese sandwich with French fries, please."

The waiter left. Marcel said, "So, Mac, I listened very closely to your rebuttal. You didn't say *anything*. I don't think I've ever heard a man speak for a solid hour and say absolutely nothing. I mean, the stuff you come up with: the Trojan Horse? What exactly does that have to do with Eddie Stephens?"

"I don't know, Marcel. It just popped into my mind."

"I always assumed the Trojan Horse was from the *Iliad* by Homer, but now I stand corrected."

"Yes, it's actually from the *Aeneid* by Virgil. Lots of people get that confused."

"Do you realize, Mac, how pedantic you can be sometimes? Always correcting people and talking about random things like Greek mythology and Shakespeare and pop culture trivia? I actually think it's quite entertaining, but, Mac, I listened hard to your closing argument and I think I know what you're doing."

"Well, Marcel, things just pop into my mind when I'm

speaking, and I can't really control that. But I've found—and this is something I'm sure *you* can relate to—giving a closing argument that keeps the jury interested is always a good idea. Don't want to bore them, right? And, keep this in mind: I'm obligated to do my duty as a prosecutor and present the best case on behalf of the State. That's what they pay me for."

The waiter soon returned with a tray and placed their dinners on the table.

Marcel spooned a small portion of lumpy, white cottage cheese into his mouth.

After a pause, Marcel remarked, "Well, they surely don't pay you enough. And that Ari Fischbein doesn't deserve to have an attorney of your caliber taking orders from an arrogant fool like him. I'm sure you could command a very high salary out on the open market. Excellent courtroom advocates like you, Mac, are much in demand. Especially around this Washington, D.C. area. Lots of criminals here, you know."

Mac put down his grilled cheese sandwich, forked some French fries, and dipped them into the ketchup. "Well, actually, I got a call from a guy downtown named Alonzo Randall-El. Ever heard of him, Marcel? He goes by Zo for short."

"Ah, Zo. Quite a character. He got a $20 million judgment last month, I heard." Marcel said, sipping from his ice water and looking directly at Mac. "Of course, he only gets 40 percent of that award with his standard civil suit contingency agreement. What's 40 percent of 20 million?"

Mac leaned back in his plush chair and turned to make eye contact with Marcel.

After a long pause, Mac said, "Well, after this cluster-fuck of a case, maybe I *should* try something else."

"You'd look very nice, Mac, in a 10,000-square-foot house on a four-acre lot down by the river. I'm sure Zo knows some nice lots near his place. Sure beats living all squished in with a cat in a tiny studio apartment."

"You know where I live?"

"Research, Mac. Research."

"I've done over 100 jury trials, Marcel. And, I mean, I've had my share of not-guilty verdicts before, but never in such an embarrassing way as this Stephens trial. Lady Justice would be offended by what happened in this case. She'd be not only blind, but, shall we say, she'd be double-blind?"

"Ah, well, I won't count my chickens before they're hatched. I've seen many a case where I thought my client was free and clear only to have the jury come back guilty. Seneca County juries almost always render a guilty verdict. And when an ASA as talented and articulate as the impressive Mac MacIntyre is center stage quoting from the *Aeneid* by Virgil and reciting lines from *King Lear*, I'd *expect* a guilty verdict, honestly."

"Your chickens are hatched, Marcel."

"Hold on, hold on. You know how they keep those juror feedback forms down in the Clerk's Office? You know they're open to the public, by statute, right?"

"I haven't looked at those for probably 18 years. Once a trial is done, it's time to move on to the next."

"But, Mac, we did some opposition investigation on you to prepare for this trial. My paralegal went down and read through your old juror evaluations. Not all of them, of course—there are too many! But just to get a flavor for how jurors relate to you. I remember one in particular. It said something like, 'I didn't know what Mr. MacIntyre was saying, but he seemed so sure of himself. I voted guilty just because he told me to."

Mac laughed. "Really? Well, I could use that juror right now! If we get a hung jury, that will give me an excuse to let this Stephens case slide. I'm telling you, Marcel, I'm not trying this case a second time."

"Well, I am telling you, these Seneca County juries find almost everyone guilty."

"I'd be shocked if that happened in this case."

"Especially defendants of color. I hate to say it, but it's true."

Mac looked at Marcel but didn't say anything in tacit agreement.

"Let me tell you about the Delpina case," said Marcel. "Ever hear about that one?"

"Yes, I think so. The guy who was charged with first-degree rape? The girl who actually cut herself with a knife and set him up?"

"There was more to it that just that, Mac. Much more."

Mac looked at his watch, and said, "Tell me what happened."

CHAPTER 60

September 26, 2022
7:17 p.m.

"Delpina was a kid at Seneca County Community College, just 19 years old. He met this girl at the bus stop. She was very pretty. Blonde, slender, young. Looked a lot like Carrie Underwood. A freshman. Well, they decided to go on a date. So the next Saturday evening, she went out with Delpina, and, after dinner, he asked her if she'd like to come up to his dorm room. She went. Willingly. Even enthusiastically, you could say. So, they got up to his room—he had a single room with no roommates. Well, you can imagine what came next."

"I can only imagine," said Mac.

"Yes, they moved very quickly. Ah, but that is the state of young people today. Not like in my day, Mac, when there was still courtship and rules of etiquette and manners and chivalry."

"What are those things? Just kidding. What happened?"

"They had sex. And it was our position at the trial that

it was completely consensual and voluntary and, well, that's that. A typical Saturday night college date, right?"

"I'm assuming something more than that happened."

"Yes. So, after they were done doing the wild deed, my client Delpina—being the gentleman that he was—offered to pay for an Uber for her to get home. So, together, they walked down the street from the dorm and found an ATM. There, Delpina took out some cash and gave her $40 to pay for the ride. She hugs him, gives him one last embrace and a kiss, gets into the Uber, and goes off on her way. Or so my client thinks."

Mac said, "Well, the ATM would have surveillance footage 24/7, so you could verify all of that if you subpoenaed the video, Marcel."

Marcel smiled. He placed his spoon down next to his plate.

"Mac, surely you can see that I wasn't born yesterday, son."

"Oh, so you got the video?"

"*Oui, Monsieur. C'est vrai.*"

"Did you show it to the State's Attorney pretrial?"

"Yes. It was that dope Ashley Nixon—you know, that giant prosecutor who never smiles and moves like a robot in court? You must know her. She's like six-foot-two and built like one of the Washington Redskins."

"Oh, her. Yes, not my favorite colleague. Terribly clique-y."

"Anyway, so the girl goes home in the Uber and Delpina goes to sleep. At about 5:00 the next morning, the police are banging on his door. He jumps up and asks what the hell is going on."

Mac was tapping his foot.

"The police say the girl's at Tomlinson General Hospital with superficial cuts on her arm. Saying she's been raped at knifepoint by my client!"

"But you have the ATM videotape showing they were all lovey-dovey *after* this supposed sexual assault, right?"

"That's correct, Counselor."

"Wait. You said she had cuts on her arm? And she told the ER docs, and I'm guessing the cops who responded to the hospital, that your guy cut her with a knife?"

"The cops searched the hell out of his dorm room and couldn't find a knife anywhere. They flipped over the mattress. They tore the place apart. Then they found a pair of scissors. A normal pair of scissors my client had in his desk drawer. So, later, they show them to the girl and she changes her story and says, 'Yes, that's what he held up to my neck. Scissors!'"

"Did they test the scissors for DNA? Was there any blood on them?"

"No. Clean. Well, of course *his* DNA is all over the scissors, but none of hers and not even a trace of blood."

"Ridiculous."

"So, we get the hospital report, the medical records. I'll never forget this: it says point blank right there in the records that she had 'active bleeding' from several cuts to her forearm. *Active* bleeding. Now, this is like five hours after she was supposedly cut."

"Cuts don't bleed that long," Mac responded. "I mean, not unless you hit an artery or a vein or something. Not superficial flesh wounds. That type of wound would coagulate in that period of time. Everyone knows that."

Marcel added, "So, that airhead Ashley says she won't drop the case. She says my client can plead guilty to a first-degree rape or it's a trial. I said the girl probably cut herself before walking into the ER. Then, I showed her the video from the ATM machine and she still wouldn't change her mind. Said she believed the girl. That the girl was credible. So, we went to trial."

"Well, I hope you kicked her ass."

"We *lost*. That's what I'm trying to tell you, Mac! These jurors find everyone guilty around here."

"Your client was found guilty? With that weak evidence? God have mercy. Who was the judge?"

"That old fat slob Barnette! Same racist moron Eddie had first time around. Always wore those pompous bow ties? The judge who hated Latinos and was all crazy about immigration and protecting the border and all of that right-wing nonsense."

"I hate to ask: what did Barnette give him?"

"Thirty years. Said he would've given him life if he hadn't had a clean record."

"Oh my God, really? That's terrible."

"So, please, don't tell me when to count my chickens. I've seen a lot of unbelievable verdicts around this county."

Mac's cell phone rang. He lifted it out of his suit pocket and saw UNKNOWN on the Caller ID.

"Mac MacIntyre here."

"We have a jury note," said Kristen. "Judge Ryan said to

call you and have you get back here as soon as you can. Can you tell Mr. St. Croix?"

"I'll let him know. We will both be back in fifteen minutes."

CHAPTER 61

September 26, 2022
7:44 p.m.

Kristen opened the door to Judge Ryan's courtroom and held it for Marcel and Mac to enter. Mac gestured to Marcel to enter first, and then he followed. As he waited for Marcel to walk down the aisle a few steps, he whispered to Kristen, "The jury has a note? What does it say?"

She glanced to see if Marcel was outside of hearing range and whispered back, "They're deadlocked."

Mac nodded but did not respond.

Great! A mistrial will work just as good as a not-guilty verdict. Anything other than a guilty verdict will do.

Kristen walked briskly across the well of the courtroom and opened the door to chambers, where Judge Ryan was standing just on the other side of the doorway. As Mac walked up to the prosecution table, Eddie was escorted out from the lockup area by two deputies. There was a creaking at the door to the hallway, and Tamika and Ophelia stood outside the double doors to the courtroom. Eddie turned his head at the sound of the door opening and tugged on Marcel's elbow. Marcel waved Tamika and Ophelia into the courtroom. There was no one else there at this time of the night.

Judge Ryan flipped open her laptop with her right hand and activated it, prompting a whirring sound. She clicked on the keyboard and said, "I understand, Ms. Voice, that we have a note from the jury. Is that correct?"

"Yes, Judge," Kristen replied, holding the folded note tightly. The paper quivered and shook in her hand as if it was windy inside the courtroom.

"Please hand it to the Court," Judge Ryan announced.

Judge Ryan stood up and reached over the edge of the bench to take the note, careful to use her right hand, which was further away than her left hand. She read the note to herself and said, "Let the record reflect that it is now 7:59 in the evening, and we are here on the case of State versus Edward Stephens. Counsel for Mr. Stephens, Mr. St. Croix, is present, as is the State's Attorney, Mr. MacIntyre. The jury is not present and is continuing to deliberate, but they have handed my clerk a note. Gentlemen, please be seated."

The room was silent.

Judge Ryan said, "I'm going to read the note into the record verbatim. It says, 'We are deadlocked and cannot come to a unanimous decision. What should we do now?'"

Tamika blurted out, "Lord have mercy! God is good." The deputy with the blond crew cut, Feeny, stood up and turned to face her, holding his finger up to his lips. Eddie turned, too.

Judge Ryan raised her voice and looked out into the gallery, "Ma'am, court is in session. I understand it's late, but we will have decorum inside my courtroom at all times. You will remain quiet. Do you understand?"

Tamika leaned back in her seat and waved her hand over her head, but did not respond.

Having quelled that outburst, Judge Ryan addressed Marcel and Mac. "Gentlemen, do you have anything you want to put on the record? Mr. MacIntyre, anything on behalf of the State?"

Mac stood and said, "No, Your Honor."

When he sat, Marcel rose and in a rambling, improvisational manner, replied, "Well, Judge, we would prefer a resolution to this matter while we have the opportunity to achieve finality. As we all know, a mistrial caused by a hung jury does not preclude the State from filing for a retrial, and I'm not sure any of us want that. So, with all due respect, I would ask that the Court give them the so-called *Allen* charge. For all we know, they are 11 to one to acquit. So, we are requesting that the Court instruct them..."

Judge Ryan interrupted, "Well, Mr. St. Croix, they could just as easily be stuck at 11 to one to *convict*. I'm not in the business of reading tea leaves, sir."

Mac didn't react and sat still.

"I will note for the record," Judge Ryan added, "the jury has only been deliberating since about, what? Approximately 4:30 this afternoon. So, that's less than four hours on a charge of first-degree murder. So, that is not an inordinate length of time." She paused and turned around to look at her stack of law books on the small shelf behind her seat. "I will give them the *Allen* charge. Let me see, that's..."

"Maryland Common Jury Instruction 2:01, judge," Mac said, still seated. "The *Allen* case, for reference, is captioned *Allen v. U.S.* It's an 1896 United States Supreme Court case."

"Thank you," said Judge Ryan without looking up as she flipped through her book of Common Jury Instructions. "OK, I've got it here. Ms. Voice, will you please get the jury?"

Mac stood, as he always did, for the jury to enter the courtroom. Marcel also rose slowly and motioned with an "up" gesture for Eddie to stand next to him. Kristen walked across the well of the courtroom and knocked loudly on the door. The buzzing sound quelled from the other side. She opened the door, poked her head inside, and said, "Come take your seats. The judge wants to talk to you."

One of the male jurors asked, "Should we take our stuff with us or leave it here?"

"You can leave it here. The judge just wants to instruct you further."

The jurors stepped out in single file, looking around the empty courtroom as they emerged from the Jury Room. They avoided eye contact with both Mac and Marcel and especially Eddie. After they settled in their assigned seats in the jury box, Judge Ryan said, "All of the jurors are present and accounted for and are now sitting in their respective seats. So, I have received your note, Mr. Foreman. I will read it into the record, 'We are deadlocked and cannot come to a unanimous decision. What should we do now?' Sir, am I reading the jury's note correctly?"

The young college student designated as the Foreman stood and said, "Yes, Judge, but we are very close to a decision now. There's only one guy who..."

Judge Ryan interjected swiftly, "Please! Sir, please do not give us any breakdown of the votes. That is not proper."

The young man stood frozen with his mouth open.

Judge Ryan quickly added, "Please sit down. Thank you."

The young man sat, his eyes wide.

"So, right now, ladies and gentlemen, this is what we will do: I am going to read you a jury instruction designed to address this situation. OK?" She lifted a small, green three-ring binder containing the Maryland Common Jury Instructions. There was a yellow sticky note marking a page. She flipped the pages over to that section and said, "The verdict must be the considered judgment of each of you. In order to reach a verdict, all of you must agree. In other words, your verdict must be unanimous. Each of you must decide the case for yourself, but do so only after consultation with your fellow jurors. Do not hesitate to reexamine your own views. You should change your opinion if convinced you are wrong, but do not surrender your honest opinion for the mere purpose of reaching a verdict."

The jurors looked back and forth. Several were staring at the man Mac had dubbed 'The Therapist,' who was furiously trying to jot down the judge's words. Noticing him, Judge Ryan said, "Don't worry about writing all of that. My law clerk, Ms. Voice, will make a copy of the Instruction and bring it back to you in the Jury Room."

The Therapist kept scribbling.

"Ladies and gentlemen," Judge Ryan added. "I note that it is now after 8:00 in the evening. This would be an appropriate moment to recess your deliberations. We will adjourn for the night and resume tomorrow morning at 9:00 a.m. promptly. Again, please do not discuss the merits of the case overnight, please do not do any independent research, and keep an open mind. Please collect your belongings, and Ms. Voice will distribute parking passes for the Jury Lot for tomorrow. Thank you."

The majority of the jurors walked back into the Jury Room to collect their jackets and personal items. Kristen had a basket containing their cell phones which she produced from behind her law clerk's desk, and each juror selected the appropriate phone as if they were choosing chocolates from a Valentine's Day box. The Therapist grabbed his phone and left quickly.

When all of the jurors had left, Judge Ryan said, "Gentlemen, please be here right at 9 tomorrow, OK? I have a feeling whoever was stuck will become unstuck overnight. We will likely have a unanimous verdict quickly tomorrow morning."

CHAPTER 62

September 27, 2022
12:15 a.m.

Mac rolled out of his bed, grabbed his phone, and stood up. He clicked autodial.

Andre's voice came through the speaker. "Man, it's after midnight. Got that damn insomnia thing again, bro? I've seen you struggle with that shit before. You can go a whole week without sleeping when you're in trial."

"Listen to me. Crazy shit going on in court."

"OK, chill. What's up?"

Mac walked across his small apartment in his underwear and stepped into the kitchen. He opened the refrigerator and took out a full gallon plastic jug of milk. He unscrewed the small red cap and chugged several gulps of cool, white liquid directly from the jug.

As he drank, he heard Andre say, "Mac? You still there?"

"Yeah. I'm here. Completely awake now. I'll never get

to sleep. So much is running through my mind. Judge Ryan recessed until tomorrow—well, I mean later today, actually. She sent the jury home around 8:00. They said they were deadlocked so she gave them the *Allen* charge."

"How does that shit work again? *Allen* charge? When I hear that expression *Allen* charge, all I can think of is Ray Allen of the Boston Celtics committing an offensive foul, y'know, a charge? You have your photographic memory, and I have my own ways to remember stuff. That's how we do it on West 127th."

"Mnemonic device. Clever. I like that."

"What'd you say?"

"Never mind. So, the judge gives the jury an *Allen* charge as a way to try to break a deadlock. To encourage the jury to compromise and find a way to agree. It's like a legal way to tell the jurors not to be stubborn. But usually it results in some charges being tossed and some sticking. Here, we only have one charge, so I don't think it's going to do any good. Actually, I don't think I've ever seen it work in a murder case like this one."

"Oh, OK," Andre replied. "So, what happens if they can't unanimously agree and it's a hung jury?"

"If they're hung, we have three options: drop the case, try it all over again, or look to work out a plea."

"Well, sounds to me like you only have *one* option: try that shit all over again. The Fish ain't letting you drop it, and Eddie Stephens ain't pleading guilty. Hey, man, let's be real: Makayla was a weak-ass witness. If you have to rack this case up all over again, she'll be even worse. And Frenchie will be even more ready to destroy her shit. So, it doesn't sound like a mistrial's going to be much help."

Mac walked back into his bedroom and sat on the edge of the bed. He said, "I know. But get this: the foreman of the jury let it slip out their vote was 11 to one."

"Did he say which way? I mean, 11 to one leaning toward guilty or toward not guilty?"

"He didn't say."

"So, maybe they're getting ready to *acquit* him. You never can tell with these damn jury trials. I gave up trying to guess a long time ago. Just when you think it's in the bag, it goes the other way."

"I know. Shit," Mac replied. "I'm ready to just fall on my sword and get this trial over with."

"What do you mean fall on your sword? What are you talking about?"

"It's an expression, Andre. It means to sacrifice yourself. It comes from the Roman way of committing suicide. If you were a general, for example, and you wanted to die with honor, you'd fall on your own sword and kill yourself. Brutus did that after he helped assassinate Julius Caesar. That's exactly how I feel about this Stephens case."

Mac leaned back on his pillow and stared at the ceiling.

Andre said, "I can't believe you went with Frenchie for dinner at the Avery Country Club. Aren't there some rules against lawyers doing that?"

"What? Fraternizing? There's nothing wrong with that. We attorneys don't hate each other. Just like you basketball players, we fight hard, might even hack each other really hard, but when the game's over, we don't hold grudges."

"Well, some of you don't. Some lawyers do. I once saw this lady lawyer—you know the one I mean—she's like six feet tall and real skinny. Got some German-sounding name like Gudrun or something. I saw her spit in the face of this other lawyer in the hallway once. It was crazy! She was yelling, 'Liar! Liar! Liar!' I thought the other man was going to deck her. I had to step in and break it up."

Mac acknowledged, "Yes. It happens. I once saw this juvenile defendant—you can't call them defendants in Juvenile Court. You have to call them respondents—I saw this big kid punch his own lawyer in the jaw really hard. Knocked him out cold. You have to watch your back at all times when you're in court."

"So, Mac, what was it like at that fancy country club? Obviously, I've never been inside that place."

"Why do you say obviously?"

"Mac! Are you kidding me? How many brothers did you see in there? I mean, dudes who weren't waiters or busboys? Ain't no Black people belong to that shit, man."

"It wasn't my type of place, trust me. I've never been there either, so we're even. Marcel had this scoop of cottage cheese with French dressing in a little, metal bowl, like the kind you serve ice cream in. It was disgusting."

"Don't tell me you ate that too?"

"Hell no. I had to order off the lunch menu. I had a basic grilled cheese sandwich and fries. It was really good, actually. Hey, Andre, Marcel told me this long story about a rape case he once did. Did you ever hear of a case where this chick said she was raped at knifepoint and then showed up at Tomlinson General with superficial slash marks on her arm that were still freshly bleeding? And she said she'd been cut six hours before?"

"No. That sounds highly suspect. They wouldn't be bleeding unless they were really deep wounds. Six hours later? Ah, I don't think so."

"Well, Marcel's whole point to the story was that his client was totally innocent, but the jury found him guilty anyway. He was trying to draw a parallel with this Eddie Stephens case. I mean, you'd have to be *blind* not to see how weak this case is."

"Blind as a bat, Dude."

"I know. I know. I told Marcel that this was the weakest case I've ever prosecuted and he picked up on the fact The Fish basically ordered me to do this trial. But Marcel was saying Eddie might be found guilty anyway. He said Seneca County juries find almost everyone guilty. He didn't come right out and say all Black people, but he hinted at it. And he has a point, I mean, he's been doing jury trials here for like 50 years. He should know."

"Yeah, he definitely has a point. And don't forget it's *you* who's the prosecutor."

"What do you mean?"

"It's *you*! The great Mac MacIntyre. You can make *any* jury come back guilty. You have that power of persuasion. They just do what you ask. I mean, did you *ask* the jury to find Eddie guilty?"

"Of course. I had to. I say that in every closing argument."

"Well, then. Don't be surprised if they do what you told 'em to do. That alone could get Eddie a guilty verdict. I'm telling you."

"Oh, man. I feel stuck. I don't know what to do. I might resign."

"What?! No fucking way."

"I've been thinking about that Alonzo Randall-El guy. Maybe it's time to leave the SAO. It would be nice to make a million bucks every year. I could win those civil trials easy. Much easier than a murder case. You only have to prove a civil case by a preponderance of the evidence."

"That's 51 percent, right?" said Andre.

"Yeah. Not like beyond a reasonable doubt. It's so much harder to win a criminal case. I would make so much money. I could afford to take you out for sushi every day, Andre."

"You'd really resign if this jury convicts Eddie? Wow. I wasn't expecting that."

"I swear, if this jury sends Eddie Stephens back to jail, I'm out. I don't want that on my conscience for the rest of my life. I can't do this anymore."

"Man, you need to think this through, Mac."

"I know. I'll be up all night. My brain is totally wide awake. Anyway, I have to write something now. Goodnight."

"Good luck with the verdict."

"Thanks."

"Goodnight, Mac."

Mac went to his desktop computer and pressed the power button. He searched in his drawer for a ream of stationery with letterhead he kept on hand.

CHAPTER 63

September 27, 2022
3:47 a.m.

State's Attorney's Office for Seneca County
18 Courthouse Square
Seneca, Maryland 20805

State's Attorney	Deputy State's Attorney
Ari F. Fischbein	Jo Newgrange

September 27, 2022

Dear Mr. Fischbein and Ms. Newgrange:

After careful consideration, I have decided to tender my resignation as a Senior Assistant State's Attorney.

Thank you for giving me the opportunity to serve the citizens of Seneca County for the last twenty years. It has been an enormously rewarding experience, and I will truly miss representing the State's Attorney's Office on your behalf and on behalf of the State of Maryland.

With my warmest personal regards,

_____

William T. "Mac" MacIntyre
Senior Assistant State's Attorney

CHAPTER 64

September 27, 2022
9:55 a.m.

Mac took out the letter from his inside jacket pocket and laid it flat on his office desk. As he was staring at it, his cell phone rang.

"Hey, Andre."

"So, did you hand in your resignation?"

"No. Not yet. I'll know soon. I have to go, Andre. I have to go upstairs now. The law clerk just called me. She said we have a verdict."

"What?!"

"Yes. The jury said they were finished after only a few minutes this morning. I was here waiting in my office. Barely had time for a bagel and coffee and then she called. Marcel is on the way over from his office right now. Once he gets to the courthouse, we will learn what they decided."

"Oh, Jesus. Good luck, Mac."

"Got to go."

"Remember, man. Whatever happens, you did your best."

"Well, that's absolutely not true. I did *not* do my best. But I know what you mean. Hopefully, Marcel pulled a Houdini."

"What do you mean?'

"Houdini was probably the most famous magician of all time. His real name was Erich Weiss, and he was born in Budapest in 1874. But he was also famous for being an incredible escape artist."

"Oh, right! The guy who escaped from a straitjacket while handcuffed and all that shit. Hey, I got some handcuffs, bro. Wanna try 'em?"

"Later. I've got to run."

Mac clicked off his cell phone and switched it to vibrate.

C'mon, Marcel, where are you? This waiting is torture.

Mac slipped on his jacket, picked up his case file, and walked down the hall to the elevators. He got off on the ninth floor and went inside Judge Ryan's courtroom. As he entered, he saw Kristen leaning against the door to the Jury Room with her ear pressed against it. She turned when Mac entered and said, "They started deliberating right at 9:00 and then knocked on the door, like, 15 minutes later and said they were done."

"You told the judge, right?"

"Yes," Kristen said. "She said to call you, and we're just waiting for Mr. St. Croix to arrive." She tilted her head towards the side door toward the lockup area and added, "She already called down, and the Defendant is waiting outside with the deputies."

"If you were on the jury, Kristen, which way would you vote?"

Kristen looked all around the empty courtroom and then said, "To be honest, not guilty. But—I don't know. I don't have much experience at this. I guess it could go either way. I mean, Mac, you were *really* persuasive, and that eyewitness Makayla was awfully confident and seemed absolutely sure he was the right guy. So..."

As Kristen left the courtroom through the door to chambers, Marcel bounded through the main doorway from the hallway with no sign of his usual labored, slow-motion movements. Tamika came in right behind him, with Ophelia Jackson Katz slowly trailing her. Tamika paused to hold the door open for Ophelia.

Marcel briskly strolled down the center aisle and said to Mac, "That was fast!"

"Which? The way you're walking, Marcel? Or the verdict?"

"Ha! Never too early for a quip, Mr. MacIntyre, I see."

There was a loud knock at the door to Judge Ryan's chambers, and Kristen pushed the door open while announcing, "All rise! Judge Roberta Ryan presiding. Court is now in session."

Judge Ryan entered, took three steps up to her chair behind the bench, and said, "Thank you. Please be seated. Deputy, please bring in the Defendant."

She opened up her laptop, and the familiar whirring sound swirled around the nearly empty courtroom. Mac stood still at his table, and Marcel turned to watch Eddie come through the side door from lockup. Marcel shook Eddie's hand and gestured for him to sit down at his place at the defense table. A gasping sound was audible from the back of the room where Tamika leaned with both of her elbows on the row of seats in front of her.

"Let the record reflect that both Counsel are present, as is the Defendant, Mr. Stephens. Ms. Voice, I understand we have a verdict," Judge Ryan flatly said.

"Yes," Kristen replied.

"You may bring the jury in. Thank you."

Kristen marched across the well of the courtroom and knocked on the door to the Jury Room. The faint buzzing of human voices and fragments of conversations halted immediately. She opened the door and said, "Please take your seats in the jury box, and the judge will have further instructions for you."

Kristen held the door open as the jury assembled and filed out sporadically in a chaotic scramble. They moved into the open space of the courtroom as if searching for fresh air, as if the oxygen in the small Jury Room was insufficient to accommodate all 12 of their lungs.

There was a cacophony of muffled coughs and the scraping of shoes on the carpet mixed with random innocuous exclamations—"excuse me" and "no problem"—as the jury reassembled in their proper seats.

Mac assessed each juror's face as they emerged from the Jury Room. Some jurors looked at him—one smiled—while most of them glanced at Eddie or Marcel as they walked across the well of the courtroom. When they had settled in the jury box, Judge Ryan announced, "Ladies and gentlemen of the jury, I understand that you have reached a verdict. Mr. Foreman, is that correct?"

The Foreman, who occupied the first chair, stood and brushed wisps of his long brown hair from his eyes. He was holding a sheet of paper with two trembling hands.

"Yes, Your Honor, we have."

Judge Ryan replied, "Who shall speak for you?"

After an awkward momentary pause to digest the archaic language mandated by the Maryland Common Jury Instructions, several members of the jury said, in unison, "Our Foreman."

Judge Ryan continued with the prescribed colloquy, "Mr. Foreman, as to the first count, Count One, murder in the first degree, what is your verdict, guilty or not guilty?"

The Foreman's hands were vibrating as if electrified.

He looked at the verdict sheet and said, "Not guilty."

Eddie bowed his head and began to mumble, "Thank you, God. Thank you, Jesus."

Tamika was wailing and attempting to suppress her voice with both palms. She leaned her head on Ophelia's shoulder.

Marcel smiled and patted Eddie on his back.

Kristen covered her mouth.

Mac leaned back and smiled slightly.

Judge Ryan said, "OK. And is the Foreman's verdict the verdict of you all?"

The jurors, aliens to this ritualistic process, nodded in agreement. Assorted fragmentary responses of "Yes, Your Honor" and "Correct" drifted from the jury box.

"Thank you," Judge Ryan stated. "That concludes your

jury service. On behalf of the citizens of Seneca County, we appreciate your dedication to the task at hand. It is a privilege and an honor to serve in the capacity as a juror, and, on behalf of all of us, I extend my most sincere gratitude. Thank you."

Unsure what to do next, the jurors looked around the courtroom.

"My law clerk, Ms. Voice, will assist you from here. She will instruct you further. Please collect your personal items and your cell phones and report down to the third floor to the Jury Commissioner. I believe you are fully entitled to the *per diem* and the modest lunch allowance even though it is not even 10:00." She checked the time in the corner of her laptop's screen.

When the jurors had all filed out—two of them stopped to say something to Tamika as they walked down the main aisle past her—Judge Ryan said, "Gentlemen, thank you very much. I believe that concludes this matter. Mr. Stephens, it will be necessary for you to do some processing—Deputy, that's done downstairs in the Sheriff's Office, right?"

"Yes, Your Honor," Deputy Feeny said. "He has some paperwork to do, but then we will release him from the basement holding area once that's completed."

Judge Ryan turned to Marcel and said, "Well, Mr. St. Croix, another excellent job. Mr. Stephens will be released shortly down on the 'T' Level. Counselor, is there anything you'd like to put on the record at this point in time?"

"No, thank you, Judge Ryan," Marcel softly said. "It has been my pleasure to appear before you this week. Thank you kindly for all of the grace that you have extended to myself,

Mr. Stephens, and to his mother. Thank you very much, Your Honor."

Jesus, Marcel. You had to thank her three times?

"Mr. MacIntyre? Anything further on behalf of the State?"

Mac rose and said, "No, thank you, Judge."

"Very well," Judge Ryan concluded. "Court will stand in recess."

She marched out of the courtroom into her chambers, with Kristen trailing. Before the door shut, Kristen turned to look back at Mac.

Mac smiled.

Kristen walked through the doorway and closed the door behind her. Marcel stepped over to Mac, shook his hand, and said, "Well done, Counselor. That was the most effective closing argument I have ever heard." He grasped Mac's arm tightly with both hands. He leaned close to Mac's ear and said, "The prosecutor's job is not to win every case, but to achieve justice. You are a good man, Mac MacIntyre."

Mac picked up his papers, left the courtroom, and turned in the other direction from the elevators. He went into the men's room, looked at himself in the full-length mirror mounted on the wall, and then entered the larger, handicapped bathroom stall. He reached into his breast pocket and pulled out the resignation letter he had written earlier that morning. He tore it into quadrants, eighths, and sixteenths. He kept tearing until the paper was reduced to confetti, and then he methodically dumped all of it into the toilet and flushed it.

CHAPTER 65

September 27, 2002
11:32 a.m.

"The press wants a statement. What the fuck am I going to say?!" Ari Fischbein shouted across his office. "The whole atrium downstairs is going to be filled with reporters for the noon news shows. That asshole Don Morris from the *Journal* said this office hasn't lost a first-degree murder case in like 25 years, and you have to do this to *me*, Mac!"

"Sorry, Boss. I gave it my best shot."

Jo Newgrange was sitting at the conference table scrolling through her phone. She said, "Ari, you should see the texts I'm getting. This is a disaster."

The Fish was red in the face and turned to look in the mirror attached to the inside of his door. He furiously adjusted his thinning, straw-like, blond hair across the top of his shiny scalp. Without turning back to face Mac and Jo, he asked, "What am I going to say? It's not *my* fault."

"Blame it on that witness," Jo offered. "That recovering addict. What's her name again, Mac?"

"Makayla. Makayla Schweitzer O'Reilly."

Jo asserted, "Ari, just say she was a terrible witness—no, don't say that. Say she was—say her memory faded over time. And you could add that she has personal problems. Everyone will know what that means. And that sounds completely plausible. Just say we, as an office, are obligated to do the best we can in old cases despite the flaws of a witness's memory. Blame her, but don't do it in an obvious way."

The Fish turned back and said, "What about Judge Bennington? What do I say about him? We're going to need him for future cases."

Mac looked down at the conference table.

Jo said, "Say we have the highest respect for the Seneca County Circuit Court bench and stand by all of our well-qualified judges. Then, if they bring up anything about what Bennington did when he was a prosecutor here, just say that was well before our administration assumed power—no, don't say power, say since our administration revised how things are now done. That should give us complete deniability."

"OK. Good. I like that," The Fish responded. "Things are done differently now. Not like in the old days. Yes, I like the sound of that. I'll just make a short statement and I won't take any questions. This should simmer down fast."

Mac asked, "Ari, do you want me to come downstairs, too?"

"No. You stay up here. Jo and I will handle this. You've

caused enough problems for now. If anyone from the media calls you, direct all calls to me. Got that?"

"Understood."

"C'mon, Jo, let's go."

The Fish and Jo marched down the hall toward the elevators.

As Mac walked back to his office, he stopped at the front desk.

"Hey, Lupe. Can you please mark me 'out' for the rest of the day?"

Lupe stopped chewing her gum and asked, "Are you feeling OK, Mac? You don't look so good."

Mac said, "I just had a meeting with The Fish and Jo Newgrange. I think I'm about to vomit."

He went to his office, went inside, and closed the door. He grabbed his suit jacket from the hook behind his door and patted his pockets to check that he had his wallet, keys, and cell phone. He left. After taking the elevator down to the basement garage, he climbed into his yellow Jeep and drove home to catch the news on the noon telecast.

CHAPTER 66

September 27, 2022
11:58 p.m.

Mac's cell phone rang. Uncharacteristically, he had fallen asleep at 4:00 in the afternoon. He had been exhausted for days.

Who the hell is calling me at midnight?

He glanced at the Caller ID. It said UNKNOWN.

Oh my God, not this fucking stalker again.

He clicked his phone and said, "Who is this? Why are you calling me so late?!"

"Mr. MacIntyre?"

Mac recognized the voice but couldn't identify it immediately. Shaking his head, he sat up, placed his feet on the floor beside his bed, and looked at Iago, who was curled up, unmoving, like a circular pillow, at the foot of the bed.

Iago, are you dead or alive?

Mac blinked his eyes and asked, "Who is this?" His mind

was now fully alert, like a car engine after a key had been flipped to start the ignition.

"It's me. Eddie. Eddie Stephens."

Mac stood and walked into the kitchen without responding. He opened a carton of orange juice, folded the waxy opening into a triangular spout, and took a long swig directly from the carton.

"Mr. MacIntyre? Are you still there?"

"Yes. Is everything all right?"

"Oh, yeah, man, couldn't be better, Mr. MacIntyre."

"Please. Just call me Mac. Can I call you Eddie?"

"Of course! Hey, the reason why I'm calling is... I was just wondering if you were free to meet for a cup of coffee or something tomorrow morning. It's the least I can do for you, buy you a cup of coffee."

"Well," Mac responded, "I'm free. And *you're* free too, Eddie. Congratulations."

"I'll meet you at the Starbucks across from the courthouse at 8:00 a.m. OK?"

"Do you mind if I ask my lead detective, Andre Okoye, to join us? That's probably a good idea."

"No problem. That's cool."

Andre waved from the back corner of Starbucks. Mac walked across the coffee shop and pulled out a chair from the table. It was a typical weekday morning downtown. The room was filled with local people with newspapers spread out across sticky tables, glowing laptops open and muted smooth jazz music softly wafting through the air.

"Got you a Grande with extra half-and-half. How many of those Splendas you take again? Five?"

"Six," Mac said. "Have you seen him?"

Before Andre could answer, Eddie stepped through the doorway at the front of the coffee shop. He immediately noticed Mac and Andre sitting in the back corner. Andre waved at him with a come-here gesture.

Eddie smiled, walked back, and said, "Do you mind if I sit against the wall instead of in this chair?"

Mac said, "Sure. Why?"

"Oh, just something you learn over the years at Broad Run. Never sit with your back facing outward. You never know what's sneaking up behind you." Eddie squeezed into the small booth-like space, flattening his back against the thick upholstery. He was wearing new slacks, a blue polo shirt, and all-white sneakers.

"Man, it's very strange being out—y'know, it's been a long, long time since I did simple stuff like this. Just going to a Starbucks. Man, that's a hell of a nice thing. You miss the simple things more than the big things, I'm telling you. But there's a lot of new stuff I gotta learn," Eddie said.

Andre asked, "Can I get you a coffee or something else, Eddie?"

"Coffee. Black. Nothing in it. Thanks, Detective."

"Cool," Andre said, as he walked away toward the counter.

Eddie said, "All these technological things are totally new to me, Mac. Never used an iPhone before. Earbuds.

Google. Home deliveries from Amazon. All this shit is new. But I like it!"

Mac smiled and said, "Well, not all of those things are necessarily improvements. When I was a kid, we actually played outside and talked to people face-to-face. Nowadays, kids are addicted to their phones and videogames and don't really have real conversations with people. They just text."

Eddie laughed and turned to see Andre's progress on the line to order.

"Mac, I wanted to talk to you alone," Eddie said. "But I get it. You need a witness. I totally understand, and I'm OK with that."

Eddie glanced down toward Andre again.

"Sure," said Mac. "It's OK."

"I just wanted to tell you, man-to-man, face-to-face, like you just said—have a real conversation. No bullshit texting. So, Mr. MacIntyre, I just wanted to say thanks. I know you're not to blame for all the shit that happened a long time ago in this case. Those police officers. Makayla. Even that Judge Bennington. Not your fault what they did."

Mac picked up his coffee and sipped it.

Eddie continued. "Marcel did a great job in court. I saw that, and I truly appreciate what he's done for me. But I also realize what *you* did for me. I know what you did. So, thank you, man."

Eddie reached out across the table and offered his hand. Mac grasped it tightly, looked in his eyes, and said, "You're very welcome."

Andre came by with a large cardboard cup of coffee and

three chocolate chip cookies. He placed the coffee in front of Eddie and dropped the cookies in the middle of the table. Andre said, "These are great!"

The three of them talked spiritedly for 30 minutes—what life was like inside Broad Run, the new job Ophelia Jackson Katz had lined up for Eddie at the Lowe's hardware store at the mall, Andre's Nigerian roots, the NBA season and Mac's loyal cat Iago.

They did not discuss the trial.

CHAPTER 67

September 28, 2022
9:35 a.m.

Mac got off the elevator and walked past the front desk of the State's Attorney's Office.

"Hey, Lupe, *que pasa?*"

"Mac! Hey, sorry about your verdict. I saw it in the *Journal* they said not guilty. You'll get 'em next time."

"Can't win them all. All I can do is try my best and then it's up to the jury, right?"

"Well, shake it off. What is that saying? If you fall off a bicycle, just get back on?"

"Something like that. Thanks, Lupe. I appreciate it. But I'm good."

Mac walked down toward his corner office and noticed a sky-blue folder lying outside his door. He picked it up.

Give me a break. A new case? Does this ever end?

He opened his door, went inside, and sat down at his

desk. Opening the file, he could only scan the first page before looking up. He didn't have the energy to start reading the Statement of Charges, but, feeling as if he was stuck in quicksand, he felt his mind sinking back down to the file. He looked at the first page as a whole unit without reading any individual words and then immediately recoiled. After a moment, he glanced down at the page, and several disconnected, random phrases jumped up and stuck in his mind like bugs splattered on a windshield.

Diffuse axonal injury, Children's Medical Center, inflicted head trauma, both parents deny allegations, autopsy reveals healed rib fractures and bruising, Preliminary Hearing set for December 1st.

Mac leaned back and closed his eyes.

His desk phone rang. The Caller ID said BLOCKED.

He lifted the receiver, placed it against his ear. There was no response, but Mac could hear the familiar faint breathing, almost a gasping sound. He said, "Hey, whoever the hell this is, can you please stop harassing me with these anonymous calls? You won the case, OK? Eddie's free. No need to bother me anymore! It's really annoying."

He heard the breathing accelerate.

Mac said, "I can tell you're still there, whoever you are. What the hell do you want?"

Kristen said, "I don't know how to tell you this, Mac—I know this is crazy! But... but... I think I'm in love with you."

Mac's mind went completely blank, and he did not reply.

APPENDIX I

STATEMENT OF PROBABLE CAUSE

On July 5, 2002, the applicant began an investigation involving Victim J'Mal Jefferson (Date of Birth August 4, 1977), a 23-year-old African American male. The Victim was found deceased from gunshot wounds to the head at location: 175 Rotterdam Street, Apartment 503, in Seneca County, Maryland.

At approximately 0230, a call for service was received by SCPD. At that time, members of the SAT/VU team were working undercover in the area. A 911 call alerted the undersigned I/O and his supervisor, Sgt. Rick York, of a shooting at the above-referenced address. The I/O and Sgt. York responded to the address at 0233. Calls were placed for EMS and backup patrol uniformed units who responded and arrived by 0245.

The individual who called 911 was subject Makayla Caitlyn Schweitzer, a 20-year-old Caucasian female (Date of birth, June 18, 1982). Schweitzer was known to the I/O and SAT/VU officers due to prior encounters along Rotterdam Street. Schweitzer has priors for Trespassing, CDS Possession, CDS Possession With Intent to Distribute, Solicitation of Prostitution, and Theft-Misdemeanor.

The I/O and Sgt. York were the first responders to the scene and secured the apartment. It should be noted that the front door was unlocked and swinging open when the I/O arrived. The scene was cleared to ensure there were no individuals inside the apartment. Multiple EMS units and backup SCPD units arrived at the scene but did not take action at life-saving measures as it was obvious the Victim was deceased. Photographs were taken of the scene, and Crime Scene Technicians were called to respond. Car #1 (Lt. Daalder) was notified. Also, per Department protocol, the SAO was paged, and the I/O spoke with Assistant State's Attorney Daniel Bennington who also responded to the scene.

There was a superficial bullet wound to the Victim's scalp which did not appear to be fatal. However, there was a second bullet wound making entry directly into the center of the Victim's face, just below his eye, which entered and exited the Victim's head. There was a large exit wound approximately the size of a fist in the rear of the Victim's head. The body was positioned on top of a broken glass table, face-down and turned to the side, as if he had been shot and had fallen on top of it. There were multiple pieces of shattered glass beneath the deceased's body. A search of the apartment revealed nothing of evidentiary value; there was no CDS in the apartment. A search of the deceased's pockets revealed a roll of U.S. currency in various denominations: thirteen (13) one hundred dollar bills ($1,300), two (2) fifty dollar bills ($100), six twenty dollar bills ($120) and four ten dollar bills ($40) for a total of $1,560.

An interview with Witness Schweitzer was conducted inside Sgt. York's department vehicle. Witness Schweitzer relayed the following narrative:

I went to J'Mal's apartment with this light-skinned Black guy I met on the street who asked me where he could score some rocks. I knew J'Mal from previous occasions when I took him customers before. This guy on the street called himself "Eddie" or "Freddy" or "E-Z" or something like that. He wanted a bag of crack. He said he would give me a small rock in exchange for hooking him up. I took him up the stairs to the apartment. It's on the second floor, like on this landing thing. J'Mal looked through the peephole and saw it was me. He opened the door and let us in. The guy said he wanted to buy $200 worth of rocks and showed us a bunch of money in a wad. J'Mal invited us into the apartment, and then he shut the door. He went into the back room, and me and this Eddie guy stood in the main room. J'Mal came back with a big bag of rocks. But, instead of buying the crack, the guy took out a small silver handgun and shot J'Mal twice in the head. One shot hit him right in the face. I saw that and then turned away for safety. J'Mal crashed into the table. Then, the guy stole J'Mal's supply of crack and dashed out of the apartment, down the stairs to the street and ran away. I had never seen this guy "Eddie" or "Freddy" guy before all this happened.

He was a young man around 18 years old with long dreadlocks, or plaits, or cornrows in his hair. He was skinny and, like I said, very light-skinned, mixed-race looking. I went down to the street where two officers met me and let me sit in their car where I gave this statement. No one coerced or forced me to give this statement and I do so voluntarily of my own volition. That's all I can remember.

The I/O immediately recognized the description of the assailant as EDWARD DELAWRENCE STEPHENS, an African American male with a light complexion and long dreadlocks who is a regular on Rotterdam Street and well-known to the I/O for a previous vandalism case involving damage to the I/O's cruiser. STEPHENS uses the nickname on the street "Eddie."

A search warrant application was filed with Judge Herrmann of the Seneca County Circuit Court for STEPHENS'S mother's residence where STEPHENS is known to reside. On July 6, 2002, contact was made with Ms. Tamika Stephens at 20257 Collegiate Way, a small single-family dwelling. Tamika Stephens became belligerent at the scene and refused entry. Forced entry was made by multiple SCPD personnel, and Tamika Stephens was placed under temporary custody in handcuffs for officer safety. She was positioned on the kitchen floor during the search.

A sweep of the house was conducted by P.O. 3 Billy Bob Wagaman and his K-9 partner, Kimba, with negative results. While searching the basement area, a small-caliber .22 handgun was recovered inside a Reebok basketball sneaker, inside a shoebox, under the sofa. The sofa was a foldout type used as a bed. Mail, with the name of STEPHENS, was found on a table next to the bed, and numerous additional clothing and other personal items belonging to STEPHENS were recovered throughout the basement area, indicating he lived there. The handgun was silver in color, matching the description given by the eyewitness at the scene of the shooting. Fingerprints taken from STEPHENS during processing subsequent to arrest matched fingerprints taken from the handle/grip of the handgun seized from the shoebox.

On July 6, 2002, a photo array was conducted by the I/O and Sgt. York with the eyewitness, Makayla Schweitzer. After reviewing the six (6) Polaroid photographs/mug shots containing one (1) photo of EDWARD DELAWRENCE STEPHENS and five (5) similar light-skinned African American males with dreadlock hairstyles, the eyewitness Makayla Schweitzer positively identified STEPHENS as the shooter in the above-referenced narrative. Upon seeing the photo of STEPHENS, Schweitzer said, "That's him! He's the guy who shot J'Mal. I'm 100 percent positive. I'll never forget his face."

Based on the foregoing information, an arrest warrant was issued for EDWARD DELAWRENCE STEPHENS, who was apprehended on July 7, 2002 two blocks from the murder scene inside Broadway New York Pizzeria on 38 Rotterdam Street. After briefly resisting arrest, STEPHENS was subdued and placed into custody. At the time of the arrest, STEPHENS exclaimed, "What the fuck are you doing? I don't know nothing about any shooting." STEPHENS was treated at the scene for minor injuries sustained resisting arrest. It should be noted that at the time of arrest, STEPHENS had cut his dreadlocks off in an attempt to avoid detection, identification, and apprehension.

Based on the above factors and circumstances, and subject to review by the SAO, the applicant is requesting EDWARD DELAWRENCE STEPHENS be charged with the following criminal offenses:

1) Murder in the First Degree

2) Murder in the Second Degree

3) Armed Robbery

4) Use of Firearm in the Commission of a Felony

5) Possession CDS: Cocaine.

APPENDIX II – GLOSSARY OF TERMS

A Fait Acompli – A thing that has already happened or has been decided.

ACL – Anterior cruciate ligament, one of the key ligaments that helps to stabilize the knee joint.

AO – Assignment Office, the authority for scheduling cases and trial in the Seneca County Courthouse.

Appellee – The party against whom an appeal is filed who must respond to and defend a legal appeal.

ASAs – Assistant State's Attorneys, the prosecutors who charge cases and prosecute them inside the courtroom.

Brady Material – Evidence the prosecutor is required to disclose to the defense, especially any evidence favorable to the Defendant. From the 1963 United State Supreme Court decision in *Brady v. Maryland*.

Batson v. Kentucky – A 1986 landmark decision by the United States Supreme Court ruling that a prosecutor's use of peremptory challenges must not be used to exclude by race.

Brown v. Board of Education – A 1954 United States Supreme Court decision establishing that segregation in public schools is unconstitutional.

Corum Nobis – A legal order allowing a court to correct its original judgment upon discover of fundamental error.

CDS – Controlled dangerous substance, what illegal drugs are called by the police, prosecutors, and litigants in criminal cases.

Charles Manson – An American criminal and cult leader who led the Manson "family" in the late 1960s; members of the cult committed a series of brutal murders resulting in a sensational trial.

Change of Venue – A legal challenge to the jurisdiction of a case seeking to move the trial to a new location to avoid publicity in order to provide a fair and impartial jury.

Code 3 – Seneca County Police Department code for an African American citizen.

Drug Rip – "Rip" as in rip-off; a crime where a robber poses as a drug buyer in order to steal drugs from a dealer.

Ellis Island – A Federally owned island in New York Harbor that was once the busiest processing station in the U.S. for immigrants, with nearly 12 million arriving from 1892 to 1954.

Ex Post Facto – A law that retroactively changes legal consequences for actions that were previously committed

In Camera Review – Latin for "in a chamber," a legal term describing when a judge alone reviews evidence and decides what action to take.

Interstate Witness Agreement – A legal process whereby prosecutors in one state subpoena a witness currently living in another state outside the jurisdiction.

Jack the Ripper – An infamous serial killer who, in the Whitechapel district of 1888 London, killed a series of prostitutes. He was never identified or held accountable for his crimes.

Judicial Nominations Commission – Also known as the "JNC," a group of attorneys who interview and recommend judicial candidates to the Governor of Maryland to select a new judge.

Julliard – A prestigious private performing arts conservatory in New York City founded in 1905.

Lindbergh Kidnapping – An infamous 1932 American crime involving the kidnapping and murder of aviator Charles Lindbergh's infant son.

Loving v. Virginia – A 1967 United States Supreme Court decision ruling that laws banning interracial marriage were unconstitutional.

MJOA – Motion for Judgment of Acquittal, also known as a directed verdict, a legal procedure whereby a judge decides that the State has not met its burden of proof and dismisses the case before the jury deliberates.

Mag – Abbreviation for magnetometer, a device used by security officials at the courthouse doors to detect metal or weapons.

Med Mal – Abbreviation for medical malpractice civil lawsuits.

Motion in *Limine* – A Motion heard by the court before the opening statements, usually requested under emergency conditions.

Nolle Prosequi/Nolle/Nol Pros – Latin for "not prosecuted," terms used interchangeably to describe when a prosecutor elects not to proceed with a criminal case.

P/I firm – Personal injury law firm.

Pansexual – Sexual, romantic, or emotional attraction towards people of all genders.

Peremptory Challenges – In jury selection, the process whereby attorneys reject potential jurors with each side having a number of challenges based on the type of case and whether representing the state or a criminal defendant.

Plantar Fasciitis – A disorder of the connective tissue in the arch of the foot, often resulting in pain in the heel and sole of the foot.

Polysexual – Sexual attraction to different kinds of genders and sexual orientations, often used synonymously with the term bisexual.

Pro Se – Latin for "one's own behalf," a legal term when a litigant chooses to represent themselves in court.

Robert E. Lee – A Confederate general during the American Civil War.

Rosenbergs – Julius and Edith Rosenberg, an American married couple who were convicted of spying for the Soviet Union in 1951, subsequently executed in the electric chair in 1953.

SAO – State's Attorney's Office, the organization in Seneca County authorized to charge and prosecute crimes.

Sapiosexual – A term to describe sexual attraction to the high intelligence of another.

Scottsboro Boys – An infamous 1931 American criminal case involving the false accusations of rape by two white women against nine African American young men.

SOC – Statement of Charges, the document whereby investigating police officers record their investigation's findings, leading to an indictment by the State's Attorney's Office.

Ted Bundy – An infamous American serial killer who kidnapped, raped, and murdered dozens of young women during the 1970s.

U/C – An abbreviation for "undercover."

Vehicle Forfeiture – A legal process whereby the police seize a motor vehicle from a suspected criminal as an asset derived from illegal drug profits.

Venire – A legal term given to the entire jury pool from whom jurors are selected to serve on the jury.

Voir dire – A legal term derived from French, meaning "to speak the truth," to describe the process of asking potential jurors a series of questions to determine neutrality and fitness to serve as a juror in a criminal case.

0100 – Seneca County Police Department code to describe a homicide.

APPENDIX III – A PREVIEW OF GAVEL TO GAVEL

CHAPTER 1

Thursday, December 20, 2018
8:22 a.m.

Mac sat in his office, appraising the tall stack of thick homicide case files piled up on his desk. Each one a tragedy. These were the most difficult jury trials to prepare. A baby shaken to death. A patient smothered in a nursing home. A hit man who killed for cash. Evil came in many forms to Senior Assistant State's Attorney Mac MacIntyre.

The worst cases haunted him and stuck in his mind like barnacles encrusted on a ship. He'd see these victims in sweaty dreams before sunrise. An angelic teenager named Violet visited regularly. Just 14 years old, she was strangled by a jealous schoolboy. She appeared at daybreak, ghostlike, her long, cascading blonde hair swishing across Mac's mind.

He glanced at his cell phone: the text alarmed him.

TUF CASE COMING IN. BRINGING LITTLE GRIL DOWN TO UR OFC NOW. SHE SAW 0100 OF DAD. EYE WITN. B THERE 10 MINS. SERIOUS SHIT.

In all the years they had worked together at the Seneca County Judicial Center, ever since Andre Okoye was an undercover cop and Mac a rookie prosecutor, Mac had never received a message with such urgency. "Tough case coming in?" he said out loud to his empty office. The sound of his own voice jolted him back to reality. 0100 was code for a murder. *A little girl saw her father killed? Concentrate. Focus.* That was one of Mac's great strengths. When necessary, he could fuse all of his brainpower together to solve the puzzle or crisis looming in front of him. Before he stood to address a jury or a judge, he would write the word "FOCUS" at the top of his legal pad. It was the best advice he could give himself, better than anything he had learned in law school. Five block letters printed in red with a plastic felt-tipped pen.

His phone pinged. The second text notified him:

CMING UP ELVTOR WITH KID. RESERVE CONFRNCE RM NOW.

GAVEL TO GAVEL: CHAPTER 1

He felt a dull pain throb in his stomach. *Not that again. Not right now.* He refused to Google "ulcer," although the instinct to do so raced through his mind.

The bright December sunlight poured through the large picture window and lit up his office. His eyes fell on a framed crayon drawing over his desk. Asymmetrical rows of square and rectangular frames displaying artwork, diplomas, various awards and newspaper articles dotted the walls: a visual roadmap of Mac's career. But the small frame directly over his desk was different, and his gaze reflexively returned to it time and time again; it gave him daily inspiration, like a talisman. It was a child's hand-drawn stick figure with a headline of scribbled words in a variety of bright crayon colors: some red, some blue, some green, in alternating serendipity. It read:

"TO THE STAIT'S ATTOURNY MAC. YOU ARE VERY NICE AND THANK YOU FOR HEPLING MY GRAMMA. LOVE MADISON."

The stick figure was the tiny girl's portrait of Mac. Even 10 years later, it was, essentially, an accurate rendering, portraying Mac as tall and thin, with a mop of bright red hair. His eyes were depicted as large crayon spirals in light green, the hue of traffic lights signaling "go."

A small flashing light on his desk phone blinked, signifying a call from the front desk. He lifted the receiver.

"Mr. MacIntyre, Detective Okoye is here to see you. He's got a little girl with him."

"Thanks, Lupe. *¿Carino que onda?* Send Andre down to

the conference room. And can you please mark me *out* on the board for the next hour?"

"*Todo bien. ¿Y tu guapo?*" Lupe replied.

Mac smiled. She called him handsome every day. He never got tired of it.

"I'm good, *preciosa*," he said, knowing how infrequent compliments were around the office.

Lupe brightened at his response; then she whispered, "Hey, Mac. I gotta tell you, Fischbein's in the office already. He asked me if you were here, like he was checking up on you."

"Thanks for letting me know. Hey, keep this between us, Lupe, but The Fish is a real *pendejo*."

"Right! He got elected, like, what? Has it even been a year yet? And, so far, he hasn't bothered to learn my name, just walks right by the reception desk. Says nothing. Pretty rude for a new State's Attorney. You'd think he'd want to be nice, especially to the support staff. I called him Mr. Fish-bean by accident when he first got here, and he stopped and corrected me. He said, 'My name is Fish-byne!' He's been real mean to me ever since."

Mac looked to confirm that his door was shut and added, "Yeah, my new boss. The Fish. As I said, this guy is a born asshole."

"Maybe he's like that because he's so short? What do they call that? A Neapolitan complex or something?"

"Napoleonic."

"What?"

"Lupe, what exactly did he say? Can you remember his exact words?"

"Mr. Fischbein asked, 'Is MacIntyre here!?' Kind of angry-like. That's it. He never says please or thank you. Just letting you know."

"*Gracias*, Lupe. Thanks for looking out for me. I know how to handle this guy. Just feed his ego. For such a small man, he sure has a big mouth."

Before Mac could put down the telephone receiver, Andre texted once more:

HERE IN CONF RM. BRING TISSUES.
GIRL CRYING. GET HERE NOW.

Mac grabbed the box of Kleenex he always kept handy in the bottom drawer of his desk, turned, opened his office door, and jogged down the hallway.

ACKNOWLEDGEMENTS

Thank you to all of those who helped to make this fanciful dream a reality. Very belatedly, I thank my original sources of influence, Ronald M. Foster, Jr. and Anne Tolstoi Wallach. Thank you to my beloved wife, Kathy Ambrose Foster, and my children, family, friends and courthouse colleagues. Much appreciation to the excellent professionals at Paper Raven Books, especially Colleen Tomlinson who has been there from Chapter 1 to the end.

Printed in Great Britain
by Amazon